♦ ♥ B Y ♣ ♠

P E T E

HAUTMAN

S I M O N & S C H U S T E R

DRAWING DEAD

A ♦ ♥ NOVEL ♠ ♣

NEW YORK LONDON TORONTO SYDNEY TOKYO SINGAPORE

SIMON & SCHUSTER
Rockefeller Center
1230 Avenue of the Americas
New York, New York 10020

Copyright © 1993 by Pete Hautman

SIMON & SCHUSTER and colophon are registered trademarks
of Simon & Schuster Inc.

Designed by Songhee Kim
Manufactured in the United States of America

1 3 5 7 9 10 8 6 4 2

Library of Congress Cataloging-in-Publication Data

Hautman, Pete
Drawing dead: a novel / by Pete Hautman.
p.   cm.
1. Swindlers and swindling—Minnesota—Minneapolis—Fiction.
2. Minneapolis (Minn.)—Fiction.   I. Title.
PS3558.A766D73   1993   93-11206
813'.54—dc20   CIP
ISBN   0-671-79374-8

For Mary Logue

THE SHUFFLE

I don't care who you are—nothing rides like a fucking Cadillac.

—Joey Cadillac

Joseph Caruso Battagno (better known as Joey Cadillac, Joey C. to his friends and customers, Mister C. to his employees, Joe Chicago to his Las Vegas investors, and occasionally referred to as "Stallion" by Chrissy Swenson, his twenty-two-year-old side-squeeze, former Miss Minnesota, recently imported from the frozen wastelands of the north) said that the copy of *Batman* #3 he held in his chubby right hand was not for reading—it was for investing.

"Oh, come on, Joey," Chrissy whined. "It's just a comic book. Open it up. I want to read about the Batman."

It was Friday night, their night, and they had just finished a late supper—takeout from Tony's—in her Lake Shore Drive condo. Joey was showing off his latest acquisition. Joey always had something new to show her. Sometimes it was a present for her, but more often it was something he had bought for himself. Last week he had brought along his new electronic cigar lighter, which Chrissy thought was the coolest thing ever. Chrissy always made it a point to be impressed by Joey's toys.

"I can't, doll. This here is called a Stasis Shield, see?" He handed her the comic in its rigid Mylar sleeve. "It's, like, permanently sealed in there so the air and the, like, pollution don't get at it. Thing's worth three grand, you don't want to fuck it up."

Chrissy was examining the plastic sleeve, her brow furrowed, glossy lips pushed out past the end of her button nose. "What good is it if you can't read it?"

"Like I told ya, it's worth money, honey. Last year it was worth two grand, this year it's worth three, next year who knows? It's like an in-*vest*ment, dollface. Like you buy gold or something. Or a classic car, y'know? Look." Joey took the comic and pointed out a small card that had been sealed into the plastic sleeve with the comic. "See the signatures? That's so you know it's the real thing."

Chrissy looked at the card. "Who's B. Disraeli?"

"That's Ben, the notary, doll. And the other one, Tommy Paine, he's the country's number-one comic book expert. That's who I got them from. What they do, they seal the book in with some kinda special gas so it stays perfect, what they call mint condition, and you can buy and sell it without its getting wrecked by people like you pawing through it."

Chrissy pushed her lips out another quarter of an inch. "I don't *paw*," she said. "I just wanted to read about the Batman, Joey."

"Well, you can't. I open this up, it loses value. Then I got to pay to have it resealed and notarized and like that." He held the sealed comic in front of him with both hands, holding it out like a new baby. "Four large for a comic book. Ain't that something. And I got twelve more like this, three more *Batman*s and a bunch of other stuff, every one of them worth two grand or more."

"Wow, Joey, that's really cool." Chrissy made her eyes go big. "That's a lot of money." Joey loved it when she got excited by his money. He liked her to be there, sitting behind him, when he used her place for poker night. He liked it when she clapped her hands when he won. When he lost, of course, he was just impossible for the rest of the week. But he still paid the rent.

Joey grinned. "Didn't cost me a dime, babe. I traded the guy one of our demos, a Fleetwood spun back to ten K on the speedometer. Got thirty K in rare comics for a ten-thousand-dollar demo."

Chrissy had the comic again and was looking at the purple cover through the thick plastic. The Batman and Robin running straight at her, looking like they were going to jump right off the comic, right through the Mylar shield. She shook her head and licked her lips.

"You're so smart. How come you're so smart, Joey?"

"I dunno." Joey grabbed a piece of cold garlic toast and pushed it

8

into his mouth, poured himself another glass of Chianti and sucked it down, feeling good about his comics, enjoying this private time with his girl, his Minnesota import with the big front end. At that moment the three K a month she cost him in rent and goodies seemed like nothing, like pocket money. About the same as one vintage comic book. He wiped his chubby fingers on the tablecloth.

"What the hell," he said, reaching for the sealed comic. "You want to read about the Batman, we'll open the fucker up." He could just call the comic guy and have it resealed. What was the guy gonna do—say no to Joey Cadillac? "Make sure your hands are clean, doll." He took a steak knife and pushed the point into the end of the plastic package and tried to slit it open, but the Mylar, twenty mils thick, resisted the thin-bladed knife. He had to saw with the serrated edge to open it all the way along the top, scratching the cover of the comic book in the process. Red-faced from the effort, he handed the open package to Chrissy.

"Oh, Stallion . . . ," she said in her little-girl voice. "You're so good to me."

Joey poured the rest of the Chianti into his glass, wiped his brow with his bunched-up napkin, then settled back and unwrapped one of his prized Cuban Montecristos. Chrissy slid the comic out of the sleeve, admired it for a few seconds, crinkled her nose at the Stallion, and opened it to page one. Joey bit the end off his cigar and, since he had already worn out the battery on last week's electronic lighter, lit it with the candle on the table. Chrissy was big on candles, always had to have one going. He settled back in his chair to watch his Minnesota import read his three-thousand-dollar *Batman* comic.

But Chrissy was frowning. She turned the page, looked at Joey, wrinkled her brow, turned another page, and pouted ferociously. "Oh, you! You were teasing me."

Joey sat forward, dropping his fifteen-dollar cigar onto his leftover puttanesca sauce. "What?" He reached for the comic, pulled it from her limp fingers, and looked at the inside pages.

"That wasn't nice," Chrissy was saying as Joey Cadillac stood and roared and threw the comic across the room. Empty, blank pages separated and fluttered to the carpet.

The Tom and Ben Show ran out of rock and roll on Interstate 35, five miles north of Clear Lake, Iowa, twenty-six miles east of the cornfield where the Big Bopper, Buddy Holly, and Ritchie Valens died.

When Mick Jagger groaned and stuttered during the *Sticky Fingers* tape, something he had done many times before but never halfway through "Brown Sugar," Tom and Ben looked at the tape deck, then at each other. The song went on to the end with no further interruptions, Tom went back to reading to his *Spiderman* comic, and Ben returned his eyes to the highway, playing the drum part on the rim of the big Cadillac steering wheel. The lemon-yellow Fleetwood slid up I-35, Cadillac smooth.

Two cuts later, during the long jam at the end of *"Can't You Hear Me Knocking,"* the Stones went into slow time. Ben pressed his foot down on the accelerator, as though by speeding up the Fleetwood he could bring the recording back into phase, but as the digital speedometer counted up, the tape deck moaned and the speakers fell silent. Tom reached out and pressed the eject button. The tape leapt from its slot, followed by a cloud of acrid smoke, which was quickly sucked into the powerful Cadillac climate control vents.

Tom and Ben looked at each other.

Ben lightened his foot on the accelerator and brought the Fleetwood back down to sixty-five miles per hour. A hot plastic reek pierced the climate control's defenses and attacked his nostrils. He sneezed, three times, violently.

"Now what are we gonna do?" asked Tom. "Middle a fuckin' nowhere." He gestured at the rolling, homogeneous farmland that surrounded them. The land was dotted with rows of small green plants. It was early May, planting time, the new growth electric green on the black Iowa soil.

Ben cleared his throat. "Are we on fire?" His voice was deep and cavernous. People who heard him over the telephone visualized him as a big-chested man with a full head of gray hair, a ruddy complexion, and crinkly brown eyes. When he spoke, words took on prodigious meaning. In person, Ben was a less impressive creature. He was six feet three inches tall but weighed no more than one hundred sixty pounds, had both hair and flesh the color and texture of overcooked wheat pasta and eyes like weak, milky tea. An uneven beard was nearly invisible on his face. He was wearing a gray T-shirt with Mickey Mouse smiling on the front.

Tom, the other half of the Tom and Ben Show, leaned forward and peered into the cassette slot. "It don't look like it," he said in his smaller, more nasal voice. He shook his head. Shanks of black hair separated, then pasted themselves back together. He picked up the ejected cassette. The case was warped and too hot to hold. He shifted it from one hand to the other, then dropped it back on the floor.

"Please get it out of here." Ben sneezed again. Tom lowered his window, flipped the tape out onto the highway, and turned to watch it skitter down the pavement after them.

The Tom and Ben Show rolled up I-35 in silence for almost five minutes before Tom slapped his knee and said, "This is no good. We got to have tunes."

"Perhaps you could turn on the radio."

"You kidding me? Do you know where we are? The middle of the fucking prairie, and you want to listen to the radio? You know what kind of shit they listen to out here?"

"Probably the same variety as is listened to elsewhere."

"Damn straight. We turn that thing on, we might hear Milli Vanilli or Vanilla Ice or something worse, you can imagine that. I might jump out the window, sixty miles an hour. Christ."

Ben shrugged and kept the Cadillac centered in the right lane. Tom watched a few mileposts flash by, then blew out his cheeks, reached out, and turned on the radio. The speakers crackled and popped. He pressed the station selector several times without results.

"Now the fucking radio don't even work. Where the fuck are we? Where's the fuckin' map?" Tom twisted in his seat and rummaged through the garbage that had accumulated in the back seat. "Where is it?"

"Perhaps you should check your door pocket," said Ben.

"Son-of-a-bitch." Tom turned around and found the wrinkled and stained road atlas folded into the passenger-door pocket. He opened it and asked, "Where are we?"

"We passed Clear Lake six minutes ago."

"What state? Gimme the state."

"Iowa. Just below Minnesota, west of Wisconsin and Illinois."

"I know where Iowa is, f'chrissake." Tom studied the map, running his finger up the blue stripe that represented I-35. "I'm sick a this, man. I feel like we been on the road a week. This really sucks."

"Consider the alternative," said Ben. "We could be back in Chicago entertaining Joey C. We could be having him and Freddy Wisnesky over for dinner. We could all sit around admiring Freddy's tie. Freddy would appreciate that."

"Freddy and his fucking ties," Tom growled.

"Maybe Joey would fix the tape deck for us. You're Joey's good buddy, right?" Ben said. "I'm sure he stands behind the cars he sells."

Tom extracted a bottle of Children's Tylenol from the pocket of his black jeans, shook out half a dozen of the purple, grape-flavored tablets, licked them off his palm, and chewed. Ben compressed his thin lips until they disappeared, and waited for his partner to finish chewing.

"We'll be in Minneapolis soon. We can get a nice room, order some food. Joey won't be looking for us there. Nobody goes looking for anyone in Minneapolis. We can make a few calls, get the Galactic Guardians thing in motion."

"So who you gonna call? Who the fuck do we know in Minneapolis?"

Ben looked at his partner, who had both feet up on the seat, chin on his knees, glaring out at the highway. "Tomas, we don't know any-one in Minneapolis. That is why we are going there."

Half a mile later, Tom said, "Yeah, we do."

"Yeah, we do what?"

"Yeah, we do know somebody in Minne-fucking-apolis."

"Who would that be?"

"Cat."

Ben frowned and adjusted his hands on the steering wheel.

"I'm gonna give her a call soon as we get there," Tom said. "Maybe she knows somebody'd be interested in the Galactic Guardians. Maybe her new hubby."

Ben cleared his throat. "Catherine got married? I doubt, then, that she'll take kindly to us going after her meal ticket."

"You think getting married is gonna change anything? You don't know Cat. She likes a good show more'n anybody. Only thing she can't stand is being bored. That's how come you two never got along. Anyways, I don't see you coming up with anything better."

Ben's pallid face turned a deeper shade of beige. "I might be bor-ing, but I thought we had a good arrangement back in Chicago. And we did, until you decided to lay the Stasis Shield routine on Joey C. For a used car that gets ten miles to the gallon." He slapped the steer-ing wheel.

"How was I s'posed to know he was going to try and read the damn things? I told him not to open 'em up."

"And *I* told *you* not to get involved with people like that."

"How was I s'posed to buy us a car without I get involved with guys like that? You know anybody sells cars isn't connected?"

They had been having variations on the same argument ever since leaving Chicago. Ben shrugged and kept the Cadillac rolling.

"You don't think Freddy'll show up in Minneapolis?" Tom asked a few miles later. "I don't want to end up eel bait like Billy Yeddis."

"Why would he do that? First, they are not likely to find us there, and if they did, even Joey C. has his practical side. How angry could he get over a few comic books?"

"All Billy did was miss a few car payments."

The Tom and Ben Show listened to the hum of the Cadillac's big wheels on concrete.

"You've got a point there," Ben said.

"You sure?" Joey Cadillac said.

Freddy Wisnesky, slumped in the chair in front of Joey's desk, rolled his mountainous shoulders and looked down at his tie. Today he was wearing his tie with the big red flowers on it. Roses. Real silk. Lots of class. "I been lookin' everywhere, Mister C. I been over to their apartment a bunch of times. I been askin' around everywhere. I don't think they're around no more." Freddy's nose, a flattened, solid mass of healed cartilage, was no longer available as an air passage. His voice sounded like that of a man with a bad cold speaking from the other end of a culvert.

Joey Cadillac picked up a memo pad and started tearing off pages, balling them in his fist, flicking them across his eight-foot-wide desk at Freddy, who let them bounce off his chest, unblinking.

"You know who Diogenes is?" Joey asked him.

Freddy contorted his face. A bit of white spittle oozed from the corner of his mouth. He seemed to swell, then collapse, sinking down a few inches in the chair. He gave his head a shake, then ventured, "One a those Greek guys, has a joint over on Halsted?"

Joey grinned. "That's pretty good, Freddy."

Encouraged, Freddy elaborated, "One a them restaurants over there?"

"Diogenes," Joey said, standing and hiking up his pin-striped linen trousers, "is this guy who walks around with this lantern looking for an honest man. He did this his whole life, looking for this one honest guy." Joey stopped and looked to see if he was making an impression.

"I musta been thinking of some other guy," Freddy said.

Joey nodded. "Diogenes doesn't own no Greek restaurant. Even a Greek knows he ain't gonna find an honest man in the restaurant business. Anyways, this Diogenes is kinda like me, Freddy. I just wish I could find one honest guy, one guy I could count on. These comic book guys, this Paine and this Disraeli, these are not your honest guys, Freddy. So what I want you to do is like Diogenes with his lantern, only instead of looking for an honest guy, which you ain't gonna find, you go find those comic book guys. You go looking for them guys and you *find* them, you know what I mean?"

Freddy contorted his face again.

"Never mind," Joey said. "Let me lay it out for you. You find out where they went. There're these stores that sell nothing but comic books, you go ask around there, find out who they know, find out where they went. You know how to do that. Just keep asking and then go find them wherever they are, and when you find them? Do like you did with Billy Yeddis, then bring me my car back."

Freddy went blank for a moment, then he smiled. "I could do that," he said.

Something Freddy Wisnesky had learned from Mister C.—if you want to know something, you do not waste your time trying to figure it out; you ask guys. If you ask enough guys, one of them will tell you. Some guys are very cooperative, they even tell you stuff you don't want to know, but other guys you have work with to get them to open up. The fat guy behind the counter at Fatman's Emporium of Comic Book Arts was that kind of guy. He had an amused, shifty-eyed look that Freddy had often noticed in small-business owners who were meeting him for the first time. Didn't take him seriously. When Freddy asked him about Paine and Disraeli, the fat guy—Freddy figured he had to be Fatman—lost interest in him just like that. Just shook his head and went back to reading his comic book like nobody was there.

Freddy's first idea was to drag the guy across the counter and bounce his head on the floor, but years of experience had taught him that it was usually safer and nearly as effective to employ more civilized, gentle tactics. He felt for the knot in his orange-and-black tiger lily tie and made sure it was tight and centered, then turned to survey his surroundings, looking for inspiration.

Fatman's Emporium was a thirty-by-forty-foot labyrinth of shelves loaded with more comic books than Freddy had ever known existed. He was the only customer in the store. He wandered through the maze, stopping now and then to flip through a row of comics. Each comic was wrapped in a plastic bag and had an orange price sticker on the upper-right-hand corner. There was a familiar cover up on the top shelf: *Captain America* #100. Freddy reached up and took down the comic. The price sticker read: "$80.00—Near Mint." Freddy thought about his mom throwing away his comic books the first time he had gone away—a lousy six months in the joint, and she throws all his junk away. He untaped the top of the plastic bag and removed the comic.

"Hey, no reading the merch." Fatman was right there, grabbing the comic away from him. Freddy held on and pulled back, ripping Captain America in half, right across his red-white-and-blue shield. Fatman stared in horror at the shredded comic. "Look what you did," he said, his already high voice rising, his big cheeks turning red. "You're gonna pay me for this, fella. That's eighty bucks you just tore up."

Freddy felt bad about tearing *Captain America* in half, since he had wanted to read it, but Fatman's shrill reaction was giving him an idea. He picked out another comic, *Batman* #163, with a picture of the Joker on the cover, and tore it in half lengthwise.

"Jesus Christ! What are you doing?" Fatman grabbed Freddy's arm and started pulling him away from the shelves. Freddy twitched his arm and sent Fatman spinning against the opposite wall. He destroyed *Daredevil* #5, #6, and #7 while Fatman was trying to get back on his feet. When Fatman came at him again, Freddy unleashed one of his size-fourteen wing tips and let Fatman have a good one on his right shin. The best wing tips were the big black ones from Sears; they weighed a ton and made his feet sweat, but when you kicked a guy, the guy went down.

Freddy destroyed *Batman* #280 while the fat guy was trying to get his act together, curled up on the floor holding his shin, drooling and moaning, tears running from his squeezed-shut eyes.

"Please, stop," he finally managed to gasp as Freddy paged through a late-1950s copy of *World's Finest*, tearing away the pages one at a time. Freddy looked down. Fatman had managed to open one eye. Freddy tore off one last page, dropped the remains of the comic on the floor.

Fatman asked, "What do you want?"

Freddy smiled. This was more like it. "I was asking if you knew where I could find a couple guys, that's all. Paine and Disraeli."

The fat guy was shaking his head. Freddy reached for another comic book.

"Wait, please. I don't remember—you got to help me out here. How come you think I know them? I mean, maybe I do. Lots of guys come in and out of here. What do they look like?"

Freddy crumpled up a copy of *Green Lantern* #10 and threw it across the store. He was kind of enjoying himself.

"No! Wait a second. These guys you're looking for—is one of them a tall guy with a deep voice? Talks like a college professor?"

Freddy shrugged. He did not know how college professors talked.

"And the other guy, kind of little and greasy and talks really fast? 'Cause it sounds to me like you want the Tom and Ben Show. I should have known."

Freddy shrugged. "Tom and Ben Show?"

"That's what they call themselves. Ben Fink and Tommy Campo. They got more names than Beelzebub."

"Who?"

"The Tom and Ben Show. I bet they're the guys you want, don't you think? They owe you money or something?"

Freddy reached down a big hand and helped him stand up. Fatman was talking now, turning into a real motormouth. " 'Cause it wouldn't surprise me. They been in the business for years and never done a deal yet where somebody didn't get screwed. Couple of comic book con men, if you ask me. They were in here just a couple days ago, come in here trying to unload a bunch of junk, bunch of those Stasis Shield things. Like I'm gonna buy something from those fuckers. I think they blew town."

"Where they go?"

"How should I know? No, wait a second. Just a goddamn second! I think they went up to Minneapolis. I'm sure of it."

Freddy reached out and placed his hand on Fatman's head. The heel of his palm covered Fatman's forehead. "You real sure?" he asked.

"I think so. Christ, man, I don't know—all I know is that they were

16

talking about it, asking me if I knew any comics people up there. I told 'em I didn't know anybody. Even if I did, I sure as hell wouldn't give their name to those fuckers."

Freddy squeezed lightly, as if by compacting Fatman's gray matter he could cause information to flow more rapidly. It seemed to work.

"You just ask around the Minneapolis comic book shops, you ought to be able to find 'em in no time. You want to find 'em, you go on up there and ask around. They'll turn up."

"You real sure?"

Fatman's head bobbed in Freddy's grip. Freddy released him.

"Okay," said Freddy.

"Okay?"

"I'm gonna find 'em in Minneapolis, right?"

Fatman nodded vigorously.

"I don't, we can talk some more."

Fatman nodded again, though with less vigor.

Satisfied, Freddy turned toward the door.

"Just a second," Fatman said. Wincing, he hopped on one leg around the counter and pulled out a Rolodex. "I just remembered something." He flipped through the cards. "I think I still got her name on my mailing list. They get to Minneapolis, she'll know about it. Most recent address . . . yup. Minneapolis." He copied down a name and address on a slip of paper, handed it to Freddy. Freddy screwed up his eyes and spelled out the name in his mind, moving his lips with each new letter.

"Cat Fish?" he asked.

"That's right. Catfish. Tom's old girlfriend. You think Tom and Ben are a piece of work, wait'll you meet her."

The way Hold 'em works is, each player gets two cards, right? That's called The Deal. *Then you bet, then three more cards are dealt faceup in the middle of the table. These three cards get used by all the players. This is called* The Flop. *Then you bet again, and another card gets turned up. They call that* The Turn. *You bet again, then a last card gets turned up. That's* The River. *Then you get one more bet. The guy that makes the best five-card poker hand out of the two cards he holds and the five cards on the table wins. It's simple. You just play your cards and you take home the money. You want to sit in a few hands?*

—*Zink Fitterman*

The Texas Hold 'em game in the apartment above Zink's Club 34 was eight hours old when Joe Crow made his most potentially expensive mistake of the night. He had folded an eight, deuce after the deal, and was watching the other guys play out the hand. Ozzie LaRose threw his hand away. Al Levin raised it up, Frank Knox and Jimbo Bobick called, Zink Fitterman raised it up again. Ozzie pulled out his wallet, nudged Crow with his right elbow, and showed him a snapshot of the big fish he had caught that weekend.

"Check it out. Right off the end of my dock," he said. "Caught it on a Dardevle."

Crow looked at the photo. There was Ozzie, skinny white legs sticking out the bottom of his shorts, long blond hair under a Minnesota Twins baseball cap, standing in front of his cabin on Crook Lake, holding up a walleye that looked to be over six pounds. Crow was impressed. He imagined himself there, throwing out a line, reeling it in nice and steady. Right about then, Crow made his big mistake.

He said, "I wouldn't mind that. Get myself a cabin on a lake, walk out the door, throw out a line, catch a little breakfast . . ." He realized too late what he had done.

Ozzie laughed and put his wallet away. Zink was scooping in the pot, having won it with queens over sevens. Crow stared down at his chips, hoping without hope that his offhand comment had gone unnoticed.

"So what kind of place are you looking for, Joe?" asked Jimbo Bobick, the realtor from Brainerd, his wide smile shining across the table like the headlight of an approaching train. "I mean, are you set on having some shoreline, or just looking for something near a good fishing lake?"

"It's your deal, Jimbo," said Zink. "You here to play cards or sell cabins?"

Jimbo laughed. "Both," he said, riffling the deck. Jimbo Bobick was a big man with a big laugh. He loved to gamble, and he didn't mind losing. "Good hand," he would say to the winner each time he watched his money migrate across the table. He was down two thousand, give or take a hundred, which was less than he'd dropped at the Minneapolis Golf Club that afternoon. Jimbo was wearing his lucky green blazer. It wasn't bringing him much in the way of cards, but it had delivered Joe Crow. He squared up the deck and offered the cut to Knox, who waved it away.

"You ever been up around the Brainerd area?" Jimbo asked Crow as he began to deal two cards to each player. "Beautiful country up there. Lakes full of fish, lots of nice folks. Ozzie loves it, don't ya, Oz?"

"Spend every weekend up there," Ozzie said. "It's the only chance I get to relax."

"What it is, it's the only chance you get to look at your porn collection," said Zink. "You guys should see the skin mags this guy's got stashed away up there. A whole room full of the things. Invites me up there to catch a stringer of walleye, and the first thing he does is show me his porn collection."

Ozzie shrugged. "Ginny made me get 'em out of our house," he said, referring to his most recent live-in girlfriend.

Jimbo laughed. Ozzie's porn collection was legendary, his pride and joy. And it was true—Jimbo had seen it—it almost filled the back room of his three-room log cabin. "That's one of the advantages of having a second home," Jimbo said. "Two separate life-styles. You never have to give anything up." He watched Crow, looking at him closely. Nothing.

"Yeah, except now Ginny's into this do-everything-together thing,"

Ozzie said. "Now she wants to go fishing with me. Next thing you know, she'll be here playing poker. Anyway, my porn collection has got to go. Any of you guys interested?"

"Just what I need," Zink said. "A room full of used pornography."

"You never know," Frank Knox said. "It might come in handy."

Jimbo noticed that Crow was riffling his chips, not participating in the banter. Joe Crow never had a lot to say. His sense of humor was too dry for most of the players—although Zink seemed to find him amusing—and he didn't know how to make small talk. Jimbo had noticed that before about Crow: the guy was there to play cards. Jimbo, being in the people business, was curious about Crow. He'd heard stories about him from the other players, but he had yet to separate the true from the untrue. Physically, Crow was on the small side—five feet eight inches and maybe a hundred fifty pounds—but he was usually perceived as being larger, especially when sitting at the card table. His stolid, expressionless face—dark-brown eyes and a wide, straight mouth—gave him a massive, dense look. At times he reminded Jimbo of a cigar store Indian, but his features were Irish—more like a petrified leprechaun than a Native American. Poker face. The only part of him that didn't fit the picture was his hair—brown, black, sometimes with a hint of red, depending on the light—always sticking out, always in need of a trim. Jimbo didn't like or dislike him. He thought of Joe Crow as a force, like water in a river, or like the weather. The guy just didn't have a lot of personality.

According to Ozzie, Crow was an ex-cokehead. Ozzie claimed that Crow had recently graduated from the cocaine program at Saint Mary's. Jimbo chose not to believe this. Crow was not his idea of a drug addict. Ozzie—one of the world's great bullshitters—also claimed that Crow was an ex-cop. Jimbo found it easier to believe the cop story than the cocaine story. In any case, it wasn't important. Whatever Crow was now, or had once been, he was starting to look a lot like a guy who was in the market for some lakeshore.

Jimbo pointed a forefinger at Zink. "Bet 'em, Zinker."

Zink checked. Crow looked at his cards and bet twenty dollars. Ozzie folded. Al Levin twitched as if he had received a mild electric shock, then called. Frank Knox considered his cards, frowned, shrugged, and called. Jimbo laughed and added his forty dollars to the pot. He was holding a pair of deuces. Deuces never looses, he said to himself. "A lot of really nice properties have come on the market this year. The recession, you know." He flopped three cards faceup on the table. Ace, jack, eight. "Your bet, Crow."

What Jimbo needed was a toehold. "They've been pulling fifteen-pound northerns out of Gull all summer," he said.

Crow bet forty dollars but gave no sign he cared about the size of the northern pike in Gull Lake. Al Levin and Frank Knox immediately folded. Jimbo laughed, called Crow's bet, and turned a fourth card. Another jack.

In an average year, Jimbo Bobick lost about twenty thousand dollars playing poker, blackjack, and golf. Fortunately, he earned ten times that selling lake properties in the Brainerd area, where a quarter of Minnesota's ten thousand lakes were located. Some of his fattest commissions had come from guys he had met while gambling. He got down to the Twin Cities every couple of weeks, usually got into at least one card game at Zink's, and in the past two years had sold properties to both Frank Knox and Ozzie LaRose. The Minnesota dream of a cabin on a lake was alive in every man. Jimbo Bobick believed this the way he believed in heaven and hell. His job was to find the dream and to nurture it.

"I had this one place, a beautiful three-room cabin." Jimbo watched Crow's eyes carefully as he said, "On an island." He saw Crow's pupils enlarge slightly. Jimbo smiled. He should have known—Crow was an island guy. He sat back in his chair. "You don't see those island properties come on the market very often. I sold it to a guy who uses it about one week out of the year. Beautiful view. I'll go forty."

Crow raised. Jimbo called and turned the final card over. A deuce.

Crow bet eighty dollars. Jimbo looked at his hand—a full house, deuces over jacks—and considered his next move. "You ever think about owning your own island, Crow?"

"It's your bet," Crow said.

"I know. I'm thinking. You know, there is a guy I know, has an island on Tenmile. I think his business is in trouble. I'll talk to him."

Crow shrugged. "You going to raise, call, or fold?"

Jimbo threw his hand into the discards. "It's all yours, my friend." He watched Crow rake in the pot. "Listen, how about if I show you a few of these places, Crow? You could drive on up, and we'll go check out some properties. What do you say?"

"Sure," said Crow, stacking his chips. "Maybe we could do that sometime."

Jimbo smiled. There was no better time to push a sale than when the other guy thought he had you by the nuts. Joe Crow had just won himself one hell of an expensive pot.

Richard Wicky drove around the block twice, finally squeezed his Mercedes into a spot between a black Jaguar and a beat-up Toyota. He had to give the Jag a little shove to get in, but what the hell. He'd paid a premium for those big German bumpers; might as well use them. He fumbled in the glove box with his right hand, came out with a sterling-silver coke vial, and treated each nostril to a little toot. He looked at his new watch—a Rolex President—sniffed, screwed the top back onto the coke vial, wiped his nose with the back of his hand, got out of the car, and inspected his parking job. The back end of the Mercedes was sticking out a couple of feet, but not too bad. He locked the doors and headed back up the sidewalk toward Club 34. The sky was beginning to lighten; the streets were deserted.

The outside door leading to the upstairs apartment was unlocked. Wicky climbed the wooden staircase, telling himself he was feeling lucky. Wicky believed in luck, especially at the card table. He believed that winning at poker came half from being able to read opponents and half from luck. He considered himself a lucky person, and he could read faces as if they were Teleprompters. He tried not to think about the fact that he almost always lost. When he did think about it, he attributed the loss to a fluke, or a single expensive mistake, or a hole in his luck.

In business, Wicky's combined luck and perceptive abilities had served him well. His clients were still buying everything he recommended, and this new thing he had gotten into—the Galactic Guardians Fund—was bringing in some sweet commissions. He was even thinking about buying some of it for himself. Business was good. But in other areas, specifically those surrounding his marriage, his luck was hurting. His wife, he was sure, was fucking some other guy. Married two years, and already she's going out on him. Two o'clock in the morning, he gets home and she's gone. He'd sat around the condo for three hours thinking about it, drinking beer, watching cable, chipping away at a quarter-ounce chunk of coke, and finally had to get out of there, hoping to find the game at Zink's still going strong.

He knocked on the upstairs door. A moment later, Zink opened it. He looked tired, which was normal for him at any time but especially at dawn, after a night spent playing cards. "Hey, Dickie, come on in."

Wicky always introduced himself as Rich, but few people called him that for long. Just about all of them, including his wife, called him Dickie. Once, when he complained, she told him, "You just don't look like a Rich, Dickie. You look like a Dickie. My little Dickie-poo." He was a lumpy man, shorter and wider than average, with coarse yellow hair and pale-blue eyes that never stopped moving.

Wicky looked past Zink at the other players. Frank, Al, Ozzie, Jimbo the realtor, and Joe Crow. "So who's got all the money?" He walked up to the table and scanned the stacks.

Zink inclined his head toward Crow, who was in the process of showing Frank Knox a winning hand, all hearts.

Wicky wrinkled his brow. "Don't you ever lose, Joe?"

Crow shrugged.

Wicky took a chair and pushed it between Crow and Zink. "You're looking good, buddy," he said, looking at Crow's pile of chips and cash. "What does a guy have to do to get a stack like that?"

Crow shifted his chair to put more space between them. "Live right," he muttered, the standard poker player's response to Wicky's question.

Ozzie said, "Nice clock, Dickie."

Wicky shot his cuff and held the Rolex out for all to admire. "You like it?"

Everybody liked it. Al Levin was shuffling the cards. Al claimed that seven good shuffles guarantees a random mix of cards. He had read it in *Scientific American*. "You in, Dickie?"

"I'm in." He pulled out a sheaf of mixed bills and laid them on the table. "Reel 'em, Alan."

Al Levin offered the cut to Ozzie, then dealt in his characteristically twitchy manner. Levin had a nervous tic that showed up in every part of his thin, dry body. He was a numbers guy, and a good one, but it made Wicky itchy just to sit at the same table. Wicky looked at his cards—the jack and ten of clubs. Not bad. Knox bet, Jimbo and Zink folded, Wicky called.

Crow raised fifty dollars. Wicky examined Crow's dark Gaelic features. Of all the guys he played cards with, Crow was the most difficult to read. Something about him made you see what you wanted, or expected, or feared. He couldn't read the man's cards for shit, but he was working on it. People were his specialty.

Ozzie folded. Wicky paid to see the flop—king, four, four. He checked, then folded when Crow bet another fifty. Frank Knox raised a hundred. Wicky was sure that Frank Knox's raise was a bluff. Crow looked again at his cards, then re-raised another hundred. Did Crow have a hand? Wicky had no idea. He watched Crow's still, calm face and let himself imagine Crow as angry, frightened, sad, confident, proud, nervous. . . . All of those things were there; he had only to think it, and the emotion would fit itself to Crow's features. The man was like a mirror. He had the perfect poker face—not a face that displayed nothing, but a face that reflected the hopes and fears of the other players.

Wicky, who considered himself a master of practical psychology, felt as though he had finally created a working theory to wrap around the enigma of Joe Crow. Not that it would help his game.

Frank Knox said, "Shitsky." He picked up his two cards, looked at them, looked at Crow's raise, shrugged, and threw them away. Crow pushed his own hand into the discards and scooped in the pot.

Wicky frowned—now he would never know. Crow rarely had to show his cards, and when he did they were usually winners. In his quiet way, he dominated the action. Wicky put his hand on Crow's shoulder. "You're one hell of a cardplayer, Joe."

Crow turned his head toward Wicky, who saw, or thought he could see, that if he didn't move his hand quickly he might lose it. Wicky lifted his hand and shook his head, smiling. "Joe, if I didn't know you so good, I'd think you didn't like me."

"I don't," said Crow.

Zink broke into a snorting laugh.

Wicky went momentarily slack, then laughed loudly and almost put his hand back on Crow's shoulder, but caught himself at the last moment.

"Well, I like you," Wicky said.

The cat that fell 32 stories on concrete, Sabrina, suffered only a mild lung puncture and a chipped tooth. One explanation may be that the speed of the fall does not increase beyond a certain point. This point, "terminal velocity," is reached relatively quickly in the case of cats. Terminal velocity for a cat is 60 mph; for an adult human, 120 mph. After terminal velocity is reached, the cat might relax and stretch its legs out like a flying squirrel, increasing air resistance and helping to distribute the impact more evenly.

—The New York Times, *August 27, 1989*

Dickie Wicky opened a new jar of pimento-stuffed olives and, using his fingers to keep the olives in the jar, poured the brine down the kitchen sink drain. He stood and watched the last drops of liquid drip away, then dumped half of the olives into a thick glass tumbler that bore the etched initials "R & C." When guests noticed the initials, he would say they stood for "Rude and Crude." People liked that. They thought it was funny. The glass was the last of a set of eight.

He set the tumbler on the counter, took a frosty green bottle of Tanqueray from the freezer, opened it, measured three jiggers of subzero gin into the glass, capped the bottle, returned it to the freezer compartment, and closed the door. Wicky stood balanced on his bare feet and watched the frost collect on the outside of the glass. The Mondo Martini was his own invention, and he always took a moment to appreciate the physics. The bottom third of the glass frosted first and thickest. The middle third, to which the olives had migrated, frosted to a lesser degree, and the top third remained clear and empty. Wicky lifted the glass by its rim and carried it through the condo and out onto the balcony, where he set it on a glass-topped table.

It was a few minutes past noon, Sunday morning, and he had just gotten home from the game at Zink's. Wired from the coke, the action, and a twenty-three-hundred-dollar loss—most of which he'd dropped on the last hand—he needed the drink to jack down, get some sleep, quit thinking about who his wife was fucking.

The mid-June sunlight was intense. He went back into the apartment and found his Vuarnets. When he returned to the balcony, the frost on the martini had begun to melt and pool on the tabletop. Wicky settled into the chaise longue, picked up his drink, and swallowed a quarter of it. The icy gin left a tingling path from his mouth to his stomach, and Wicky smiled. He fished out three of the olives and pushed them into his mouth. Chewing, he looked down through the balcony railing at the swimming pool twenty-five floors below.

The outdoor pool, a shallow, obese boomerang—useless for swimming—was empty. A half-dozen sunbathers were lying on the adjoining patio. Wicky could not distinguish their faces, but the body shapes and swimsuit designs were distinctive, and he immediately picked out the black-haired woman. She was on her back now, arms held a few inches away from her sides. Her bikini bra featured two neon colors, green on her left and orange on the right. The bottom half of the bikini was neon yellow, an eye-searing triangle even from twenty-five stories up. The back, he knew from earlier observation, was an equally compelling neon pink. A deeply tanned young man with blond hair was crouched beside her. They were drawn to her like dogs to a bitch in heat. Wicky took another gulp of his martini. The man was resting one hand on her leg. Wicky munched another olive and watched. After a few minutes, the man stood up and went toward the bank of vending machines concealed behind a tall hedge at the far side of the pool area. Wicky kept his eyes on the woman, who remained motionless. The man returned and handed her something. Wicky knew that it would be a Diet Pepsi, an invariable element in her poolside flirtations. She sipped it and set the can under her lounger, out of the sunlight, then turned her face directly toward Wicky and waved. The blond man looked up, shading his eyes. Wicky scowled and shifted back from the railing.

When he looked back over the edge a minute later, the man had disappeared and the woman was lying on her stomach, mooning him in pink neon. Wicky ate another olive and examined the inscription on the glass. The tumblers had been a wedding gift. To Richard and

Catherine. It had taken them two years to break the first seven glasses in the set. The penultimate tumbler had shattered a week ago when he had made the mistake of inviting Jack Mitchell, one of the other salesmen at Litten Securities, to drop by for cocktails after work. He and Mitchell and Catfish had been sitting on the balcony, sipping gin and tonic, when Mitchell asked him what the etched "R & C" stood for.

"Guess," Wicky had said, grinning.

"Runt and Cunt?"

What really pissed Wicky off was how hard Catfish had laughed—Laughing so hard she had to hold herself up by grabbing Mitchell's thigh, causing him to drop the glass.

"Jesus, Dickie, I'm sorry," he had said, not sounding sorry at all, Catfish looking at the shattered glass, still laughing, digging into Mitchell's thigh with her red nails.

Wicky squeezed his eyes shut and drained the rest of the martini, still cold, letting the last six olives roll into his mouth, then he looked down again at his wife, Catfish, and wondered how close he could come to hitting her with the glass. He knew from having thrown other objects off the balcony that accuracy from such a height was difficult. The poolside was farther out from the building than it appeared.

He looked again at the glass, now warm and smudged from his fingers. Richard and Catherine. Rude and Crude. Runt and Cunt. He shrugged and walked back into the condo, where he still had half a jar of olives waiting beside the kitchen sink. He would have another martini. He thought about how rich he would soon be, and that made him feel better. He would have another martini and think about that. He looked again at his Rolex and felt the power of ownership warm his groin. He would have another martini and think about some other things he could own.

Catfish's goddamn cat, Katoo, was sitting in the sink, lapping water from the dripping faucet. When Wicky stepped into the kitchen, Katoo panicked, launched himself from the sink, hit the floor running, and disappeared into one of the bedrooms. The jar of olives shattered on the tile floor, olives rolling in all directions. Blinking, Wicky looked at the explosion of green-and-red spheroids. He said, as though answering a question, "The goddamn cat."

Cautiously circling the broken glass, Wicky pulled a new jar of olives from the rear of the refrigerator and made himself a fresh Mondo Martini. He took it to the balcony, set it on the table, and looked down over the railing. Catfish was on her back again, this time attended by a thin man with a bald spot on top of his head. Wicky thrust out his lower jaw and ground his teeth. Then he went back inside to get the cat.

THE DEAL

I'll play for any kind of money, even dimes and nickels, so long as everybody agrees that a nickel is worth something. Otherwise it's not fair.

—Joe Crow

Joe Crow was sitting at the kitchen table in his underwear, eating a peanut butter sandwich and paging through a brochure from Bobick Realty, when the telephone rang. It rang four more times before he managed to swallow what he had in his mouth and answer it with a passable, if slightly thickened, "Hello."

"Joe?"

"Yeah."

"This is Rich."

"Who?" Crow turned the page in the brochure.

"Rich Wicky."

"Dickie?"

It took Rich Wicky a second to reply. "Right. You got a minute?"

Crow looked at the clock radio on his kitchen table. Two-thirty in the afternoon, and he hadn't thought of a reason to get dressed yet. He had been looking at photographs of lake properties, reading the brief descriptions. It wouldn't hurt to look, he thought. A guy had to have a dream. His head was full of acres, feet of shoreline, elevations, and abbreviations such as "FP." Fireplace? Front porch? Either would be fine. None of the listings in the brochure was for an island. That would be something, to have his own island, a place to be with himself. No phone. No Dickie Wicky.

"Joe?"

"Yeah, I'm here."

"I need to talk to you about something." Wicky paused.

Crow waited, trying to imagine what it could be. He had never seen or talked with Dickie Wicky other than from across a card table, nor had he ever wanted to. He didn't even like playing cards with the guy. Wicky was everything Crow had avoided becoming—overweight, overfamiliar, overpaid—and he was a user, both of people and of substances. Crow liked users about as much as he had liked himself when he was using, which was to say, not at all. He decided in that moment to buy an answering machine. He had never liked the things, but if it would screen out one call from a guy like Dickie Wicky, it was worth the price. He turned to the next page of the brochure: "Bird Lake, 210' lksh, secluded, on pt, cozy 4 rm getwy, FP, grt fshng." It was hard to see the cabin in the picture because it was surrounded by trees. He liked that. "$140,000." That was a bit of a problem, since his entire net worth would come in at something like twenty thousand dollars, most of it tied up in his Jaguar XJS. The three thousand he had won last night was a start, but not nearly enough. Was there such a thing as a cabin on an island for ten or twenty thousand?

"You still there?"

"I'm here. What's on your mind?"

Wicky cleared his throat. "I got a little problem. Listen, Joe, you do, like, odd jobs, right?"

"I'm not really looking for work, Dickie." Milo, Crow's oversize black tomcat, bumped against his leg.

"I heard you did some investigating work for Frank Knox."

"I did him some favors." Crow set the peanut-butter-covered knife on the linoleum floor. Milo set to work, scraping it clean with his rough tongue. Crow had served some papers for Frank Knox and chased down a reluctant witness to an auto accident, but that was about it. Aside from his poker winnings, he was professionally and financially adrift, waiting for something to inspire him.

"You used to be a cop, right?"

"Not much of one. Dickie, what is it you're looking for?"

"It's sort of complicated. Do you think you could come down here?"

"Where is 'here'?"

"Litten Securities."

"That's downtown, right?"

"We're in the Mills Building."

"Maybe you ought to tell me what you want to talk about. I don't want to waste your time."

"A business proposal."

"I don't have any money to invest, Dickie."

"You won't need any money. But there might be something in it for you."

"You want me to sell Amway, you can forget it."

"I don't want you to sell Amway. Look, I'll pay you for your time. A consultation fee. What would you charge me for a half hour of your time? Just to listen."

"Three hundred dollars," Crow said, hoping to discourage him.

Wicky did not hesitate. "How about ten o'clock Friday morning?"

After agreeing, reluctantly, to meet with Dickie Wicky, Crow put on his gray sweats, brewed a cup of strong coffee, and went out onto the porch to drink it. He brought the real estate brochure with him. Milo, who had finished with the peanut butter knife, followed, his kinked tail held proudly aloft.

Crow rented the top half of a duplex on First Avenue, an eighty-year-old clapboard house that, unlike most of the properties in this marginal neighborhood, retained all of its windows, was vermin-free, and sported a coat of white paint less than a decade old. His porch, which ran the length of the house, faced a row of rapidly aging brownstones, each building containing its own unique mix of humanity. Crow could sit in his wicker chair for hours, watching his neighbors live their lives.

He looked again at the brochure from Bobick Realty. In the north woods, sitting outside his cabin, he would be watching the birds and the squirrels. He would see a deer, or a fox. Or maybe he would be on the dock, watching a red-and-white bobber dance on the afternoon chop.

Was that what he wanted? The idea of isolation was seductive. If he could be alone with himself, away from all the crazy people, maybe he would find out what he wanted from life. If he could capture that long quiet moment, all would become clear. Here, in the city, the distractions ruled.

People like Dickie Wicky were everywhere.

What did Dickie want?

Sipping his coffee, wishing he had quoted a five-hundred-dollar consultation fee, Crow watched four kids from the building directly across the street holding the corners of a blanket, moving up and down the sidewalk, their faces tilted skyward. He watched them for several minutes, his mind drifting from Dickie Wicky to the north woods, before he started to wonder what they were doing. At first he couldn't see it; he was looking too high. The four blanket holders, three blond girls and a little Hmong boy with a purple Batman cape, were shouting something at the sky, but Crow could not understand their words over the steady stream of cars and buses roaring down the avenue. Finally he spotted the object of their attentions, a calico kitten on a ledge between the second and third stories. As the kitten moved along the ledge in one direction, the blanket crew would follow, trying to remain in rescue position. Now that he had a context, Crow could hear what they were shouting: *Jump, kitty, jump!*

He sighed and let a smile melt across his face. "Jump, kitty, jump," he said. Milo, sitting on the porch rail, twitched his tail. Crow watched until the kitten, the first to become bored with the game, followed the ledge around the corner of the building to the fire escape and descended to safety. Crow drained the last of his coffee, let his head hang over the back of the wicker chair, felt the muscles in his scalp and face loosen. He closed his eyes and willed his body to go slack, hazily remembering an afternoon, thirty years before, spent trying to rescue a cat from its comfortable perch twenty feet up a shaggy walnut tree. Had the rescue succeeded? He couldn't remember, but he suspected it hadn't. Perhaps the cat had found his antics entertaining, a good way to pass a summer afternoon.

"So how you doing on these comic book guys?"

Freddy went blank.

"The comic guys! The comic guys!" Joey Cadillac shouted. He was having a bad day. His best customer, one Bubby Sharp, had been pulled over while test driving one of the new Cadillac Allantés, a slick little cherry-red two-seater with the Italian body and a sixty-thousand-dollar invoice. He'd lost his best car and his best customer, just like that.

And now Freddy Wisnesky, mind like a fucking color crayon, needed something to do. Joey picked up a pencil and broke it into two pieces, then broke the halves into quarters. He could not break the quarters, so he crushed them between his desktop and a brass paperweight shaped like a 1959 Cadillac.

"I dunno, Mister C." Freddy shifted uncomfortably from one foot to the other. "The guy I talked to a few weeks back, he said they went to Minneapolis." He didn't like it when his boss was disturbed, which was most of the time. "You want me to go up there?"

"Minneapolis?" Joey couldn't get his mind off Bubby Sharp, the dumb shit taking the red Allanté, two days off the truck, less than a hundred miles on the speedometer, taking it out and running it up to a hundred miles per on the Kennedy, getting his ass stopped by the cops. Fucking cokeheads, Joey thought. If they weren't half his business, he wouldn't have nothing to do with them.

"That's what the guy said. He said he heard 'em talkin' about it. He said the one guy had a girlfriend up there."

"Who's that?" Joey wasn't tracking. He kept thinking about his red Allanté. The way Joey heard it, when the cops start flashing him, Bubby panics and cans it, which in the Allanté takes him right up to one twenty, and the next thing, he's got every cop on the North Side coming at him.

"Catfish."

"Catfish?" Sounded like one of his customers. The guys he sold cars to all had goofy names—Dogboy, Tacoumba, Mohammed. Or Bubby. Fucking Bubby, gets himself boxed in at the tollway entrance, gets the shit beat out of him, which he deserved by all accounts, and then they find a quarter pound of coke in the gym bag on the passenger seat. Of course, Bubby says he never saw it before. Shit. With a little luck, Joey might get the Allanté back from the cops in three months. Even worse, Bubby would be spending his next decade in the joint instead of paying cash for a new-color Caddy every time he moved a key.

"So now you want I should go up there?" Freddy asked again.

Joey forced his mind to the business at hand, the comic book guys. Unfinished business. A few weeks back, when Freddy found out that they had fled to Minnesota, Joey decided that he had more important

jobs for Freddy right here at home. As much as he'd wanted to take
care of the comic book thing, sending Freddy all the way up to Minnesota seemed like a lot of trouble. Besides, he'd had a few large and
uncertain payments coming due, and Freddy's presence had ensured
their prompt receipt. Also, Jimmy Spencer, his chop-shop manager,
had a guy on a six-to-nine-month state-funded vacation, and he had
needed an extra hand in the shop. But two weeks of Freddy Wisnesky
was more than enough for Spence, and he'd sent him back to Joey
with a note: "No thanks. I want my cars taken apart like that, I'll get
a guy in here with a backhoe."

So now Freddy needed something to do. It wasn't like you could
tell him to go hang out until needed. A guy like Freddy had to be kept
busy, or he'd get in some kind of trouble. The comic book guys were
perfect. What the hell, Joey thought, it would get Freddy out of his
hair for a while, and it would take care of that stabbing sensation he
got in his stomach every time he thought about the Stasis Shields.
The memory of opening the phony comic book up, Chrissy sitting
right there watching, made his veins bulge. Now was the time.

"You want to go to Minneapolis? Why the fuck not? Isn't that what
I told you before? Didn't I tell you to find those guys?"

"Uh-huh."

"Then do like I told you. I don't care if you have to go to fucking
Timbuktu."

"What car you want me to take?"

"Take whatever you want. Wait a minute. Don't take an Allanté,
f'chrissake. Take something I can afford to lose. You like convert-
ibles?"

"Sure."

"Go over to Spence's shop and tell him to give you the blue ragtop
we just took from Ohio. Have him throw on a new set of plates.
Needs a muffler, but it ought to get you to Minneapolis. Okay?"

"Okay. Can I have some money?"

"Everybody wants money. Didn't I give you some money a week
ago? My fucking wife wants money. My squeeze wants money. The
cops want money. My lawyers want money." He swept the shattered
remains of the pencil off his desk. "How much money you want?"

Freddy shrugged. "Whatever you think I'll need, Mister C." Math-
ematical reasoning ability was not Freddy's strongest asset.

Joey Cadillac glared at Freddy. How do you argue with a guy like that? He unlocked a desk drawer and pulled out two packs of twenties. "There's two thousand. Try not to spend it all on ties."

Ellis Ward's Big and Tall was having a slow day. Ellis Ward, former third-string tight end for the Bears, was standing in the window looking up Clark Street, thinking, as he did on a daily basis, that it was time he got into some other business, something he could make some real money at, when he heard a sputtering roar, then saw Freddy Wisnesky pull up in a baby-blue Cadillac convertible that must've been fifteen years old. It sounded like the muffler had been blown out.

"Thank you, Lord," said Ellis Ward as he watched Freddy, a decidedly big and tall man, extract himself from the Cadillac and lumber toward the front entrance. Ellis moved to the door to greet him. "Mr. Wisnesky, how are you today?"

Freddy looked down at himself. "I'm okay," he said. "You got any new ties?"

"I sure do. We just got in some real beauties. Genuine Chinese silk. Take a look, right over here, Mr. Wisnesky. I've got our florals in their own little section now, just for you. Check out the daisies, one of our classiest new patterns."

Freddy picked up the bright yellow-and-white tie, held it up against his chest. It glared cheerily against his rumpled, unevenly gray suit. "I like it," he said, handing it to Ellis. "I'll take it. What else? What's this one?"

"Those are carnations," Ellis said. He had no idea what flower had inspired the pink explosions, but then neither would Freddy.

"I like it," Freddy said. He picked out another tie, a darker floral pattern that was actually not too bad. "This too. What else you got?"

"Take a look at this beauty." Ellis had a theory: The uglier and duller the customer, the uglier and brighter the tie. Freddy Wisnesky, with his sideways nose, muscled lips, and lightless eyes, illustrated this theory vividly. He didn't even need the hair between his eyebrows or the wart on his chin. Ellis thought that Freddy and his ilk might be using the ties to distract people, and maybe it worked.

Twenty minutes later, Freddy had selected every floral-patterned tie in the store, a total of nineteen ties. He always did. Ellis always kept a good supply of bright florals in stock for Freddy Wisnesky, who always bought every last one of them and never questioned the price, a fact that Ellis had noted early in their relationship. As he was wrapping the ties, he asked, "When are you going to let me fit you with a new suit, Mr. Wisnesky?"

Freddy looked down. "Something wrong with my suit?"

"No, of course not," said Ellis. "I just thought you might feel like a change of pace. You know, maybe a double-breasted, or something in a tropical weight . . ."

"You don't like my suit?"

"I do, I like it."

"You sure?"

Ellis Ward experienced a moment of indecision. He was reasonably certain that Freddy Wisnesky owned only one suit, the wrinkled and stained gray polyester he was wearing, and, possibly, two or three cheap, dingy-looking white shirts. And about five hundred ties with flowers on them. Ellis decided not to risk a good thing. "I like it a lot," he said, ringing up the nineteen ties. The tie thing was too good a deal to risk by offending Freddy. Ellis bought most of the floral ties from an importer working out of Hong Kong. He paid about $2.50 apiece.

"With your discount, that comes to nine hundred dollars even, Mr. Wisnesky."

Freddy handed him the bundle of twenties. Ellis Ward counted off forty-five of them and handed the rest back. Ellis Ward never short-changed a customer.

I'll try anything twice, unless it's Crow's idea of pizza.

—Laura Debrowski

The Litten Securities waiting room was long and narrow. Crow introduced himself to the ice queen who ruled the business end of the room from behind a complicated-looking desk. She flickered her subzero eyes at him, answered a phone call on her microscopic headset, then paged Mr. Wicky. Her impressive halo of hair inclined toward the far end of the room. Mr. Wicky would be right out, and the visitor could have a seat. Crow smiled and said, "Thank you." The ice queen did not smile back.

Crow shrugged and looked down at the far end of the long waiting room. The large abstract print above the fake-leather camelback sofa looked like an original Picasso lithograph. Crow wasn't big on the fine arts, but Picasso always made him grin. Was it really an original? Probably just another poster. He started across the room to examine it more closely.

"Joe!" Wicky stepped through a door into the carpeted waiting room and grabbed Crow's hand. His handshake was firm and energetic, but moist. "Thanks for coming down. I really appreciate it."

"No problem." Crow withdrew his hand.

Wicky threw back his head and laughed. Crow couldn't find the joke, but Wicky had an infectious laugh, and he found himself chuckling along, feeling like a fool.

"Let's go talk in the conference room," Wicky said, touching him lightly on the back, guiding him through a paneled door into a large open room full of desks, computers, and young men with carefully combed hair talking on streamlined white telephones. The room was surrounded by glass-walled cubicles, most of them occupied by other young men. Everyone seemed to be on the phone, staring into VDTs.

Wicky pointed at one of the more cluttered offices as they passed. "Mine," he said.

The conference room was barely large enough to contain the sixteen-foot oak-laminate table. One long glass wall faced the main room; the other was paneled and decorated with three large LeRoy Neiman prints: a baseball scene, a football scene, and a basketball scene. Something for everybody—Picasso in the waiting area, LeRoy Neiman in the conference room. The duck paintings, Crow reflected, would probably be in the rest rooms. At the far end of the table, an easel supported an enormous pad of white paper.

"I've been having one hell of a week," Wicky said. "I got hooked into this very hot product. An investment pool called the Galactic Guardians Fund, if you can believe that. I figure to have every last unit gone by the end of the week. Figures to make over two thousand percent. I had to buy a chunk of it myself. In fact, I bought most of it. Got both Ozzie and Al in on it. Very sexy deal. I might have a few units I could shake loose for you, if you're interested."

"Is that why you asked me to come down here?"

"No! No, I'm just mentioning it. I mean, I don't care. Like I said, I'll have every unit sold before I go home tonight. I just wanted to run it by you."

"Consider it run."

"Okay." Wicky took a deep breath and lowered himself into the chair at the head of the table. "Here's what I wanted to talk to you about. You don't know my wife, do you?" He held his breath and raised the short, furry yellow patches that served him for eyebrows.

Crow shook his head and sat down, leaving one empty chair between them.

Wicky let his breath whistle out and seemed to relax. "Good," he said. "Here's the thing, Joe. We've been married, Cat and I, two years now, and she's a hell of a woman." He held Crow's eyes, nodding slowly until Crow, too, nodded. "Hell of a woman," he repeated, his eyes shifting off beyond the walls of the conference room.

Crow focused on Wicky's nose and waited. Had he started the day with a little toot up each nostril? Probably. Crow would have.

"You know what I mean?"

Crow shrugged and let his eyes drop to Wicky's watch. Wicky noticed and pulled his hand below the edge of the table. "Do you have to be someplace?"

"Eventually," Crow said.

"Okay. I'm not getting to the point, am I? You used to be married, right? Your wife ever go out on you?"

"Not that I ever knew about." Crow paused. "She might've."

"Damn straight," Wicky said, rapping the tabletop with a knuckle. "You got to tie them down." He slapped a palm on the table, pushed his chair back, stood, hiked up his trousers, and turned his back to Crow.

Crow said, "Look, Dickie, I don't know what you've got in mind here, but I'm getting the impression it's not something I'm going to be interested in."

Wicky walked around the table to the easel at the end of the room and picked up a red marker. He drew a small triangle and, a few inches to the side, a small circle. "You agreed to hear me out," he said without turning away from the easel.

Crow shrugged, wishing it were not so. He had a feeling that listening to Dickie Wicky's proposal would not be the easiest three bills he had ever earned.

Pointing at the triangle, then at the circle, Wicky said, "I married Catfish two years ago." He drew two parallel horizontal lines connecting the circle with the triangle. "You used to be married, so you know what I'm talking about. You fall in love, you do just about anything."

Crow nodded. The shapes on the paper looked familiar, like something from a math class he had taken fifteen years before. Or was it chemistry? He had been there for ten minutes now. Another twenty minutes and he could say No, thank you, to whatever it was, collect his three hundred dollars, and go back home for a nap.

"Cat needs a lot of attention," Wicky said. "I can't always be there for her. I have to make a living, you know? Like, this last couple weeks I been so busy with this Galactic Guardians deal, I don't know, I don't always get home at five, y'know?"

"Galactic Guardians?"

"That deal I mentioned. Very sexy. You sure you aren't interested in a good short-term investment?"

"Yes."

Wicky shrugged. "Anyway, I've been working my ass off. One thing Cat knows how to do is spend my money."

Crow nodded, thinking that Dickie knew how to spend money

too. The Rolex on his wrist had probably cost him more than Crow had won in the last three months, and that suit fit his lumpy body so well it had to have been custom tailored. Add to that the silver Mercedes he drove and the money he dropped every week at Zink's card game . . .

". . . you know what I mean?" Wicky was saying.

Crow, who had not been listening, nodded. Wicky had been drawing more lines and shapes. Now there was another triangle, with a dotted line leading to the circle. The new triangle, Crow decided, was cuckolding the Dickie triangle. He remembered now why the symbols were familiar; they were the symbols used by anthropologists to describe familial relationships. So, college had not been a complete waste of time after all.

"Were you an anthropology major?" Crow asked.

"Psychology," Wicky said. "Are you going to help me?"

Crow shook his head. "I don't know what it is you want me to do."

"I want you to save my marriage."

"I couldn't even save my own marriage, Dickie. What makes you think I can help you?"

"You can help me, Joe."

"Have you tried talking to her?"

"Cat doesn't like to talk. She's a body person."

Crow wondered which tabloid personality test had produced that insight. "If you're going to try to catch your wife with some guy—assuming she's seeing anyone at all—it might not do much for your marriage."

"That's not what I want to do. That's not why I called you."

"Exactly what is it you want me to do?"

"I want you to talk to the guy she's seeing. I don't even want to know who he is. I just want you to find him and get rid of him."

Crow jerked his head back. "You want me to *kill* him?"

"I want you to *pay* him," Wicky said.

"You want me to pay him," Crow repeated, somewhat relieved.

Wicky turned to the pad of paper and drew a dollar sign over his wife's lover's triangle. "Pay him to go away," he said.

Crow cleared his throat and looked off to the side. He felt as if Wicky was showing him a sore on his cock. Paying him to look at it. He was embarrassed to be in this sterile room with this lumpy man, taking his money, looking at his circles and triangles and dollar signs.

"This isn't my sort of thing, Dickie," he said, wondering as he said it what his sort of thing was.

"Joe, I trust you." Wicky caught Crow's eyes and held on. "I know you can handle it. Professionally. If I tried to do it myself I'd lose it. I'd kill the son-of-a-bitch. I can sit here and talk about it with you all rational like and calm, but if I saw the guy face-to-face I just don't think I could hold myself back. I'd be like a wild animal." He paused, his little eyes flickering back and forth over Crow's face.

The image of Dickie Wicky becoming a wild animal was almost too much, but years of poker playing enabled Crow to hold his face rigid.

Wicky continued. "Look, Joe, I can afford to make it worth your while. And you'd be doing me a huge favor. Wait . . ." He held up a palm, halting Crow's refusal. "Don't give me your answer now. I just want you to think about it. Would you do that for me? Think about it?"

The way he put it, it seemed so reasonable and fair. Crow tried to shake his head no, but found himself nodding. Why was he so gutless in the hands of a salesman? Was it the eyes? Later, on the phone, he could say no and he wouldn't have to look at those pale, quivering eyes.

"Okay," he said.

Wicky stood up and gave Crow's hand a firm, moist shake. "Thanks, Joe. Thanks for listening."

Crow felt as if he had just paid too much for something he didn't need. Wicky was still holding on to his hand. He clapped his other hand on Crow's shoulder. "Say, do you like to have a good time?"

"Not particularly." Crow pulled his hand away and stepped back. Wicky held his palms out, facing Crow as though to show him that they were empty, a magician about to perform sleight of hand.

"We're having a little wingding tonight. Lots of food and booze. Or whatever you want. I'll even have some of that fake beer stuff that you drink. Bring a friend if you want, or come alone—there'll be plenty of women there. Besides, it'll give you a chance to get a look at Catfish. Here." He produced an expensive-looking pen and wrote on the back of a business card. "You know where The Summit is? Where I live? It's right downtown, right on the river. Here's my ad-dress and security code. Just buzz yourself in and go right on up to the twenty-fifth floor. We got the whole floor opened up—swimming pool, game room, whatever—so come by anytime." He held out the card.

"I'll try to make it," Crow lied, dropping the card in a pocket, not looking at it. "What's the occasion?"

"It's my birthday," Wicky said. "I'm going to be twenty-seven."

Crow blinked. Twenty-seven? He would have guessed closer to forty. "Congratulations," he said, apropos of absolutely nothing.

"Thanks!" Wicky opened the conference room door.

"What about my fee?" Crow asked.

Wicky furrowed his brow, then brightened. "Oh, of course. How much was it?"

"Three hundred."

"Ouch! You want to flip for it?"

"No, thanks."

Wicky opened an oversize ostrich-hide wallet, and looked inside. "Oops! I'm gonna have to stop at the bank. I'd write you a check, Joe, but I'd just as soon not have Cat asking me about it. How about I have it for you tonight? Come on, I'll walk you out."

In the waiting area, Wicky insisted on shaking his hand again. The receptionist was staring into the screen of her word processor, tapping her perfect front teeth with the end of a plastic pen. She looked up, but not at them, and wrinkled her nose as though detecting an unpleasant odor.

Wicky said, "Janet's our best girl, isn't that right, Jan?" Wicky was leering at her.

Janet snapped her eyes at him. Crow could almost hear the eyelashes clatter. She turned back to her machine and began typing furiously.

It occurred to Crow that both he and Janet were there to serve the whims of Dickie Wicky. He felt a surge of empathy and decided to revise his feelings about Janet the Ice Queen. She was who she was for reasons he was beginning to understand. To distract Wicky, he pointed across the room at the Picasso print hanging above the fake-leather sofa. "Is it real?" he asked.

Wicky looked and laughed. "Are you kidding? Nothing in this business is real."

"I didn't think so."

"Besides," he said, "they're getting so good with vinyl there's really no point. It looks just like leather, don't it?"

• • •

On his way home, Crow stopped at a discount electronics store on Lake Street and bought an answering machine. He spent most of the early afternoon getting it hooked up and then trying out an assortment of announcements ranging from the clever to the offensive to the absurd. He soon tired of hearing his own voice and settled for the mundane and minimal.

"Wait for the beep."

Debrowski said, "Are you asking me out, or do you just need a chaperone? Don't answer that. Just bang on my door when you're ready; I got nothing going on. I'll be around all night."

Crow broke the connection. A moment later, the booming from the apartment below returned to its previous level, or perhaps a notch higher. Debrowski, his downstairs neighbor, was a breath of rock and roll in a Muzak world. Crow had first met her at Cocaine Anonymous, back when he was going to three, four meetings a week—not because he was afraid of fucking up but because it bored him stupid to be sober alone. Lately, things had been better. He hadn't been to a meeting in over a year.

Laura Debrowski still attended her weekly meetings. Before checking herself into Saint Mary's two and a half years before, Debrowski had looted and all but destroyed her one-woman booking agency, "and had one hell of a good time doing it," as she put it during one group session. Crow had liked her right away. Debrowski had held on to a bit more fire than most of the CA people. She met her recovery with backtalk, tears, and laughter.

Crow's return to sobriety was more sullen. He was rarely heard from at the meetings. When he confessed to his former profession, the news was greeted by most of the others with hostility. Cokeheads didn't like cops, period. Crow couldn't blame them. He didn't like cops, either.

Debrowski had said, "You don't look like a cop to me, Crow."

"I'm not now."

"It shows."

A few weeks later, pushed out into the gray, pallid world of mineral water, coffee, and cigarettes, they had stayed in touch, doing regular lunches at Emily's Lebanese Deli, where they satisfied a mutual craving for olives, feta cheese, and company of a kind. Friendship formed around the seed of their shared addiction and continued to grow. They discovered in each other a sense of humor so dehydrated that to laugh out loud would cause a joke to crumble. To others, their conversations at Emily's looked serious, even somber, but Crow always remembered them as scintillating, comical, humorous.

Debrowski had rebuilt her booking business within a few months. In the rock-and-roll business it was generally understood that drug problems are a hazard of the trade, and her past was quickly forgotten. She was representing a dozen groups already, including the Coldcocks, Bad Dream Danny, and Bad Beat. Drug-addicted cops were not so quickly pardoned for their sins, and Crow had been drifting from one thing to another for the past two years, none of them real jobs, none of them with even the pretense of permanence. So far he liked it that way. When Debrowski had mentioned the vacant apartment upstairs from her place, Crow abandoned his sterile suburban efficiency and moved into the city.

He didn't want to go to the party, but the idea that Dickie Wicky might be trying to stiff him for a lousy three hundred dollars was sticking in his throat. Going with Debrowski made the prospect a bit more appealing. She kept him from taking people like Wicky—or himself—too seriously. He was comfortable with her. Her boundaries were solid and clear. They were friends. They could go to the party, stay sober, have a good time, and be back in their respective beds by midnight. Besides, there were no good poker games around, and it was Friday night.

If he had a cabin on a lake, he would now grill a few walleye fillets, sauté some wild mushrooms, sit and listen to the loons calling. Instead, he dialed Peroni's Pizzeria.

"P'roni's." Crow could hear crashing pans and loud voices in the background.

"One small anchovy and pineapple, light on the cheese."

"This must be Crow."

"Just take it easy on the cheese this time, okay, Jake?"

"Small anchovy pineapple, easy cheese. Got it. Anything else?"

"That's it."

"You still living in that dump down on First?"

"You calling my place a dump?"

"You kidding? My driver won't go down there 'less I make him a loan a my piece. Oughta drop a bomb on that neighborhood."

"You don't want my business, Jake?"

"Keep your shirt on, Crow. We'll get you your pizza."

Forty minutes later, a tall kid with greasy hair and a pizza showed up at the door. Crow asked to see his piece. The kid looked confused.

"Jake didn't loan you his six-gun?" Crow asked.

The kid shook his head and stepped back. Crow took the pizza. It was enormous. "I ordered a small," he said.

The kid shrugged. "You want I should take it back?"

"Forget it." Crow handed him a twenty.

"Pizza's sixteen bucks. You want change?"

"Forget it." He closed the door and carried the pizza into the kitchen, picked up the phone, and made another call to his downstairs neighbor.

"Debrowski here," she shouted into the phone, rock music pouring across her voice.

"What's that you got on down there?"

"What?"

"This is Crow. What are we listening to?"

"Just a second." He heard the receiver drop. A few seconds later, the music stopped and Debrowski got back on the line. "Hello?"

"This is your upstairs neighbor. What were we listening to?"

"Bad Beat. I got them booked into First Avenue in front of Concrete Blonde."

"Congratulations. You eat yet?"

"You gonna take me out to dinner, Crow? This must be a date."

"I've got more pizza than I can eat here."

"What kind of pizza?"

"Anchovy and pineapple."

"Jesus, Crow, you ever hear of sausage and mushroom? Thanks but no thanks. I'll make myself a peanut butter sandwich for dinner."

"I had that for lunch."

"Couple of gourmet cooks."

Crow managed to eat all but three slices, which he folded back into the box and put in the refrigerator. It might start looking good again by morning.

His first idea was to throw on a jacket and a tie. He was, after all, going there to collect a business debt. But he didn't want to overdress, wind up looking like some nerd. His second idea was to go in shorts and a T-shirt. Crow vacillated for about three seconds between slob and nerd and ended up in jeans, open-collar shirt, and faded black cotton sport coat. He would cover all bases, look like a slob *and* a nerd. Locking his door, he walked downstairs and pounded on Debrowski's door until it opened.

"How was the pizza?" Debrowski never had to wonder what to wear. Short, spiky blond hair streaked with blue, thick slabs of mascara, black leather jacket, shredded jeans, big black boots, chains and pins and dangling jewelry everywhere.

"Salty and sweet." Crow looked at her face, small and childlike behind the rock-and-roll facade. "Was your peanut butter okay?"

"I didn't eat. You think they'll have any food there? God, I sure hope so! What kinda party is this? Jesus, Crow, you look even nerdier than usual. You trying not to impress somebody or what?"

"That's pretty close. Actually, the guy owes me some money." They walked around the house to where his black Jaguar XJS squatted adjacent to the alley. Originally, the car had been a custom-ordered soft pink with matching leather upholstery. Crow had received it in lieu of payment from a former client—a pudgy liposuctionist named Bellweather with a taste for flesh tones. Bellweather had fled town, but he had left his Jaguar—decorated with several bullet holes from a nine-millimeter Glock—behind. Crow's body-shop man, a tall Hmong nicknamed Swede, had plugged up all the holes, then painted the outside of the car black.

Debrowski waited for him to unlock the door, frowning at the fleshy-pink leather interior. "Back to the womb," she said. Chains jangling, she ducked into the low-slung cockpit and slammed the door. Crow twisted the key, turning the engine over for almost thirty seconds before it hiccuped, caught, and instantly roared up to seven thousand rpm. He waited for the twelve cylinders to settle back down.

"Car sounds all excited, Crow. I never know if I'm going for a ride or about to be digested. You sure you don't want to take my bike?"

"It'll be okay." He'd been on the back of Debrowski's Kawasaki once and wouldn't forget it anytime soon. He dropped the Jaguar into gear and pulled away from the curb, rear wheels spinning. "It wants to go all the time, like there's a ghost on the gas pedal. I keep taking it in, and they keep charging me more money, but it goes like it wants to when it wants to."

"Sort of like you."

"It goes when it goes, though." He tapped his foot on the accelerator and made her chains rattle.

"Jesus, Crow, when you gonna grow up." She pulled a Camel out of one of the forty or fifty zipper pockets that decorated her leather jacket and a farmer's match out of another. She struck the match on a zipper and sucked the flame into the end of the cigarette. The tiny interior immediately hazed blue with smoke. "I suppose you're gonna get in another card game and leave me hanging out with a bunch a bozos, huh?"

"If the party's no good, we can leave."

"We always have so much fun together."

◆ ♥ 6 ♣ ♠

One thing I like about cats—they know what they want.

—Joe Crow

Most of the men looked as if they had come to the party directly from their downtown jobs, a lot of gray suits and big black shoes. The women, fewer in number, sported more colorful attire. The scene looked and felt like an office party, men and women who had to work together trying to get drunk enough to like one another.

"Real hip crowd, Crow."

Crow shrugged and grinned. People were distributed in small clumps around the three-lane lap pool, drinking and talking in loud voices. No one was swimming.

"Which one's your friend?" Debrowski asked.

"I don't see him. Let's look around."

The party spread throughout the twenty-fifth floor, with groups of people gathered in the hallways. They found Wicky in his crowded kitchen, demonstrating the proper way to mix a martini. He was wearing a pair of neon jams under a Hawaiian-print beach robe.

"Joe Crow!" Wicky said. He handed the half-shaken martini to a woman with glazed blue eyes in a matching pale-blue suit. "Just shake it till you get thirsty, sweets." He turned back to Crow. "Great! You came! Who is this?"

"My friend Laura Debrowski," said Crow.

"Call me Debrowski."

"Great!" Wicky held out his hand; Debrowski shook it, giving her chains a good rattle. "Great jacket," Wicky said. He looked at Crow. "You see Catfish yet? No? She's wearing this little black dress, hair up on top of her head. You can't miss her."

"I'll look for her. You think I could get that three hundred from you now?"

"Your consultation fee?" He looked at Debrowski and winked. "The guy costs me six hundred bucks an hour. You believe that?"

"You really charge that much, Crow?" Debrowski asked.

Crow shook his head. "Dickie gets a special rate."

Wicky laughed, a little too loud, and slapped Crow on the back. "I'll be right back." He maneuvered his way through the crowded kitchen and disappeared into one of the bedrooms.

"What an asshole," Debrowski observed. "Who are these people, anyway?"

"Friends of Dickie's, I guess. He's a stockbroker." The woman to whom Wicky had passed the cocktail shaker was pouring martinis into plastic glasses. Crow looked past her, through the living room, out onto the balcony. A woman in a black cocktail dress was standing at the railing smoking a cigarette, looking out over the Mississippi River. The sky beyond was the deep gray of dusk's final moments. Something in her shape, or in the way she smoked the cigarette, made him want to keep looking at her. Her hair was black, like her dress, and her skin looked flushed, as though she had spent the afternoon in the sun. She had an extraordinarily long neck. Debrowski was complaining about the music, some new-age stuff with a rock-and-roll backbeat. Crow said, "Uh-huh," but kept his eyes on the woman on the balcony, who he had decided must be Catfish Wicky. He was watching her when she turned and looked into the apartment. Her eyes raked over the crowded room and caught his. To his own surprise, Crow looked quickly away.

"You hear this kind of shit in grocery stores," Debrowski was saying.

"What?"

"Muzak, Crow. Where the hell have you been?"

"Sorry. Where'd Dickie go? I have to take care of some business."

"You didn't tell me we were here on a collection call. Do I get a piece of it?"

Some time later, Crow found Wicky in one of the bedrooms, laying out a few lines of cocaine. The sight hit him like a bellyful of cold; he took a quick step back and collided with the martini woman.

"Hey!"

"Sorry," Crow said, turning and making his way back out into the living room. Debrowski had disappeared, and Catfish Wicky was no longer on the balcony; Crow took her place, watching the line of headlights streaming up and down the East and West River Roads, trying to erase the image of the white lines of coke from the screen in his head. He imagined himself walking back into the room, Wicky handing him a rolled-up hundred-dollar bill, clapping him on the back, offering him the biggest, fattest, purest line in creation. . . . Crow shook his head violently, dislodging the fantasy, forcing himself to watch the traffic twenty-five stories below. "That was before," he said out loud. "This is now."

"Hey, Crow." Wicky's voice. Crow took a breath and turned to face him. Wicky was holding out his hand. "Sorry, I got hung up. Three hundred, right?"

"Right." Crow took the cash, three hundreds. The top bill was curled up, as if it had recently been rolled into a tube. Crow folded the money and pushed it into the front pocket of his jeans.

"Where's your girlfriend?"

"I don't know."

"Maybe she's out by the pool. You see Catfish yet?"

"She's wearing a black dress, right? Yeah, I saw her."

"She's really something, isn't she?"

"I didn't get that good a look at her."

"You hang around very long, you'll get a real good look. I guarantee it."

Debrowski was not at the swimming pool. Crow leaned against a cool tile wall and watched a very drunk woman explaining to a very drunk man how drunk he was. The couple stood unsteadily near the edge of the pool, taking turns talking, arms churning in dangerous gesticulation. Crow thought it was close to a sure thing that one or both of them would fall in before the night was over—about six to five that the man would get wet first. He was enjoying this thought when he felt something warm behind him. Turning his head, then his body, he looked into a pair of uneven black eyes. She was too close; he stepped back and crossed his arms.

Catfish Wicky smiled, thick red lips stretching across small, even teeth. Crow thought, again, what an odd-looking woman. Something about her features—their relative size or shape, maybe—was alarming, as though at any moment he might discover that she had two different-color eyes (though both now looked solid black), or that her nose had the wrong number of nostrils (but he counted two), or that her teeth had been sharpened. And perhaps they had. He had the strong sense that her parents ought not to have met.

"Do y'all find me attractive?" she asked.

Crow's eyes went to her lips. They looked swollen and soft, as though she had just been making love. They seemed to add a soft Southern buzz to the words passing between them. He remembered the way his lips had felt after eating a wide bowl of peppery crawfish étouffée somewhere far south of New Orleans in the toe of Louisiana, some low, tangled place where humans mated with swamp creatures. Crow's eyes dropped to the spray of freckles across the tops of her breasts and tried to make sense of her question. Did he find her attractive? One thing he knew for sure: he was no way going to answer it.

She took a step toward him. "I saw you watching me," she said. "When I was on the balcony you were looking right at me. My name is Cat Fish." She said her name distinctly, tearing it apart, making two separate words. "Do you know me?"

"No." She was not a person he would forget.

"What's your name?" She smelled of cigarettes and spice.

"Joe Crow."

She swiveled her head slowly, taking in the room. "People are so boring, Joe. I get so bored I want to take my clothes off and scream. I saw you were watching me, Joe. I thought I'd better introduce myself. I don't mind if you look at me. I kind of like it."

Crow thought it safest not to reply. There was something odd about the way she talked, as if her accent and her speech mannerisms had come to her late in life. It was there, and then it wasn't. Catfish smiled and punched him lightly on the arm. "Y'all come on over here, Joe Crow. I want to show you something." She grabbed his wrist with a hot, dry hand and pulled him toward a door at the far end of the pool area. Crow made a feeble attempt to disengage, but her grip was determined; he let her guide him down the length of the room.

The door led into a game room with a Ping-Pong table, a pool table, and three card tables. A noisy group of men was gathered two deep around the pool table. "The lady says she's hot," he heard. "She wants those bones, cool her down." Then he heard a familiar jangle of metal links being shaken together and Debrowski's husky voice: "Come *on* you mother*fuck*er . . . yes! Four-three for me!" Then a man's voice: "You sure you never played this game, lady?" and a chorus of male laughter.

Catfish was beside him, still gripping his wrist. "That's who y'all were looking for, right?"

Crow nodded, moving around the table, Catfish staying with him. He decided that the problem with her voice was that she didn't say "y'all" like a real Southerner. The contraction came and went, as though she was using it consciously. But the buzz in her voice, the sound of forgotten French, sounded real. Cajun? Now he wasn't sure. Debrowski was at the end of the pool table, shaking the dice hard in both hands. "Shake them puppies, baby, heat 'em up," urged a flushed young man, his unknotted maroon-and-black rep tie hanging over the lapels of a light-gray suit.

"I's born in sixty-one, six-one for the vix-un! Yeah!" Debrowski let the dice fly, pitching them hard down the length of the table, bouncing them off the chests of the men crowded against the opposite end. Six and one: seven spots. "Yes!" She thumped her fist on the table and collected from three of the bettors.

"How are you doing?" Crow asked.

Debrowski grinned and gave him the thumbs-up, then her eyes snagged on Catfish and went narrow. It lasted only an instant, and Crow was not sure he hadn't imagined it. Crow watched her throw two more naturals. He tried to keep his mind on the dice, calculating odds, wanting to bet but adhering to his personal proscription on games of pure chance. His body, at the same time, was acutely aware of Catfish Wicky standing close by his side. She was like a furnace; he could feel her body heat warming his entire right side. Her hand, resting lightly on his hip, felt as though it would leave a blistered palmprint.

"Are y'all going to play?" she asked, her mouth inches from his ear.

"I don't play craps. Just poker."

"Poker's boring. But I bet Dickie could probably get up a game, if you want to play. Dickie loves to lose our money at poker."

"That's okay." Crow brushed her hand off his hip. Catfish smiled and crossed her arms over her freckled breasts. Now her eyes were pitched at different angles, and the right one looked noticeably larger. Crow felt as if he was going to fall into it. "Excuse me," he said, stepping back. He turned and started toward the pool area, came face-to-face with Dickie Wicky.

"Dickie!" Crow was discomfited, as though he had been caught undressed with the man's wife.

Wicky was grinning broadly, showing too many of his peglike teeth, holding a large, frosted glass full of olives and gin with both hands.

"You see what I mean?" he whispered loudly.

"Excuse me." Crow made a detour around him, headed back through the pool area. The man who had been in conversation at the pool's edge was now standing in four feet of water, wearing his suit, his hair plastered to his skull, still talking to the woman, who sat with her feet dangling in the water. Crow kept moving; he had the idea that a glass of cold water would make the feelings go away, the memories triggered by the cocaine and the sense of inevitability brought on by the heat of Catfish Wicky's body.

The martini woman was still in Wicky's kitchen, holding herself up by leaning forward over the butcher-block counter that separated the kitchen from the living room. She watched Crow fill a glass from the kitchen tap, drink it, and fill it again.

"What's the matter with you?" she asked. "Where did everybody go?"

"They're all over by the pool and in the game room. Having a good time."

"I doubt that," the woman said.

Crow shrugged, silently agreeing with her but not wanting the conversation.

"I'm a stockbroker," she said. "I got my license to steal. What do you do?"

"Lately, I've been a marriage counselor."

"Yeah, me too," she said. "My husband keeps asking me why we got married. I tell him it was for the silverware and toasters. Look, there's that cat again."

Crow followed her gaze. The cat was looking at them from the opposite side of the living room, a big tom with a sleek, handsome coat. Crow started toward it, needing to make contact with something sober. When he was a few steps away, the cat hissed at him and took off, clawing its way across the carpet, dragging its hindquarters, which were strapped to a tiny wheeled cart.

A gentleman is a man who will pay his gambling debts even when he knows he has been cheated.

—Leo Tolstoy

Alone, Crow reclined on a lounger by the outdoor pool. Twenty-five stories above him, he could see Wicky's brightly lit balcony. People appeared and disappeared, leaning on the rail, looking out over the river. Crow wanted nothing more than to go home, crawl into bed, and lose consciousness, but he knew that the images from the party—the coke, the cat, Catfish, and the man standing in the pool—would keep his head buzzing for hours.

Debrowski had refused to leave. "No way, Crow. I'm hotter'n a Thai chili here. These guys just can't stop giving me their money." Her face was pink, her eyes bright.

"You sure?"

"What's the matter, Crow, you eat some bad dip or something?"

"I've got to get out of here."

"So take a walk. I'll have these guys cleaned out in an hour."

He had left the party drunk on bad air and memories. He didn't like to see Debrowski like that, all wound up from her run at the craps table. It was too much like getting high. What the hell—it *was* getting high. He closed his eyes. The faint party sounds drifted down through the summer air like flakes of artificial snow.

"Have you seen Cat?" Wicky asked, swaying at the edge of the lap pool.

Jack Mitchell, sitting on the lip of the pool with his feet in the water, looked up and shook his head. He had taken his shoes off but was still wearing his sodden navy-blue suit and matching socks. "Sorry, Dickie. You checked all the bedrooms?" The woman sitting beside him, her bare toes wiggling in the water, giggled. They put their heads together and laughed. Wicky staggered off toward the game room, almost colliding with a similarly inebriated man moving in the opposite direction.

"You seen my wife?" Wicky asked. The man kept walking, listing toward the pool. Wicky pushed into the game room. "Catfish?" he called. A few of the poker players looked up momentarily, returned their attention to their cards. None of the craps players seemed to hear him. Wicky approached two men who were leaning against the Ping-Pong table, talking.

"Jimmy, Dave, you seen Catfish anyplace? I can't find her."

Dave shrugged and looked away. Jimmy, one of Litten Securities' most junior RRs, said, "You don't look so good, Mr. Wicky. Maybe you ought to go lay down."

Wicky shook his head and touched the side of his nose with his finger. "I just need a little blast to get my head straight. You guys want to do some lines?"

Jimmy and Dave looked at each other. Dave's eyebrows went up, and Jimmy smiled. "What the hell," Dave said, pushing himself off the Ping-Pong table.

"Then let's get straight," Wicky said, moving away.

Dave and Jimmy followed. "Nothing like doing a little blow with the boss," Dave said to Jimmy. " 'Specially when it's his coke."

Debrowski was still winning when Crow returned to the party.

"You're looking good, Debrowski," he said.

She grinned and punched the man standing next to her on the shoulder. "A half hour ago I had a bad run and tapped out. Then Loman here loaned me a lucky tenner."

Loman was about Crow's size, but rounder and softer. An initialed collar bar held his tie in place. He grabbed Crow's hand and gave it a sincere shake. "My name is Ron Lipke, but Laura here calls me Loman. She says I'm the perfect salesman," he said proudly. "I'm with Centennial Life."

Crow let his eyes go unfocused. Debrowski tugged on his sleeve. "I'm up almost five hundred bucks!" she said in a hoarse whisper. In a normal voice she added, "Loman here won't even let me give him his tenner back."

"It was a gift," Ron Lipke explained.

"Good for you," Crow said to both of them. "You want to go anytime soon?" he asked Debrowski.

"You kidding me, Crow? I'm hot. Listen, why don't you hang around, play some cards or something? These guys got the runs with their money like you wouldn't believe. I been fading six-eights at even odds all night long. Imagine what you can do to that stud game over there."

Crow looked over at the card game. Five players, all strangers. He could feel the buzz coming on, the adrenaline edge that a good card game brought out. He walked over to the table and watched them play a hand. All of the players looked as if they shopped at Brooks Brothers, except the guy who was wearing a Mickey Mouse T-shirt. He was a tall, thin man with hair, flesh, and eyes the color of weak, milky tea. An impressive pile of cash was stacked in front of him.

"Anybody seen Catfish?" called a voice from behind Crow. Dickie Wicky was walking toward the craps table, his head twitching back and forth, his jaw pulsing. Crow knew the recipe by heart, having applied it to himself more times than he cared to remember: Take one human being, add a generous handful of dry martinis, a few hours of inane conversation, and a gram or two of good coke. From the inside, Wicky would be feeling as if he was turbocharged, running at the red line, hitting hard on all cylinders. Sometimes Crow missed that feeling. Seeing it in Wicky made him feel flat and insubstantial.

Wicky's eyes jerked back and forth and landed on Crow. A moment later, his body changed direction, following his eyes.

"Crow! Where you been? You seen Cat?"

Crow shook his head.

"Well, fuck 'er, then." He looked at the cardplayers and weaved from side to side. "Hey, Crow, what do you say we show these guys how to play poker. What are you guys playing?"

"Seven stud, ten-buck limit," said one of the players without looking up.

Wicky looked at Crow and winked broadly. "You guys want some of our money?" he asked.

Crow started losing from the first hand, when his ace-high flush lost to a concealed full house held by the very drunk man sitting to his left, the guy catching the case jack on his last card. Within an hour Crow was down over four hundred dollars.

Ten hands later, he was down eight hundred. He had lost three big hands, one right after another, two of them to the tall man with the Mickey Mouse T-shirt and the other to Wicky, who was playing his usual horrible game of poker but getting lucky for once. The guy with the Mickey Mouse shirt controlled the biggest stack—he had been winning steadily all night. Crow, sitting immediately to his left, watched him take a small pot with wired aces.

"Nice hand," said Crow as the man swept in the pot. "My name's Joe Crow."

The man shook Crow's hand and said, "Benjamin Cartwright," in a deep, mellifluous voice.

"You play a hell of a game of seven stud, Ben," Crow said. "You learn that on the Ponderosa?"

"I have been fortunate this evening."

"You guys want to kick up the limits?" asked Wicky, shuffling the deck. He nudged the man next to him. "What do you say, Mitch? Want to up it to twenty bucks?"

"Fine with me," Mitch muttered.

"I could do that," said Cartwright.

The other three players—a red-faced man holding a dead cigar in his mouth, an extremely drunk older man who might have been a good cardplayer had he been sober, and a dried-out-looking fellow with a frayed collar who folded every hand he was dealt—all shrugged their assent.

"Crow?"

"Fine by me, Dickie."

On his next hand Crow got a pair of aces facedown and a deuce showing. He bet twenty dollars and got three callers. Cartwright looked at Crow's cards and folded an exposed ace. Somewhere in Crow's mind an alarm went off. He looked carefully at his down cards, the two aces. Was that a nick on the top edge? He didn't think so at first; it was so slight he was not even sure he was seeing it. But the same faint irregularity appeared on the edge of both his aces. He looked at the ace that Ben Cartwright had turned over when he folded. It had the same faint impression on the edge. Crow looked at the other cards that had been dealt, but could not find the case ace. Someone was nicking the aces, making money with his fingernails. Crow played out the rest of the hand cautiously, winning a small pot with aces and deuces. Before passing his cards to the next dealer, he nicked the two deuces with his fingernail.

Ben Cartwright dealt the next hand, giving Crow a deuce, ten down, and a queen showing. Crow dropped, nicking the deuce as he threw away the cards. Since Cartwright was winning most of the money, it was a good bet that he was the cheat. Crow watched him bet into a pair of aces, one of them concealed, held by the red-faced man, who raised back. All the others threw their hands away, Cartwright re-raised, and his opponent called. Crow thought he detected a nick on the top card of the deck and wondered if the red-faced man was about to catch an ace or a deuce.

Cartwright dealt his opponent an eight; Crow could hear a faint *hist*, the sound signature of a deuce dealer, as Cartwright thumbed the card off the deck. The sound of the second card from the top of the deck being pulled from between the first and third card was distinctive, and Crow realized with some embarrassment that he had been hearing it all along, every time Cartwright dealt, without consciously identifying it. The guy had been dealing seconds all night. He heard the hoarse voice of his father. *You catch a deuce dealer with your ears, not your eyes, son.*

Cartwright gave himself the nicked ace. A card nicker *and* a deuce dealer, Crow thought, wondering how he was going to recover his eight hundred dollars. Cartwright won the hand with kings full of aces.

"What do you do for a living, Ben?" Crow asked, gathering the cards for the next deal. "You still in the cattle business?"

Cartwright squared up his pile of cash and said, "I am an investment counselor. I specialize in collectibles. Investment-quality ephemera. What do you do, Mr. Crow?"

"Odd jobs."

Ben Cartwright smiled. "I used to do that," he said. "A difficult way to make a living."

"You doing better in ephemera?"

"Much better, thank you."

Crow shuffled the deck and dealt. Using his peripheral vision, he watched Cartwright pick up his down cards, both of which were nicked. The ace of spades was his up card. Cartwright looked quickly at Crow, who appeared not to notice.

"Ace bets," said Crow. Cartwright reached for his stack, hesitated, bet ten dollars. Crow, with a jack of clubs showing, raised twenty. The man to his left folded, the red-faced man called, the other two players folded. Cartwright hesitated, then called the raise.

On the next round, Crow dealt the red-faced man a rag, gave Cartwright the case ace and himself an eight of clubs. "Pair of aces bets."

Cartwright was looking at him suspiciously. "I check."

Crow shrugged and bet twenty dollars. The red-faced man folded. Cartwright glared at Crow, his weak-tea eyes quivering.

"You in or out?" Crow asked. The other players, sensing something between the two but uncertain what it was, were watching carefully. Cartwright looked again at his down cards and called the bet.

"You're not raising?"

"I am not."

Crow shrugged and dealt a fifth round—a nicked deuce to Cartwright, the seven of clubs for himself. "Possible straight flush for the dealer. You're still high," he said to Cartwright. "You gonna bet those aces this time?"

Cartwright chewed his lip before answering. "I think not."

Debrowski came up behind Crow. The craps game was breaking up. "I lost it all, Crow. How are you doing?"

"Not bad." He bet twenty dollars.

Cartwright picked up his down cards and threw them faceup on the table: ace, deuce.

"I fold," he said.

"You're folding a full house?" said Wicky.

Cartwright was staring at Crow, his pale eyes quivering. "He has a straight flush," he said in his big voice. "Show them your hand, Mr. Crow."

Crow raked in the little pot with one hand and flipped over his down cards with the other. The three of hearts, the five of spades.

"Rags!" the red-faced man said, laughing around his cigar. Ben Cartwright sat back as though he had been chest-punched. He reached for the deck and turned over the top four cards, the cards they would have received had they played out the entire hand: three of diamonds, eight and nine of hearts, queen of spades. No clubs, no possibility of a straight flush.

"Excuse me, gentlemen. I have to be going." Ben Cartwright stood, folded the pile of money in front of him, pushed it into his hip pocket, and headed for the door.

"What was that about?" Debrowski asked.

Crow stood up. "You want to play my stack? I have to go see a man about a debt."

"Sure," she said, sliding into his seat. She watched him follow Ben Cartwright out of the room.

"There go two of the three weirdest guys I ever met," Dickie said. He picked up the deck and started shuffling.

Ben Cartwright entered the elevator and pressed the ground-floor button. The doors had almost closed when a hand appeared and tripped the safety bar. The doors slid open and Crow stepped into the elevator. "How you doing?" he asked. The doors hissed shut and the elevator began its descent.

"I'm doing fine," Cartwright replied. The two men watched each other, leaning against opposite walls.

Between the fifth and fourth floors, Crow pressed the red emergency button and the elevator chattered to a stop.

"Maybe I'm not doing as well as I thought," Cartwright said. He looked at the elevator control panel. "I always wondered what would happen if you pressed that button."

"What happens is, the elevator stops, you pay a guy eight bills, the elevator starts up again."

"That how much you dropped?"

Crow smiled.

Cartwright stared down at the smaller man. After several seconds, he nodded, returned Crow's smile, and pulled a folded sheaf of bills from his hip pocket.

"You should have seen it sooner," he said, as though delivering a critique on Crow's performance. "It's been years since I did this for a living. I thought for sure you could hear me pulling out those cards. Noisy deck."

Crow took the money and pressed the button for the twenty-fifth floor. "I thought it was a friendly game. I wasn't looking for a trim job."

"Trim job?" Cartwright seemed surprised and offended. "You call that cheating?"

"What do you call it?"

"I call it poker, Mr. Crow."

As Crow returned to the game, Debrowski counted off a stack of bills and threw it down in the middle of the table. "Five hundred forty. All-in."

"What happened to twenty-dollar limit?" Crow asked.

"We got bored," Wicky said. "Laura, here, wanted to play some no-limit."

"Why not, since she seems to be doing it with my money. What the hell you doing, Debrowski?"

"Winning."

"She sure is," said the red-faced man. "Where the hell did you find her?"

"I forget," Crow said. "Let me see what you're betting my money on."

Debrowski showed him her cards. Crow nodded, crossed his arms, and stepped back to watch the hand played out.

The drunk sitting to Debrowski's left looked at his cards, then at the pot, then back at his cards, then folded. Debrowski's crap game sponsor, Ron Lipke, a.k.a. Loman, had taken the next seat. He gazed sadly at his cards, threw them away. The red-faced man, his cigar burned down to a one-inch stub, looked as if he was about to explode. "I don't believe this shit," he muttered, slamming his cards down on the discard pile.

Wicky was not looking at his cards, or at Debrowski, or at the money on the table. His eyes were fixed on Crow. Slowly, he counted out five hundred forty dollars, then counted out another five hundred. "I raise," he said.

"You can't raise," said the fat man. "She's all-in. Aren't we playing table stakes here?"

Wicky was looking at Crow. "What do you say, buddy?"

"I'll cover your light," Crow said to Debrowski.

Debrowski leaned forward and examined the pile of cash in the middle of the table. "How much we got here? About two thousand?"

"Something like that," Wicky said.

Debrowski smiled. "I'm light the pot."

Crow felt as if his stomach had detached itself, turned to ice, and started spinning. He focused on keeping his face neutral and his body upright. The cards Debrowski had shown him were a lousy pair of deuces—any decent hand would beat them—and she had just raised fifteen hundred dollars. Wicky was staring not at her but at Crow, drumming the table, staring at him, waiting for him to snap into focus. Crow tried to slow time, astonished by the effect Debrowski's bluff was having on him. He had been in hundreds of bigger hands, but this effect was new to him. He was furious with her for risking his money, he admired the guts it took to run this bluff, and he was flattered by her confidence in him—they both knew that Crow was the active player from here on out. Wicky's pale-blue irises floated on pink scleras, picking at Crow's face, seeking access. Crow felt a warm wave of confidence rise from his groin to his belly; the spinning inside slowed to a stop. Wicky was finding nothing; his eyes were skittering across Crow's shield like water droplets on a hot iron skillet. He was going to fold. Crow could read it in Wicky's eyes as clearly as he could see the chains on Debrowski's jacket. He didn't have shit. The shield was holding; Wicky was coming up empty; the only play that made sense now was for him to fold.

Wicky dropped his eyes to his cards. It was all Crow could do to keep himself from reaching over Debrowski's shoulder and scooping in the pot. It was as good as his.

Hunches are for dogs making love.

—*Amarillo Slim Preston*

Crow sat on his porch and watched it rain. It was coming straight down, thick but oddly quiet. The First Avenue traffic hissed by on slick black asphalt. It was Saturday, early afternoon, but none of the neighborhood kids were out. The only foot traffic was the postman, shrouded in his gray-blue raincoat, walking through the wet as if he owned it. Crow watched him deliver to the apartments across the street, then lost sight of him as he crossed over to Crow's side. A few seconds later, he heard the clank of his mailbox downstairs. He thought about going down to look at his mail, but he could not think of anything he was hoping to receive. Still, it would be something to do. He visualized himself getting up from his chair, opening the door, walking down the stairs.

An hour later, he was still thinking about it when he heard a door slam, footsteps in the staircase, pounding on his door, a muffled voice: "Open up, Crow."

He got up and opened the door.

"I brought your mail," said Debrowski, handing him a slim assortment of envelopes. She was wearing a sweater, white cotton with a cowl neck, and a pair of khaki slacks that had no holes, patches, studs, chains, or graffiti. Crow could not detect any makeup, and her usually spiky hair was combed down and held back by a tortoiseshell barrette.

He took the mail. "Thanks. What happened to your basic black?"

"I got to go out and see my mom today."

"She doesn't like leather and chains?"

"Actually, she doesn't mind them. She's pretty cool for an old lady. I just like to surprise her now and then."

"The penny loafers ought to blow her mind."

"You think I should put some pennies in them?"

"Too retro."

"That's what I thought. I don't want to scare her. She's got this heart thing, has to take all these pills."

"Uh-huh." Crow sorted through his mail.

"Crow? I'm sorry about last night."

"You already said that about twenty times. Forget about it. It wasn't a bad play, but you should never try to bluff a drunk. You never know what he's going to do. Best thing is to play your cards tight and wait for him to give you his money. I wasn't thinking, either."

"Yeah, well, it was mostly my fault. It was my hunch. Listen, I want to cover it. What was it we lost—about five thousand?"

"More like four. Forget it, Debrowski. You were playing with my stack. You don't owe me anything. We were both a part of it. He had no business calling us with a lousy pair of fours."

"I shouldn't have bet your money. Especially pulling light that way. I want to pay you back. I can give you a check for fifteen hundred right now and the rest of it in a few weeks." She opened her purse and took out a black leather checkbook.

"I don't want your money, Debrowski," he snapped.

Debrowski jerked as if she had been slapped.

Crow looked up. "Sorry."

"Me too," said Debrowski, putting away her checkbook.

"It was my stack," Crow said again.

"It was my play. You aren't the only asshole in this universe, you know."

Crow shrugged. Debrowski turned and walked out. He listened to the soft sound of her penny loafers on the stairs, feeling more than a little ill. He looked at the mail in his hand, tore open an envelope from Bobick Realty of Brainerd, Minnesota, looked at the photographs. Pictures of an island and a small cabin. He read the note from Jimbo.

"Great," he said to the empty room. "All I have to do is come up with a hundred thirty thousand bucks and a boat." He laughed and threw the letter and photos in the wastebasket. Milo stalked into the room, sniffed the wastebasket, stretched.

"I'm afraid old Jimbo's wasting his time on this one," Crow said. "He wants my money, he's going to have to get in line behind Dickie."

He winked at Milo. "You believe it? I'm talking to the damn cat." He picked up another envelope, and his usually expressionless face went white.

"Mrow?" Milo asked.

Crow swallowed and stared at the return address of the Internal Revenue Service.

"I think the line just got longer," he said.

At nine o'clock that evening, Crow was awakened by someone pounding on his front door. It used to be, when Crow had troubles, he just got high. Now, hooked on sobriety, he went to sleep. He rolled off the sofa and staggered toward the sound, more to make it stop than because he wanted to know who was there. It was Dickie Wicky, wearing a neon baseball cap.

Crow's half-open eyes went to the cap and got stuck there for an eternal moment. He shook his head to clear it. "Nice hat," he said, his voice thick with sleep.

"Thanks!" Wicky stepped inside and looked over the room. "I've been trying to call you all day. You ever listen to your messages?"

"Not often," Crow muttered.

"I thought so. You got a minute?"

"I was asleep," said Crow. "What do you want, Dickie? Is this a collection call?"

"Yeah, I came over to break your arm—just kidding! I have this idea I want to run by you."

"Excuse me." Crow went to the kitchen and mixed two teaspoons of instant coffee into a mug of hot tap water. He sipped it, made a face, sipped it again.

Dickie Wicky was looking curiously at the prints, posters, and paintings that hung in haphazard array on the walls, and at cardboard boxes that were stacked along the baseboards. Each of the boxes was labeled: Books, Kitchen Junk, Misc, Mags, Towels. . . . Some of the boxes had been opened and partially emptied, others were still sealed with brown plastic tape.

"Moving?" he asked.

"Still unpacking," Crow said. He had been unpacking for months. He took another pass at the lukewarm coffee, gestured with the mug. "You want some?"

Wicky shook his head, looking closely at a deep frame that held five dog-eared baseball cards: Harmon Killebrew, Roger Maris, Zoilo Versalles, Whitey Ford, Willie Mays.

"These might be worth some money," he said. "I've got some friends that are into this kind of stuff. Collectibles. Comic books. You know that there was one comic that sold for over a hundred thousand dollars last year? You find an attic full of the things, you could retire. Baseball cards too. You want me to get them appraised?"

"No. You want to tell me your idea now?"

"You sure? Maybe you've got a fortune hanging there on your wall."

"No, thanks," said Crow, making a mental note to find out what his baseball cards were going for now. When he'd had them framed five years ago, they had been worth less than a hundred dollars. The frame had cost him more than the cards were worth.

Wicky shrugged, then sat down on the sofa. Crow remained standing. Wicky cleared his throat.

"Remember we were talking about Catfish before? At my office?"

Crow nodded.

"Did you get a chance to think about it some more?"

"Yeah, I did." He took a breath. "I'm really not interested in that kind of work." Actually, it wasn't the work he minded; it was the thought of working for Dickie Wicky.

Wicky nodded, but continued as though Crow had said nothing. "Because I was thinking that you could take care of that two thousand pretty quick that way. I'd even be willing to trade you straight up. You take care of my problem, I tear up your marker. What do you think?"

Crow forced down another ounce of the rapidly cooling coffee and thought about his financial situation. The IRS wanted $3,575 in back taxes, claiming that the Jaguar left behind by Bellweather, his former client, was unreported income. How had they found out about that? Bellweather had probably declared it as a business expense. Crow remembered receiving a 1099 for thirty thousand dollars from someplace called Eternal Enterprises in Honolulu. He had assumed it was a mistake, thrown it away, and hadn't given it a thought since. How did he get involved with these people?

"Joe? What are you thinking?" Wicky said.

Rent was due in a week. Things were looking bleak. He wouldn't be buying that island anytime soon, but the idea had become more attractive than ever. Getting Dickie Wicky paid off, at least, would be a positive step. Crow raised his eyes and stared at him over the rim of his coffee mug, playing with the balance in his mind. He wished he were a little more awake. Or maybe he didn't. He stared at Wicky, trying to imagine himself in his employ, fighting the stomach-rolling sensation as he realized that he was going to do it.

"Nothing," said Crow.

Wicky held Crow's gaze for several seconds before his eyes fell away. He cleared his throat and said, "Catfish didn't make it home again last night, Joe." His voice had suddenly changed, as if he had a mouth full of pudding, and his eyes were wet. Crow looked away. It was the way it had been the day before in the Litten Securities conference room—he was uncomfortable with the forced intimacy. Wicky's emotion was probably genuine, but that didn't mean he wasn't using it, consciously and with premeditation, to manipulate and to control his audience.

Now he was staring off over Crow's right shoulder, his eyes uncharacteristically still. "She finally got home this morning. I could smell him on her. Some kind of crummy cologne." He cleared his throat and leaned forward, staring down at the hardwood floor.

Not fair, thought Crow. He shouldn't have to see this stuff, especially in his own home. He said, "And you want me to find this guy and pay him off."

"Yeah. That."

Crow closed his eyes. "I charge five hundred a day," he said.

"You find the guy and get it taken care of, I tear up your marker, even if it only takes you half an hour."

"Suppose I don't find him."

"You will. I'll tell you what. If you have to put more than four days into it, I'll go your regular rate for the extra time."

"And if I don't find him?"

"Oh, you'll find him, Joe. I know my wife."

THE FLOP

*Every time you play a hand differently from the way you would
have played it if you could see all your opponents' cards, they
gain; and every time you play your hand the same way you
would have played it if you could see all their cards, they lose.*

—*David Sklansky*, Poker Theory

In the bright summer daylight, from a distance, Catfish Wicky
had an ordinary, almost dowdy look about her. She could have
been any young woman in Reeboks and a baggy cotton dress
running her Thursday afternoon errands—a long visit to the mall, a
trip to the Porsche dealership for an oil change, an hour spent window-
shopping at the Galleria, a stop at Sherman's Bakery for scones and a
baguette, then downtown to Gaviidae Common. Her driving, however, was not in the least bit dowdy. She hit thirty miles per hour in
the Gaviidae parking ramp, her little red-on-red Porsche 944
screaming past rows of Audis, Volvos, and Mercedeses.

For the past week Crow had been keeping Catfish Wicky under sur-
veillance, waiting for her lover to appear. He had worked off his two-
thousand-dollar debt within the first four days without producing any
results, but Wicky wouldn't let him quit. "Don't leave me hanging,
Joe. I think she's going to meet him this afternoon. I want you to stay
on her, Joe. You just stick with her, and she'll lead us to him."

So far, Catfish had been leading him in circles. She did a lot of
sunbathing, and a lot of shopping, and a lot of fast driving. Bored,
Crow fantasized seducing Catfish himself. He would become her
lover, take her to his island cabin, then offer himself the ten thousand
dollars to give her up. Technically, it was a good plan. The ten thousand dollars Wicky had budgeted seemed low, but Crow was willing
to sacrifice if necessary. He let the fantasy run while he was standing
behind a potted avocado tree in Gaviidae Common, watching her
through the glass front of a shoe store. Catfish was trying on sandals.

For the first few minutes, he thought she might have a thing going with the shoe salesman. She was such a compulsive flirt it was hard to tell. He watched her putting the salesman through his paces, holding her leg up to look at the sandal, giving him the peek up her dress, getting him all steamed up, finally buying a pair of red leather sandals and leaving the store. Crow ducked behind the avocado tree until she passed. Two kids with designs shaved onto the sides of their heads were watching him. One of them started laughing, looking right at him. After an intensely angry moment, Crow took a look at himself hiding behind a potted plant. What the hell. He would have laughed too. He followed Catfish toward the parking ramp.

Apparently, adultery was not a daily thing with her. Not unless she was making it with the invisible man. The red Porsche screamed out of the ramp, onto Marquette, narrowly missing a taxi. Crow followed, pushing the Jaguar through the downtown traffic, staying with her until she had crossed the river and was turning into the parking ramp at The Summit.

Crow parked by a phone booth at the corner of Hennepin Avenue and called Litten Securities. Janet answered the phone and informed him that Mr. Wicky was taking a meeting. He asked her how she liked working for Dickie Wicky. She said she didn't work for Mr. Wicky, she worked for Litten Securities. He asked her if she thought Dickie was any good at his job. She said Mr. Wicky had been with the company for six years and was one of their top performers. Crow hung up, then dialed the number again.

"Mr. Irwin Jacobs calling for Mr. Richard Wicky," he said, invoking the name of Minnesota's high-profile corporate raider.

Wicky was on the line within ten seconds.

"Rich Wicky speaking." The voice was so contrived, so artificially deep, that Crow had to laugh aloud. He could almost hear Dickie's face collapse.

"Sorry, Dickie. It's me."

"Jesus Christ, Joe, don't do that!"

"Your wife was a good girl again today."

"She didn't meet anybody?" Wicky asked.

"You're disappointed? You should be happy, Dickie. She bought herself some sandals. I'm sure you'll like them."

Wicky snorted, a wet sound that made Crow hold the phone away from his face.

"She set a new speed record for the Gaviidae parking ramp," Crow added.

"Sounds like Cat. Spending my money as fast as she drives." He paused. "Listen, I've got to take a couple guys out for dinner tonight. Cat knows I won't be home, so she'll probably go out. How about you stay on her, see where she goes?"

It was a familiar conversation. "That's what you said yesterday, and she stayed home all night. You sure you want me to keep spending your money on this?"

"Don't worry about it."

"I'm going to need a check from you."

"I said no problem."

"She's at home right now. You want me to just sit here?"

"She won't stay long, buddy; you can count on it. You just wait awhile, and she'll be out and about."

"Okay, *buddy*."

Wicky laughed. The sound came over the wire like a cartoon balloon: "Ha ha ha!"

Catfish Wicky's red Porsche was parked at an angle on the second level of The Summit's ramp, taking up the parking spaces marked C. Wicky and R. Wicky. Crow found a slot in the next row where he could keep an eye on both the car and the elevator lobby. He passed the time by rereading Sklansky's *Poker Theory*. Four cars over, a man was sitting in a big blue car, also waiting for something. Crow couldn't see him clearly, but he could hear the radio, the foamy, pulpy sounds of lite rock echoing off the low concrete ceiling. He tried to push the music from his consciousness, focusing on Sklansky's brilliant but nearly impenetrable tome. Lite rock oozed over the chapter on Game Theory and Bluffing. Crow was about to get out and ask the guy to turn down his radio, when the elevator doors opened and Catfish Wicky stepped out into the parking ramp.

She had transformed herself from dowdy young housewife into what Debrowski would call, wrinkling her nose, "Tits and lips." Crow tried to identify the elements of her metamorphosis. Red lipstick, a little something on the eyes, a black cotton dress that looked like it would crawl up her thighs at the slightest provocation. Her dark hair, which during the day she had worn tied back in a loose ponytail, was now piled casually on top of her head, as though she had pushed it up there to get it out of the way, then forgot about it. She was wearing her new red sandals. Was that all? Was she walking differently? The superficial changes were slight, but there was nothing minor about the lump that had formed under his stomach. The Porsche swallowed her up, and Crow let his breath escape.

He started his car and followed her down the ramp. A big blue convertible was crowding his rear end. The lite rock guy. Catfish waved at the attendant and drove through the exit without stopping. The gate arm dropped in front of Crow; he had to pay three dollars to get out. The guy in the convertible, an ugly guy with a big head, was right on his back bumper. The Cadillac hood ornament was level with the top of Crow's head; his rearview mirror was full of bug-spattered chromium grillwork. Crow paid the attendant and resisted the urge to turn and give the guy behind him a look. He got the Jaguar out onto Hennepin just in time to see the Porsche turning right at University Avenue; by the time he made the corner, she was a quarter of a mile ahead.

Crow punched the accelerator and brought the Jag up to fifty, passing a little green Honda. Catfish was still pulling away, moving her Porsche deftly through and around the slower traffic. Feeling a seductive jolt of adrenaline, Crow shifted into fourth gear, prepared to follow her at any speed, when he heard a screech, a metallic thud, and the piercing sound of sheet metal on asphalt. He took his foot off the accelerator and flicked his eyes to the mirror. The Honda he had just passed was on its side in the road, still spinning, and behind it he could see the blue Cadillac convertible, its proud grille riding up over the remains of a small ash tree. Crow pulled to the side. Other cars were stopping. The windshield of the Honda had popped out in one piece and skidded across the four-lane avenue; the driver, a kid in a red T-shirt, was climbing shakily out through the front of his car. The Cadillac man, uglier than ever with blood running from his nose, was already out of his car, glaring at the ash tree that was jammed under his front bumper. A group of energetic young men came out of a frat house across the street and ran to the aid of the drivers. Crow dropped the Jag in gear and took off.

Catfish's Porsche was nowhere in sight.

Crow frowned and continued east on University Avenue, through the campus and toward Saint Paul, relying on luck and instinct. She could be going anywhere. If he didn't stumble on her within the next few miles, he decided, he would give it up, save Dickie some money.

As he crossed the invisible boundary between Minneapolis and Saint Paul, the character of the neighborhood changed. The businesses on the street got older, the buildings became more varied and peculiar, the trees fewer, and the signs at the intersections were no longer numbered streets but names. It was like sliding back in time. Some blocks seemed unchanged by the last half of the century. Tiny service-oriented businesses—shoe shops, tailors, TV repair, beauty salons, hobby stores—were sandwiched between red- and gray-brick factories. The Turf Club, "The Best Remnant of the '40s," featured country dancing seven nights a week. Porky's Drive-In, still painted like a giant red-and-brown checkerboard, had been feeding people burgers and malts in their cars since 1953.

Crow was looking for a convenient place to turn around, when he passed the Twin Town Luxury Motor Hotel, another fifties relic, and saw what looked like Catfish's Porsche parked in front of one of the rooms. The car was empty. Crow circled the block and drove past again, checking the license plate. It was hers. He parked on the street and entered the motel lobby. An old man wearing a Minnesota Twins baseball cap was sitting in a swivel chair behind the counter. He lowered his newspaper and raised his eyebrows.

Crow decided to use the direct approach.

"Did the woman driving that red Porsche just check in here?"

The man stared back at him, black eyes buried in a whorl of wrinkles.

"That's her car parked outside. Are you sure you didn't see her?"

The old man shrugged. Crow stared glumly through the lobby window at Catfish's car. He didn't want to sit there all night waiting for her to show up. The Porsche was parked next to a lemon-yellow Cadillac Fleetwood that needed a wash and wax. It had an Illinois license. Crow turned back to the desk clerk, who was still watching him over the top of his newspaper.

"You know whose Caddy that is?"

The old man slowly smiled. He had nice yellow dentures—they almost looked real.

Crow took out his wallet and put a twenty-dollar bill on the counter. It was worth a try. The old man sat up in his chair and stretched his neck to see the bill. He put it in the cash register and handed Crow ten dollars in change.

"Fella named Tom Aquinas in there now. Number twenty-two." He smiled again and went back to his newspaper.

Crow looked at the ten-dollar bill in his hand. He had never before received change on a bribe.

"You ever see the girl in the Porsche before?"

"Yup."

"She usually stay in there long?"

"Nope."

Crow decided to wait around. After Catfish left, he could approach "Tom Aquinas" and make him an offer. If all went well, he would be out of Dickie Wicky's employ by the end of the day.

"Thanks," said Crow, starting toward the door.

"He's a strange one," the old man said.

Crow stopped. Apparently, he hadn't used up his ten bucks yet.

"Never stops moving," the old man continued. "Like he's got ants in his pants."

Crow drove across the street to Porky's Drive-In. In its heyday, Porky's had been a full-service drive-in, complete with carhops, multicolored neon lights, and a fistfight every other Friday night. Their burgers had been the juiciest, their fries the crispest, and their malts the thickest. Somehow it had survived the onslaught of McDonald's and Burger King and was still serving its high-fat delights, although the carhops were ancient history. You could eat at one of the umbrella tables set out on the fenced-off patio area, or you could use the drive-up window and eat in your car. Crow ordered a bag of french fries and a Coke. He set the bag on his passenger seat and drove around to the end of the hundred-foot-long corrugated-metal awning, parking where he could see across the street to room 22 of the Twin Town. The underside of Porky's awning was decorated with colored neon bulbs. Crow picked a limp french fry out of its red-and-white-checkered paper tray. Contemporary reality could not compete with memories. Or maybe he had lost his tolerance for saturated fat. He squeezed the foil packet of catsup over the fries.

Twenty minutes later, he was looking at the last catsup-soaked french fry, daring himself to eat it, when Catfish Wicky stepped out of room 22. She was followed by a compact, dark-haired man in a bright-orange polo shirt. They walked between the yellow Cadillac and the Porsche and crossed the street on foot, heading directly toward him. Had she seen him following her? It was possible—he hadn't made much of an effort to remain unnoticed, and the Jag did not exactly blend in with the traffic—but they weren't looking at him. Every few steps, the man reached up with his right hand and pushed a slab of glossy black hair from his forehead; the hair would almost immediately fall back down over his thick eyebrows. He was talking, gesturing with one hand and working his hair with the other. Once across the street, they turned, entered the patio area, and sat at one of the umbrella tables. Crow could just see the tops of their heads over the low cedar fence; he pushed the french fry into his mouth and chewed.

So he was real. Crow had started to think of Catfish Wicky's mysterious lover as a Dickie Wicky delusion. But Tom Aquinas was real, even if his name was not. What kind of guy would he turn out to be? An intellectual, interested in theology? What did he have that Catfish wanted? The man he had seen crossing the street didn't look like anything special. He wasn't particularly good-looking, unless you went for the greasy look. And he wasn't rich, or they wouldn't be shacking up at the Twin Town. Would Dickie's ten thousand dollars be enough to make him take his urges elsewhere? Crow frowned. His job was to get the guy alone and make the offer; that was it. The guy could take it or leave it; it made no difference. Either way, Crow could simply report back to Wicky and be done with it. He didn't plan to get any deeper into the Wickys' domestic problems than was absolutely necessary.

He let his thoughts drift, staring off into the distance. Of all the things he had done for money, he decided, this was far and away the silliest. The more he thought about it, the closer he came to laughing out loud. Hiding behind potted plants. Maybe he should buy one of those Groucho Marx glasses with the nose and mustache, go up to the guy, and offer him a rubber chicken full of money. He was thinking that one day this would be really funny—something that would make him laugh while he was casting for walleye off the end of his dock—when Catfish Wicky suddenly appeared at his open window, reached in, and wiped a spot of catsup from his cheek with her forefinger. Crow jumped, hitting his head on the Jaguar's low roof.

Catfish laughed. "Small world, huh?" She licked the catsup from her finger and grinned. "Y'all got a minute, Joe? I want you to meet a friend of mine."

10

You remember Milli Vanilli? I was the guy introduced 'em.

—*Tomas Campo, a.k.a. Thomas Jefferson, a.k.a. Tom Aquinas*

The old man was right. It was like the guy had ants in his pants. Catfish introduced him as "Mah love stud, Tommy." She buried the fingers of her left hand in his thick black hair. Her other hand gripped Crow's wrist.

Crow nodded, thinking, At least there's no misunderstanding here—it's not like she's claiming he's her spiritual adviser or something. He wished she would let go of him.

Tommy had a quick white smile that used up most of the bottom half of his face. "I knew a guy named Crow," he said. "Apache. Real fuckin' nut. You Apache? You don't look Apache, you look like a mick. How do you know Cat? Cat? Where you know this guy from?" He bit into a chicken leg and chewed audibly.

Catfish sat down, still gripping Crow's hand.

"Crow's a friend of Dickie's," she said, squeezing. Her palm was hot and moist.

"Stockbroker, huh? That's a tough business. I used to be a stockbroker. You know Michael Milken? We did a deal together once, back before he got famous. I made a fuck of a lot of money in that business." His knee was going up and down.

"What did you do with it?" Crow asked, speaking for the first time since Catfish had dragged him out of his car.

"Spent it. Got something better now. Doing my own deals. The only way to go, bro. Don't invest in nothing you don't control. You a player?"

Crow did not respond. He had no idea what a "player" was in Tommy's lexicon.

" 'Cause I got a deal you wouldn't believe. Some of my deals, guys made a fuckin' fortune." He attacked his fried chicken. Catfish's grip slackened, and Crow was able to twist his hand away. "This is fucking great. I love this place," Tommy said through a mouthful of chicken. "You don't get food like this at your McDonald's. Anyways, you remember the Pet Rock? That was me. I did the Berlin Wall thing too. Brought forty tons of it over, busted it up, and sold it by the pound. People thought I was crazy, but I made a fucking fortune. Now I got this other deal."

"Tommy's got a lot of ideas," Catfish said.

"I can see that," Crow said.

"My love stud." Catfish ran a red-nailed hand through his hair.

"Fucking right," Tommy said, picking up a handful of sagging french fries. "You want to make some major cash, Crow, you come talk to me sometime." He pushed the mass of fries into his mouth and chewed, blinking his black eyes.

"I'll do that," said Crow, backing away. "It was nice meeting you."

Tommy waved a chicken leg at him. "Good meeting you, Crow. Keep me in mind, you want to make some serious money."

Catfish's eyes seemed to go off in two different directions, but they were both landing on Crow. He could feel them plucking at his neck as he walked to his car.

Tommy sucked the grease off his fingers.

"So who the fuck was that?" he asked, wiping his mouth with the back of a hand.

Catfish shrugged. "Some guy I met. He's doing some kind of work for Dickie. I think he's cute."

Tommy looked back over his shoulder and watched Crow drive his Jaguar out of Porky's lot onto University Avenue. "He don't look like a stockbroker. What's he doing for Dickie?"

Catfish smirked. "I think he's following me."

"Yeah? What for?"

"Dickie's going through one of his jealous streaks. He probably wants to know who I'm fucking."

"What's he want to know that for? Hope this don't ice our deal."

"I don't see why it should." Catfish sipped her Coke, sucking until the straw drew air. "Dickie'll work it out. He always does. He'll have this big temper tantrum, kick the cat, break something. I don't mind. It's kind of exciting."

"You sure minded when he gave that cat a yours a flying lesson."

Catfish smiled, but her eyes went dead. "He won't do that again."

"You sure?"

"I'm sure he better not."

Freddy Wisnesky had ordered the Double Twin Bacon Deluxe Basket, a jumbo root beer, and two of Porky's Big Brownies. It was his reward to himself for a job well done. One day in Minneapolis, and already he had found one of the guys he was looking for. The little one, Tommy Paine. Sitting right there with the broad, the one Fatman had told him about. With the weird name. Cat Fish.

He'd found her just like Mister C. had told him to. Like Dodge-a-knees, the guy with the light. Looking for a chance to get her alone. The only thing too bad was, he'd been looking forward to making her talk to him, and now he didn't have to. The guy was right there. And Freddy'd smashed up the Caddy trying to keep up with her. A little green car had got in his way, and then he had run over the tree.

Freddy grunted at the memory and proceeded to demolish the Double Twin Bacon Burger. He chewed methodically, biting through each mouthful three times before swallowing. He kept his eyes on the woman and the comic book guy.

A bunch of college kids with weird haircuts had helped him unhook his front bumper from the tree. They had been worried about the tree. It hadn't broken off completely, but the Cadillac had bent it nearly parallel to the ground and torn off most of the bark on one side. The consensus was that the tree was history. Freddy didn't give a shit. He was worried about the car. The left headlight was smashed in where it had hit the Honda.

The guy in the Honda had been upset when Freddy drove away. Freddy saw him writing something down. Probably the Cadillac's license number. Freddy didn't give a shit about that. He continued up University Avenue. No idea where he was going—it was pure luck when he spotted Tommy Paine and Catfish Wicky crossing the street.

Freddy ate his warm, sweet coleslaw and waited. Maybe the other one, Ben Disraeli, would show up too.

Crow drove out of Porky's and headed east on University Avenue, drove a few blocks, then doubled back and parked a block down from Porky's and the motel. Ten minutes later, Catfish and her "love stud" crossed the street. Crow waited. After a few minutes, Catfish's

Porsche pulled out onto University and headed east at high speed. Crow got out of his car and walked to the motel.

Aquinas—or whatever his name was—answered the door wearing nothing but a big white smile and a pair of purple briefs with the Batman logo printed across the crotch. He lost his smile when he saw Crow, and craned his neck to see past him into the parking lot. Apparently, he didn't see what he was looking for. He shook his head as if he was trying to shake a fly off his nose.

"Cat just left. You just missed her, man. The chick moves fast, you know?" He was chewing on something, crunching it between his teeth.

"That's okay," Crow said. "I came over to talk to you. What are you eating?"

Tommy Aquinas popped up his dark eyebrows and grinned. "Aspirin." He held up a bottle of grape-flavored Children's Tylenol. "I got a bad back. You want some? No? I bet you're thinking about that deal I mentioned. Didn't think you were interested. Listen, I forgot your name. Some Indian thing, right? I'm not so good on names. Forget my own sometimes. You want to come in so I don't have to stand out here in my fucking underwear?"

Crow stepped inside. The room smelled of perfume, Ivory soap, and sweat. Both beds were unmade. The floor was strewn with assorted clothes. Aquinas was talking.

"I got a few deals going now, but only one of them is for sure. Hell of a deal—two thousand a unit gets you ten thou by this time next year. That's five bucks on the dollar. Only thing is, I don't know if we got any more units. I gotta check on that. But don't worry, I got some other deals coming."

Crow had no idea what he was talking about. "You have so much money, how come you're staying here?"

"What, you don't like this place?" He looked around the room. "They got HBO, a nice bed, hot and cold running water. What more do you want?"

"You staying here by yourself?"

"What, are you some kind of cop? You gonna tell me your name?"

"Joe Crow."

"Yeah, that's right. I thought I remembered it was something like that. I knew a guy named Crowe. With an *e* on the end, right? Guy was a limey. What can I do for you, Crowe?"

Crow said, "Did you know that Catfish Wicky is married?"

"Does the pope shit in the woods?" He looked bored.

"I'm working for her husband."

"Dicky. Nice guy. So? What's his problem—he not getting enough goodies? I can't hardly feature that. Cat's got enough Tabasco for ten guys. The fuck's his problem?" He was moving around the room, picking things up and putting them down. He sat on the bed and used the remote control to turn the television on and off repeatedly. "So you supposed to beat me up or what?" He flipped through the cable channels, not pausing long enough to see anything.

"He wants you to stop seeing her."

"So we'll do it in the dark."

"And he's willing to extend himself to get you to leave her alone." Crow was still feeling around, trying to find out where Aquinas stood. He hated the idea of giving this sleazebag money, even Dickie's money. Let him draw his own conclusions about what it meant for Dickie to "extend himself."

The channel clicking stopped. Crow had his full attention now.

"He extended himself a little more often, he wouldn't have this problem," Aquinas said.

Crow almost smiled.

Aquinas clicked off the TV and looked up at Crow. "So Dickie wants to pay me off, huh?"

"I didn't say anything about money." He didn't like being anticipated.

"You didn't have to. I know how guys like that think. He's got the car, the nice watch, the big paycheck. He thinks everything is for sale."

"And you're not?"

"I didn't say that. I agree with ol' Dickie on that one. How high will he go?"

Crow thought, As crazy as these two are, they speak the same language. He decided to start low.

"Three thousand dollars. You break it off with Mrs. Wicky, and you get it in cash, tomorrow." He knew immediately that the offer wasn't going to fly. No surprise there. Aquinas had his mouth open. He started to laugh. Someone was knocking at the door.

"You want to get that while I consider your offer?" Aquinas said.

Crow opened the door. It was Catfish. She was holding a small brown bag in her hand.

"Joe Crow," she said. She pushed past him into the room and tossed the paper bag toward Aquinas. "I had to go to three places to get the kind you like, darlin'," she said. "You owe me twenty-five bucks." She looked at Crow, then at Aquinas, who was reclined on the far bed, grinning. "What's going on?"

"Crow here has made me an offer." Aquinas bobbed his eyebrows and smirked.

Crow wanted very much to be anywhere else. This was the kind of prideless situation that came of working for Dickie Wicky. Catfish picked up on his embarrassment.

"Tell me about it," she said, patting him on the shoulder. "This has got to be one of Dickie's deals, right?"

Crow hid behind his face, saying nothing.

Aquinas said, "He just offered me three thousand dollars to give you the kiss-off. He works for Dickie."

Crow felt something turn over in his belly. *He works for Dickie.* What could be worse?

Catfish frowned at Crow. "Three thousand? That doesn't sound like Dickie. I bet he told you ten."

Aquinas asked Crow, "Will he go ten? For ten I could see it."

Catfish took a swat at him, but Aquinas rolled away, laughing.

"Don't bullshit a bullshitter, Crow," she said. "He told you ten, didn't he? Dickie thinks in ten-thousand-dollar units." She was right in his face; her lips were enormous.

Crow shrugged. "I can ask him." He wanted to go home.

"What do y'all think, Tommy? We can split it, okay?"

"Okay with me." He grabbed Catfish around the waist and pulled her onto the bed. She kicked off her red sandals. "But the action don't stop till we get paid."

Crow backed toward the door. Catfish had picked up the paper bag and pulled out a box of condoms. She tossed it at Tommy.

"You better get busy, big guy. This store's about to close."

Crow backed up to the door, opened it, and stepped out into the evening sun. The musky sweet smell of Catfish Wicky choked his nostrils. His mouth was slick with the taste of Porky's french fries. He spat onto the asphalt parking lot, then walked down the block toward his car, the texture of the sidewalk stabbing at him through the soles of his shoes.

11

You wanna know what this business is all about? It's about attitude. You got the right amount of attitude, you control the action. It's that simple.

—*Joey Cadillac*

Joey Cadillac had given Freddy Wisnesky a set of clear, if contradictory, instructions—find the comic book guys, do to them what he had done to Billy Yeddis, then bring the Fleetwood back to Chicago.

The contradiction was that Billy Yeddis had ended up with two broken arms and a shattered face inside his car under thirty feet of Lake Michigan. The first part, the arm breaking and such, was no problem. But did Mister C. really want him to push the car into a lake? And if so, how was he to get it back to Chicago? Freddy thought carefully. He was pretty sure that Mister C. wanted the yellow Caddy back. And so it followed that he would not want it to be immersed in a lake. He concentrated, keeping in mind that Mister C. did not always say exactly what he meant.

He decided that the method was unimportant. Mister C. wanted the comic book guys dead, and it didn't matter how he did it. Freddy was pleased with his analysis. He would perform his duties one at a time and, if he got stuck, he would call Mister C. and ask him what to do next.

Freddy had been sitting in Porky's lot watching the door to room 22 for half an hour. The short one, Paine, was in the room. The woman had left, then the guy with the Jaguar had come, then the woman had come back. They were all in there now.

Freddy was getting tired of sitting. His legs were cramping, and he had to take a dump. When the Jaguar guy left the motel room and walked up the street, Freddy decided to get up and do something. He decided to ask Tommy Paine about his partner. He drove across the street and parked next to the yellow Fleetwood.

Catfish released her grip on Tommy's ears and rapped her knuckles on the top of his skull.

"Hey! We got company, Captain Muff."

Tommy raised his head and squinted up at her. "Tell me your buddy the private detective ain't back already. He's only been gone two minutes."

The knocking on the door repeated, this time louder. Catfish closed her legs and swung them over the edge of the bed. The knocking continued.

"I can't concentrate with that banging. Answer the door." She tugged her black dress down over her hips.

Tommy growled and crawled across the carpet to the door. He stood up and opened the door a few inches, peered through the opening, and slammed the door shut with a gasp. He took two steps backward, and the door exploded inward. Tommy stumbled back, tripped, and fell to the floor, as Freddy Wisnesky stepped into the room.

Catfish was sitting with her back against the headboard, lighting a cigarette. She inhaled, then, letting the thick blue smoke trail from her nostrils, looked up at Freddy's massive structure.

"Nice tie, big guy," she said.

Freddy looked down at his tie, then at Catfish. Tommy was skidding himself back on the carpet, heading for the bathroom. Freddy grabbed him by the feet. Tommy said, "Freddy, waitaminute, just hold on a second, okay? Joey's got a problem, we'll make it right. Listen to me a minute, would you . . . ?" He was hanging upside down, his face bright red. "You don't got to do this. I just talked to Joey on the phone. Five minutes ago I was talking to him, I'm not kidding you."

Freddy gave him a shake, snapping his head back and forth.

Catfish said, "How tall are you, anyways? Are you seven feet tall? I never met a guy as big as you." She made her eyes go round.

Freddy paused. "I'm six six," he said.

"I ain't kidding you," Tommy whined. "You don't believe me, you can call him. We made a deal. In fact, he said I should tell you to call him. Freddy? You hear me, guy? You got to call Joey."

"Shut up a minute." Freddy delivered a light kick to the head; Tommy groaned and went slack.

"I got a cousin six foot eight," Freddy said to Catfish. "Use ta play center for the Bulls. Tallest white guy on the team."

"Really? He give y'all that tie?" She hugged her legs.

Freddy held Tommy's bare feet out away from his chest and looked again at his tie, tiger lilies, bright-orange flowers on blue silk. "I picked it out myself. You like it?"

"I like it a lot," Catfish said. "Who's Joey?"

"I never heard of him," Freddy said. Joey Cadillac was always telling him to say that.

"Oh. That's too bad, because he just called for y'all. Y'all're supposed to call him back, like Tommy said."

Tommy moaned. Freddy lowered him so that his shoulders rested on the floor. "That right?" he asked.

Tommy coughed and said, "I told you, man. Your boss, Joey, you're supposed to call him. We made a new deal with him."

Freddy let Tommy's hips and legs thump to the floor. "Stay put," he said. "Okay?" He circled the bed and reached for the telephone.

Tommy said, "Sure, Freddy, no problem. You just call Joey and ask him." Slowly, he rolled onto his belly and rose to his hands and knees. "We're all friends now. Isn't that what he said, Cat? We're all supposed to be friends, right?"

"That's right," said Catfish. "We're all friends now."

Freddy had the phone in his hand. "Where did he say to call?" he asked her.

Catfish lapped up smoke from her cigarette and shrugged. She gestured at Tommy, who said, "Area code three one two . . ."

Freddy squinted at the telephone dial pad and picked out the numbers with his thick fingers. When he looked to Tommy for the rest of the number, all he saw was the ass end of a pair of purple Batman briefs disappearing out the door.

Joe Crow was still sitting in his parked car, trying to find Whiting Lake on a road atlas. That morning he had retrieved Jimbo Bobick's letter and photos from his wastebasket and attached them to his refrigerator door with a magnet shaped like a walleye, Bobick's address and phone number printed on its side. The island was on Whiting Lake, but he couldn't find the lake on the map. That probably meant it was a small lake. A little cabin on a little island on a little lake. Perfect.

According to Jimbo, all he needed was a thirty-thousand-dollar down payment. The seller would contract for the other hundred, which would probably cost him about eight hundred a month. Crow had no idea where he might get thirty grand, but if it came his way, he'd first have to pay off the IRS, get caught up with the people at American Express, take care of the rent, get the Jag tuned. . . .

Crow sighed. He imagined himself sitting in his dream cabin, too worried about how he was going to make his monthly payment to enjoy the scenery. He closed the atlas. His first priority was to finish up this Wicky business—get the money, pay off Catfish's love stud, take his fee, and leave it all behind. Find a nice, clean card game and go back to living right.

He started the Jag and pulled out onto University Avenue. As he passed the Twin Town, he saw Tommy Aquinas dash across the street in front of him, barefoot, wearing nothing but his purple underwear. Crow slowed down and watched him run through Porky's parking lot, weaving among the cars, then crash through the bushes at the back of the lot.

That's different, Crow thought.

He looked toward the motel. A large, ugly man with a bright orange-and-blue tie was charging straight at him. Crow goosed the accelerator and shot forward to get out of the way. The big man, who looked awfully familiar, passed behind the Jag and crossed the street at high speed. Crow pulled over and watched him run through Porky's lot into the bushes, leaving a large, ragged gap where he had penetrated the foliage. Crow looked back toward the motel, half expecting a third, perhaps even larger, runner.

Catfish was standing in the door to room 22, leaning against the jamb, laughing smoke. She waved at him.

Crow put the Jag in gear and continued down University. He wasn't even going to think about it.

The accessories man was pushing rubies.

"You got your diamonds, Mister C., and I got to say for investment they are your top of the line. But if you really want to get a lady's attention, you got to be talking rubies. You give some chick an emerald, and she wants you to take her out on the town, spend some more money, show it off to her girlfriends, y'know? You hang a diamond on her, and what's she thinking? Right. She thinks you're gonna marry her. All she can think about is the big white dress. But your ru-bies, you give a chick a ruby and she's got one thing in mind, and that's how it's gonna look without nothing else on her body, you know what I mean? You give a chick a ruby, and she says, 'Do me.' "

Joey Cadillac was working on his cuticles, shoving them back just so with the tip of a letter opener. He was in a good mood, a mood to buy something nice. The accessories man had his black velvet spread on Joey's desk. He was laying out a row of rings set with bright-red jewels, talking them up.

"A lot of people don't know this, but a perfect ruby is actually rarer and costlier than your perfect diamond. Take a look at this." He pointed at a ring carrying one of the larger stones.

Joey leaned forward and looked. A red rock, like glass, set into a slim gold ring. He picked it up and held it to the light. "How much you get for this one?"

"That item was selling for eighteen at Cartier. I could let you have it for ten."

Joey dropped the ring. "I got cars I sell for less than that. What else you got?"

The accessories man was thrown, but only for about a tenth of a second.

"Whatever you want, Mister C. I got some nice Sulka ties in. I got in some Davidoff Havanas. You know, Davidoff doesn't make Cuban cigars anymore. They're into selling that Dominican crap now. Once these are gone, crop of '90, that's it, my friend."

"How much?"

"Five hundred a box of twenty-five."

"Jesus. Okay, get me a couple boxes. You got any sunglasses? I lost my goddamn shades."

"I got whatever you want, Mister C. I got every major manufac-turer. I got your Ray-Bans. I got your Vuarnets. I got your Porsche Design." He rolled up the velvet and put it away in his jewelry case. "What kind of sunglasses did you want?"

"Something with attitude," Joey said. "But not too much attitude."

The accessories man closed his eyes, accessing his inventory data base.

"I got just what you need." He smiled.

"Something in blue," Joey said. "Blue frames. Maybe like a teal color. And those lenses that change color, you know?"

"Perfect," said the accessories man. "That's just what I had in mind."

The intercom buzzed. Joey said, "Yeah?"

"I have Mr. Wisnesky on the line."

"Okay." Joey motioned the accessories man toward the door. "Pick me out a nice pair, have them sent over with the smokes." He waited for the accessories salesman to close the door, then pressed the speakerphone button.

"Frederick," he said, smiling in anticipation. As he listened, the flesh on either side of his mouth moved slowly toward the floor, making his face look a lot like a Richard Nixon Halloween mask.

The odds are, the guy who makes the first play is the guy who's going to win. My problem is, I only remember that when I'm playing cards.

—*Joe Crow*

"I don't want to know his name. I don't want to know anything about him." Dickie Wicky made out the ten-thousand-dollar check, left the payee name blank, slid it across his desk.

Crow said, "I told the guy it would be cash."

"This is better than cash," Wicky said. "It's got my name on it."

Crow looked at the check doubtfully. It was nine o'clock in the morning, too early to argue. "What about my fee?"

"You got your retainer. Bill me for the balance when you get the job done," said Wicky, straining to give the impression of a busy man who had been bothered enough already. He looked out through the glass wall of his office. Dickie Wicky at nine o'clock in the morning was not a pretty sight. His eyes were crusty, his face bloodless, and he needed a new knot in his tie. He looked like a man with a swollen brain and a liver to match. Crow felt a wave of vicarious nausea.

"Did she get home last night?"

Wicky blinked and turned his face toward Crow. "Cat? I don't remember. She was there when I got up."

Crow folded the check and put it in his shirt pocket. "Maybe this will take care of it," he said, not believing it.

Wicky shrugged. "For a while."

Crow stood up.

Wicky said, "What kind of guy is he? Is he big?"

"He's a runt, Dickie. Just like you and me."

On his way out of the Litten Securities offices, Crow told Janet the receptionist that she looked like Michelle Pfeiffer the actress.

"I've heard that before," she said, her glacial demeanor thawing slightly.

Crow grinned. "I bet you have. And you know who I think Dickie looks like?"

"He *thinks* he looks like Nick Nolte," she said, with a sour twist to her polished lips. "He told me that."

"Nick Nolte?" Crow tried to see it but failed. "I was going to say he looks like a blond Buddy Hackett."

"I could see that. Buddy Hackett bleached." She gave a sharp nod. "I like that. So who do you look like?"

"Me? I was thinking Cary Grant."

She squinted at him critically. "Really?"

"How about Mel Gibson? Clark Gable? Sidney Poitier?"

She laughed. "I don't think you really look like anybody, Mr. Crow."

"Nobody?"

"Well . . . maybe a little Wayne Newton."

"No!"

"Just around the eyes, when you're surprised."

Crow drove directly from Litten Securities to the Twin Town Luxury Motor Hotel. The yellow Cadillac was gone, but the blue convertible with the smashed-up front end was parked in its place in front of room 22. He decided to check with the desk clerk before knocking on the door.

The old man watched him enter the lobby. "Back again," he pointed out.

Crow nodded and leaned over the counter. The clerk was holding the new *Reader's Digest* in his lap, a mug of milky coffee in his right hand.

"I'm looking for my friend Mr. Aquinas," Crow said. "Is he in his room? I don't see his car out there."

The old man sat up straight and looked past Crow. "Nope," he said. "You don't."

"It looks like somebody else might be in there now."

The desk clerk shrugged and sipped his coffee. The beige mug was printed with the Twin Town script logo. He looked down at the *Reader's Digest* and thumbed the pages.

Crow reached for his wallet, extracted a twenty-dollar bill, slid it across the counter.

The old man smiled. "Your friend took off," he said.

"He checked out?"

"Nope. Just took off. Seemed sorta upset. His face was all scratched up."

"Like from fingernails?"

"More like he'd been running through the woods. Little scratches. Just grabbed his stuff, jumped in his car, and took off like somebody was after him. That little gal took off too."

"You don't know where they went?"

"Nope."

"They owe you any money?"

"Nope. This other fellow, he just moved right on in."

Crow looked out the window at the blue Cadillac convertible. "A big guy? Face like a pot roast?"

"Pot roast? I never thought of that. He's in there now."

"You've never seen him around here before?"

"Nope. He just moved right on in. Paid me for two nights."

"What's his name?"

The old man shrugged. "According to my guestbook here, it's Thomas Aquinas, on account of the other fellow never checked out like he was supposed to. And the big guy, he never actually checked in. So it says here his name is Aquinas. But it ain't. Fact, he's looking for the Aquinas fellow too. Thought he was gonna try to rough me up for a minute there."

"He thought better of it?"

"I got to admiring his tie. Damnedest thing you ever saw. Daisies.

Big guy like that, and he's got these little yellow daisies sprinkled all up and down his front. Real proud fellow. Nasty but proud. We got on pretty good after that."

Crow picked up one of the business cards on the counter, turned it over, and wrote down his name and phone number. "If you see Aquinas, give me a call, okay?"

"Whatever."

Crow started for the door, then turned back. "Do I have any change coming?"

The old man shook his head slowly and let his lips roll back from his dentures. "No change today."

Crow walked out into the late-morning sun, stood in the parking lot beside his car, and considered the door to room 22, ten yards away. From the few glimpses he'd had of the big man, he knew he didn't want to know him better. He had a feeling that Aquinas would not be returning to the Twin Town. How was he going to deliver Wicky's check? Through Catfish? He found the concept disturbing. The ten-thousand-dollar paper rectangle in his shirt pocket pressed uncomfortably against his left nipple.

The curtain covering the window to room 22 accordioned to the left. A large face appeared, then disappeared. A moment later, the door opened and the big man, the same man he had seen before, filled the doorway.

"Hey, fella." The voice was something between a rumble and a croak. "Got a minute there? Can I talk to ya a minute, fella?"

Crow said, not moving, "What can I do for you?" He was standing on the passenger side of his Jaguar, wishing he had the car between them.

The big man looked up and down the parking lot, then stepped out of his room and moved toward Crow, walking slowly the way you would approach a runaway dog. He was wearing a soiled blue oxford shirt, gray pants gone shiny at the knees, and an eye-searing red-and-gold necktie. No daisies today. Crow took his hands from his pockets and let them hang. It was late morning on a busy street, and they were in full view of the motel office, but he did not want to be in the same parking lot with this man, who, with each forward motion of his enormous black wing tips, got bigger. All of Crow's alarms were going off. If he had still been a cop, he would have had his holster unsnapped, a hand on his baton, and been calling for backup.

The big man was still coming, but moving slower now.

Six feet away, he stopped and twisted his face into a strange new configuration. After a breath, Crow realized that it was a smile. He tried to smile back. He suspected that his version didn't look much better.

"I'm lookin' for a guy," the big man said. "Maybe you seen 'm."

Crow said, "Who are you?"

The big man thought about that. "Freddy," he said at last.

"Who are you trying to find, Freddy?" In his mind, Crow was reviewing the escape route used by Tom Aquinas. Cross the street, don't bother to look both ways, run as fast as possible through Porky's parking lot, crash through the bushes, don't slow down—not a bad plan, all things considered.

"Couple fellas named Tom and Ben. These comic book guys."

"Comic book guys? You mean like Batman and Robin? Sorry, can't help you there." The big man was standing six feet away, and Crow still had to tip his head back at an uncomfortable angle to look at that face. Apparently, the big man had not caught up with Tommy.

"I seen you with the one."

"The one?"

"The little one." Freddy shuffled closer, rocking back and forth from one wing tip to the other. Crow let his hand drift back and feel for the handle to the car door. Could he get into the car, close the door, and lock it before Freddy was on him? Probably not. He looked toward the motel office. Was the desk clerk watching? All he could see was the sun blasting back at him from the window. Cars passed down University Avenue, anonymous and oblivious.

"Oh, him," said Crow. "With the purple underwear, right?"

Freddy stopped. "That's the guy."

"Tommy, right? I saw you chasing him."

"That's the guy."

"I'm going to go see him right now. You want to come along?"

Freddy smiled. "Sure," he said. His shoulders sank to a relaxed position.

"Hop in." Crow opened the passenger door. He circled the car, climbed in on the driver's side, pushed the key into the ignition switch. "You coming?"

Freddy was bent forward, his hand gripping the top of the open car door, peering into the tiny pink cockpit. He shook his head. "We got to take my car," he said.

Crow shook his head and started the engine. "It's too big for me. I don't think I could fit."

Freddy crumpled his brow. He was holding on to the door with both hands.

"That's a real nice tie you got there," Crow said, slowly pressing his foot on the accelerator, bringing the engine up to 4,000 rpm.

Freddy looked down at his tie and reached to stroke it with one hand.

Crow dumped the clutch. The car lurched forward a few feet, then stopped. The rear wheels were spraying gravel back toward the motel office.

Freddy had a grip on the doorframe, the composite soles of his Sears wing tips welded to the asphalt. Crow stared at the bratwurst-size fingers wrapped around the top edge of the door, unable to comprehend that the giant was actually capable of holding the car in place. For what seemed like several seconds, the rear wheels smoked blue. Freddy shifted his grip, got one foot into the car, started to swing his great body inside, as the tires finally caught and propelled the Jag forward. But Freddy wasn't letting go. He had one leg in the car, one in the air, and was holding on to the door with both hands. Crow hit the brake. The car stopped, Freddy and the passenger door continued forward. The ear-twisting metal sound of the door being opened wide in the wrong direction felt like a knife in his wallet. He slammed the shifter into reverse, heading directly for the motel office. Freddy had a death grip on what was left of the door, his shoes leaving black skid marks on the asphalt. Crow hit the brake again and the car skewed to the side, knocking Freddy into the air and onto the hood. Crow took off again, going forward, and bounced over the curb onto University Avenue, tires spinning, the rear end fishtailing. Narrowly missing a pizza delivery van, he ran through two gears, trying to see past Freddy, bringing it up to forty miles per hour.

Freddy was glued to the hood, glaring in at Crow, gripping the slick front end of the Jag like a sex-crazed wolfhound. He let go with one hand and brought his fist back. Crow didn't doubt for an instant that he was capable of putting the cantaloupe-size fist through the windshield. He braked and cranked the wheel to the right. The Jag's nose dipped, and the car whipped around in a tight U-turn, riding up on two wheels.

Freddy disappeared.

The Jag was balanced on two wheels; the world turned sideways, all things gone to slow motion, slow enough for Crow to say, out loud, "Please don't roll." The Jag shuddered and dropped back onto all fours, like a good cat.

Freddy was still rolling down the street. Crow, gripping the wheel of his car, let his lungs empty and watched through the mangled car door as Freddy came to a stop, lay still on his back for a long moment, then sat up, shook his head, climbed to his feet, and started toward the Jaguar.

Crow shivered, turned the car around, and headed in the opposite direction. The front end was shaking, and so was he. The passenger door hung open at an angle, promising never to close again. This was going to be expensive. He kept going, though, until he had left Freddy far behind. The car could be repaired.

A few blocks later, he stopped and tied the door closed. The top edge showed a row of depressions where Freddy's fingers had distorted the sheet metal. He kept thinking about how it would feel to have those thick white fingers wrapped around his throat.

Beep.

"Joe, this is Rich. I gotta talk to you, buddy. It's important. Gimme a buzz."

Crow sighed, hit the rewind button on his new answering machine, picked up the phone, dialed Litten Securities.

"Rich Wicky, please."

"I'm sorry, Mr. Wicky is in a meeting."

"Tell him Michael Milken is on the line."

There was a pause. "Is this Mr. Crow?"

"If it is, will he pick up his phone?"

He could hear her tapping her front teeth with a pen. "I'll see what I can do," she said. "He'll usually pick up for his wife."

A few seconds later, Wicky's voice came over the wire. "Hey, baby."

"Hi, Dickie," said Crow.

There was a long silence.

"I'm gonna get that dumb broad's ass canned," he said at last. "She told me you were my wife."

"That's who I told her I was."

"Well . . . what did you want?"

"I'm returning your call. You said it was important."

"Oh. Did you get the job done?"

"Not yet. I'll let you know. Is that why you called?"

"Just checkin' on you, buddy."

"I'll call you when I have something to tell you, Dickie."

"Well, when do you think that'll be?"

"I have no idea. Depends on how much time I have to spend on the phone."

There were several seconds of silence, then Wicky said, "Oh. Listen, I gotta go, Crow. I've got a couple guys waiting for me in my office."

After hanging up, Crow called Litten Securities again.

"Thanks for putting me through," he said.

"You're welcome."

"Dickie says he's gonna get you fired."

"God," said Janet. "I wish."

That evening Crow sat on his porch with Debrowski and told her about the job he was doing for Dickie Wicky. Crow was reclined on the porch swing; Debrowski was balanced on the railing, drinking a Moussy.

"I don't understand you, Crow."

"What do you mean?"

"I mean I don't know how you can work for a guy like that. It's not you, Crow."

Crow contracted his neck and squeezed the corners of his mouth together.

"Now don't go getting all small on me, Crow. You know I'm right."

"I know I owe a lot of money."

"So play cards. You're supposed to be such a hotshot poker player. Why abase yourself? You get mixed up with a bunch of losers like Dickie, you're going to wind up a loser too. You just told me, what that guy did to your Jag is going to cost you more than what you'll collect from Dickie. And that's assuming he even pays you."

"Yeah, well, it's done. All I have to do is find the guy and give him the check."

"And that's it? I don't think so, Crow. You still have to collect from Dickie. And you've still got Freddy the Terminator out there. Guys like that have a way of turning up. Besides, after what he did to your car, I can't see you letting go of it."

Crow shrugged, wishing he hadn't told her what he was doing, thinking that if she hadn't tried to bluff that pair of fours he wouldn't be working for Wicky at all.

"I know what you're thinking, Crow. It was all my fault, right?"

Crow raised his eyebrows and tipped his head.

"Well, fuck you. You didn't want to take my money, I don't feel sorry for you."

They sat for a few minutes without talking. The air was thick and warm, muting the hiss of First Avenue traffic. Debrowski had found a wedge of early-evening sunshine. She was leaning against the corner post, both feet up on the railing, a slash of sun falling across her black leather jacket and jeans. Tonight she was barefoot and chain-less. Her toenails were unpainted, her short blond hair looked soft in the yellow light.

"You look nice tonight," Crow said.

Debrowski made a face. "Screw you, Crow." She tipped up her near beer and swallowed. It was hard to tell in the yellow light, but he thought he detected a rise of color in her cheeks.

"How's your mom?" he asked.

"She's all right. She liked my penny loafers. Sometime you got to meet her, Crow. You'd like her." She paused and looked over the railing. Crow heard a car door slam. "You know anybody drives a big yellow car, Crow?"

He stood and looked past Debrowski's knees. The yellow Cadillac was pulled over to the curb, engine idling. Tommy Aquinas was coming up the walk, his head moving back and forth like a hopped-up radar dish. Crow called over the railing, "Come on up."

Aquinas flinched and took a step to the side, looked up at Crow, nodded. He scanned the area again, then opened the downstairs door. Crow stared at the Cadillac, trying to make out the driver. He could see a long, pale hand resting atop the steering wheel. Not Cat-fish. Not Freddy.

"Is that the guy with the Batman underwear?" Debrowski asked.

Crow nodded and went into the front hall to open the door. Tommy Aquinas was on the stairs a few steps below the landing. He stretched his neck, trying to see past Crow into the apartment.

"Listen, you seen this big guy, ugly as shit, wears these wild ties, drives a big blue Caddy? You seen anybody like that hanging around?"

"Not here," Crow said. "You want to come in?"

Tommy looked back down the stairs, then climbed the last few steps and entered the apartment. He stalked the perimeter of the room, stopping at Crow's framed baseball cards, looking at each of the cards for five seconds, grunting after each brief scrutiny. "Worth a few bucks," he said, rubbing his fingers together. His face was decorated with several shallow horizontal scratches.

"He a friend of yours?" Crow asked.

"Who? Harmon Killebrew? Yeah, I know him."

"I'm talking about the guy with the ties."

Tommy jerked his head up. "You seen him?"

"His name is Freddy, right?"

"You got it, man. Fucking Freddy Wis-fucking-nesky. You seen him?"

"He's waiting for you back at your motel room."

"No kidding?" Tommy shrugged. "Oh well, it was a shit place anyhow. Fuck 'm."

"Who is he?"

"Just a guy, works for a guy that fucked me over on a business deal. Old business."

"He says he wants to get ahold of you."

"I bet he does," Tommy said, putting a hand to the base of his throat. "I gotta get going," he said suddenly. "You want me to sell those for you?" He pointed at Crow's cards. "I can get you top buck."

Crow shook his head.

Debrowski came in from the porch and introduced herself.

Aquinas pumped her hand vigorously. "Call me Tommy," he said. "You remember the Pet Rock? That was me."

"What happened to your face?" Debrowski asked.

"I got in a fight. A couple guys jumped me. I beat the crap outta the one guy, but the other guy got away." He turned to Crow. "You got something for me? I gotta get going."

Crow held up Wicky's check. Tommy frowned. "What the hell happened to cash? Doesn't anybody do business in green anymore, f'chrissake?"

"You don't want it?" Crow asked.

Tommy looked at Debrowski. "What do you do for a living, Deb?"

"I'm in rock and roll." She crossed her arms, holding one tight fist in front of each breast. She didn't like being called "Deb."

"I used to do that shit. You remember that song '96 Tears'?"

"Question Mark and the Mysterians," Debrowski said. "I remember, sure."

"Question Mark, that was me. I was just a kid. Made a lot of money on that tune, but I couldn't handle the bullshit." He looked at the check in Crow's hand. "What the fuck. I suppose it's good. Tell Dickie thanks, man." He reached for the check, but Crow had made it disappear.

"Tell me more about Freddy," Crow said.

"What's this shit?" Tommy's eyes bounced around Crow's body, looking for the check. "You gonna pay me or not?"

"Soon as you tell me who this guy Freddy works for."

"Freddy? He works for Joey Cadillac," Tommy said, astonished that this was not common knowledge.

"Joey Cadillac?"

"Yeah. You know. Out of Chicago. We had a little misunderstanding. Joey sent Freddy up here to talk about it. But fucking Freddy, he don't talk."

Crow looked at Debrowski. "You ever hear of a guy named Joey Cadillac?" She shook her head. Crow looked back at Tommy. "Me neither," he said.

"You gonna pay me or not?" Tommy demanded. "I got somebody waiting on me. I gotta go."

"Who's Joey Cadillac?"

"Joey Cadillac is Joey Cadillac, man. He runs a bunch of car lots down there, sells Cadillacs to the dealers and pimps, you know? Now *there's* a cash business. Joey loves cash."

"Joey Cadillac is a car dealer?"

"That's what I said, man. New or used. Cash or stash."

"You know how I can get ahold of him?"

"Why? You in the market for a car?"

"Maybe I am."

"Well, you go on down there, then. He's got a place on Franson. J.C. Motors. Tell him I sent you."

"I thought you were having problems with him."

"Just a misunderstanding. Joey's a friend of mine."

"You got his address?"

"What do I look like, a fucking Rolodex? I gotta go. You gonna give that check or what?"

Crow hesitated, shrugged, made the check appear, and handed it to him. Tommy jammed it in his pocket. "You ever want to sell those baseball cards, you let me know. I got connections all over the country. You ever hear of Wayne Gretzky? He buys all his baseball cards from me. You want to make some serious money, you got to look me up. Anything else I can do for you, guy?"

Crow grinned and shook his head. "You got it coming out your ears, don't you?"

"You betcha. Isn't that what you say up here?"

"You betcha." Crow opened the door. "Where should I look you up? Where are you staying now?"

Tommy stepped out onto the landing and started down the stairs. "I'll be around," he said over his shoulder.

Crow closed the door. "What do you think?"

"You better go check your silverware, Crow."

"If I had any, I would. You get down to Chicago now and then, Debrowski. You never heard of this guy Joey Cadillac?"

"Chicago's a big town, Crow. There are a lot of sleazy characters down there. I only know maybe half of them."

"Weren't you just giving me shit about associating with Dickie Wicky?"

"I said I know 'em, Crow. I don't work for them."

"I suppose I could get the address out of the phone book."

Debrowski smirked. " 'Why? You in the market for a car?' "

Crow shook his head. "I'm getting my Jag fixed. I'm thinking I'll send this Joey Cadillac a bill."

Freddy ain't been the same since he was born.

—*Joey Cadillac*

Freddy Wisnesky glared at the ringing telephone. On the third ring he set his tweezers on the nightstand, picked up the receiver, and held it gingerly to his right ear.

"Hullo?"

He listened.

"Not yet, Mister C." Freddy winced and pulled the phone away from his ear. Joey Cadillac's voice screeched from the handset.

"I dunno, Mister C. I ain't seen 'em since," Freddy said. "I don't think they're coming back here, Mister C."

Freddy listened, his face twitching every time a new epithet exploded from the handset.

"I dunno, Mister C. There was this other guy come by that was with 'em, but he got away."

Freddy was sitting on the bed in room 22 of the Twin Town Luxury Motor Hotel. The television was on, the sound turned off. Freddy was wearing only a pair of yellowish boxer shorts. Several large areas of his body were raw and oozing. The bed was stained red and pink in several places. His shredded shirt and pants lay in a soiled pile on the carpet.

"I s'pose I could go ask the lady." He listened for a while, holding the handset a few inches out from his ear. "I s'pose I could ask him too. Only I don't know who he is." He listened again. "Okay, Mister C. Uh-huh. Okay. Okay. Okay."

Freddy hung up the phone and leaned carefully back against the headboard. The bed groaned. He raised his left knee, examined the saucer-size abrasion, and picked up the pair of six-inch tweezers from the nightstand. They looked tiny and thin in his hand. Biting his lip, he removed another small gray flake of stone from his knee and dropped it on the nightstand.

"Ouch," he said. He had been cleaning his wounds all afternoon and into the night, picking them clean a speck at a time. Freddy looked at the collection of rock flakes, grains of sand, and unidentified deleterious matter, all of which had been embedded in his skin. He put down the tweezers, opened and swallowed another can of beer. Arsenio Hall was delivering a silent monologue on the television, talking and laughing, wearing this shiny plastic leisure suit.

"Shut up," Freddy said. Arsenio kept on talking. Freddy shrugged, picked up the tweezers, and probed his wounded knee. He wanted to get all the rocks out before he went to sleep. In the morning he would be all scabbed over, and it would be too late.

By eleven o'clock that night, Dickie Wicky was down two thousand dollars. The usual guys were sitting in at Zink's Club 34. Al Levin was winning modestly, as usual. Ozzie LaRose had a nice stack—playing stupid but getting lucky. Zink was quietly riding the rail, and Frank Knox seemed to be controlling more than his share of the cash. Wicky was financing the game. He looked quickly up at Crow, who had just stepped in through the doorway, then back at his cards, then he bet fifty dollars on a baby straight. Frank Knox hesitated, peered closely at his cards, and raised.

Knox was a tall, loose-jointed lawyer who played a painfully conservative game of poker. He rarely won, never lost, and could be counted on to run a bluff about once in every fifteen thousand hands. When Frank Knox raised, anybody with less than perfect cards was well advised to fold.

On some level Wicky knew this, but he was on tilt, staying in on every hand, going for the long odds, and losing heavily. He called Knox's bet, and he lost again.

Al Levin picked up the cards and shuffled.

Zink turned to Crow. "Sitting in, Joe?"

"Sure," said Crow. He took the seat across from Wicky. Levin spread a hand of Hold 'em. Crow peeked at his two cards. Ace, king of diamonds. It looked like this was going to be his night. He bet ten dollars. Al Levin folded. Ozzie LaRose folded. Wicky called. Zink stared at his cards for several seconds, shuffled through his cash, folded.

Levin flopped three cards. Ace of hearts, three of diamonds, five of diamonds. Crow watched Wicky as the cards were turned. Wicky looked back at him, raised his short, pale eyebrows, and bet twenty. Crow raised.

On the turn, Crow caught a fifth diamond, a jack. This was almost too easy. Wicky, probably trying for another baby straight, was drawing dead. Even if he made the hand he was looking for, he had already lost to Crow's nearly perfect hand.

Unfortunately for Wicky, the four of clubs came on the river, making his baby straight. He re-raised five times before realizing that he might not have the best hand. Crow scooped a large pot, including a hastily scrawled IOU from Wicky.

Three hours later, Wicky got up from the table, mixed himself another vodka tonic, and went to sit on the sofa.

"You gonna play anymore, Dickie?" Zink asked.

Wicky shook his head. He owed Zink five hundred and Crow thirty-eight hundred. Pouring the rest of his drink into his mouth, he stood up. "I'm out of here."

Ozzie LaRose said, "Give me a call tomorrow, Dickie. Let me know what you've got left of that Guardians stuff."

"Okay," Wicky said. "I think I got five units for you."

"I'll take whatever you got."

Crow followed Wicky to the door. "Got a minute?" They walked down the stairs and out onto the sidewalk. "You Ozzie's broker now?" Crow asked.

"He throws me a bone now and then. I'm getting him into this Galactic Guardians deal. Very hot property. He's taking the last few available units." He put his hands in the pockets of his sport coat and squinted up at the streetlamp. "So how you doing on our deal? You pay the guy off?"

"I paid him. You owe me nineteen hundred for the extra time I put in."

"Jesus Christ, Joe, what are you trying to do to me? What about the two K you owed me from before?"

"I told you that was used up four days ago. I put over a week into this."

"Christ, all I asked you to do was give a guy some money."

"Dickie, I don't have time for this shit. I told you what I was charging you. You should have complained about my rates back then.

You're lucky I'm not making you pay for my car."

"Car?"

"I damn near totaled it. Your guy has some hood after him, some guy about the size of a buffalo. I accidentally got between them."

"You got in a fight in your car?"

"Something like that."

"Jesus," said Wicky, shaking his head. "Maybe we should just get the two of them together, save me ten grand."

"Too late now. Your guy came by and picked up the check a few hours ago. Said to say thank you."

Wicky scratched under his Adam's apple. "How do we know he's going to live up to his end of it?"

"This was your idea, Dickie. I never said I thought it was worth a damn."

Wicky shook his head. "I'll have to get back to you on this, Joe."

"Dickie, don't do this to me. It's not worth it."

"I'm going to pay you, Joe. If I'd got a few good cards, I'd've maybe even paid you tonight. Only thing is, I've got my liquid assets all tied up in this Galactic Guardians deal." Wicky frowned. "I had to tap my IRA to come up with the ten thousand you just gave away, Joe. I'm one hundred percent invested in Galactic. Opportunity of a lifetime."

"Your lifetime, maybe. But no money for me."

"No money for you *right now*." He fixed his eyes on Crow's face, blue irises muddy in the yellow light. "But I'll have something for you tomorrow," he added.

"What do you mean, 'something'?"

"I mean I'll pay you. Come by my office tomorrow. What do you say?"

"You shouldn't play cards when you're tapped, Dickie. It makes bad poker. You're into me for a total of fifty-seven hundred so far. I could use the money."

"Lighten up, Joe. It's just a little cash-flow thing. We're all in the same boat here."

Crow thought about being in a boat with Dickie Wicky, out on the ocean someplace. You wouldn't want to fall asleep.

"Come on by my office tomorrow. I'll buy you lunch."

"How about I just stop by and you pay me. Then I can afford to buy my own lunch."

"Whatever. I'll see you tomorrow, then?" Wicky smiled, cuffed him on the biceps, and moved off down the sidewalk. Crow watching until Wicky reached his Mercedes and drove off, then walked back up the stairs and rejoined the card game with the forty dollars he had left in cash. It took him nearly an hour to lose it all. He tried to sell some of Wicky's markers to Frank Knox, who had most of the cash. Knox laughed.

At three-thirty in the morning, Dickie Wicky fumbled his way through the door of his condominium. Catfish was reclined on the sofa in her black velour bathrobe with Katoo, her cat, stretched out beside her. A zombie was hulking its way across the television screen. Catfish watched her husband close the door, shuffle into the kitchen, and mix himself a vodka and Alka-Seltzer on the rocks. The cat kept its eyes and ears trained on the master of the house. When Dickie carried his drink toward the sofa, the cat clawed its way down and wheeled itself toward the bedroom.

Catfish watched Katoo disappear, her lips pressed tight together, the corners of her mouth drawn back and down. Dickie crossed the room to the recliner and fell into it. He sipped his drink, squinted at Catfish, and belched.

"How much did you lose tonight?" she asked.

Dickie belched again. "What makes you think I lost?"

"I can tell," she said. "You're drunk."

"I'd be drunk either way."

"How much did you lose?"

Dickie pressed the cold glass against his forehead. "Sixteen thousand dollars," he said.

Catfish sat up. "What?"

"Six thousand I lost to Joe Crow; the other ten I spent on you."

"You bought me something?"

"I bought *me* something."

"I thought you said you spent it on *me*." She pouted. "What did you buy?"

"I bought you."

Catfish narrowed her eyes. "You're drunk," she said.

Dickie drained most of his drink. "Not drunk enough," he said. "I'm celebrating. I sold the last of the Galactic Guardians units last night. Your friends Tom and Ben should be pretty happy about that."

Catfish was surprised. "You sold them all?" But then she wasn't. One thing Dickie was good for, he could sell anything to anybody.

"Yeah. I sold them to myself."

"You what?"

"I figure it's about time I get to be a millionaire." He grinned at her. "Don't you want us to be millionaires?"

"You actually *bought* Galactic Guardians?"

"Why not? I had to liquidate the Keogh, but it's going to be worth it. You don't get rich by squirreling it away. Got to spend it to make it. This is our chance to go ballistic, Cat. Comic books are just going to keep going up and up. And up."

"You bought it with *our* money?" She thumped her chest with a fist.

"Yeah. What's the problem?"

Catfish sank back onto the sofa, shaking her head. "You bought your own story. I don't believe it. I thought I told you about those guys."

"You did. You said we could make some easy money."

"That's right. You made thirty percent on the units you sold, right? They gave you a hundred twenty units at two thousand each, right? Your commissions would have added up to over seventy thousand dollars. Right?"

"Seventy thousand is nothing. This deal is worth millions."

Catfish sighed. "Dickie, Dickie, Dickie. It's a story, don't you get it? It's a paper chase. It's just a little thing Tommy came up with so we could all make some money. You were supposed to sell the story, not buy it. It's not real."

Dickie's eyes seemed to swell. "Sure it is," he said. "Isn't it?"

Catfish shook her head.

"How come you didn't tell me?"

Catfish smiled ruefully. "I didn't think you'd want to know. You better figure out a way to get rid of those shares, Dickie. And you better do it in a hurry, 'cause if this is like all of Tom and Ben's other deals, it's gonna blow up big-time. Do they know you bought the shares?"

"Who?"

"Tom and Ben."

Dickie shrugged. "Probably. They get records of all the limited partners. So what?"

"So right now Tommy's got to be laughing his little Italian ass off."

"I don't get it. Since when is Jefferson an Italian name?"

Catfish shook her head. "Never mind," she said. "Have another vodka Alka-Seltzer. Mix one for me too."

Despite its race-bred handling and spirited response, today one of Jaguar's most admired aspects is a financial one.

—Advertisement

According to Charles, the Customer Service Specialist at Jaguar Motor Cars of Minneapolis, repairs to Crow's XJS were going to cost $4,385. It would be two days before they could get the parts and another two weeks before they could finish the bodywork. He took Crow out into the immaculate shop, where they had the car up on a lift, and showed him the damaged strut on the underside of the Jaguar.

"Jaguar parts are expensive," Charles pointed out unnecessarily. He pronounced it *Jag-you-are*. Crow stood under the lift and stared gloomily at the twisted strut.

"You can't just straighten it out?"

Charles laughed at Crow's little joke: "Ha ha."

Crow scowled and looked down at the spotless floor. "How much of that forty-four hundred goes toward keeping this floor clean?"

"Jaguar parts are very expensive," Charles repeated. He seemed happy but was unable to infect Crow with his good cheer. "It's not just a matter of replacing a few parts," he explained. "I don't know what you were doing, but it looks to me like somebody picked this vehicle up by the door, shook it, then threw it back down on the street."

"Yes, that's what happened," Crow said.

Charles laughed: "Ha ha ha." He showed Crow the other damaged parts, describing in detail the work that would have to be done.

"What about a loaner?" Crow asked.

"No problem." Charles smiled. "I can let you have an old XJ-6. We charge our repair customers a nominal thirty dollars per day."

The idea of letting Jaguar Motor Cars of Minneapolis have any more of his money sizzled. Crow left the shop in a dark mood. After waiting at the corner for twenty minutes, he paid eighty-five cents to squeeze into an overfilled bus and rode downtown between a twitchy young woman with a pointy nose and a beery-smelling, bug-eyed old man who bounced against him every time the bus swayed to a stop. Crow had never liked being touched by strangers. He kept thinking about Freddy Wisnesky's huge white fingers holding the Jaguar in place.

After enduring a few more blocks of public transport, Crow got off at Eighteenth Street and walked the last mile to the Mills Building. He hoped that this would be his last professional interaction with Dickie Wicky.

Janet was still working the front desk.

"Aren't you supposed to be fired?" Crow asked.

"Mr. Wicky can't fire me," she said with a hard smile. "I'm the only one that knows what's going on here."

"That doesn't surprise me. What's going on?"

"The usual. Sell low; buy high. Whatever runs up the gross."

"Is Dickie in?"

"He's expecting you. Do you remember where his office is?"

"I can find it."

Wicky was sitting on the edge of his oversize leather office chair, hunched over his desk, staring at a miniature snowstorm. From outside the glass front of his office, Crow saw him pick up the tennis-ball-size glass sphere, shake it, set it back on the center of his maroon leather desk blotter, watch the white flakes settle slowly onto a tiny plastic church.

Crow opened the door and stepped inside. Wicky jerked his head up. The whites of his eyes were red, the flesh below looked bruised. He returned his attention to the paperweight, the fingers of his right hand drumming on the blotter.

"Morning, Joe," he said as the white flakes precipitated.

"Rough night?"

Wicky shook the paperweight again and set it aside. "I was up late." He opened his desk drawer, took out a roll of Certs, popped two in his mouth. "Want one?"

"I just stopped by to pick up a check," Crow said.

Wicky sagged for an instant, then lifted his shoulders, sat forward, crinkled up his eyes, and laughed. It was one of his practiced expressions, the laugh that was not a laugh. Crow had often seen him use it after losing a large pot. "Always the practical one, aren't you?" He rolled his shoulders, as if loosening up in preparation for some feat of physical strength. "So tell me, Joe, do you ever think about your future? I mean, do you ever just step back and take a good hard look at the big picture? Or do you just count today's pennies? You know, the guys with a lot of money, they all thought long-term when it counted, Joe." He pushed back in his oversize chair, crossed his arms, wiggled his eyebrows, and crunched down on the Certs.

"Why do I get the feeling you're not going to pay me?" Crow said.

Wicky leaned forward again, pressing down on his blotter with both palms, and pushed his face halfway across the desk. His breath was minty, with undertones of funk. "I'm gonna do better than pay you, Joe. First I'm going to buy you lunch. Then I'm going to make you rich."

15

Prices extended their steady upward trend during the first half of the year as the economy continued to expand. Led by huge increases in the Silver Age area, sales remained at a brisk clip throughout the marketplace. As the second half of the year began, sales above the previously achieved highs became less frequent. Sell offers began to exceed want list requests for the first time in years as the economy slipped into recession.

—The Official Overstreet Comic Book Price Guide

"What would you do if you had, say, a quarter-million dollars, Joe?" Wicky asked.

They were seated in one of the high-backed wooden booths at Myron's Pub. Myron's did a huge lunch business with the lawyers and stockbrokers who officed in the Mills building—a sea of gray and blue suits, hunched over plates piled high with Myron's famous fries, getting their daily dose of cholesterol.

Crow tried to ignore Wicky's question. It was a tough one to get past—questions like that tapped directly into his island fantasy. With a quarter-million dollars he could buy the island, a little boat, get his Jag fixed, and have enough left over to fill it with gasoline. He looked up at the menu, a chalkboard screwed onto the wall, and tried to decide between the steak sandwich and the walleye fillet.

"How's the fish here?"

Wicky pushed out his lips. "I don't know. I always get the cheeseburger." He looked past Crow, grinned, and waved. A waitress, big and blond, wearing a pair of eyeglasses with glittering red frames, pushed the front of her thighs against the edge of their table.

"Afternoon, Mr. Rich," she said, flipping back a page in her order pad. "What can I do you for?" She laughed. Wicky laughed. Crow smiled painfully.

"My usual, Melly, with a martini, up, four olives, and a beer with the food."

"You got it, Mr. Rich." She looked at Crow. "How about yours, honey?" She winked.

"I'll have the walleye. And a Coke."

They watched Melly move away, her big hips swinging gracefully. "They know me here," Wicky said.

Crow rested his big hands on the table and watched Wicky's face, saying nothing.

"So, Joe, how's it going with your girlfriend?" Wicky asked. "What's her name again?"

"Who?" The image of Catfish Wicky flashed across his retinas.

"What's her name? Doberman?"

Crow sighed. "You mean Debrowski. She's a friend, not my girl-friend."

Wicky's martini materialized on the table, followed a nanosecond later by Crow's Coke. Neither man looked up.

"And she's fine," Crow said.

"She seems like a nice person." Wicky lifted his martini, saluted, and drained half the glass in one swallow.

"She's a very nice person."

"I can always tell." Wicky fished out two olives with his soft little fingers and pushed them into his mouth. Crow watched as the alcohol brought color flooding back into Wicky's nose and cheeks. Wicky chewed his olives and smiled. "So what do you think you'd do with a few hundred thousand bucks, Joe?"

"I'm more concerned about what I'm going to do if I don't get the fifty-seven hundred you owe me."

Wicky frowned. "You think small, Joe."

Crow was getting tired of hearing his own name. "I'm a small guy, Dickie."

Wicky shrugged and finished off his martini, closing his eyes as the last two olives slipped between his lips. It looked to Crow like the windup before a pitch. He was right. Wicky cleared his throat, squared his shoulders, and launched into it.

"Joe, did you by any chance read that article in the *Journal* about comic book collections?"

"What journal?" Crow asked.

Wicky drew back. "The *Wall Street Journal*." He frowned at Crow, sighed, and continued. "Anyway, as investments go, comics are the sexiest thing going. Last year a comic book that sold for ten cents back in 1939 went for $108,000. The first *Batman* and *Superman* comics sell for over eighty thousand each. Sotheby's, Christie's, all the big auction houses, are into collectibles now. Comic books, baseball cards, old bottles and cans, you name it. It's where the money is these days, Joe. Used to be you could make your money buying stocks, precious metals, stuff like that. These days the only real opportunities for the small investor—that's you and me—are in stuff people used to throw out."

Crow thought about the boxes of comic books and *Mad* magazines his mother had given to the church rummage sale while he was away at college. At the time, his only concern had been whether she had dug deeply enough in the boxes to discover his collection of *Playboy* magazines.

Wicky was watching him, a knowing smile distorting his lips. "You're thinking about the comics you used to have when you were a kid," he stated.

"I never used to read comics," Crow lied. Wicky was getting alarmingly good at reading him. He yawned and looked at Dickie's Rolex. "Why don't you just give me your watch and we'll call it square, Dickie."

"Are you kidding? This baby's worth fourteen big ones."

"Pawn it."

"Joe, I didn't say I couldn't come up with your money. I said I had something better. You want to hear about it?"

Crow shrugged, inviting the inevitable. The sad fact was, Wicky had him hooked on the idea of a six-figure comic book. He wanted to hear more.

"Okay," Wicky said. "I got this deal—"

"What do you mean, you 'got' it?" Crow would listen, but he wasn't going to make it easy.

Wicky cleared his throat, threw a glance over his shoulder, leaned forward and dropped his voice. "I've got the exclusive. I'm putting a few of my best customers on this, and I'm one hundred percent invested myself. That's why I don't have any liquidity, Joe. Every nickel I could get my hands on, I put it into this deal. That's how solid it is."

He pushed his jaw forward. "Fact is, it's sold out. The only way you can get in now is for you to buy some of my units. You know anything about limited partnerships?"

"They're a device used by shady promoters to rip off investors," Crow said.

Wicky smiled and shook his head, but his eyes stayed on Crow's face. He sat back and let his voice return to normal volume. "Only if you're buying condos in Florida or gold mines in Colorado, and even then not always. What it is, basically, is a bunch of people put together an investment pool, put the money to work for a period of time, and then cash it in. When it works it can make a lot of money for everybody. Most LPs are real estate deals—shopping centers, apartment complexes, that sort of thing—but you can put one together for whatever investment you want. You heard about that sunken treasure that was recovered off the Dry Tortugas a few years back? That was funded as a limited partnership. They sold five-thousand-dollar units to a bunch of small investors, raised about a million bucks, put together a high-tech boat and crew, and went out and found it. Two hundred ten million in gold bars and coins. Every partner became an instant millionaire. Of course, not all of them pay back quite that good."

"Most of them don't pay back at all, the way I hear it."

Wicky shrugged. "They used to be a better deal taxwise. Back in the early eighties. That's when you heard about all the real estate scams. The tax consequences were so attractive that nobody cared if the partnership paid off. That's history. Anyway, this deal I came across is a sure thing, and the best way we knew to put it together was as an LP."

"Who is 'we'?"

Wicky dropped his voice down again and pushed his face across the table. "I put the package together for a couple guys I know. A couple of very sharp guys named Franklin and Jefferson." He drummed his short fingers on the tabletop. "Industry insiders. You'll meet them. I'm going to get them to come to one of our card games."

"Sounds illegal. How about if you just loan me your watch until you come up with the cash?"

"Nothing illegal about it. This isn't like trading stocks or commodities. These guys I met, they know the market inside and out. This comic book market is exploding. It used to be that only these nut-job collectors cared about the things, but now you got your in-vestors, big guns, guys with real money, buying the things up. Comics you could've bought five years ago for a couple bucks are now worth hundreds each. You know what the first *Spider-Man* comic goes for now? Five thou."

Spider-Man? That sounded familiar. Crow was reasonably certain that his copies had gone for a nickel each at the Church of Saint Mary annual rummage sale.

"The what?" Crow had tuned Wicky out for a moment, thinking about his lost comic books.

"That's what it's called," Wicky said in a near whisper. "The Galactic Guardians Fund. See, there are unknown comic collections scattered all over the country, just sitting in people's attics and base-ments. The fund will buy these collections for two to five cents on the dollar, maybe less, then sell them either privately or through the auction houses."

"So this whole deal is to finance some kind of comic book treasure hunt? No, thanks."

Wicky was smiling, shaking his head. "There's more to it. They've already located a *major* unknown collection. Money in the bank."

Melly appeared and slid two plates onto the table. Crow's walleye was curled up. It looked like a deep-fried tongue. Wicky opened his cheeseburger and squeezed a layer of catsup over the beef patty. An instant later, a frosted mug of beer landed beside his plate. He drank a third of the beer, picked up his burger and pushed it into his mouth, then continued his pitch, talking in a low voice and chewing simulta-neously.

"I'll tell you how this whole deal came together, but you got to keep it to yourself, okay? A few months ago, Jefferson—that's one of the general partners—is buying a paper from this newsstand, down-town Chicago, and the newsstand guy is selling a whole stack of new comic books to this weird-looking old guy in a raincoat. I swear to God this is true. Jefferson is in the comic book business, so naturally he's interested. He tries to talk to the old man, but the guy takes off like he's scared. Just then, this CTA bus comes along and runs the old guy over. Comic books and blood all up and down Michigan Avenue.

"Now most guys would've got the hell out of there, but Jefferson hangs around and after they scrape the guy up he starts quizzing the newsstand guy. Seems the old guy was one of his best customers. He tells Jefferson that the old guy's been buying up doubles of every comic he gets in. Says he'd been doing it for years. Says he saves two copies of every new comic for the old guy. So Jefferson finds out the guy's name and where he lived. Big old house, about the only private home left in the Loop. Turns out the guy has a sister lives there. House is full of comics, all perfect condition, filed and catalogued, like a dream.

"What he finds out from the sister is, back in the thirties, this guy, name is John Jones—he was just a kid then, of course—started saving comic books, every comic book he could get his hands on, which was pretty much every comic book that was ever published from 1936 up until he got run over. He was a real nut about it, treated the things like they were sacred documents, which was unheard of back then. Who cared about a bunch of comic books? But this Jones wasn't exactly a normal kid. His sister says he used to boil his marbles every time after he played with them. Some kind of germ phobia. He lived with his sister in their parents' house, living off the trust fund their parents left them, never went outside except to go to the newsstand for more comics. His whole life he didn't do anything except buy comic books and wash his hands. Imagine it: a house full of comics, every comic ever published, in perfect condition. That's what the Galactic Guardians Fund is going to acquire. They've got the collection located and are in contact with the sister. And she's agreed to their offer."

Crow was intrigued. "How much is this collection worth?"

"Twelve million, *minimum*."

"Twelve million dollars' worth of *comic books*?"

"The collection is extraordinary. He had over fifty thousand titles, with two of every issue published after 1941. In perfect condition. Absolute pristine mint condition. This is a one-of-a-kind collection, absolutely without equal, Joe. You run into something like this once in a lifetime, if that. And the Galactic Guardians Fund is buying up the entire collection."

"So you're trying to raise twelve million dollars?"

Wicky grinned and shook his head. "That's the beauty of it, Joe. The sister has agreed to sell the collection for three hundred thousand dollars in cash. We've got a purchase agreement. We've got the money. Nobody else knows about this collection. Even the sister didn't know what she had until Franklin and Jefferson contacted her."

Crow examined Wicky's flushed face. The excitement was genuine, he was sure, but was it excitement over the investment or over the prospect of selling him on the fund?

"Why would this woman sell twelve million worth of comics for three hundred thousand dollars?"

"Are you kidding? Because she doesn't know what she's got is why."

"Does that bother you?"

"Why should it? That's what investing is about. You buy low and sell high. Every time you buy something, the guy who's selling it thinks he's getting the sweet end of the deal. Once this old lady agrees to sell her dead brother's comic books for three hundred thousand—which, incidentally, she doesn't need—what are we supposed to do, raise the offer? All we needed to do was come up with the money, which we have. We'll be taking possession within a week. When Franklin and Jefferson came to me with this deal, I knew right away to structure it as a limited partnership. It's very clean, Joe, very sexy. Once in a lifetime. I owe you six K, right?"

Crow nodded.

"What I'm saying I'll do is, I'll transfer three units of Galactic Guardians into your name and we'll call it square."

"What's a unit worth?"

"The payback should be sixty to eighty thousand per unit."

Crow couldn't help thinking about the things he could do with that much money. "If it's so clean, how come they don't just borrow the money from a bank, buy the comics, and keep all the profit for themselves?" He could buy a boat. He would need one to get to the island. One of those bass boats with the fancy seats.

Dickie nodded seriously. "Good question, Joe. There are reasons why they don't do exactly that. One, the deal is complicated—"

"I thought you said it was simple."

"It is, from the point of view of the investor. But from the point of view of negotiating a loan from the bank, it's complicated. They would have to do a formal appraisal of the comic collection, and that would create a couple of problems. For one thing, you'd have the problem of the seller finding out what her collection was really worth and backing out of the deal.

"The second reason is that bankers simply don't take comic books seriously."

"Hard to imagine."

"Really. If they were able to get through the appraisal process, which as I explained is not a good idea anyway, they'd probably turn down the loan just because if something happened they don't want a comic collection showing up on their inventory one day. Loan officers do not like explaining that sort of thing to their superiors.

"The third reason they don't want to use a bank is that these guys want to be able to buy and sell the comics quickly, and they don't want a bunch of blue suits hanging over them asking questions. See, a collection of this size is going to flood the market, so to get full value for it, it's going to have to be sold nice and quiet. You get an institution like a bank involved—for one thing, it's going to be harder to turn the stuff around for cash, if you know what I mean." He rubbed his thumb and middle finger together.

"Okay, so they don't go to the bank." Crow found himself wanting to believe. He forced his skeptical side to the foreground. "It still sounds too good to be true."

Wicky shrugged. "Deals that sound too good to be true go down every day, Joe. How do you think people get rich?"

"I always assumed they stole it."

"Let me tell you the rest of it. The Jones collection, which is going to get you thirty times your investment, is just the tip of the iceberg. Back in the forties, this John Jones started a fan club. Over the years he built up a list of pen pals that he called the Galactic Guardians. Then, in the fifties, when these fans grew up and quit buying comics, he got disgusted and turned into a sort of hermit. According to his sister, that's the way he was headed anyway. But he kept on buying those comics. And he kept his list of pen pals."

"Let me guess," Crow said. "You think you're going to mine a list of pen pals that's four decades old, right? Find them and buy their old comics, right?"

"Right," said Wicky.

Shaking his head, Crow said, "A list of kids' names from the forties and fifties? How many of them do you think you're even going to find, never mind that their mothers probably already gave the comics away for the church bazaar. It'll be a waste of time." Crow crossed his arms.

But Wicky was smiling. "Joe, you have to appreciate what a nut this Jones guy was. He didn't just make a list. He had a file on everyone he ever wrote to. He wrote down their addresses, their parents' full names, names of brothers and sisters, how many comics they had, everything! And these weren't just your average kids that read a few comic books; these were collectors. A lot of those comics are still out there, Joe, all boxed up in attics and basements, just waiting for us. And best of all, we aren't talking a few dozen names here. He had files on eight hundred names."

"Eight hundred?"

"At least. And even if we strike out on every single one of them, we still have Jones's own twelve-million-dollar collection in the bag."

Crow shook his head, hard, pushing back the greed that was threatening to overrun his common sense. "It sounds to me like somebody's getting ripped off."

"Somebody's always getting ripped off. But this case is a win-win situation. Everybody comes out ahead."

"Except for the old lady."

Dickie was shaking his head. "It doesn't work that way, Joe. The guys that started the fund, if they hadn't discovered the collection, the old lady would have probably let it sit there till she died. She had no idea what she had. In fact, they could have bought the entire collection for a few thousand dollars if they'd wanted. The fact that they offered her a fair price tells you what kind of guys they are."

"What kind of guys are they?"

"They're a little strange, but they know comic books. I think Franklin is the smartest guy I ever met. He lives and breathes numbers. A real gentleman. And Jefferson . . ." He shook his head, smiling. "You remember the Lava lamp? Jefferson invented it. And he was the guy who had the original idea for Pac-Man, even though he never got a dime off it. You know those Teenage Mutant Ninja Turtles? That was his idea too. He was sitting around one night drinking beer with the two guys that started the comic book and he came up with the idea of the turtles. They send him free copies of all their comics. He's one of the most creative minds I've ever met."

"They sound like quite a pair."

"They're really something. So what do you think, Joe? Do you want in?"

Wicky had demolished his burger and fries and was sucking down a second beer, staring at him. Crow sat back in the booth. "I just want my fifty-seven hundred dollars, Dickie."

Wicky rolled his eyes and shook his head. "I can't believe what I'm hearing, Joe. I offer you a sure thing, six figures, and you can't get your mind off a measly six K. Let me put it to you this way. I will personally guarantee you that the fund will pay off for you. If it goes sour, which it won't, I'll still pay you the six K, okay?"

"How about you pay me now?"

"I don't have it, goddamn it. I'm offering you the opportunity of a lifetime, Joe, and I'm personally guaranteeing it. Christ, I'm even buying your goddamn lunch. What more do you want from me?" He was glaring across the table, red-faced, a spot of catsup on his chin.

Crow shrugged. "Your Rolex." He smiled and looked down at his plate. The walleye was gone, but he couldn't remember eating it. A hand appeared, and the plate slid away. Another mug of beer materialized in front of Wicky, who was trying to hold his face perfectly still. His eyes looked ready to burst.

"I'll give it back to you when the Galactic Guardians thing pays off," Crow said. "I promise."

Wicky lifted the beer, sipped, banged the mug down on the table not quite hard enough to spill any. He unclipped the watchband, jerked it off his wrist, dropped it on the table.

"There. You satisfied?"

Crow lifted the watch. It was astonishingly heavy. He clamped it onto his wrist, checked the time.

"You lose that baby, you're out fourteen big ones, Crow."

"Don't worry about it. I won't bet it on less than aces full of kings."

Wicky winced and drained his beer. "You want anything else? My car? My wife?"

"I could use your car. Mine's in the shop, you know."

"Christ, here I'm offering you the deal of a lifetime, giving you my personal guarantee, giving you my fucking Rolex President, and you want my fucking car."

"I'm just kidding, Dickie. Relax. The watch will do me fine. First dividend I get from this Galactic thing, I give it back."

"Yeah, right."

"So how long will it be before I see some money?"

"Right away."

"Like next week?"

Dickie frowned. "That's not what I meant. Be reasonable."

"When, then?"

"Soon. All we have to do is take possession of the collection and start selling it. You don't want to just dump it on the market, understand. Sell a few titles at a time, keep it quiet, that's how you make the money. You don't want to flood the market with top-quality comic books. But as soon as the money starts rolling in, we start dividing it up. The fund's number-one top priority is to take care of the limited partners. That means you and me and Ozzie and all the other guys I got into the deal. We get paid even before the founders. By the way, I invited them to play cards at Zink's. Give you and Ozzie a chance to meet the guys that're going to make us rich."

"These guys play cards?"

"Sure. They love to gamble. One time Jefferson threw seventeen straight passes at the Horseshoe in Vegas. He was up sixty-three thou, so he passed the dice, walked over to the sports book, bet it all on the Cubbies. Easy come, easy go."

"I thought you said this guy was smart." Crow was thinking he knew how he was going to pay Charles for the "Jag-you-are."

"Oh, he's smart. But he gets stupid behind a bet, just like anybody. Except you, of course." Wicky grinned and winked. "You're going to like being rich, Joe. Trust me."

It's not what you think, it's what you see—
It's not what you see, it's what you be.

—*The Coldcocks, "Existentionalized"*

Crow's feet hurt. He propped them up next to Milo on the railing and let the afternoon sun warm his soles. At times, Minneapolis felt like a small town, but not when you had to walk it. Milo, his tail twitching, examined the bare human feet, sniffing each of them with tremendous concentration.

Crow was feeling sorry for himself. He had no woman, no car, and very little money. Times like these called for a cocaine fantasy, but he resisted. The fantasy, he had learned, became reality. And vice versa. He picked up one of the sheets of paper balanced on his lap and tried, again, to read it. The documents looked good, pages filled with columns of numbers, copies of news articles about the investment potential of rare comic books and baseball cards, biographical data on F. B. Franklin and T. K. Jefferson, the founders and general partners of the Galactic Guardians Fund, plus an impressive foldout page featuring a four-color bar graph projecting the value of golden-age comic books well into the next century. It was a nicely designed package, very sober and official-looking. Crow turned again to the most astonishing page of all—the one on which he had scrawled his own jagged signature. He swayed between a gambler's greedy joy at the potential windfall and the poker player's sure knowledge that you're not a winner until you're out the door with the cash in your pocket, and sometimes not even then.

He forced his mind to the more immediate and practical problem of transportation. He wouldn't have the Jag back for a couple of weeks, and maybe not even then unless he could figure out a way to pay for it. In the meantime, did he know someone who might have a spare vehicle? Only one name occurred to him: Sam O'Gara. Crow made a sour face. He hadn't called Sam in weeks. Could he pick up the phone now and ask to borrow a car? Not yet, he decided. All the shit going down in his life, he wasn't quite ready for Sam.

A banging at the door interrupted his thoughts. He pulled his feet down off the railing, let the Galactic Guardians Fund documents fall to the floor, and went to answer the door.

It was Debrowski, looking stark in black leather and red lipstick. "You got a beer?"

Crow went to the refrigerator and opened a Moussy. Debrowski wandered out onto the porch and sat in Crow's chair. "Hi, cat," she said to Milo. Milo flicked his tail and squinted. Crow handed her the Moussy and leaned his hip against the railing.

"Dressed for action," he said, looking at the five feet of motorcycle chain wrapped twice around her hips.

"I've got a couple business meetings tonight. I'm trying to put together a midwestern tour for the Coldcocks, and they keep running me around. Don't want to play this town, insist on playing that town, won't do outdoor—bunch of prima donnas. What the hell happened to rock and roll, anyway? I don't want to talk about it. How you doing with your buddy Dickie? He pay you?"

Crow pointed at the papers on the floor. Debrowski scooped them up and paged through.

"Comic books?" she said. "What the hell do you know about comic books?"

"Not much," he said. "This is how Dickie has decided to pay me off."

She flipped through the pages, frowning. "What the hell have you gotten yourself into, Crow?"

Crow cleared his throat. "Well," he said, "there was this comic collector named John Jones—"

"John Jones? You got to be kidding me."

"You want to hear this or not?"

"Sorry." Debrowski crossed her arms. Crow waited for the sound of clicking chain links to subside, then told her, as best he could remember, the story of the Galactic Guardians.

Debrowski listened, asking few questions, taking tiny sips from her Moussy. When Crow had finished, she said, "So the idea is to rip off some old lady for her brother's comic books."

"Something like that," Crow said gloomily. Repeating Wicky's sales pitch had underscored its absurdity. "They say she would have just let them rot if they hadn't made her an offer."

"Huh." She scratched Milo behind the ears and drank the last of her beer.

"So what do *you* think?"

"You really want to know what I think?"

"Yeah," said Crow, knowing from her tone of voice that he really didn't.

"I think you're getting sucked into the sewer. I think you'll be lucky to come back up with your pockets full of shit. I think Dickie Wicky is leading you around by the nose, and I think you're letting him do it."

Crow searched his mind for a withering comeback. "Yeah?" he said.

"Yeah," said Debrowski. Her "yeah" was the more convincing. She lit a cigarette and let the thick smoke trail from her nostrils.

"What was I supposed to do, break his fingers?"

"I don't know, Crow. Collection work is a little out of my area. All I know is, this Galactic Guardians thing smells a lot like eau de merde."

Crow pulled back his left sleeve and held up the gold Rolex. "How does this smell to you?"

Debrowski shook her head. "It's not you, Crow. It stinks. You get it from Dickie?"

"Collateral."

"Right. I hope it's real. Listen, I know a guy that's into comic books in a big way. Natch Jorgeson. Has a little shop down on Fourth, just up the street. Do me a favor and go see him, ask him what he thinks of these 'Galactic Guardians.' You want me to give him a call?"

Crow looked at the agreement he had signed. He didn't want to know any more about the Galactic Guardians. The whole deal was making him queasy. He started to tell Debrowski to forget it, but she was already on the phone, punching numbers.

"In the first place, dude, the nums are all wrong," said Natch, fingering his gold earring.

Crow asked, "What do you mean? Which numbers?"

"All the ones you told me, and probably the rest of 'em too." Natch paged through the Galactic Guardians prospectus and agreement. "This is some weird shit, man. People actually buy this, huh?"

"I guess they must."

He squinted and stabbed a long-nailed forefinger toward Crow's chest. "How long you known L.D.?"

"Debrowski? Not long. About a year."

"You two an item?"

"We're friends."

"Yeah? She likes you, man. I could hear it in her voice. You don't know shit about comics, do you?"

Crow shook his head. He had been sitting right there when Debrowski had made the phone call to Natch, and *he* hadn't heard anything in her voice.

Natch pulled his bare feet off the countertop and stood up. He circled the end of the counter, locked the front door, and motioned Crow to follow him toward the back of the shop. "Show you something, dude."

Natch was a thin, pale, angular creature wearing vintage bell bottoms and a T-shirt that read: HARD ROCK CAFE—MIDDLE EARTH.

Long gray-blond hair radiated out from a bald patch at the top of his head and trickled down over his shoulders. According to Debrowski, he'd been in the comic book business since the late sixties. His storefront business had survived several location and name changes—its present incarnation was called Ephemera—but it had retained that special sixties flavor. Perhaps it was a cone of strawberry incense burning somewhere among the piles of magazines, or the half-smoked joint propped behind Natch's right ear. Crow followed him past uneven stacks of comic books and magazines. Overfilled boxes were jammed into narrow, sagging shelves, and piles of assorted magazines, books, and newspapers covered the baseboards. Dust bunnies scurried for cover. Natch pushed a stack of cardboard boxes to the side, revealing a metal door. He selected a key from the ring hanging at his belt, unlocked and opened the door. An invisible cloud of cool air touched Crow's face. Natch flipped up a light switch, illuminating a bright white stairwell.

"Check it out, my man," said Natch as he descended the steel staircase. "Close the door behind you. This is a controlled environment—constant fifty-five degrees and sixty percent relative humidity. I've got an electrostatic precipitator that'll knock the lint right off a gnat's pecker." Crow closed the door and followed Natch down the steps. He could hear the hum of the climate control kicking in, restoring the atmosphere to its prescribed parameters.

The basement of Ephemera was a single rectangular room twenty feet long by twelve feet wide. The walls were pure white and, with the exception of a row of filtered vents, featureless. A set of flat files, chin high, ran the length of the room on two sides. A flat white table, nothing on it but a blue notebook, sat in the center of the room. After the barely controlled clutter and reek of the shop upstairs, this was like stepping into the far future. Crow gave Natch the stunned look he was waiting for.

"This is where I keep all my good shit," said Natch, showing a set of long, smoke-stained teeth. "Check this out." He opened a file drawer, gently lifted out a flat plastic package, and set it on the table. It was a comic book, yellow cover, Batman and Robin swinging from ropes high over Gotham City.

"You were talking about *Batman* #1? Well, there it is. Kind of gives you goose bumps, don't it?"

Crow leaned closer and inspected the comic. It looked to be in perfect condition, but it also had a dated look, like a visitor from the past. "This is worth eighty thousand dollars?"

Natch shook his head. "You don't get it, do you? Man, I look at these things and I get a rush you wouldn't believe. Guys like you, all you want to know is how much it's worth. That's how come this business has gotten so fucked up the last decade. You know those prices you were quoted? They told you this comic is worth eighty thousand, right? Well, I am ever so fucking sorry to tell you this, my man, but comics like these do not *sell* for, they *trade* for."

"I don't get the difference."

"Look, man, this here is what you call a key issue. It's got historical significance, it's got a primary character, and there're only about a dozen other mint-condition copies on planet Earth. But if I wanted to sell this comic for cash money, I could get fifteen, maybe twenty thousand for it—assuming I could even find a buyer. And this is the good shit."

"How come I keep hearing these big numbers thrown around?"

"Those are trades, man. All these old comics get rated by *Overstreet's* or one of the other price guides. They're worth anything from their cover price up to maybe ten or twenty thousand dollars. If that. There are maybe four or five very rare and important comics that could sell for fifty thousand in perfect condition. Not many comics are worth more than a few hundred. When you hear about these huge figures, a hundred thousand dollars, what you're hearing is what the comic *traded for*. That means that a guy who trades *Batman* #1 for eighty thousand dollars probably got a little bit of cash, if any, plus a stack of comic books that is supposed to be worth the eighty thousand."

"And the comics he gets aren't worth that much?"

"It's in everybody's interest to pump up the nums, my friend. Except for the small collector. The guy who really loves comics, he gets screwed. Big trades kick up the value for the pros but leave the little guy sucking air. But nobody ever pays a hundred thousand cash for a comic book. I'm not saying it won't ever happen—with these auction houses getting into the act, there are some real cash-for-comics sales happening, but the true nums aren't like that. That's one of the reasons comic values have been inflating like crazy the past few years. You get a few responsible dealers that say 'Now wait a minute,' but those guys get left in the dust. It's like the stock market, only without the SEC."

"I can see why Dickie likes it."

"That's the dude sold you this shit? Those guys are raising four hundred thou, spending three quarters of it to acquire a collection that sounds like a dealer's wet dream and probably is. You ever hear of Edgar Church? This John Jones character sounds an awful lot like Edgar Church. Too similar. The Church collection is legend in the comics business. It surfaced about twenty years ago. Hit the market like a goddamn tidal wave. We'll never see a collection like that again, my friend. Only in our dreams. This Galactic Guardian thing? Dreams, dude."

Crow nodded glumly, staring at the *Batman* comic on the table. A memory tugged at him.

"Do you have any old *Spider-Man* comics?" he asked.

Natch said, "Spidey? I've got most of the older ones. You have a particular issue in mind?"

"There was this one with a green guy that flew around on a little rocket. The Green Goblin."

Natch put the *Batman* comic away, then opened the blue notebook and flipped through it. The pages were covered with tiny, cramped entries. It looked like an accountant's ledger. He ran his finger down a page of entries, stopped, and said, "Far out." He went to a file on the other side of the room, opened it, and handed Crow a comic book in a plastic sleeve. "Number fourteen," he said. "Introduces the Green Goblin."

Crow looked at the cover. Spider-Man clinging to the top of a cave, being attacked by the Green Goblin. He felt the hair on the back of his neck rise. He had once owned this comic book, or one exactly like it. It was as if he was looking through a window back onto his childhood. He looked at Natch, who was grinning.

"Can I take it out of the plastic?"

Natch smiled and said, "Maybe there's hope for you yet, dude."

The walk home from Ephemera seemed to take hours. Crow let himself in, walked out onto his porch, picked up Milo, draped him over his shoulders, and stood watching the traffic pass below. After a time, Milo grew impatient and inserted a set of claws into his perch. Crow bent forward and let the cat dismount. What the hell, he decided. He swallowed his pride and phoned his old man to see if he could borrow a car. The way he was feeling, there wasn't much to swallow.

Sam O'Gara answered the phone with his characteristic unintelligible croak.

"Sam, this is Joe."

"Son!"

"How you doing?"

"I got a devil in my belly. Doctor says it's acid, on account of the snoose, but I think it's the Big C, son."

"Sounds rough. Say, you got a vehicle I could borrow for a few days?"

"Your old dad's dying, and you want to borrow his car?"

"Sam, you've been dying since the day I met you. You'll still be dying ten years from now. I'll have it back before then."

He listened to his father's harsh breath.

"Welp, I got this big red fucker you can use."

Sam O'Gara lived across the river in East Saint Paul—an hour and a half on the bus—in a former shotgun shack that he had expanded in every direction. It looked like a piece of dirty popcorn. Sam shared his home with four cats, two dogs, and an occasional girlfriend. He boasted that he could make one cat last longer than any three women.

Sam made his living as a shade-tree mechanic and used-car dealer, buying, fixing, and reselling as many cars as it took to meet the monthly food bill. He always had two or three vehicles in various states of disassembly in his backyard and had been at war with the city housing inspectors ever since Crow could remember. "Ain't no car. It's a sculpture," was one of his favorite and most effective lines.

Crow found him back by the alley, with most of his wiry little body inside the engine compartment of an old Ford flatbed truck. It was the only red vehicle in sight, so Crow assumed that this was the "red fucker" he had come to borrow. The body looked as if it had been painted in the dark with a stiff brush. A matching set of spotted yellow mutts that looked more like hyenas than dogs jumped up from their resting place in the shade of a rusted-out blue Chevy and charged. Crow froze and waited, ready to protect his groin with one hand and his throat with the other if they failed to recognize him.

Sam looked up and shouted, "Chester! Festus!" The dogs stopped a few feet away, growling. Crow had to run this gauntlet every time he visited Sam. He slowly lowered himself into a crouch. The dogs consulted each other, then one of them came forward slowly, sniffed his proffered hand, and started to wag its tail. The other mutt joined in. Crow rubbed the dogs' heads, stood up, and joined his father. He leaned over the grille. Sam was pulling the valve cover.

"What's going on?" Crow asked.

"Just a little adjustment I got to make." This was a typical Sam O'Gara ploy. If he wanted to borrow the truck, Crow would have to spend the next hour passing tools over the fender, listening to the old man's bullshit.

"I just need it so it runs, Sam."

"Yep. Just a little adjustment's all she needs. You want to grab that fucker for me?" He pointed a grease-blackened forefinger toward a row of tools on the far fender. Crow handed him an open-end wrench.

"Not that fucker, t'other one."

Crow had never heard his father call a tool by any other name. He put his hand on a smaller wrench.

"That's the fucker," Sam said, looking full into his son's face for the first time.

As always, Crow felt a javelin of recognition pierce his gut. Strip away the wrinkles, whiten the teeth and eyes, and add a few pounds— it was as if he was looking into a mirror made of slow glass, seeing his future in this foul-mouthed old man. Crow had been eighteen years old the first time he met his father. The old man had come to watch him graduate from Westland High School. Until then, Crow had not even known he was alive. The first thing the old man had said to him was, "I'm the fucker knocked up your mama, son."

Since then, they had maintained a cautious and distant relationship, trading favors back and forth, keeping the scales in balance. Crow had never been comfortable with his father, never felt quite the way he imagined a son should feel, but he stayed in touch. Whenever he asked the old man for help with something, it was with a measure of shame, as if suddenly he was not complete without the part that had sired him.

"How come you need wheels all of a sudden, son? Thought you had some fancy-ass fucker you was driving."

"It's in the shop."

"Shoulda brought it on over. I'd a fixed 'er up for you."

"It's a Jaguar, Sam."

"So what?" He pulled a tin of Skoal from his pocket, snapped his

forefinger against the tin top, opened the can, and took a pinch between grease-blackened fingers.

"So it'd be like asking a veterinarian to take out my appendix, that's
what."

Sam inserted the Skoal into his cheek, then pulled a Pall Mall from
behind his ear, lit it with his battered stainless-steel Zippo. Crow
could almost feel the double dose of nicotine ripping through the old
man's arteries. "You got trouble with your appendix, son?"

♦ ♥ **17** ♣ ♠

*Deep down, everybody thinks they deserve to make as much
money as the next guy, and they're scared to death they won't
make as much. That's what you got to tap into. That's why when
one guy hears that this other bozo bought five hundred shares of
Dumb Ass, Inc., he's gotta do it too. It's like those . . . what do you
call them? Lemons. Like when the lemons march into the sea.*

—*Richard D. Wicky, V.P., training a new registered representative*

"Yeah, Oz? Listen, I'm glad I caught you. You know that
Galactic Guardians? No, no, I got you the three units, just
like I said I would. I said I would, didn't I? Yeah. Yeah.
Yeah. Listen, the reason I called, some more units just became available. No. No. No. What happened is, one of the guys that bought a
bunch of it ran into a cash problem and he's trying to unload a few
units. Uh-huh. Uh-huh. Uh-huh. I don't know yet—how many
would you be interested in? Uh-huh. Yeah. No, he just wants to get
his money back. Two thousand a unit. I don't know. Sure, I'm pretty
sure he could let loose of three more. And, Oz? You can just make the
check out to me. I run it through Litten here, you got your transaction cost. We don't need that, right? Yeah. Okay. Three units. You
got it, buddy. You want any more, let me know, okay? Yeah. Thanks,

Oz. See you tomorrow night at Zink's. Right. Bye."

Wicky set the phone back on its cradle, shook his paperweight, watched the snow settle. He picked up the phone and dialed another number.

"George! Rich Wicky here! You been watching the market today? It's looking real shaky. I'm thinking it's about time to sell that Unisys. Yeah. Uh-huh. At least you'll get the tax break. Yeah, I really think you should. In fact, I'm getting a lot of my people out of the market altogether—things are just too uncertain right now. They're saying it could go down another three hundred points before it makes a new bottom. Uh-huh. Uh-huh. Well, you know, the money markets aren't paying much now. I'm getting a lot of guys into this limited partnership I found. Yeah, I know. I know. I know. The thing is, this one's different. You read that article about comic books in the *Journal* a few days ago? Well, let me tell you . . ."

It was after six o'clock when Wicky left Litten Securities. His efforts to unload the rest of his Galactic Guardians were not going well. He still had another eighty-six units to dump, and he'd used up most of the juice he had with his existing clients. They weren't buying his line. Something must be coming through in my voice, he thought—they can smell fear right through the phone lines.

He decided to stop at Myron's Pub for a martini, something to get his mind off his troubles. Jack Mitchell was sitting at the bar with one of the new guys—a wimpy-looking kid, all decked out in his new Brooks Brothers suit, wearing it like it was alive. First day on the job, out for a few drinks with one of the big boys. Mitchell introduced Wicky as Litten's number-one sales animal. Even called him "Rich" for once, so of course Wicky had to buy a round of drinks. It was the kid's first martini. Mitchell was wearing his cherry-popping smile. In about twelve hours, the kid would be experiencing a hangover to die from. Mitchell was keeping his hand on the Brooks Brothers shoulder, keeping the kid focused, saying, "You can talk on the phone all day long, read your script to every little old lady from Thief River Falls to Winona, but the real business happens right here in Myron's. This is where the deals are made. Right, *Rich*?"

Wicky smiled and saluted with his martini.

Another round, and the kid loosened up and started talking macroeconomics, a bunch of shit he'd learned in college. Wicky ordered some shots of tequila to shut him up. It worked, but then Jack

Mitchell started in about Las Vegas. He went there for two weeks every year, acted like he owned the place. Wicky shared some of his hot stock picks with the kid, who dutifully typed them into his new electronic memo pad, punching the tiny keys one at a time. By seven o'clock the kid was zonked, complaining in slurred sentence fragments about women in general and about his new wife in particular, who hadn't gone down on him since the day they were married. A smiling Jack Mitchell kept prescribing new drinks for the kid's problems. "Ever had a Zombie, kid?"

Wicky said, "I gotta get going, guys. Gotta go win the rent money. You guys interested in playing some cards tonight?"

The new kid had never been this drunk before in his life—not even in college—and, after what awaited him in the morning, would likely never be this drunk again. But he wasn't so drunk that he didn't know he was too drunk to play poker. Unable to form words clearly by this time, he simply shook his head.

Mitchell laughed. "This kid's no dummy," he said.

When Wicky floated out of Myron's, Mitchell was suggesting that the kid buy another round of Glenlivet for the road. No deals had been made.

♦ ♥ 18 ♣ ♠

Cars are like dogs. You can walk 'em around a ring, give 'em funny haircuts, pick up their do-do with your hand inside a plastic bag. I don't give a shit. A dog's a dog, and so's your car if it don't run right.

—*Sam Crow, explaining the nine cars in his backyard to a city inspector*

B*eep.*
"Joe, this is Jimbo Bobick. You get that package I sent you? Call me!"
Beep.

"This is Cat Fish. You and me, we need to talk. Don't call me, I'll get back to you."

Beep.

"Son? This is your daddy. I maybe forgot to mention, that red fucker's got a sticky gas pedal. I was gonna tie a cord to it, case it gets stuck down. Maybe you oughta do that, before it goes and takes off on you. Okay, son? Bye."

The first time the red fucker took off on him, Crow was on the Ford bridge, crossing the Mississippi. He wasn't used to the truck, and it took him two critical heartbeats to realize that even though he had pulled his foot off the gas pedal, the truck was still accelerating. He was almost climbing up the trunk of a little Mitsubishi when he stood hard on the brake and stalled the racing engine. He sat there for a minute, then another minute, waiting for his heartbeat to slow, then reached down and pulled the accelerator pedal off the floor, worked it up and down. It seemed fine. He restarted the truck and drove home slowly, working the pedals gingerly. It took off once again on Hiawatha Avenue, but he was ready for it this time and flipped the gas pedal back up with the edge of his shoe sole.

After hearing Sam's message, he found a piece of clothesline, tied it to the pedal, ran it up over the steering column so it hung within easy reach. A typical Sam O'Gara repair. He drove the truck around the block a few times, thinking about his dad, practicing with the cord. It worked fine. One thing about old Sam—as foul-mouthed, irresponsible, and full of bullshit as he was, he cared enough to call and warn his son about the gas pedal. Crow was touched.

He parked the truck, went inside, made himself a sardine, onion, and tomato sandwich, ate it, drank a fake beer, listened to an old Tim Buckley tape, and tried not to think about the message from Catfish. She got to him like a drug. The night stretched before him, huge, empty, and grim. He wished fervently for a crisis, solvable and impersonal, to give him purpose, but would have to settle for the poker game at Zink's.

Maybe he would drive up to Brainerd when he got his Jag back, look at that island. It would be something to do. It would get him out of town. Drive up for a day, about three hours each way, and get a few lungfuls of that northern air.

Crow showed up at Zink's a little after ten. He didn't like sitting at a table, waiting for the other players to show, so he always tried to be an hour or so late. Waiting at the table made him anxious and too ready to gamble his money, and he didn't have a hell of a lot to work with, so he liked to walk in on a game in progress—that was the way to control the action.

Tonight he was feeling cocky and ready for play. A dangerous attitude when it came to cards, but the feeling was good and he decided to go with it. He found a parking space for the red fucker right in front of Club 34. A good omen. Had he still been using, he would have done a couple of quick spoons, one in each nostril, right now. Instead, he sat in the truck cab with his eyes closed, letting his mind go flat. He pushed away all thoughts of broken cars, dark-haired women, islands, and empty pockets. He let the gray nothing rest in his head. A clean mind was a winning mind, a mind attuned to probabilities, strategies, and the intent to deceive.

Ozzie LaRose opened the door at the top of the stairs.

"Crow! All right, guys, we got ourselves a real game now."

The other four men sitting at the table all looked at him. Zink was shuffling through a deck, ready to deal the next hand. Dickie Wicky waved at Crow with what looked like a gin and tonic. To Wicky's right, Catfish's former love stud Tom Aquinas—or whatever his name was tonight—winked at Crow. Across the table, stacking a pile of chips, Ben Cartwright looked at him mildly.

"These are the fish?" Crow asked, looking at Ben Cartwright. He could feel his meditative calm crumble, breaking into chunks of illusion.

Dickie looked embarrassed. "Hey, who said anything about fish?"

Ben Cartwright smiled and looked down at his long-fingered hands.

Wicky said, "These are the guys I was telling you about, Joe. This is Ben Franklin, and this is T. K. Jefferson. Guys, this is Joe Crow, a good friend of mine."

Crow stared at Cartwright/Franklin, then shifted his eyes to Aquinas/Jefferson. He could hear the clicking of broken information re-sorting itself in his mind, the sound of pieces thudding painfully into place. Jefferson was grinning at Crow, riffling his chips with one hand. Crow wondered if he was wearing his purple Batman underwear. Franklin, big and languid and pale, was stacking towers of chips, keeping his eyes averted, a faint smile showing through his sparse beard.

Crow waited for his mind to sort it out. One thing he knew for sure: if Catfish Wicky's frenetic "love stud," Tommy, and the pale-eyed card mechanic, Ben, were behind the Galactic Guardians Fund, his units weren't going to make him a rich man anytime soon.

Ben Franklin cleared his throat. "Good to see you again, Mr. Crow," he said in his deep voice.

Wicky looked surprised. "You two know each other?"

Crow looked at the Rolex on his wrist. He made a decision. "I gotta go," he said.

"What the hell?" Zink said. "What's going on, Crow?"

"I don't think I want to play. This fellow"—he pointed a thumb at Ben Franklin—"plays a different brand of poker than you or I. Check your aces, Zink."

Wicky looked quizzically at Ben Franklin.

Franklin stood up. "No big deal. You don't want me to play, I'll cash in my chips and leave."

"Hey, who said anything about not playing? What are you talking about?" Wicky looked up at Crow. "Joe, what makes you think you can just walk in here and call my friend a cheat? You just got here. This is a friendly game, isn't it?"

Crow crossed his arms and shrugged. Zink was holding the ace of spades, feeling along the front edge with his thumb, looking past it at Franklin, his neck turning slowly red.

Counting out his chips, Franklin said to Zink, "You don't mind, I'll just cash in now."

Tom Jefferson drummed his fingertips on the green baize surface of the table, holding his face in an uncomfortable-looking grin, his little black eyes jumping like fleas.

"I think you better pass on the cashing in, fella, and just cut right to the part where you leave," said Zink.

Franklin froze. "I have invested two hundred dollars in this game," he said slowly, pitching his voice so deep it seemed to emanate from his belly.

"That don't quite pay us for the time we've wasted entertaining you, fella." Zink's complexion had advanced from red to a deep maroon, making his blue eyes seem to jut out and float a few inches in front of his face.

For a moment, Franklin fixed his pale eyes on Zink's face. Then he sighed, held up two long-fingered hands, palms forward, and stood up. "No problem," he said. He walked softly past Crow, opened the door, disappeared down the stairs.

Tom Jefferson cleared his throat. "You want to cash me in?" he said to Zink.

Zink fixed his eyes on him. Jefferson gestured toward the door. "My ride," he said apologetically. Zink pulled out a roll and cashed his chips. Jefferson took the money and followed his partner down the stairs.

Wicky said, "Jesus Christ, Joe, you sure know how to bust up a game."

"There was no game." Crow turned to Zink, whose color was just starting to mellow. "Zink, you know where I can find a pawnshop still open?"

"There's one up on Broadway," he said. "Al's Loans. They're open till midnight."

"Thanks." Crow said, looking again at the Rolex on his wrist. He headed out the door. He saw the yellow Cadillac pulling away as he reached the street.

Wicky caught up to Crow as he was unlocking the door to the truck, "Hey, Joe, wait a minute."

Crow turned and looked at Wicky, his eyes tense.

"You aren't going to sell my watch, I hope."

"You want to buy back those units of Galactic Guardians?"

"Hey, Joe, give it a little time."

"Don't bullshit me anymore, Dickie. That fund is worthless, and you know it. You owe me fifty-seven hundred bucks, and I need the money now."

Wicky drew back. "Joe, I thought you would understand that there is some risk involved in any speculative investment."

"You told me you'd make it good, Dickie. Now's your chance. Where's that personal guarantee you were pushing yesterday?"

"Joe, I don't know what you think you heard, but I don't remember it that way. You say the fund is worthless, I don't agree. Give it time. If you aren't willing to let the vehicle perform, I certainly don't feel any obligation to honor any 'personal guarantee,' even if I'd made such a statement, which I don't think I did. As far as I'm concerned, the marker's paid."

Crow said, "I'll mail you the pawnshop ticket. You come up with the money, you can buy the watch back from Al's Loans." He opened the door and climbed up into the truck cab.

Wicky sighed. "I'm really disappointed in you, Joe," he said as the truck door slammed.

Crow found a forward gear, revved the engine, and pulled out onto the street, one hand on the clothesline, holding it like a rein, jerking back on it every time the truck tried to take off without him.

Debrowski's lights were on and her walls were thrumming. Crow slammed the side of his fist against the door five times. No ordinary knock could compete with the rock and roll. After a second round of knocking, which left his hand numb, the music stopped and she answered her door.

"Music too loud, Crow?" Her standard greeting, and usually a good guess. Tonight she was wearing a pair of gray sweatpants and an oversize Iggy Pop T-shirt, Iggy's staring face covering the entire shirt, eyes the size of grapefruit, the shirt spotted with perspiration. Her face looked flushed, her eyes blue and bright.

Crow shook his head. "I need company."

"Come on in." She held the door wide, and Crow stepped inside, his nostrils flaring at the smell of fresh, healthy sweat.

Debrowski was still in the doorway, looking toward the street. "What's that big red thing doing parked in front of my house?"

"It's mine. I mean, I borrowed it from my dad."

"It's really ugly, Crow." She closed the door.

"What were you doing?" he asked, looking around the living room for a place to sit. Debrowski's few furnishings had all been pushed back against one wall. Her Oriental rug was rolled up against the other wall, leaving the center of the room open.

She closed the door. "My tai chi sets."

"You do tai chi while you listen to the Coldcocks?"

"That was Jane's Addiction, Crow. Get with it. You want some coffee or something?"

"I thought tai chi was supposed to be the mellow martial art."

"I mix in some Muay Thai kick boxing. They actually aren't all that different. Hey, I got some of this wild Cameroon Arabica, little tiny beans that'll blow your head off. You want a little blast?"

Crow nodded. Debrowski, like a lot of ex-dopers, talked about coffee that same way she had talked about the real stuff—Peruvian Flake cocaine, China White heroin, Lebanese Blond hashish. Crow sat at the kitchen counter and watched her prepare two sugary doses of black energy. She operated her complicated-looking espresso machine with quick, efficient movements, running the superheated water through the finely ground beans, letting the dark liquid flow into two tiny brass cups. She added three teaspoons of raw sugar to each cup, stirred, handed one to Crow with a conspiratorial smile. The unspoken question: Was this cheating?

They sat on the floor, resting their backs against the rolled-up rug. Crow sipped and waited for the fingers of energy to climb the back of his neck. He felt something, but no one could ever mistake it for the real thing. If this was cheating, then so was a married man cheating when he shook hands with another man's wife.

Debrowski sipped and shuddered, acting out the buzz. "So what's going on?"

"You were right about the Galactic Guardians thing," Crow said.

"You talked to Natch? Kind of like going back in time, isn't it? What did he think of the Galactic Guardians?"

"Pretty much the same as you. I just met the two guys behind it. Guess who they turn out to be? The guy with the purple underwear and that deuce dealer from Dickie's party. I should've known. The thing is a scam from square one. Has to be."

She shrugged. "You've still got Dickie's watch." She pointed with her cup at the Rolex on his wrist.

Crow smiled wryly. "Yeah, I got the watch. I took it to a pawnshop last night. I was going to hock it for a few thousand, then give the ticket to Dickie. The guy in the pawnshop looks at it and says it's a good one, probably made in Singapore. He says it's 'not like that crap coming out of Hong Kong.' I said, 'What are you talking about? This is a Rolex, made in Switzerland.' The guy laughed. Offered me fifty bucks."

"Fifty bucks for a counterfeit? Maybe you should've grabbed it."

He shook his head. "Dickie's such an airhead he probably thinks the watch is real. I might be better off keeping it. I can always go back to Al's Loans for the fifty if I need it."

"You ever send that guy in Chicago a bill?"

"Joey Cadillac? Nah. I figure he's about as likely to pay it as I am to win the lottery. Fact is, Debrowski, I've been fucked."

"The way you've been acting, Crow, any jerk with a high card and a pair of feet is gonna know to walk all over you. You're wimpin' out on me, Crow."

Crow swirled the last inch of black liquid in the brass cup, tossed it back, felt it land in his stomach, solid, bitter, and cold.

"I'm not wimping out, Debrowski," he said. "I'm thinking."

"Yeah, you're thinking you're fucked.'"

"That's right—I'm fucked, and I'm thinking. I'm remembering what you told me about getting mixed up with a bunch of losers. Only so far they aren't losing, and I have to figure out how to change that. I keep remembering something about Dickie, the way he buys into his own bluffs. He could be playing a pair of deuces and they'd be aces in his mind. Or they could be aces. That's how he can sell a fantasy like Galactic Guardians. He believes his own pitch." Crow could feel the espresso beans running relays up and down his spine. "I keep seeing his goddamn face. Him and that Freddy Wisnesky."

Debrowski climbed to her feet, took Crow's empty cup, spooned another measure of Cameroon Arabica into her espresso machine, and lit a Camel as the device hissed and belched steam.

"The thing is," Crow continued, "Dickie and Freddy are just messenger boys. Those other guys are the ones pulling the strings."

"The purple underwear and the deuce dealer," said Debrowski, handing him another cup of espresso.

"And the car dealer," said Crow, sipping from the brass cup.

"You want me to check him out, Crow, I'm going down that way tomorrow. I've got a couple bands booked at an outdoor gig in Joliet. I could take an hour and go car shopping."

"Forget it. If this guy has people like Freddy Wisnesky working for him, you don't want to mess with him."

Debrowski rolled her eyes. "The Lone Ranger rides again. You ever think about asking a friend for help, Crow?"

"My problems aren't your problems, Debrowski."

Debrowski stared back at him, her eyes level, flat, and frozen.

• ♥ 19 ♣ • ♠
THE TURN

J.C. Motors does not sell used Cadillacs. We sell demos. You
know what the difference between a used car and a demo is?
About five thousand bucks.

—*Joey Cadillac, explaining company policy to a new salesman*

"What's he want? You tell him, you ask him if he's got good news. He don't got the good news, I don't wanna talk to him. No. Wait a second. Put him on. Freddy, you dumb shit, what the fuck are you doing up there? Well, you find 'em. I don't care. You stay with the woman. Find her, make her tell you where they are. You don't eat, shit, or sleep till you find those fuckers!"

Joey slammed the phone down, pushed a thumb knuckle against his front teeth, squeezed his eyes closed, and tried to jack down. Fucking Freddy. He jumped to his feet and circled his desk. The phone rang again. Joey snatched it up. It was Margie, the receptionist downstairs. Joey listened, blinking, then said, "Yeah. Yeah, okay, she's been waiting, big deal. I been busy. What's she want to see me for? Okay, okay, send her in." Joey flicked a bit of lint from the lapel of his new teal-colored silk jacket, shot his cuffs, looked at himself in the wall mirror, straightened the gold chains around his neck, fluffed up his chest hair, got back into his chair, and pretended to be reading a sales contract. The door opened, and a woman wearing a motorcycle jacket with a bunch of junk hanging off it jangled into his office. Joey examined her briefly, gestured toward a chair, and continued to examine the contract, occasionally making a random tick mark with his thick gold pen. His visitor dropped into the chair and waited, perfectly still, watching him. Joey kept running his eyes over the contract, waiting for her to get restless, to stand up and move around the office or something, so Joey could look up and say, "Relax."

Joey liked to tell women to relax.

But this one was so relaxed already there was no place for her to re-lax *to*. Fuck it.

He looked straight at her. "What can I do for you, sweets?" She had so much junk hanging off her jacket—buckles, zippers, buttons, chains, pins—it was hard to focus on her face. She leaned forward and reached out a hand. "Debrowski," she said, smiling, red lipstick, not showing her teeth.

Joey pinched her hand between his thumb and fingers and held it. A small hand, but not soft. Her eyes were bright and blue. She was looking right at him, right in his eyes. He waited for her to pull her hand back, but she didn't seem to be in any hurry for it. Joey held it for another five seconds, gave it another squeeze, then let go. "What can I do for you, sweets?" he asked again. He didn't feel the need to introduce himself. The name plaque on his desk said it all: MR. CADILLAC.

"I'm interested in a car." She seemed amused, as if she was playing some game.

"You're interested in a car," Joey repeated, smiling but not getting the joke, if there was one.

"Yes. I want to buy a Cadillac. Maybe something the color of that jacket."

Joey looked down at his jacket—iridescent teal, 100 percent silk. He shook his head. "I got three salesmen out there, honey, all on draw. Every one of them would love to sell you a car. Any color you want. So how come you got to talk to me?"

"I always talk to the man in charge. I've got a little excess cash, and I thought maybe I could move a bit of it your way."

"Who have *you* been talking to?" Joey was enjoying this. He'd had this conversation dozens of times, but never with a woman, especially not one dressed like this. Usually it was some guy with a bunch of flashy jewelry and no way to legitimize the income from his crack house. Guys with a cash problem.

She shrugged. "A lot of people."

Joey sat back and crossed his legs. "Name one."

"Bubby Sharp."

Joey had managed to not think about Bubby Sharp and the red Al-lanté for almost a whole day. Fucking Bubby. Out on bail now, and not at all interested in helping Joey get his Allanté back from the cops. Times like these, Joey missed Freddy.

Freddy would bring Bubby around in no time.

"Bubby ain't what you'd call your sterling reference."

"You want a letter from the mayor?"

"Look, you want to buy a car, that's fine, sweets. We can go back out in the showroom right now. I'll have Wes show you the new Seville. You want to pay cash, that's fine too. We don't mind filling out a few forms for the federales."

"I was thinking you could skip that part."

Joey narrowed his already tiny eyes. Was it possible that this leather-clad young woman had a badge in her wallet? Joey looked at the seven rings and studs decorating the rim of her left ear and decided that this was highly unlikely. Even the most fanatical of the IRS agents would only go for three holes in the ear, if that. He put a hand on his '59 Cadillac paperweight and rolled it back and forth across the desk.

"I hope you're not suggesting I do anything illegal," he said.

She laughed. "Little Joey Battagno do something illegal? Perish the thought."

Joey's features darkened. What the fuck was this? Nobody called him Little Joey anymore, not since he was a kid. Hadn't liked it then, didn't like it now, especially from some wise-ass leather bitch.

"You're a real firecracker, ain't ya, sweets?"

"I just want it clear who I'm dealing with here. Are you interested in my trade, or should I go up the street?"

Joey held his breath for a few beats, then blew it out in a snort of laughter.

The woman said, "Fine, you don't want my business. I can always go buy myself a Lincoln." She stood up and looked down at the name plaque on his desk. "*Mister* Cadillac." She laughed. "I suppose if you were selling Jeeps you'd call yourself Mister Jeep."

Joey pushed out his lower lip. That did it. Nobody walked into his office and talked to him that way. The bitch was way out of line. He stood up and walked around the end of his desk and put his hands on her shoulders. He felt her body go tense. Good.

"Relax," he said. He pushed on her shoulders until she sank back down into the chair.

"That's better," he said, pressing his right thumb to the base of her skull and massaging gently. She was very tight, her hands were white, gripping the arms of the chair. He thought he could feel her start to shake. "No reason for us to get all upset now, is there? You don't want me to report a little ol' cash transaction, we can work that out. You got a little dirty money, honey?" He touched her cheek with his left hand and continued to massage her neck with his thumb. "Let's see now, why would I want to do that for you? You ever hear the expression 'tit for tat'?"

Debrowski was regretting her visit to J.C. Motors. After hearing about Joey Cadillac from several of her local sources, she had become curious enough to pay him a call, get the flavor of the man, thinking of it as a little cheap entertainment before lunch. Maybe she would learn something useful, and maybe not. Crow would be impressed that she'd walked right into the man's place of business and asked him a bunch of questions. He wouldn't like it, but he'd be impressed. It was the sort of thing *he* would do. As it was turning out, though, she was getting a close-up look at behavior best observed from a distance.

Maybe she shouldn't have mentioned Bubby Sharp. She had heard the story about Bubby from a recovering crackhead who was working the door at the Big South Club. It was all over town that Joey Cadillac was foaming at the mouth over the loss of his Allanté, and it had been fun to drop his name, watch him go all red in the face, but now she was wishing she had been more circumspect. But she had figured that in broad daylight—before lunch, even—acting like a customer, telling him she wanted to buy a car, what could happen?

Stupid damn idea to come here. Stupid to piss him off.

Now he was asking her, did she have a boyfriend?

Yes, she told him. I have this enormous fucking boyfriend.

She reassured herself. What could he do? Just below them, down a short flight of carpeted stairs, Cadillacs were being sold to the public. All the dark streets she had walked, all the low-life acquaintances she had survived, why should she let this balding little fat man worry her? He was a joke, not a serious threat. She should stand up calmly, brush his hands aside, and walk away.

Joey C. chuckled, still behind her, counting her earrings with his fat little fingers.

"But you mess around, don't you?" he said, holding her shoulders now, pressing his crotch against her shoulder. His breath fell on her, a cloud of cinnamon with undertones of morning eggs and last night's ragù. "I could give you a real sweet deal on a new Seville. I bet you want a nice black one, don't you? Gold wheels? Take a drive up the shore, look out over that nice long front end? You like 'em long, don't you?"

"I'll tell you what I'd like. I'd like it if you'd get your fucking hands off me." She hoped her voice sounded tougher to him than it felt to her. She was looking for an opening, waiting for a slack moment in his attentions. If she stood up now he would grab her. She could feel it in his hands. Any sudden movement and he would be all over her. She needed the knock at the door or the ringing phone. Something.

"Now you don't mean that," he said. "You could cut yourself a real nice deal right here and now. You wanted to talk to me personal, didn't you? I know what you girls want. You'd be a real pretty one, you got dressed up a little. Grow your hair out. Get rid of those boots. You shave your legs? I like a smooth shank, but I'm not fanatical about it. Isn't this jacket a little warm?" He reached down and yanked one of the lapels to the side, pulling open the top three snaps.

Debrowski jerked her body forward, spun, and faced him, gripping the lip of his desk, fingers pressing up against the oak grain. She knew what her face looked like: hard and white, like marble, red slash of lipstick, chin thrust forward.

"Whoa," Joey said, his face breaking into a grin. "She's a tough one!"

"I'm leaving now," Debrowski said, her body shaking, held in check like an overwound spring. Her voice sounded hollow, too much treble, painfully bright.

"Don't be in such a hurry," Joey said. "We haven't even talked options. Leather seats are very sexy, sweets. What's a matter, you don't like guys or something? Hey now, where you going?" He grabbed her with one hand as she tried an end run around him, clamping down hard on her left wrist. The power of his grip sent a shock wave up her arm.

Debrowski let her body go slack, falling toward him.

Joey had braced himself for the opposite force; he staggered back, momentarily surprised, and saw a black boot coming off the floor, heading toward his face. His street fighter's instinct kicked in; he brought up a forearm, deflecting the kick, then jerked hard on the wrist he was holding and swung her against the paneled wall. A framed Certificate of Appreciation from the Chicago Area Auto

Dealers Association fell to the floor, glass shattering.

"Bitch!" He swung his fist in a hard, short arc and hit her face, bouncing the back of her head against the paneling. "Try to kick me, bitch? Huh?" He brought back his fist and drove it forward, all his weight behind it, into her chest.

Debrowski felt the air explode from her lungs. The office tilted as she slid down the wall, tasting blood from her crushed lip. Joey Cadillac, red-faced and slit-eyed, was holding on to his left arm, the one she'd kicked—at least she'd hit something. She tried to take a breath, but her lungs were paralyzed, her ear was ringing, the room was tipping over, all the way now, the floor nearly vertical.

Center.

Focus.

Five years of martial arts classes had come down to this—knocked on her ass by a fat, balding little man in a silk jacket. She could hear Sun, her Muay Thai instructor, telling her, *You too damn fancy, Deblowski.*

Center.

She should have gone for the knee in the groin, simple, direct, and effective. But she'd always wanted to kick a guy like Joey Cadillac in the face. She'd wanted to feel his nose through the sole of her boot. Violent impulses. Her chest was spasming—no air. She saw Joey turn away from her toward the door. For a moment, she let herself believe that he was about to open it, to order her out of his office. Instead, as she managed to draw her first ragged breath, she saw him turn the lock on the doorknob.

Focus.

Again, she heard Sun's reedy voice: *Too fancy! You get in a fight, you fight dirty, Deblowski. You use a two-by-four, you have to!*

Joey didn't want Margie or one of his salesmen walking in on them. They all knew better than to walk in without warning, but he felt more comfortable with the door locked. Christ, the little leather bitch had damn near broke his arm with her goddamn boot. He looked back at her. She was getting up—the bitch had spunk. He shook out his left arm, getting the feeling back in his fingertips. She was grabbing the edge of his desk, trying to stand up. He hoped she wasn't going to get sick on his Oriental rug. He started toward her. She was on her feet now, looking at him over her shoulder, unfastening something. Taking her clothes off? Maybe she liked it rough. Rough her up a little, she gets turned on. He'd seen it plenty of times before. She pulled something loose from around her waist, something long and black.

Joey stepped back, saying, "Hey, take it easy with that now. . . ."

She was swinging it over her head, the thing whipping like a snake, alive. Christ, a fucking bike chain. He hated a bike chain worse than anything. He'd seen it wrapped around her waist, but his eyes had read it as decoration, something to go with the pins and badges. Better she should have a knife, something he could take away from her. He backed away, grabbed the chair she had been sitting in, held it up in front of his face. "Easy there, girlie," he said, forcing smooth on his voice.

She shifted to his left, got to the desk, grabbing the '59 Caddy paperweight, her arm going back, whipping forward, as he ducked behind the chair. The heavy brass weight hit the bottom of the chair, knocking it to the side. Joey twisted away, at the same time trying to get the chair back up between them—not fast enough. He heard the hissing sound of air being cut by chain, felt it hit his hand. The hand went numb; the chair fell. Joey ducked his head and charged, trying to get inside her reach, get in close now, before she could swing the chain again. Get in there where the chain would do her no good. He saw the boot coming up, but this time he was too off balance to deflect it, and he took it on the ear. As if from a distance, he heard the hissing of the chain again, felt a blow, infinitely heavy, across his back and shoulders, felt himself go down, his upper body suddenly powerless. His face hit the rug, then something came down on the back of his neck, pushing his face into the thick pure-wool pile of the handwoven Persian rug, three thousand bucks, right off the truck. From the corner of his eye, he could see the sole of her boot.

"Let me up, bitch," he said, his voice muffled by the pile. He could hear her ragged breaths raining down on him. He could hear the soft clicking of the bike chain. After several seconds the weight lifted from his neck. His shoulders were buzzing, everything felt wrong. He should launch himself up and at her, get inside the arc of the chain now, before she was ready for it, but he didn't think his arms would obey. He heard the snap of the door lock being unfastened, heard the door open and close. He lifted his head. His back was really starting to sting now. Fucking bike chain. His new jacket would be ruined.

Ten days in Minnesota, and Freddy Wisnesky was getting nowhere. It was obvious even to him that the comic book guy wasn't going to be returning to the Twin Town Motel anytime soon. Like Mister C. said, his only hope of getting his hands on them was through the girl. He drove down the street to a SuperAmerica and bought himself a twelve-pack of Barq's root beer, a couple bags of tortilla chips, three cans of bean dip, and a handful of Slim Jims. The kid who rang up his purchases was giving his shredded and bloodstained shirt a look, so Freddy added an XXL Minnesota Twins T-shirt—$12.99—to his purchases. Another thing he had learned: you got to try to blend in. He drove down University to The Summit and parked his car in the ramp where he could keep an eye on her little red Porsche.

Mister C. had really been pissed off. Freddy screwed a forefinger into his left ear. He could still hear Joey Cadillac screaming at him, voice like a mad Chihuahua. Sometimes he thought about letting the little wop have one, right on his fat little chin. Freddy felt his wide lips curve up into a smile. He enjoyed the fantasy in the same way he enjoyed thinking about having lunch with Dolly Parton, and she takes her top off. It wouldn't ever happen. Life without Mister C. to tell him what to do was beyond his ability to imagine. He pulled his finger out of his ear, looked at it, wiped it on his chest. That reminded him of his new shirt. He climbed out of the car, carefully unknotted, removed, and folded his tulip tie, then took off his torn shirt. It stuck a little to his left arm and to this one place on his back. He peeled it away slowly, trying to leave as much scab as possible on his body, threw the tattered shirt under the Caddy, and pulled the new Twins T-shirt over his head. It was tight, but at least people would stop staring at him. He would look just like a local, another Minnesota Twins fan sitting in his car, chewing on a Slim Jim.

Look at the way they follow her. It must be pheromones.

—Laura Debrowski, speculating on the charms of Catfish Wicky

A full belly gives a man a sense of focus.

This highly focused thought carried Crow much of the way from the Black Forest Inn to his apartment. Something about the potential energy in a stomach full of good German food made the world seem no more than a manageable extension of his life. His car would be repaired. Dickie would make good on his marker. The cards would fall his way. Soon he would have time to think about things like falling in love and discovering meaning in his life.

Walking down Nicollet Avenue past a cluster of Vietnamese and Hmong businesses, gut full of spaetzle, paprika schnitzel, and cabbage, Crow smiled in the fading evening light. It was another hot one. He walked slowly so as not to break a sweat, and he let his mind drift.

Debrowski was in Chicago, baby-sitting two of her bands, and would not be back until tomorrow. He wished she were here now. He wanted to tell her about his idea, his answer to the Galactic Guardians. He wanted her to know that he wasn't wimping out, that he could take care of himself. So far, his scheme had all the substantiality of a cokehead fantasy. Still, on this warm night, even the insubstantial felt as solid as a gut full of paprika schnitzel. If he told it right, she would be impressed. If he could pull it off.

Crow was wearing his red-and-pink short-sleeved polyester bowling shirt with the name HAL embroidered in blue thread over the pocket and PARK TAVERN printed on the back. It was his favorite shirt. He had found it folded into one of his dresser drawers during the early years of his ill-fated marriage to Melinda Connors. Who was Hal? Jealous and suspicious, he had worn the shirt that day, parading her guilt before her. Melinda's only reaction had been to ask, in an offhand, disinterested way, "Who's Hal?"

"You don't know?" he had asked, putting some edge into his voice.

She had smiled vacantly. "Do I know? Is it your dad's name or something?" Melinda had always been weak on names. Crow had stared at her face, then a smooth twenty-three, still healthy and in love, and had seen only mild curiosity and befuddlement. She had no idea who Hal was. Hal was, and would always be, a mystery to them both. Inwardly embarrassed, Crow had concluded that the shirt had gotten mixed in somehow at the laundromat. To teach himself trust, tolerance, and patience, Crow had worn the shirt at least once a month for all of his seven-year marriage. The heavyweight polyester was indestructible. He had come to like it, to feel comfortable swathed in thick synthetic fiber, and he still wore it as often as possible. He loved it when people called him Hal. The Vietnamese woman at the drop-off laundry where he now took his clothes called him Hal Crow: "Tank you, Mr. Hal Crow." She would smile, handing him his tied-up bundle of clean clothes. He liked the way they ironed everything, even the jeans, then folded it up into a package the size of a cereal box.

He was thinking about his ex-wife, bowling shirts, and Vietnamese laundries, going up the walk to his front door, digging for keys in the front pocket of his ironed blue jeans, when a voice said, "Where'd y'all get that shirt? I sure do like it."

Crow stopped. Catfish Wicky was sitting on his front steps, smoking a cigarette.

"I do too," Crow said, after a moment. He remained still, feeling awkward. She was wearing loose black cotton shorts and a white short-sleeved shirt, the top several buttons unfastened. Her legs were tightly crossed and her elbows pulled into her lap, making her appear small and compact. He had the impression that she was cold, though the air temperature was easily eighty-five degrees. She was barefoot; her red sandals sat obediently beside her on the concrete step. He looked around, and at the cars parked on the street, looking for a Cadillac, a Mercedes, a Porsche. He saw nothing but the usual beaters that lined his street.

"Where's your car?"

"I left it at home."

"You walked here?"

"I took a cab. You want to offer a girl a cup of coffee or something? I've been sittin' here near an hour, waiting." She put her lips to her cigarette and inhaled deeply, then let the smoke trail over her red upper lip and into her nostrils.

He walked around her and unlocked the bottom door. "I don't have any milk."

"That's okay, Joe Crow." She hooked her fingers through the thongs of her sandals and stood up. He heard her following him up the narrow staircase, her bare feet soft on the hard wooden steps. "Just make it hot and strong, okay?"

Milo couldn't get enough of her. It was as though she—half cat, half fish—was the most fascinating thing he had ever encountered. He covered her lap, kneading her thigh, both of them purring. Crow set a mug of reheated coffee, blistering hot, strong, and bitter, on the glass-topped table before her. She picked it up and let Milo sniff it, then took a sip.

"It's hot," Crow warned, a little late.

"It's perfect. Good coffee."

Crow sat down across from her with his coffee, waiting for her to get to it, whatever it was.

"I sure do like this kitty cat," she said. Her accent seemed to come and go. Sometimes she sounded like any other Minnesotan except for the persistent "y'all"s, then she would leap a thousand miles south between sentences, and he could almost smell the swamp in her voice. There were even a few words, like *caw-fee*, that sounded as if they'd been learned in Brooklyn, or maybe Newark.

"He likes you."

"Cats do. Did y'all ever meet my kitty cat?"

"I saw him."

"He's a good cat. You know how he got himself all crippled up? I'll tell you. Dickie threw him right off the balcony. Dickie says Katoo just fell, but that man's got more shit in 'm than a Cajun privy. Katoo never fell off nothing. He's a good cat." She scratched under Milo's chin. "You're a good 'un too, Mr. Milo."

"He threw the cat off the balcony?" Crow was shocked. He liked cats.

"Twenty-five stories. I was down at the pool. Poor Katoo landed right next to me. I saw him coming down, feet first. Broke his poor kitty spine. They told me I should have him put down, but I found a vet who fixed him up with his wheels. You should see that cat go." She smiled with her mouth, put a cigarette between her swollen lips, and lit it with a disposable lighter. Milo jumped down from her lap. "Kitties don't like smoke," she said, sending a thick brown plume toward the ceiling.

Crow held up his mug and looked at her through the curls of steam coming off his coffee. Milo jumped back up onto the sofa and sat at the far end, watching Catfish smoke. She reached over and scratched the top of his head.

"You know that big ugly fellow was chasing Tommy?"

Crow nodded and set his cup down.

"Well, he's sitting in this big old blue car in the ramp at my building, watching my poor little Porsche. I go down to get in my car and there he is, the biggest ugliest sight a girl could ever hope for. He didn't see me, though. I got right back in that elevator and got my sweet butt out of there. That's why I had to cab it on over here."

"Freddy Wisnesky."

"That's him." She let a languid stream of smoke drift into her nostrils. The skin between her lip and nose was stained soft yellow; Crow wanted to take a tissue and wipe it away. Beads of oily perspiration showed on her forehead. "He's still looking for Tommy. I'm scared of him." She didn't look scared.

"You should be. Why don't you tell the security guys about him?"

She shook her head. "Right now I know where he is."

"You're going to not go home again?"

"Not till he leaves."

She put out her cigarette, stood up, pushed her hands deep into the pockets of her shorts. Milo walked across the sofa to the cushion on which she had been sitting, sniffed it, turned two circles, and sank into a black ball. Catfish walked around the room, touching things: books, a vase, his framed baseball cards, a blank wall.

"Why are you here?" Crow asked.

"I wanted to see you. I liked the way y'all were looking at me that night. Like I was real. When Dickie looks at me, I feel like a martini."

"Which way do you mean—like you are one or you want one?"

"Like I'm a martini and he's looking at me, staring at the olives. I need a real man in my life." She walked past him, behind his chair, leaving a vaporous trail of smoke and sweat. "A guy like Joe Crow."

Crow watched her moving away from him, toward the doors leading out onto the porch. She stood with her back to him, letting him have a good look at her.

"All the time while you were following me, I kept thinking about you, thinking about you and me." She turned and walked directly toward him. He had the sense that her moves were choreographed, but that didn't prevent his heart from speeding or his mouth from going dry. It was as though he were watching a bad movie—but he was in it. Her hands, hot and moist, pressed in on either side of his face; she bent down and kissed his lips. Her saliva was acid; he could feel his lips burning. Then she was gone, back on the sofa with Milo on her lap, both cats watching him and smiling.

Crow cleared his throat and crossed one ankle over his knee to conceal the sudden swelling in his groin. His body was betraying him. "What is it you want, Catfish?" His voice was thick, the back of his throat numb, as if he were on his fourth, fifth, sixth fat line of coke.

"I need a place to stay tonight."

He pointed at the sofa. "You want to sleep with Milo, it's fine by me."

Catfish smiled, a big smile showing all of her little white teeth, and hugged Milo to her breasts.

Crow lay naked on his bed, unable to sleep. He had opened the window, but the air outside was congealed and there was no movement. Perspiration pooled in his navel. His jaw bulged; he stared through slitted eyes at the water stain on the white plaster ceiling. It was shaped like a butterfly, a flower, a seashell, a woman's sex.

It had been over a year since the last time he had had any, or wanted it. When his marriage to Melinda Connors ended, he'd left his desire behind, or locked it away, or destroyed it.

No, not destroyed. The woman Catfish had found it. He closed his eyes and let the images flicker across the movie screen. Catfish in her black party dress, her breast pressing against his biceps. Catfish in her red Porsche, punching through traffic. Catfish reclined on the undressed bed at the Twin Town, kicking her sandals across the motel room. Catfish standing in the motel room door, laughing. Catfish small on his front steps, smoking. Catfish with too much red lipstick, nicotine staining the underside of her wide nostrils; Catfish with small sharp teeth, hot sweaty hands, breasts tart as grapefruit swinging against her white shirt.

He opened his eyes and looked toward the bedroom door, at the slit of light at its bottom. Why Catfish Wicky? She had the predatory, utterly self-centered perspective of a female cat. She smoked cigarettes, drank, jumped in the sack with every swinging dick. She was not particularly good-looking—swollen lips, protruding eyes, burnt-looking flesh, stained upper lip. She was married. He tried to twist her image into a gargoyle, a Medusa, a hag. The effort left him with a knot in his chest and an erection. He licked his lips—an hour after her kiss, they still burned. He rolled onto his side, away from the damp center of the mattress, and forced his thoughts to Dickie Wicky. That should help him chill.

At Crow's insistence, she had called Dickie to tell him she wouldn't be home. Dickie wasn't there, but she left him a message:

"Can't make it home tonight, honey. Remember that big fella I was telling you about? That Freddy Wisnesky fella? Well, he's sorta lookin' for me, and I got to make myself scarce for a day or two. I'll be in touch."

After she hung up, he had said, "Why didn't you just tell him where you were?"

"He'd freak, darlin'." Then she had laughed. "But maybe then he'd pay you ten thousand dollars to leave me alone. Y'all want me to call him back?"

"Forget about it."

"Anyways, he'll be drunk as a mash-fed opossum when he gets home."

Crow had let it go. He tried to imagine Dickie, drunk, alone in his condo, listening to the recorded voice of his nymphomaniac wife. It wouldn't be so bad, though, because Dickie would quickly render himself unconscious and oblivious. Crow envied the man his drugs, his liquor, his peace.

A soft thud came from the living room, then the sound of bare feet padding down the hall, the sound of the toilet seat going down and, a few seconds later, the tinkle of urine falling into the bowl. The image of Catfish sitting on his toilet. The sound of the toilet flushing.

She had said he looked tense. She had wanted to rub his neck. She had sat on the sofa, curled her toes over the edge of the glass-topped coffee table, put the palms of her hands together, squeezed them between her thighs.

"Don't you want me?" she had asked.

He had brought out a blanket and a pillow and said good night.

He heard her now, padding back toward the living room. He could feel the muscles in his abdomen relax. He swallowed, and half-thoughts tumbled unidentified through his mind like clothes in a dryer. As though in a memory, he again heard the sound of bare feet on a wooden floor. The door to his bedroom opened, closed, and he felt a hot hand press his shoulder back against the mattress. He opened his eyes, drew a ragged breath, stared at her dark shape. She moved her hand down his chest, paused at his belly—"You're all soaking wet, honey"—and continued down to stroke the length of his swollen penis. He heard her husky whisper, "I thought you might be waiting on me, Crow," and then her tongue was in his mouth, deep and soft and wet, and he hoped he would drown.

◆ ♥ **21** ♣ ♠

Thing I always wish, son, was I coulda been there to teach you how t' handle a woman.

—Sam O'Gara

In the morning, tangled in his sheets, Crow sought to reestablish the connection between his anxious mind and his sated body. What had he gotten himself into? He was alone on the bed, but he could still smell her. His penis lay against his thigh, long and flaccid, blooming with the crusted oleo of their bodily fluids. Was she gone?

He thought about herpes, about AIDS. No disease seemed, in that moment, to be as serious as the fact that he had been betrayed by his body. Over a year of celibacy—waiting for love or some other noble impulse to return him to the world of feeling—and he had wallowed in the depths of this black-haired Catfish creature, this married woman, this cigarette-smoking estral female who would fuck, as she had told him in the postcoital dark, anybody with a dick longer than his nose. At the same time, the memory of her lying there on his bed asleep, her quiet, abbreviated snores, came with a wave of desire—of the urge to protect, to preserve, to own. Could she help what she was?

He felt strong in his body, an engine enjoying a long-overdue tune-up. Another illusion? Another drug? He thought back to his walk home from the Black Forest Inn, his belly full of food. He had been happy then. Or, at least, at peace. Thinking about his Vietnamese laundress.

Last night, in the dark, Catfish had talked but said nothing. He had asked her questions. "What do you want?" "I want you." "Where do you come from?" "New Jersey, Phoenix, Mexico, Louisiana, Tampa." "How do you know that guy, that Tommy?" "I've known Tommy forever." "What do you know about his business?" "Nothing. Business is boring." He had asked her more questions, thinking himself clever, but had learned nothing. She had quickly grown bored and fallen asleep.

Was she gone?

He listened, searching with his ears for clues to her presence. Someone was talking, but he couldn't identify the direction or the source. He rolled out of bed, pulled on a pair of jeans and a T-shirt, and went into the kitchen. The smell of coffee was overpowering. He poured a mug full, tasted it, shuddered. Thick and bitter. She must have used half a pound of grounds. He could already feel the caffeine plucking at his synapses.

Catfish was sitting in the wicker chair on the porch, wearing nothing but his red-and-pink bowling shirt and a pair of suntanned legs. She held a coffee cup near her mouth, and she was talking to someone. Crow put his head out the porch door. Debrowski stood at the railing, looking down First Avenue. Catfish smiled up at him, her rubbery lips big and red as cayenne peppers.

Debrowski's face was white stone, her mascaraed eyes slitted. A cup of coffee balanced on the railing beside her, untouched. She was holding a quart of milk, her hand squeezing the waxy carton.

"Morning, darling," Catfish said. She hooked a forefinger through his belt loop and pulled. "Laura, here, came up looking for you this morning. I told her you were sleeping. I've never seen a guy sleep like that, like you were never gonna wake up. I invited her to have a little coffee with me, long as she brought her own milk. This gal's got to have milk with her morning coffee, you know." Crow looked down at the coffee in her mug. It was paler than her thighs. He detached her finger from his belt loop and stepped to the side, out of range. Catfish shrugged, wrapped her mug with both hands.

Crow said, "Welcome back, Debrowski." He felt like a boy caught masturbating.

Debrowski turned her face toward him, her mouth drawn into a twisted gash, the left side swollen and purple. Crow started toward her, reaching out, but she jerked back, shifted her hips, and her eyes fixed on a place above his head and a foot to the side. He stopped as if he had struck a force field. She did not want to be touched.

"What happened?" he asked.

"I ran into a door," she said, her voice flat.

Catfish rubbed an ankle with the sole of her foot.

Crow smiled uncomfortably.

Debrowski pushed off the railing. She handed Catfish the milk carton. "I'm going to bed. I've been driving all night." She walked between them and through the door to the staircase. She looked back at Catfish. "I just wanted to make sure you were still alive, Crow. Nice meeting you, Fish. You can keep the milk."

Crow listened to the heavy sound of her boots descending his stairs.

Catfish said, "Fish? Who's she calling 'Fish'? Sort of a tense little thing, ain't she? Can you imagine doing it with all those chains?"

Crow was staring at the cup of coffee balanced on the railing.

"I get all sore just thinking about it," Catfish said.

"I think you had better go now," Crow said. His voice sounded harsh and distant. He was seeing Debrowski's face, bruised, hard-eyed, bloodless.

"What? Isn't that a little rude, darlin'? I'm not even half done with my coffee. Y'all make love to a woman, you ought to buy her breakfast, don't you think?" She seemed more amused than offended.

"No. I don't know. You have to go. I'm sorry."

"You want me to go back home, with that Freddy fellow waiting on me?"

"You can go wherever you want. This was a mistake. Go to the police, or take a vacation." He went inside, picked up the phone, punched in the number printed on the back of every third cab in the city. Catfish came up behind him and put her arms around his waist.

"I'm calling a cab," he said.

"Y'all leave a lady feeling a bit cheap, Joe Crow."

"I'm sorry." Her arms were two hot bands across his belly. He stepped from her embrace, turned, pressed her palms together. "Last night was a mistake. You have to go now. I'm sorry."

She looked at her hands pressed between his. "Did I make trouble with your girlfriend, darlin'? Maybe I shoulda had my coffee black."

He released her hands. "She's not my girlfriend."

Catfish smiled. "What ever can I have been thinking?" She pulled the bowling shirt up over her head and handed it to him. Her body was as sensational in daylight as it had been in his dreams, in the dark. He could feel the pulsing begin in his groin. "I'll get dressed," she said, scratching her dark and tangled pubis with red nails. Crow looked away; Catfish snorted. "You know, darling, I never realized y'all were such a prude."

"I'm not a prude," Crow said as she walked toward the bedroom. But he knew it was true even before he heard her laughter.

Ten minutes later, she was gone in a blue-and-white cab. Crow picked up the phone and called Debrowski. No answer. He went downstairs and pounded on her door. No answer. He went back upstairs, turned on the shower, and let it hammer at his chest until the water went cold.

♦ ♥ 22 ♣ ♠

*Be sure to be nice to the people you step on on your way up, be-
cause you're gonna have to step on them again on the way down.*

—*Richard D. Wicky, V.P., training a new registered representative*

Wicky sipped his instant coffee, winced, added a shot of brandy, a dollop of milk, and a handful of sugar cubes, sipped again. He was sitting out on the balcony in his silk Calvin Klein boxer shorts, staring across the river at downtown Minneapolis. Things were looking a little fuzzy, though no fuzzier than usual. It was one of those windless, cloudy days, thick with atmospheric moisture, eighty-three degrees and rising, a good day to skip work, hang out in front of the air conditioner, nurse a hangover, maybe take a couple of naps. Not a good day to be jump-started by a call from Catfish, phoning from some motel, or so she said. She'd wanted him to get out of bed, seven o'clock in the morning, and run downstairs to the parking ramp to see if Freddy Wisnesky, the ogre from Chicago, was still sitting there. He'd told her to call the cops, but she wouldn't do it. "You don't call the cops on these kind of guys," she'd said. "Look, I just want to know if he's still there. You can't miss him. He's the biggest, ugliest guy you've ever seen, and he's driving a blue Cadillac convertible with a smashed-in grille. If he's gone, I can swing by and get my car out of there."

She wasn't even thinking about coming home; she just wanted her car. He'd told her he would call her back. "Where exactly are you?"

"I won't be here," she had said. "I'll call back in ten minutes."

"Make it an hour."

She didn't want to come home, that was her business, but he wasn't going to go running downstairs half asleep to look for some guy who broke arms for a living. His life was falling apart already; the last thing he needed was a broken limb. He looked down the river, then across at the old courthouse, trying to read the red hands of the clock against the purple brick of the tower. Seven-thirty. The buzz and rumble of rush hour traffic drifted across the river and climbed the brick walls of The Summit. His head felt as if someone was sharpening a pencil in his ear. Wicky closed his eyes and waited for the brandy to kick in.

Even forgetting about his marriage, if you could call it that, he was looking forward to some serious complications when the Galactic Guardians thing hit the fan. All the guys he'd sold units to would be looking for someone to blame, and even though he was both scammer and scammee, nobody was going to care that he'd believed in it himself. Old Man Litten would throw him to the wolves. The SEC, the IRS, the BCA—all those three-letter guys with the one-color business cards and a hard-on for anybody who'd made a few bucks—man, no way would Catfish stick around for any of that shit! She'd be long gone in her little red Porsche before they closed the cuffs around his other wrist. And then there was Joe Crow. Their last conversation had been distinctly uncomfortable.

No question about it, old Rich Wicky had some nasty incoming to deal with.

Thank God for brandy in the morning. That reminded him to check his pockets. He found his suit coat lying over the edge of the bathtub; found the remnants of last night's coke folded into a piece of paper and tucked into the watch pocket. Hands shaking, Wicky unfolded the square of paper. Looked like about an eighth of a gram. He lowered his nose to the powder and snorted it right off the paper.

Yow.

He licked a finger and wiped the few remaining grains from the paper, rubbed them onto his gums.

Yow. That was more like it. Once again, proof positive that attitude is chemical. Matters pertaining to Freddy Wisnesky, the Galactic Guardians Fund, his philandering wife, Joe Crow, and other imminent disasters were quickly reduced to manageable proportions. A light bulb, about three hundred watts, flashed to life in Wicky's buzzing frontal lobe.

All he had to do was make a deal. What had he been worried about? There was no situation so bleak that a sharp guy couldn't cut his way out of it with the right deal. He ran down the elements of the deal according to Rich Wicky:

Talk to the right people in the right order.

Find out what they all want.

Find out what they think it's worth.

Show them a way they can get it.

And charge admission.

It was simple. He yawned, a dry-eyed cocaine yawn with no trace of weariness in it. He wasn't sure how he was going to get out of this one, but he was convinced that, as always, the solution would present itself. He just had to recognize it when it came knocking.

A guy had to eat, sleep, and shit, Freddy decided. Especially shit. There was just no way around it. The strident echoes of Mister C.'s voice were fading, and things were moving down there in his intestines, approaching critical mass. Just a quick run up the street to the SuperAmerica, use their john, and pick up some doughnuts or something. He let the idea settle in. What the hell, he'd had to leave the ramp to make the call to Mister C. anyway; what was another ten minutes? He started up the sidewalk, his bowels humming.

When Freddy got back, bowels empty and a sack of doughnuts clutched in his hand, he found a smiling blond-haired man sitting in the back seat of the Caddy, drinking a Moosehead beer. The man grinned and saluted Freddy with the green bottle, pointed at the six-pack on the seat beside him.

"You care for a beer, my friend?"

Freddy tossed the doughnuts on the front seat and considered how best to remove this person from the car.

"Now take it easy," the little man said. "I just noticed you sitting out here earlier, and I thought you could maybe use a brewsky."

"You gotta get outta the car," Freddy said.

"You work for a fellow down in Chicago, right? A Mr. Cadillac?"

Freddy shrugged. "I don't know him. You gotta get out now."

"Well, I guess I must be wrong, then. You sure you don't want a beer?"

Freddy reached into the car, grabbed the little man under the armpits, and lifted him out. To Freddy, nearly all men were little men. He set the man down on the concrete floor of the ramp. "How come you think I know Mister C.?"

"Call me Rich. You're Fred, right? I like the way you handle yourself, Fred."

Under ordinary circumstances, Freddy would have ended the conversation some time ago—possibly by opening one of Rich's beers on his head—but he'd sat all alone in this parking ramp going on two days now, and even Freddy's primitive mind craved stimulation.

"You do?" he asked.

Rich took a swig from his Moosehead and grinned. "You got class," he said. "I can always tell when a guy's got class."

Even Freddy could understand that. He screwed up his face and thought of a question for the little man. "How come you know me?"

"You kidding? Your reputation precedes you. Everybody up here knows Fred Wisnesky. You and Mr. Cadillac are like movie stars. We even hear about you way up here in Minneapolis. A guy like you, a guy who can just go in there and get it done, he gets a lot of respect. You sure you don't want a beer?"

Freddy liked the little man.

"Sure," he said. A Moosehead disappeared into his fist.

"Attaboy!" said Rich. He pointed a finger at Freddy's T-shirt. "Say, how about those Twins, huh? You a Twins fan?"

"Sure," said Freddy.

"We oughta go see a game sometime, you and me."

Three acre island on beautiful Whiting Lake, cozy 3 rm cabin with bthse, sauna, grt fshng. $130,000/bo. Call Bobick Realty.

Wicky made it into the office by eleven-thirty that morning, which wasn't bad. Freddy Wisnesky, so far as he knew, was still haunting the parking ramp, waiting for Catfish, drinking the rest of the Mooseheads. A nice guy, Wicky had learned. Just needed a little direction. When Catfish called back, he had told her that Freddy just needed to ask her a few questions, that was all. He was just trying to locate somebody.

"You ever had Freddy Wisnesky ask you a question?" Catfish had asked.

"Sure. He asked me lots of questions."

"And you're still talking? I'm surprised."

Their conversation had ended ambiguously. Was she coming home soon? She couldn't say. Every time they talked, it seemed, they pulled a few more pegs out of their marriage. Soon only paperwork and inertia would bind them.

Wicky picked up his stack of pink message slips from Janet and was trying to decide which ones he could throw away, when he noticed that she had an odd expression on her face. She was looking right at him, and she seemed to be enjoying herself, a combination that Wicky had never before observed on her usually chilly features. Wicky smiled back, uncertainly.

"You have a customer waiting for you in your office, Mr. Wicky," said Janet, sweetly.

Wicky frowned. "What the hell? Who?"

"A walk-in," Janet said.

"A *walk-in?*" They had about one a month, every one a waste of time. "What the hell's he doing in my office? How come you didn't just give him to Frank or one of the new guys?"

"You were up on the rotation, Mr. Wicky."

"F'chrissake. Listen, I've got work to do." He waved the handful of message slips at her. "What the hell did you let him in my office for?"

Janet said, "Sorry, Mr. Wicky. He was out here for a while, but I just couldn't get anything done, with him asking me all these questions. You were up, so I asked him to wait in your office."

"You coulda stuck him in the waiting room, f'chrissake."

"Gee, I didn't think of that." She examined a fingernail, frowning.

Wicky pressed his lips together and let the air whistle in and out of his nose a few times. What the hell, might as well get it over with. He pushed through the door into the big room, followed its perimeter around to his glassed-in office.

The man sitting in his chair was wearing bib overalls over a long-sleeved T-shirt, and at least a week's growth of grizzled, uneven beard. His feet, encased in a pair of greasy-looking running shoes, were propped on Wicky's desk. He was smoking a cigarette, in violation of the Minnesota Clean Indoor Air Act. Wicky took a deep breath, opened the door, and brought up a smile.

"How do you do. I'm Rich Wicky," he said. He couldn't quite bring himself to offer his hand. The man sitting in his chair raised his eyebrows and grinned. "Hope it's okay I smoke in here." He brought his feet down and stood up, pushed out a big hand. "Sam O'Gara."

Wicky hung on to his smile and clasped Sam O'Gara's hand, allowed the man to squeeze and pump it vigorously. O'Gara laughed around his cigarette. Wicky wondered where he had been ashing it. As if in answer, O'Gara let a long ash fall onto his palm, slapped the ash against his thigh, and rubbed it into the denim fabric.

Wicky pointed to the visitor's chair. "Would you like to sit down, Sam?"

"Oh, sure. I was sittin' in the boss's chair." He came around the desk, cackling. "Sorry 'bout that. Look, I ain't gonna take up a lot of your time here, Rich. Richard Wicky? I bet they call you Dickie. Your folks musta had a sense of humor, eh?"

"I don't know what they had," Wicky said. He wanted Sam O'Gara out of his office. "What can I do for you, Sam?"

"Welp, I just happened to see one a your ads, y'know, on one a them MTC buses?"

Wicky sighed. The dreaded bus ads strike again. One of old man Litten's less-than-great notions had been to advertise financial services to people who couldn't afford to drive a car.

"And I happened to be downtown, picking up my license tags. Don't get down here all that often, y'know. Traffic going every which way. Anyways, I seen your ad and I figured, what the hell, I'd drop on by!"

Wicky lowered himself into his chair, still warm from O'Gara's body. He could feel the morning's hangover, which had almost subsided, climbing through the maze of his digestive system, headed for a return engagement with the base of his skull.

"So what's the story, Rich? You want to tell me about these 'income opportunities'?"

Wicky cleared his throat. "Well, first we should talk about whether or not you qualify, Sam. You see, to make money with Litten, you must have some relatively liquid assets. How much were you thinking of investing?"

"Well, hell, you tell me! How much you think you can handle?"

"We have clients who have invested several million dollars with us." Wicky smiled. Best to get it over with quickly, add a zero to his usual routine, get rid of the guy. "I'd say you should have at least a hundred thousand dollars to open an account with us." He watched Sam O'Gara's eyes. Something about them, deep in their wrinkly nests, seemed familiar. They glittered, seeming, for a moment, amused. "Do you think we have a basis for further discussion, Sam?" Wicky finished.

Sam pinched the tip of his nose and pushed his lips into a shriveled pout.

"Way-ell," he said slowly, "you had me scared there with that 'several million' stuff, but I think I might come up with a couple hundred thousand. I give you that to work with, how long you think it'd take you to double 'er up?"

"You'd be willing to invest two hundred thousand?" Wicky asked.

"Two or three. Ain't counted it lately. It ain't making any money sitting in my safe-deposit. Always meant to do something with it, just never got around to it till now."

Wicky said, "It's in cash? No, that's no problem." He was thinking about the $140,000 worth of GGF he still had to unload. "No problem at all. In fact, your timing couldn't be better. I've got an investment vehicle here that should help you achieve your financial goals and then some."

"I don't want no junk bonds, now."

Wicky nodded soberly. "I can see you've thought this out. You want a safe, secure investment that will protect your capital and, at the same time, provide maximum opportunity for growth. That's very intelligent, Sam. I have many clients, doctors and lawyers, who aren't nearly so sophisticated in their investment strategies."

"Never met a doctor or lawyer I thought was worth more'n a good bird dog when it came to common sense," Sam said.

As it happened, Wicky agreed with that. "As I was saying, Sam, your timing couldn't be better. I've got a limited-partnership opportunity right now that should fit you like a glove. You know, the usual investment vehicles—stocks, bonds, CDs—they simply aren't producing the returns they once did. The smart money is moving into collectibles."

"You mean like plates? I had a girlfriend collected them fuckers."

"Plates, coins, artwork—they've all had their day. The hot item these days is comic books."

"You mean like *Superman*?"

"Exactly. I have some units of a limited partnership that is in the process of buying up a major collection. They're pretty much un-available now, but I happened to put away a few units in case one of my good customers wanted to increase their position."

Sam O'Gara laughed. "Shit, Rich, I got too damn many a them things already. Don't you got something like de-benchers or some-thing where a guy can make a lot of loot? What about these, whataya-callem, annuities?"

Wicky was confused. "You got too many of what?"

"Comic books! Christ almighty, I got a whole damn room full a the things. I come down here to talk serious now, Rich. Tell me about them annuities. A friend a mine told me, he said annuities was the way to go. How about it, Rich?"

"You've got a room full of comics? Where'd you get a room full of comics?"

Sam O'Gara placed a Pall Mall in the center of his lips. "Had 'em for years. My brother Vince used to save the damn things. He died, I put 'em away." He lit the cigarette with his Zippo and gazed thought-fully at Wicky through the smoke. "You saying they might be worth something?"

Wicky shook his head. "Not a lot, but maybe something. When did your brother die?"

"Fifty-one."

Wicky felt his heart jump. "And you have a *room* full of his comic books?"

"Damn near. Vinnie was a nut for comics."

"Where are they? You have them at your house?"

Sam hesitated, then said, "Took 'em all up north. Got 'em all put away at my cabin. Take out a box now and then and read 'em. Have a few shots of Jack and read about the Superman. Vince, he wouldn't let me read 'em when he was alive. I think old Vinnie had just about every *Superman* comic ever made. You think they might be worth a few bucks, eh?"

"Maybe," Wicky said. "It's worth taking a look at them. I might be able to get you a good price for them. Maybe three or four times the cover price. What do you say?"

"Well, sure, if you want to," O'Gara said slowly. His eyes shifted back and forth, landed on Wicky's tie. "Only I'm thinking more like a buck a book." He blew a plume of smoke across the desk.

Wicky was shaking his head sadly. "Sam, that's ten times the cover price. They'd have to be in pretty good condition to warrant that kind of markup."

O'Gara pushed out a wrinkled lower lip. "I don't mind keepin' 'em."

Wicky watched the old man filling his office with smoke. This was it, he realized. This was the solution. He could hear it, the knocking on the door. It was too perfect—comic books had nearly destroyed him, and comic books would save him. Superman to the rescue. A *room* full of comics. How many comics did it take to fill a room? And all of them bought before 1951. Had to be worth a lot. A lot.

He opened a desk drawer and set a glass ashtray on his desk. "Sam, if you want a buck a book, then that's what you ought to get. You stick to your guns, buddy. If there's a buyer out there, I'm going to find him for you, okay?"

O'Gara stubbed out his cigarette in the clean ashtray.

"I knowed you was a good man, Rich."

Crow was unpacking a box of miscellaneous junk—old cassette tapes, a collection of twelve-step books he had never opened, an empty photo album, two marksmanship plaques from his days with the Big River Police, a coffee can full of pens and pencils, a stoppered test tube containing one cigarette, five years old now, a souvenir from his smoking days. If it had been fresh, he might have lit up at that moment. He was suffering from a shortage of active vices. He kept thinking about Debrowski, waiting for her to wake up, listening for the sound of footsteps, or music, or the penetrating hiss of the espresso maker. The telephone rang. Crow stood up, knees cracking, and answered.

"Welp, I done 'er, son."

"Sam? Good. What did you think of Dickie?"

"Son, it were like foul-hooking a carp. I give him so much line he could go in the rope business. Took me out to lunch, one a them fancy places, had myself a New York steak and a couple Leinenkugels. You know that fellow drives a Mercedes-Benz? Now what would make a guy go out and buy a spendy car like that, he could get himself three, four Chevys for the same money? Course, maybe I'm asking the wrong guy."

"You think he bought it?"

"What are you saying, son? You think he stole it?" Sam sounded as if he'd had more than a couple Leinenkugels.

"I mean the story, Sam. You think he bought the story?"

"Hell, yes! He wants to see them comics awful bad. He wanted to go look at them right then, but I told him they was up north at the cabin. Figure we get that city boy up in the woods, he won't know what's going on. You don't want him to know what's going on, do you?"

"Wait a minute. You told him what? You told him the comics were where?"

"Up north at the cabin. Had to tell him something, son."

"What cabin?"

"Welp, I figured we could use your place. Besides, I figure it's the only way I'll ever get a chance to see it, since you never invite me up there."

"Sam, I don't *have* a cabin. I told you I'm *thinking* about buying one. I haven't even looked at one yet, and I'm not going to until I get some money. *Now* what are we supposed to do?"

"You'll think of something, son. You're a smart boy."

"Yeah, right. I was so smart, I probably wouldn't be doing this shit."

"You don't sound so good, son. You got something else on your mind?"

"Women troubles, Sam. Nothing you can help me with."

"Son, there's only one thing you got to know about a woman."

Crow sighed and braced himself.

"You got troubles, you got to give 'em flowers."

That wasn't what he had expected. Crow blinked, trying to imagine grizzled, greasy Sam O'Gara offering a dozen roses to a lady friend. "I can't imagine you buying flowers, Sam. Doesn't seem like your style."

"Course not, son. I don't *have* women troubles."

After hanging up, Crow sat still and let his mind work. After several minutes, he picked up the phone and punched in a number.

"Ozzie? How you doing, man? This is Crow. Yeah. Say, I was wondering if my dad and I could borrow your cabin for a couple days, say next week sometime? Yeah? That would be great. I'll send my dad by for the keys, you can give him the directions. Right, wiggle the handle after you flush the toilet. You better mention that to him. Say, Oz? You still got that porno collection stashed away up there? No, no, it's no problem—I was just wondering if I should bring along my own reading material."

At four o'clock that afternoon, Crow heard some noises from downstairs, then the floor started to vibrate. He decided to give Debrowski another try. He got the lavender paper cone of roses out of the refrigerator and went downstairs to see her. She was awake, but not by much.

"I just woke up, Crow. Can it wait?" The music she had playing, her wake-up music, was a sort of rhythmic drone with some spacey female voice flitting in and out of the beat. She was wearing a Coldcocks T-shirt and leggings. The cut on her lip was healing. It looked darker now, not as red or as angry.

"No. I have to talk to you."

Debrowski looked at him for a long time, and at the lavender paper cone from Bachman Florists. She shrugged and turned away, but left the door open. Crow followed her inside. She lit a Camel, sat on her black leather couch, and blew a plume of fresh smoke into stale air. "So are you and Mrs. Fish an item now?"

"No. Here. Welcome back." He handed her the flowers.

Debrowski made a sour face and tossed them on the table. "You think Dickie'll pay you ten grand to quit screwing his wife?"

Apparently, the flowers were a lousy idea. That would teach him to listen to Sam. Crow took a breath. "I want to know what happened to you."

"I told you. I ran into a door."

"Debrowski—"

"If you want to spend your nights in the sewer with Pricky Dickie and his nympho wife, that's your business. I don't give a shit. But leave me the fuck out of it. I don't want to know about it." She winced and put a hand to her lip, turned her face away.

What was she talking about? Did she think he had come down to give her the details on his Catfish experience? Crow felt an angry retort gathering in his throat. He choked it back. He did not want to argue. He wasn't going to let her off the hook that easily.

"What happened to your face, Debrowski?" His voice was husky, concern layered over anger. He thought he knew what she had done.

He did not know how he knew, but he knew. "Did you go chasing after Joey Cadillac?"

Debrowski puffed angrily on her Camel, using the unbruised side of her mouth.

"You did, didn't you?"

"I went to ask him about buying a car," she said.

Crow sighed. "Jesus, Debrowski, I told you to leave it alone."

"You're very fucking welcome, Crow. Anytime I can do you another favor, you just ask."

"I didn't ask you to go see him. I asked you to forget about it."

She shrugged. "Fuck you."

"What happened?"

"Joey Cadillac fell in love with me." She stood up. "You want a cup of coffee?"

Crow's heart was sledgehammering. "He . . . what?" Debrowski was heading toward the kitchen. Crow got up and followed her. His mouth tasted strange, as if he was sucking on a nail. "He . . . What did he do?"

"He didn't rape me, if that's what you want to know. Not that it's any of your business. You want coffee or not?"

"Uh . . ." His liver seemed to have disappeared, leaving a cavern in his abdomen.

"You want a cup of coffee or not? Maybe you want me to make some for your girlfriend too."

"If you mean Catfish, she's gone. I made her leave this morning. Look, she just showed up looking for a place to stay. Told me Freddy Wisnesky was waiting for her back at her apartment."

Debrowski shrugged and poured water into the espresso machine. "So she goes running to Joe Crow, protector of oversexed and lonely women."

"I told her she could sleep on the couch. Whatever else happened—it wasn't what I wanted. I made a mistake. Do you understand what I'm saying?"

"You accidentally fucked her, now you wish you hadn't. It could happen to anybody. No problem. It's none of my business anyway. I just hate to see you making a jerk of yourself, Crow." She measured three tablespoons of coffee into the filter cup, her mouth drawn down in a short, distorted arc.

"You going to tell me what happened in Chicago?"

1 6 3

"With Joey? I had a wrestling match."

"Looks more like you had a boxing match," Crow said.

"He's got a mean punch. You should see my left tit." Something must have happened on Crow's face; Debrowski laughed. "Don't worry about it, Crow. I've been hurt worse. Like they say, you should see the other guy. I finally got to use my bicycle chain. He didn't like it." She flipped the switch on the espresso machine. Black liquid trailed into a brass cup.

"Jesus—is he alive?"

"Unfortunately, I think he's fine."

"Why did you go see him? What was the point?"

She gave him the same flat, frozen look he had seen on her three days before when he told her he didn't want her help. She had called him the Lone Ranger then.

"I owe you, Crow."

"You don't owe me."

"I owe you, and I don't like it. I cost you a chunk of money. You don't want me to pay you, I'll give it to you some other way. You want to know what I learned about Joey Cadillac?"

"You don't owe me, Debrowski."

She handed him a cup of espresso. "You want to hear about Joey Cadillac or not?"

Crow nodded. At least they were off the subject of Catfish Wicky.

"He wasn't hard to find out about. In some circles down there, he's high-profile. I didn't have any problem at all tracking him down. All the drug dealers know him. All that crack money down there, they can't just go out and spend it, you know. Anytime they pay more than ten thousand cash for something, the seller has to report it to the IRS. Joey manages to avoid all that unnecessary paperwork. And I found out why he's looking for your friends Tom and Ben."

"Yeah?"

"Yeah. They scammed him, stuck him with some phony comic books."

"So I'm in good company."

" 'Good'? I don't think so, Crow, although you'd probably appreciate his taste in women. He's got a blond bimbo with a pair of hooters that'd make Mrs. Fish's look like limes." She sipped her coffee and raised her eyebrows, looking up at him. "You know, Crow, I don't know what bothers me more—the fact that you climbed in the sack with her or the fact that it was probably her idea."

How had they gotten back on the Catfish subject? Crow shifted uneasily, spilled a drop of espresso on his jeans. There was no way out—he was guilty either of seducing Catfish or of being seduced by her.

"Leading you around like a prize bull," she added.

"Leave it alone, Debrowski."

"Sure. No problem. I forgot, you told me last week you were fucked. I just didn't know who was doing the fucking. So what do you think about Joey Cadillac?"

Crow jerked his mind from the Catfish problem to the Cadillac problem. Think? He imagined himself walking into Joey Cadillac's office, bouncing the guy's head on his desk blotter. Was that what she wanted? If so, he thought he might even do it. He felt as if he was threading a maze and somebody kept moving the hedges.

"I think I don't like him."

"Let me tell you more. First, I found out that they used to call him Little Joey. His real name is Joey Battagno."

"Is he connected?"

"He's one of these on-the-fringes guys. A guy I know down there, Lanny Lepert—owns a dance club now, used to be in the liquor business—asked a couple of his wise-guy suppliers about Joey. The word is, Joey has some relatives that have relatives, and maybe a couple customers that are hooked in, but no solid connections other than he pays a mob-owned security service to have a car drive past his lot once a night. My opinion is, he's out of the loop. Fact is, the organized crime scene down there is about as organized as festival seating at a Guns 'n' Roses concert. All the bright boys have gotten into politics, and what's left is a bunch of no-clout assholes like Joey C. running these quasi-legitimate operations with a few tough guys on the payroll. I mean, Joey's claim to fame is he sells Cadillacs for cash. Big deal. Plus, he puts out a few loans, mostly car loans, a few thousand bucks, which is what he needs Freddy for, mostly. It's not like he's controlling any kind of serious action. No big-time dope deals, no phony paper, no gambling action." She paused. "Except I did hear he likes to play cards."

"Cards?" said Crow. The espresso had his heart ticking like a manic metronome; he hoped it wasn't true that a man's allotment of heartbeats was decided at birth. If it was, between his three years as a cokehead and Debrowski's caffeinated depth charges, he'd be a goner anytime now. The Catfish problem, as he had come to think of it, was tabled for now. Crow set his cup down and stared into it, trying to get a clearer picture of Little Joey Battagno, a.k.a. Joey Cadillac.

"You want another one?"

"I'd better not. You got any bread? My stomach feels like there's somebody down there poking at it with a bad cigar."

Debrowski laughed and brought him a Moon Pie. Crow looked through the crinkly plastic wrapping.

"You're kidding."

"You don't like 'em? It's the closest thing I've got to bread."

Crow tore open the plastic and took a small bite.

"He plays cards?"

Debrowski lit another Camel. "Hosts a regular poker game. He keeps his bimbo in a condo over by the lake. That's where they have their games. Lanny said he played in a couple of them, lost his ass. They play for some big money."

"Is the game fixed, you think?" asked Crow, chewing Moon Pie.

"Does it matter?"

Crow examined the remaining half of the Moon Pie. "You know, this isn't all that bad. Sort of like an inflated Oreo."

Debrowski smiled wryly and crossed her arms. "I thought you'd like it. Anyway, I'm thinking that this girlfriend of his might be useful. I could probably get next to her."

"I don't want you getting into this any further."

"Crow, you're disappointing me. The son-of-a-bitch hurt me. I'm in it."

Crow tipped his head back and stared at the white ceiling. A water stain the shape of France spread across its center. He tried to think what was above it. His kitchen? Something he had spilled? He had the feeling that he was poised on the edge of a high balcony, looking up at the stars.

"What do you say, Crow? You want a seat at the table?"

"Let me think about it." He thought about Freddy Wisnesky tearing the door half off his car. Debrowski being knocked around by some guy named Little Joey Battagno. He remembered the scheme he had dreamed up the day before. Was it any crazier than playing cards with a guy who called himself Mr. Cadillac? The storm of feelings raging through his mind and his body was distinctly uncomfortable. Was he protecting her, or excluding her? Neither was acceptable. He turned and looked at Debrowski. Her crushed lip sneered at him, her eyes were bright and expectant. He pictured her swinging a bike chain. Suddenly, the idea of protecting her seemed ludicrous.

"I'm working on something else," he said slowly.

"You're changing the subject."

"I'm not. You want me to play cards, I'll play cards. But I want to tell you, I think I have a way to get some money out of Dickie. I'm going to get back the money we lost, plus what he owes me, and then some. If it works, it'll more than make up for losing to that pair of fours. What I'm saying is, it's going to work out. You don't have to pay me back. It's not necessary. I've got it covered."

"It's not about the money, Crow."

"I was afraid of that," he sighed.

24

Most humans are clearly more intelligent than horses. I therefore believed that a patient and intelligent person, by devoting a reasonable amount of time and energy to research and calculation, could do quite well financially. Was my research of poor quality? Who can say . . . who can say?

—Ben Fink, talking to an empty seat during the ninth race at Canterbury Downs

"What I want to know," said Ben Franklin, folding his copy of the *Racing Form*, "is why we are still here."

Tom Jefferson's tongue was sticking from between his lips, moving back and forth, up and down, in and out, with the efforts of Shamino the Ranger. He made little grunting sounds and puffed out his cheeks whenever Shamino had to jump.

"Would you please put that down for a minute?" Ben said. He was sitting under the umbrella, his long, pale legs carefully tucked in out of the sun. The evidence of seven shrimp cocktails, a dozen oysters, and a club sandwich rested on the table. An empty bottle of Dom Perignon lay on its side atop a silvered ice bucket. A few yards away, the empty swimming pool glittered bright green in the midday sun.

Tommy lowered his Game Boy and looked over at his partner, pushing the red frames of his new Ray-Bans up his oiled nose. "What's going on? Hey, should we order another bottle of that stuff? You want to?" He set the Game Boy on his lap and shook out his hands. "Man, my thumbs are fuckin' pooped." He pulled up the back of the lounger.

"I'm thinking we should move on," said Ben.

"You don't like it here? I like it here."

"The show is sold out, Thomas. Standing room only. Once we start selling the lobby, it's time to roll. We stayed with the Stasis Shield routine a few weeks too long and look what happened. Now we've got Freddy Wisnesky. You ever try to lose a pet dog?"

"Only reason we hadda blow Chicago was fuckin' Joey Cadillac," Tommy said. "There's no Joey Cadillac here. What are you worried about? Freddy's dumb as a stump. Tell him he's got a fly on his nose, and he'll knock himself out trying to slap it. Let's just issue some new units, call them bonds or something. No, we'll call them Galactic Convertible Subordinated Debentures, keep Dickie out there humpin' for us. We got a good story, we got a guy that can sell it, why fuck with it? Besides, the way you been droppin' money at the track, we're gonna need all we can get."

Ben ignored the shot. He was having a bad run, but so what? "You put the dog in your car, take him a hundred miles away, tie him to a tree, drive home, and next week he shows up at your back door, so happy to see you he urinates all over your leg. It's a proven fact that the dog will always find you in the end. You have to shoot the dog. Freddy Wisnesky won't ever go away. I can't even go out for a paper without thinking about how hard it would be to read the thing with two broken arms. In my opinion, we should move on while we are still able, or we'll have more than Freddy Wisnesky to worry about."

"What are you worried about? Dickie Wicky? He doesn't have a fuckin' clue. And if he did, so what? He's the scam man. Anything goes down, the heat's gonna be on Dickie-boy. He's the man with the license. I don't know what you're worried about. We have to, we just evaporate."

A waitress, dressed in a uniform that looked like a short-sleeved green tuxedo, arrived with a large tray and began loading it with their used plates. Both men stopped talking and watched her.

"Is there anything else I can get for you gentlemen?"

"Yeah," Tommy said.

The waitress looked surprised. Mr. Tucker's appetite had been re-marked upon by other members of the Whitehall Suites staff, but this was the first time she had witnessed it firsthand. "Yes, sir," she said, quickly composing herself.

"Another bottle of that fizzy stuff. And a shrimp cocktail. Wait a sec. You got anything like a lobster cocktail?"

"I could have the kitchen come up with one, I'm sure, Mr. Tucker. Will there be anything else?" She had also heard about Mr. Tucker's lavish tips.

Tommy looked at Ben. "Don't ya love the way they remember your name? It's like going to Cheers. You want anything?"

Ben shook his head. After the waitress left, he said, "I don't think Dickie is buying the GGF line anymore. You know, he's not as dumb as he acts."

"He was, he'd forget to breathe in and out. If he was gonna be a problem, Cat woulda let us know."

"I do not trust Catherine, and neither would you if you weren't suffering from an overabundance of testosterone. The other night, when we went to that place to play poker, Dickie didn't even ask us about how the acquisition was going. Every other time we've seen him, it was all he wanted to know: When were we going to take pos-session of the Jones collection? When was the money going to come? All of a sudden he doesn't even mention it. This sort of thing con-cerns me greatly."

"He was drunk, man."

"With Dickie, I don't think that is relevant. He's used to process-ing large quantities of alcohol. My point is, he might very well be onto the scam, and I think we should collect our assets and move on to someplace where they do not know us. We have close to two hun-dred thousand in the box right now. I don't want to lose it all just be-cause you got your pecker out of joint over our friend Catherine."

"My pecker's fine." He looked over his shoulder toward their pool-side room. "Speaking of which . . ."

"Please try to restrain yourself. I'm trying to make a point here."

Ben's voice was becoming even more cavernous than usual, due to the cigar and the champagne. "She's not going anywhere. Why should she? We're paying for everything. You can go flush your tubes after we decide what we're going to do."

"I say we milk it till Dickie burns."

"It's not just Dickie I'm worried about."

"What, are you talking about that guy Crow? He's a wimp."

Ben watched the waitress coming across the patio with a two-hundred-dollar bottle of champagne in a bucket and what promised to be another twenty dollars' worth of lobster cocktail. She showed them the bottle, opened it, and poured them each a glass. Tommy forked a quarter of a lobster tail into his mouth and washed it down with a gulp of champagne. The waitress twisted the bottle into the chromed ice bucket.

When she was out of earshot, Ben said, "You're thinking with your testicles again, my friend."

"What? What are you talking about?"

"Crow. He is not a wimp."

Tommy shoveled the last of the lobster into his mouth, chewed audibly, poured himself another glass of champagne. "Here she comes," he said. "Would you look at that suit? Man, I ain't seen nothing like that since Key West."

Catfish was crossing the patio, carrying a towel under her arm, her face concealed behind a giant pair of round mirrored sunglasses, her breasts swinging back and forth in minute triangular pouches suspended from shoulder straps the thickness of fishing line. The bottom of the swimsuit was similarly designed. As she came closer they could see curly dark hairs escaping from every side of the triangle. She kissed Tommy and wiggled her fingers at Ben, who smiled back without enthusiasm. He regarded her bare bottom with only clinical interest, having learned years ago that a quick fifty-dollar blow job once a week was all it took to keep his glands in balance. He picked up the *Racing Form* and tried to ignore the spit exchange going on at poolside. After enduring too many minutes of their giggling and whispering, he snapped the paper closed.

"Catherine."

"Yes, Benny-poo?" She looked up and fluttered her eyelids at him. Tommy cracked up.

Ben glared. "Did you tell Dickie that the GGF collection was a fabrication?"

"Well, sure I did."

Ben nodded and jerked back in his chair, both triumphant and alarmed.

Tommy's mouth fell open. "Whadja do that for?"

"Somebody had to. He was spending our own money on it. I got to look out for *moi* too, y'know." She pulled a lounger over beside Tommy's and laid herself out facedown. The Tom and Ben Show stared at each other, then looked down at Catfish's ripe, sun-darkened glutei maximi.

"Ben, did you know Dickie was putting his own money into the thing?" Tommy asked.

"It was his money. Caveat emptor, as they say."

"I don't know what y'all are so worried about," Catfish drawled. "Dickie's just going to sell them all over again. You all oughta get him to sell some more. He's good at it."

"See?" Tommy said. "It's okay, Ben. Nothing's changed. Only thing is, the scam man is wise now, but that don't mean we can't keep it going. We just got to whack it up a little different is all. Give him a bigger chunk."

"I don't like whacking it up at all."

"Hey, business is business, pod. Ain't you the one always telling me not to get greedy?"

"I don't like it."

"Benny-poo, you can be such an ol' stick stuck in the mud." Catfish rolled onto her back and looked at him through her upraised knees. "Why don't you just loosen up a bit, have a little fun? Find yourself a little ol' card game." Ben looked at his reduced image, twice, in the lenses of her enormous mirrored sunglasses.

"I seem to have some difficulty finding a game in this town," he said. "Your Mr. Crow has a hard-on for me."

"I hear he's a pretty good poker player."

Ben shrugged and poured the last of the Dom Perignon into his glass. "In a straight game, he would undoubtedly do well. I personally do not care for straight games. It's far more challenging and exciting to bend the odds. That is what poker is really about."

"Cheatin'?" Catfish grinned.

Ben inclined his head. He noticed the waitress coming toward them. She addressed Ben. "Mr. Hogan? You have a telephone call. A Mr. Rich Wicky. Do you want to take it?" She was holding a cordless telephone, offering it to him.

Ben took the phone, turned it on. "Dickie," he said in his deeper than deep telephone voice. Tommy and Catfish leaned forward. Tommy's right thigh was going up and down; Catfish had a grip on his left.

"Could you hold a moment?" Ben said. He pressed the mute button. "He wants to know what a set of *Detective Comics*, numbers one through one hundred twelve, would be worth. He sounds quite excited."

"Ask him a few questions. No. Gimme the phone." Tommy snatched the phone away from Ben and turned it back on. "This is Tom Terrific, Dickie. What the fuck you talkin' about?" He listened. "Uh-huh. You kidding me? Yeah. Yeah. Well, if they were *near mint*, which is about as good as the golden-age stuff gets, it'd be worth about, I'd guess, a hundred thou, maybe more. Could be more. Depends if you're buying or selling. Why, you pitching the fund to some *Batman* freak?" He listened, nodding, his knee going up and down, foot slapping on the stone patio. "Well, f'chrissake you can tell *me*, Dickie. Aren't we partners? Yeah. Yeah. Uh-huh. Well, come on over, then. We'll have a few pops and talk 'er out. Right. Later, man." He turned off the phone and dropped it on the patio.

"Well?" Ben said.

Tommy had his hands over his ears. "Shut up a minute. I'm thinking. Cat, you better scoot. Your old man's on the way over. I don't want to have to give him back that ten K."

Ben said, "What ten K is that?"

"Shut up. I gotta think." He waited until Catfish was out of range, then said to Ben, "That meathead says he wants to *buy* the Galactic Guardians Fund."

From the pay phone in the Whitehall lobby, Wicky could see through the back wall, all glass, out onto the pool patio. He hung up the phone and watched Catfish, swimsuit the size of a sanitary napkin, kiss Tommy Jefferson and walk away. It was impossible, unthinkable, but he was seeing it. Smiling bitterly, he crossed the lobby to the piano bar, hiked himself onto a stool, and ordered a gin and tonic. When his drink arrived, he asked the bartender if she thought that women were more devious than men.

"Absolutely," she said.

Wicky smiled and sipped his drink. "You're wrong," he said.

Just keep telling yourself, "They want to believe. They all want it. They want it so bad it hurts. They're scared to death they're going to be left out." Pretty soon you get so you can smell it right over the phone wire.

—*Richard D. Wicky, V.P., training a new registered representative*

Sometimes, especially while they were lying in bed, Joey Cadillac liked to ask Chrissy Swenson for advice. He would explain his problem carefully, laying it out point by point, then tell her what he thought he should do. Chrissy would nod, frown, laugh, and shake her head at the right places, then think carefully before telling him that what he was about to do was the right thing. Joey always told her she was a smart girl, and he never kicked about the rent.

Sometimes, she knew, the stories that Joey told were not exactly true. Like the story about the bruise on his back.

What he'd told her was, he'd been robbed by two big black guys with bike chains and guns. They'd cornered him in his office, after hours, nobody else around. One of them had kept a gun on him while the other one hit him with the chain and kicked him in the head. He said they took two thousand bucks off him.

The bruise was nasty. She believed the part about the chain, but she'd heard from Margie, her friend at J.C. Motors, that the person who had done the damage was a girl in a motorcycle jacket. According to Margie, the perpetrator was neither large nor black.

She didn't believe what Joey was telling her about the comic book guys, either.

"What I wanna do, what I was gonna do, was I was gonna find 'em and, you know, have a face-to-face with the both of them, make sure they understand that it ain't right to fuck a guy like me over. Only Freddy, he can't seem to connect. It's like they been avoiding him. Like, they don't return his phone calls. I dunno, you just can't figure some of these guys out. What, do they think Freddy's some kind of dangerous animal or something?"

Chrissy, who had met Freddy Wisnesky, thought that they proba-bly thought exactly that, if they had any sense.

"Anyways, sooner or later I figure Freddy will get the message across and I can forget about it, put the whole stinking mess behind me, maybe even get my car back. Except it's taking forever, and Freddy's up there in Minneapolis—"

"Minneapolis?"

"Yeah, your hometown, babe. So I'm stuck down here with busi-ness negotiations to take care of, and Freddy's sitting in some park-ing ramp, waiting for some crazy broad to show up."

Chrissy said, "Huh?"

"Never mind. So then I get this call from this guy I never heard of before, says his name is Rich Wicky, if you can believe that, says he knows a way I can get hold of the two guys and my car and make a bunch of money, all at the same time. He's got this big plan, he says. All he needs is to borrow Freddy for a few days. It sounds like bullshit to me, but I say I'll think about it. So I been thinkin' about it, and I don't know. Whadaya think, babe?"

"Hmmm," Chrissy said, making two lines appear on her forehead.

" 'Cause I think the guy's full a shit, calling me up that way, feedin' me a bunch of crap."

"That's what I think too," Chrissy said.

"Only there might be something to it. I told Freddy, I told him to go along with the guy for a few days. Might be this guy knows some-thing. But now I'm thinking I ought to talk to Freddy again, have him put the question to the guy."

"Hmmm," Chrissy said.

Joey shook his head sadly. "You can't count on nobody."

"You can count on me," Chrissy said.

Joey nodded. "I guess that's right. By the way, I got a few guys lined up to play some cards next Friday. You want to make sure we got lots a snacks and booze and stuff?"

"Sure, Joey," Chrissy said, keeping her face carefully composed. She hated poker night. The games lasted till morning, sometimes all the way into the next night, and her condo always reeked of stale smoke and male sweat for days after. "You want me to get anything special?"

Joey thought. He was lying on his back, looking at his belly. Somewhere on the other side of the fleshy mound, his pecker was hanging all limp and happy now. "How about some a them Cheetos," he said. "The things that get your fingers all orange. I like them. And maybe a couple extra bottles of Remy. And some Coke." He looked again at his formidable gut. "Make that diet Coke, doll. Some a the things you been doing, I'm getting kind of curious what my pecker looks like these days."

Tom and Ben looked at each other, then back at Wicky.

Tom said, "It sounds like we got us another John Jones Collection."

"Only difference is, this one's real," Wicky pointed out.

"The Jones Collection is real," Tom insisted.

During their earlier, occasionally heated discussion, it had become apparent to Wicky that, on some level, Tom actually believed in his own invention. Wicky was familiar with this phenomenon, having often observed it in the brokerage business. One minute Tom would be laughing at some poor fool who believed the story, and the next he would be making an earnest effort to convince him that it was, in fact, true.

After four lobster cocktails, a tray of nachos, and two more bottles of Dom Perignon, the three men were still sitting outside near the pool. Wicky had his suit jacket off, his tie and collar loosened, shoes and socks off, and his trousers rolled up to expose pasty shins to the last rays of sunshine. Several vintage comic books were strewn carelessly on the patio.

Ben was paging through an old five-ring notebook, pausing, making a clucking sound now and then with his tongue. "You want us to sell them?" he asked, keeping his eyes on the notebook.

"You keep asking me that," Wicky said. He was enjoying himself. "All I want you to do is find the buyers. I handle all the paper."

"You've seen the comics?" Ben asked.

"Some of them. He had a few of them at his house in Saint Paul, said he kept them there for his grandkids to read. And he had that notebook. His brother kept every comic book he owned catalogued right there in that notebook."

Ben paused and pointed at one of the entries. "Look at this. The first seventy-four issues of *Captain America*. Incredible. Cap, he's my favorite. You say they're all boxed up?"

"He's got them all stashed at some cabin up north, he says. Most of the boxes haven't been opened since 1951. He says as far as he knows they're in perfect shape."

"But you haven't seen them."

"They're real, Ben. You met the guy, you wouldn't doubt it for a minute."

Ben nodded and turned a page. "A lot of junk here," he said.

"Like I told you, it includes damn near every comic published during the forties, all the way up through 1950."

Ben closed the notebook.

"And you want us to sell them," Ben said again. "Let me ask you this: what's in it for us? Are you thinking of us as partners?"

Wicky shook his head. "Not exactly. I want you to handle the marketing as part of the merger agreement."

Tom laughed. "You mean the takeover." He looked at Ben. "I don't want to listen to any more of this shit. We don't need this guy."

"Sure you do," Wicky said, pouring the last of the champagne into his glass. "The GGF, as you both know, has no assets other than the cash, or whatever's left of it, that you've accumulated from our investors. The Jones Collection itself does not exist. We could keep selling partnership units, but within six months, a year at the most, the whole thing is gonna come tumbling down. We could start paying off the original investors, turn it into a Ponzi scheme, keep it going a few months longer, but eventually it's gotta come down. None of us wants to be around for that one." He tossed back the champagne. "So what we do is, we absorb the whole GGF thing into my new Justice Society Fund, merge the two entities, then market the new collection and use the proceeds to get the original partners their money back—or at least enough of it so it won't be worthwhile for them to come after us. You follow?"

Tom snorted. "Yeah, we follow, all right. I say why the fuck should we bother? You made your cut on the GGF sales, we got ours, so why do we need this Justice Society bullshit? Let's just buy the old man's collection, whack it up three ways, and be done with it."

"That's fine for you guys, but I've got a career here. I've got a job, condo, a wife. I got roots here and a name to protect."

Tom laughed. "Yeah. 'Dickie Wicky.' Why the hell you want to protect a name like that?"

Wicky smiled and let it roll off. "I'm not looking for you guys to kick back any money here. Whatever you siphoned off the GGF, which I assume is just about the whole quarter million plus, you keep. All I want is for you to sign your general partnerships in the GGF over to the Justice Society Fund. And find me some buyers with ready cash. And maybe make a short-term loan, say fifty or sixty thousand, to make the purchase."

"No fucking way," said Tom.

"Why do you need our money?" Ben asked.

"Because I want you guys to help me market the collection. And because if you're personally invested in the program, I know you'll make it happen. Call it good-faith money."

Tom looked at Ben. "He doesn't trust us," he said, eyebrows ascending.

Wicky shrugged. "If I wanted to, I could do it on my own. I'm just trying to create a paper vehicle so that I can take care of my investors without the whole thing coming down around us. You guys don't seem to realize the position you've put me in with this Galactic Guardians thing. When it hits the fan, and it will, I'll be lucky if I just lose my license. I hang around and wait for it to happen, I might end up in jail. Selling blue sky is one thing, selling a black hole is another. You guys got me into this mess, I'm offering you a way to do the right thing, plus cover your own butts and make a little money too."

"No fucking way," Tom repeated.

Ben was still paging through the book. "Basically, you want us to gift you the GGF, is that correct?"

"Right," said Wicky. "Gift it to me."

"And find a buyer for this collection."

"Yes."

"And loan you some cash."

"Exactly."

"Short term."

"Very."

"And if we don't, you attempt to implicate us in the resulting legal difficulties."

"I would have no choice."

"But we would be long gone by then."

Wicky shrugged.

Ben said, "We have to think about it." He handed the notebook back to Wicky. "I'd like to meet this person."

"No problem. But if you guys think I'm going to let you within a mile of my little old man before we've got a solid deal, you can forget it." Wicky rolled down the bottoms of his trousers. "You guys think it over and call me in the morning. I gotta get going. I'm taking a friend of mine to the Twins game tonight. I haven't been to a ball game in years. You guys interested in coming along? You might enjoy meeting my friend Freddy."

"Freddy?" Ben asked.

"Freddy fucking Wisnesky, man—I can't believe it," Tom said for perhaps the twentieth time. They had moved inside, to the bar just off the hotel lobby. Tom was drinking rum and Coke with a slice of lime, a cherry, and a handful of filberts floating on top. He took a plastic bottle of Tylenol from his pocket and shook a few purple tablets into his drink.

"You shouldn't eat those with alcohol," Ben said, sipping his Perrier. "It erodes your stomach lining. You'll get bleeding ulcers."

"I get ulcers, it's on account of that fucking Dickie and Freddy." He swirled his drink and swallowed. Most of the customers in the small bar were suited business types coming down off a day of phone calls and meetings. Tom and Ben were wearing their bathing suits, Hawaiian shirts, and flip-flops. The cocktail waitress, a slim redheaded woman, stopped at their table and gave Tom her best smile.

"How is your drink, Mr. Tucker?" Like everyone on the wait staff, she had gotten the word on his tipping habits. The tall one, Mr. Hogan, never tipped at all, but Mr. Tucker let loose of fifties like they were ones.

Tom told her it was great, the best drink he'd ever had. She smiled happily and walked off, giving him a little ass wiggle to remember her by.

"I don't understand why they're so nice to you," Ben said. "They act like I'm invisible."

"That's 'cause you're a cheapskate."

Ben frowned and sipped his Perrier. He cleared his throat. "This proposal of Dickie's, it might be to our advantage," he said. "It would get our names off the Galactic Guardians Fund."

"What the fuck are you talking? They aren't our names anyway, *Fink*."

"Good point," said Ben Fink. "In any case, the only thing that really concerns me is the front money. If our man Dickie wants to run his own fund, I really don't mind. But I do worry about the money. I don't like putting it up, even short term. If we do that, we'll have to have control of the collection."

"What the fuck is he doing, going to a baseball game with Freddy Wisnesky?"

"I have no idea. Also, I've been considering how we might get next to this old man. I want to find out who he is and have a talk with him."

"If there *is* an old man. I think he's making the whole thing up."

Ben shook his head. "I don't know about that. If you were telling the tale, I wouldn't believe it for a minute—"

"Thanks a lot."

"—but Dickie does not have the imagination to dream up something like this. And that notebook he had—that was real. You could tell that whoever listed all those titles knew their business. Some of the titles listed were pretty obscure. Dickie doesn't know comics well enough to invent something like that. The collection is real, all right, and I think we should figure out a way to acquire it."

"He probably has Freddy Wisnesky sitting on it with a fucking bazooka. Promised him a new tie or something."

Ben stood up. "I think it's time to talk to Catherine. Let's go wake her up."

"Not that I know of. Of course, I haven't seen Dickie in three days," Catfish said, picking bits of yellow from the corner of her eye. "I mean, not to talk to I haven't. Except just calling him to, you know, let him know I wouldn't be home. Have y'all had dinner yet? I'm starving."

Tommy moaned. He was lying on the other bed, digesting four

lobster cocktails, a tray of nachos and four hundred dollars' worth of champagne.

Ben said, "Catherine, are you sure? He's never talked to you about an old man with a comic collection?"

"Just the story you laid on him. Tell you what—if that Freddy's gone, I can go home and talk to him, find out what he's up to."

"Freddy's not gone," said Ben.

"Then I'm not going near the place. Maybe I could call Dickie and meet him for dinner someplace." She shook a cigarette loose from the pack on the end table. "You got a match, Benny-poo?"

Ben pointed at the book of matches in the ashtray. She picked them up and lit her own cigarette. "I'll call him right now."

"I wouldn't bother," said Ben. "He went to the baseball game."

"Dickie? You're kidding. He hates baseball."

"But Freddy Wisnesky loves it," said Tommy. He sounded ill.

"Freddy is with Dickie?" She thought about that. "It makes sense, when you think about. They have a lot in common."

♦ ♥ 26 ♣ ♠

MINT (M): Absolutely perfect in every way, regardless of age. The cover has full lustre, is crisp, cut square and shows no imperfections of any sort. The cover and all pages are extra white and fresh; the spine is tight, flat, and clean; not even the slightest blemish can be detected around staples, along spine and edges or at corners. As comics must be truly perfect to be in this grade, they are obviously extremely scarce and seldom are offered for sale.

—The Official Overstreet Comic Book Price Guide

Chrissy was looking forward to meeting her new friend, Laura, for happy hour down at The Parrot. That Joey. God. The stuff she had to put up with. She drove her Miata, top down, out of the ramp and headed south on Lake Shore Drive, her head buzzing with things to say.

The thing about Laura, which wasn't true of any of her other so-called friends, was that Laura understood what it was like to have a boyfriend like Joey. First off, most of her other friends just didn't get it. They would say stuff, always wanting to remind her that he was married, always wanting to introduce her to some guy with round glasses, a yellow tie, and a BMW. She'd gone out with a few of them. They were like kids. Joey was a fat, self-involved slob, but at least he was a grownup, and he knew how to take care of a girl. Chrissy had enough problems in her life; why should she have to worry about paying the rent? With Joey, at least she knew where she stood, and if he was married, well, so what? That gave her that much more time to herself.

But Laura understood. They had met only a few days ago, at Antonio's, and already Chrissy considered Laura to be one of her closest friends.

Joey had taken her out for once, to his cousin Antonio Battagno's new restaurant over in Old Town. Chrissy bought a new dress for the occasion, a stretchy blue sheath with sparkly gold threads woven into it. The blue was for her eyes, the gold for her hair, which she'd had done special by Robert at the Hair-Um. She didn't know what was keeping it up there—Robert could do amazing things with hair. And new shoes with really, really high heels that, with the hair, put her a full six inches over Joey's modest five feet six. When he'd picked her up in one of his limos, he was so knocked out he'd wanted a quickie right there in the back seat. It had taken every trick she knew to get him calmed down. She hadn't wanted to get all messed up, walk into Tony's new restaurant looking like a mid-shift whore, with her hair all knocked down and lipstick on her teeth.

She'd met Laura in the ladies' room while she was checking her face.

"Isn't that Joey Cadillac you're with?" the woman next to her had asked.

Chrissy had arched her eyebrows, preparing to deliver a cold, dignified *Yes*. But the woman had looked at her with such wide-eyed wonder that Chrissy found herself smiling.

"Yes, it is," she said politely.

"Wow!" the woman said. "He's a really important guy, isn't he?"

"I suppose he is," said Chrissy, who had never actually thought so before but liked the idea that someone did.

"I've heard a lot about him. A guy I used to go with bought a Cadillac from him. He got a really good deal. By the way, my name's Laura." She'd stuck out her hand. Chrissy thought it was weird, shaking hands like that in the ladies' room, but she'd liked this Laura.

They started talking, and it turned out they both belonged to the same health club. The next day they'd found themselves on adjacent StairMasters, and they'd talked and talked. They were both from Minnesota, land of ten thousand boring lakes, and that gave them both plenty to complain about. And Laura, talk about your coincidences, had a boyfriend who paid her rent every month, so she understood exactly how it was.

"It's like having a *job*." Chrissy panted. The machine reported that she had climbed one hundred seven flights of stairs and burned two hundred twenty-seven calories.

"You ain't kidding, honey," Laura gasped.

It was good to have a girlfriend, someone to confide in.

Laura was sitting at the bar at The Parrot, drinking some kind of tropical fruit thing. Two guys were with her, a slim black man and a gangly blond man in shredded jeans and a motorcycle jacket. They looked out of place in The Parrot, which catered to the yuppie crowd. Laura waved, happy to see her friend Chrissy. Chrissy waved back. Laura said something to the black guy. He looked toward Laura and glided away, followed by the tall blond man. Chrissy joined her, two very foxy chicks at the bar, girls' night out, ready to make the animals wail and gnash their teeth.

"Who were they?" Chrissy asked.

"Some guys I don't know."

"What do you have there? Is that a Mai Tai?"

"A Virgin Island," said Laura, offering it to Chrissy. It tasted like mango juice. Chrissy ordered a Mai Tai, staying with the tropical theme but going for the alcohol. When the drink came they decided to move to one of the tables.

"So how's Joey doing?" Laura asked as they sat down.

"Oh, God." Chrissy rolled her eyes. "He just told me he's gonna have another poker game next weekend."

"Really? Maybe we should go out that night."

"I can't. He likes me to be there. I'm his luck, he says. And guess where the game is. My apartment."

"Oh, God. Really?"

"He's always had them there. His wife doesn't like the smell of seven or eight guys smoking cigars. You believe that?"

The two women looked at each other and laughed. A few drinks later, Laura mentioned that her boyfriend was going to be in town in a couple of days. "He plays poker too, except he always loses. Good thing he can afford it."

"What does he do?" Chrissy asked.

"He makes deals. He's like a businessman. Say, wouldn't it be a kick if we could get your guy and my guy together? We could double date."

Chrissy laughed at the idea of going with Joey on a double date. It was so high-school. But after another Mai Tai she started liking the idea.

"I could ask Joey if he needs another player," she said. "Maybe if they played cards together they'd get to be friends."

"His name's Joe Crow," said Laura. "I just know Joey's gonna like him. I bet they get to be best friends." She put her hand on Chrissy's wrist, suddenly serious. "Sometimes I think about what's going to happen when my guy gets tired of me. One of these days he's going to pull the plug and leave me with rent due. Do you ever think about that?"

Chrissy shrugged and shook her hair. "I can take care of myself. I'm saving up."

"Are you sure you're saving enough?"

Chrissy sucked her Mai Tai dry. She was not enjoying this conversation, but she respected Laura for bringing it up. In fact, the prospect of being cast loose by Joey had occupied her thoughts on many sleepless nights. She had stashed away a few thousand, but that wouldn't last for long.

Laura said, "I was thinking of a way you might make some pretty good money, fast, no risk."

"I don't do tricks," Chrissy said.

Laura shook her head. "That's not what I mean. Look, Joey's got more money than he knows what to do with, right?"

"He's rich," Chrissy said. "What he gives me is nothing. He bought his wife a diamond necklace; you should've seen it. He showed it to me, the jerk. Looked like something the queen would wear. Then he goes and buys me this ruby about the size of a poppy seed." It felt good to complain to someone who understood.

"You deserve more," Laura said. "All the stuff you do for him."

"I sure do." Chrissy waved at the bartender and pointed at her empty glass. "What do I have to do to make all this money?"

"Do you know how to wink?" she asked.

Chrissy winked.

"That's good. That's all you have to do."

Beep.

"If you could see me now, Crow, you'd be yawning colors in about three seconds flat. These heels are killing me, and so is listening to Chrissy 'for cute' Swenson. I look like a goddamn fluffhead. On second thought, maybe you'd like it—all the guys at The Parrot did. It was all I could do to get out of there with my virtue, such as it is, intact. Anyway, we're all lined up for a game this Saturday. Chrissy the bimbo is on, and she says they bet the big stuff, so bring plenty of money. I'm at the hotel now, going to bed. Call me tomorrow."

Beep.

"Mr. Crow, this is Ben Franklin. I have a business arrangement I'd like to discuss with you. Could you call me at the Whitehall Suites, please? Ask for Mr. Hogan."

Beep.

"Mr. Crow, this is Charles at Jaguar Motor Cars. Got a little problem here with your XJS. We're going to have to replace *both* front struts, it looks like. Also, were you aware that you have a blister on this right front tire? Anyway, we'll hold off here until I hear from you. That other strut is going to run you about . . . let's see . . . about two forty. Give me a call. Thanks!"

"I'm sorry, sir, Ms. Debrowski isn't answering her phone."

"Keep ringing her," Crow said.

"I'll try again, sir."

Fourteen rings later, a husky voice answered, "Hello."

"Debrowski?"

"That you, Crow?"

"Are you all right?"

"Just a second."

Crow heard a cough, some shuffling, the sound of her clearing her throat.

"I'm back." Her voice sounded a little better. "I swear, spending a night in a bar without having a real drink gives me a worse hangover than I ever had while I was using. I must've smoked three packs of cigarettes."

"You got a cig going now?"

"Yeah, I got a cig going. You get my message?"

"I got it. You want to pick me up at O'Hare?"

"Sure. Hey, I'm finding out all kinds of new stuff about Franklin and Jefferson."

"They owned slaves, I know."

"Ha ha. His real name is Tommy Campo. I spent some time in a place called Fatman's Emporium of Comic Book Arts. Fatman's a real guy. He has one leg in a cast, courtesy of your friend Freddy Wisnesky. Fatman didn't have much to say at first, but he loosened up after I told him I worked with the Coldcocks. He's a fan. Anyway, he says those guys' real names are Tommy Campo and Ben Fink, and had nothing good to say about either of 'em. You ever hear of something called a Stasis Shield?"

"Sounds like something out of a science fiction novel."

"You got the fiction part right. Seems that Campo and Fink—Fatman calls them the Tom and Ben Show—they developed this special system for preserving investment-grade comics. They used these heavy Mylar sleeves, put the comic inside after grading and notarizing it, and sealed it in with a pure nitrogen atmosphere. The idea was to 'inert' the comic book so it could be bought, sold, and displayed without losing its grade. They claimed that a Stasis Shield–protected comic book would stay in perfect condition well into the twenty-third century. According to Fatman, the idea wasn't all that bad. Apparently, they use something like it to package chickens—Modified Atmosphere Packaging.

"The way it worked, collectors would leave their best comics with Tom and Ben to have them 'inerted,' and what they'd get back would be a color copy of their cover wrapped around a blank interior. Part of the pitch was that the extra-thick Mylar sleeve distorted the colors, which was supposed to explain any slight color differences, and since the collectors paid forty bucks a crack to have their books inerted, nobody was inclined, at first, to open the things up and take a closer look. Fatman says the guys that would want their comics shielded weren't your hard-core comics fans—guys like that want to be able to read their books. Most of them were investors, who could give a shit about what was inside. He said no real comic fan would be fooled. Tom and Ben went after the investment-oriented collectors, guys who don't care what's between the covers so long as they can re-sell it for more than they paid. You ever hear the sardine story? A guy marries into a family that's in the sardine business. He goes to work in the family business, buying and selling sardines, making tons of money. They got millions of cans of sardines, making a fortune trad-ing back and forth on the sardine market, buying low, selling high. One day he gets hungry, so he goes out in the warehouse and grabs a can of sardines. He opens up the can, and it's full of dry sand. He tries another can, and it's full of sand too. All the cans are full of sand. So he goes to his father-in-law, all upset, and shows him this can full of sand. The father-in-law laughs and says, 'Those sardines aren't for eating; they're for *trading*!'"

"What did they do with the real comics?" asked Crow.

"You don't like the sardine story? I probably told it wrong. Ac-cording to Fatman, they shipped the real comics off to collectors on the West Coast, making sure not to offer them back to the original owners. They ran this scam for three or four months without getting any wires crossed, until a couple months ago."

She paused. Crow waited a few seconds, then asked, "You gonna tell me the rest of it?"

"Just a minute. I'm trying to light a cigarette. . . . God, could I use a cup of coffee. . . . Okay, you still there? So what happened is they got greedy—big surprise, huh?—and they started making extra copies of the covers, sealing them into Stasis Shields, and selling them to investors that were totally out of the comics loop, selling them like they were precious metals or bearer bonds or something. Selling them to guys that don't know the difference between Green Lantern and the Flash."

"Guys like Joey Cadillac."

"Right. They traded a bunch of the things to him for a car. Chrissy the bimbo— You know she was a Miss Minnesota? I asked her what she did for the talent part of the contest, and she said she couldn't re-member. Anyways, Chrissy the bimbo says she was actually sitting there when Joey made history by being the first guy to open up a Sta-sis Shield and find out he'd been suckered. She says he was a little out of control that night."

"He's got a short fuse, huh?"

"Microscopic."

"Mr. Hogan, please."

Crow stroked Milo, letting the smooth feel of the black coat mod-
ulate his excitement. He had that tight feel of being in control, just
barely, like a race car driver running the perfect lap, forty laps yet to
go, expecting a tire to blow or a flag to come down at any moment.
Milo purred, his body vibrating.

"Hello?" Ben Hogan's subwoofer of a voice came through the
handset like paste forced through a pinhole.

"Ben Fink?" Crow asked.

A full five seconds later, Ben said, "Is this Mr. Crow?"

"This is Joe Stalin."

Another silence.

"I see," said Ben. "Would you like to join me for a drink?"

"For what purpose?" Crow dug his fingers in around Milo's ears.
The cat responded by extending his claws through Crow's jeans into
his thigh. Crow relaxed his grip; the cat retracted its claws.

"I want to hire you," Ben said.

27

*STOP TIME NOW! Your comics are slowly deteriorating.
Polyethylene, polypropylene, even Mylar sleeves are no match for
Father Time. Only total stasis can save your valuable books
from the ravages of time, and only one product offers this state-
of-the-art technology—the Stasis Shield®.*

—*Advertisement in* Comic Marketing Quarterly

At eleven o'clock in the morning, Zink's Club 34 was home to
those who knew how to get numb before noon and stay that
way for the rest of the day. Late in the afternoon, when the
workers from the printing plant up the street dropped in for their
Miller's, the Club 34 day shift would filter out and wander back to

their rented rooms, bridges, or doorways to nurse a forty-ouncer, a half pint of vodka, or a bottle of Thunderbird. During the day, however, Club 34 was their home.

Crow parked the red truck, got out, plugged the meter. He stood on the sidewalk and felt the late-morning sunshine on his face. The cool morning air was quickly warming, promising a scorching afternoon. He took several long, slow breaths, then walked through the smudged tinted-glass door. The cold, sour smell of beer-stained carpeting and alcoholic sweat instantly coated his nostrils. Blinking, breathing shallowly, he waited for his eyes to adjust to the dim light cast by the pink fluorescent tubes running across the top of the long, greasy mirror. Only four of the barstools were occupied. Two men were playing backgammon at a small round table near the door. Cory, Zink's daytime bartender, stood behind the bar with her arms folded, listening to one of her customers, an aging, loose-limbed Swede wearing overalls, a down vest, and a navy watch cap. He was telling her a story, using his long arms to illustrate it. Crow caught Cory's eye and nodded. She winked.

Cory White was a tall, slim, handsome, buttoned-down black woman in her early fifties who would have been cast perfectly as the courageous principal of a troubled inner-city high school. She was one of those people but for whom the word "unflappable" might have disappeared from the language long ago. Cory had been working days for Zink Fitterman for nearly a decade, and she claimed to like it. She said it kept her busy, she didn't have to think, and her customers liked her. They called her "Teach." Crow liked her too, but the few efforts he had made to get to know her better had failed. Cory had battlements that made Crow's defenses look like wet Kleenex. He bellied up to the bar and waited for her to finish listening to the big Swede's story. He was describing something he had built, a house or some other building, many years ago. Crow imagined him twenty years younger, without the red nose, a leather carpenter's tool belt encircling his waist. Something about an argument he'd had with the architect. An argument he'd won. The story ended when he drained the last of his beer, Adam's apple pulsing, and ordered a whiskey, goddamn it.

Cory delivered a shot of Ancient Age to the carpenter, poured a Coke for Crow.

"You looking for Zink, honey? He'll be back in a few minutes. How you been?"

"Not bad."

"You got a girlfriend yet?"

"Not yet, Cory. How about you?"

"I just been worrying about you, honey."

"You should worry more about yourself."

"I leave that to you, honey."

Crow laughed; Cory smiled. He had come to understand that Cory had a file of brief, circular conversations in her head, with a special variation for everyone she knew. Every time he saw her she read from the same script. If he were to disappear for ten years, then show up one morning at Club 34, they would have the identical conversation again.

Zink stepped in through the back door, carrying a case of cigarettes. He saw Crow, set the cardboard box on the floor by the cigarette machine, and joined him at the bar.

"Crow! What's going on?"

"Just stopped by for a Coke."

Zink wrinkled his face. "Come for the ambience, huh? By the way, thanks for busting up the game the other night."

"No problem."

"I mean it. That guy Ben was sucking up chips like a Hoover. What was he doing?"

"The first time I met him he was nicking aces and dealing seconds. But with his partner there, who knows. Could've been doing anything. One thing for sure, he would've kept on winning."

"Anyway, thanks. That's the first time we've had a problem like that."

"The first time you've known about."

"Uh-huh." He looked back at the case of cigarettes he had left on the floor. One of his customers, a yellow-skinned man with a sparse reddish beard and a navy-blue kerchief tied around his scrawny neck, was standing over it, weaving slightly, staring down at the assorted cartons as if he were a prospector who had discovered gold.

"Three bucks a pack, Jack," Zink snapped.

A full second later, the man jerked as if he had been touched by a whip. He looked toward Zink, who was shaking his head, then drifted back to the bar and held on to his last inch of beer.

"God, do I love this business," Zink said. "He'll make that beer last another hour, or until I kick him out." He pointed an index finger at his own temple. "Pow."

Zink could be morbid at times. Crow sipped his Coke.

"You want to help me load the cig machine?" Zink said.

"Sure. What do I do?"

"Stand guard."

Crow followed him to the end of the bar and watched him open the machine, tear open the cartons, and load the packs of cigarettes into the machine five at a time. After a few minutes, he reached past Zink's shoulder, grabbed a pack of Marlboros, walked over to the man with the blue kerchief, and set it on the bar. The man did not seem to notice.

Zink frowned and said, "He'll see it after a while. Probably think he bought it himself. You start giving stuff away to these guys, it never ends, Crow. It's like trying to fill a sink with no stopper in it."

"That's okay. I don't mind."

"Yeah? Well, you owe me three bucks for the smokes, pal."

"Take it out of my loan."

"What's that?"

"I've got a special game lined up, only I don't have the cash."

"What kind of game?"

"No limit. Probably draw poker. They still play a lot of that down there."

"Down where?"

"Chicago. A man down there owes me, but he's not the kind of guy that'll send me a check. I'm going to have to go take it."

"How are you gonna do that?"

"Live right."

Zink scratched his nose and loaded a column of Kools. "How much do you need?"

"Ten."

Zink winced.

"I'll have the ten back to you in three days, plus two for your trouble."

"Suppose you lose?"

"I've got insurance. It won't happen."

"Suppose it does?"

"Then I owe you ten grand."

Zink closed the face of the cigarette machine. "You must think I've got a lot of confidence in you, Crow. You know, if this doesn't work out, it's going to be real hard on our friendship, my friend."

"It'll work."

"When do you have to have it?"

"Tomorrow."

Zink carried the empty case to the back door and threw it out into the alley. The man with the blue kerchief had discovered the pack of Marlboros and was trying to open it. The big Swede was telling Cory another story about something he had built a long time ago.

Zink said to Crow, "Come by tomorrow, after two."

"Thanks. By the way, I'm having a little business meeting here in a few minutes. Hope you don't mind."

Zink squinted at Crow, then did a slow pan of his establishment, as though he had never been in it before. "You meeting one of your big clients or something?" he said.

Crow laughed. "Actually, I'm meeting with Ben Franklin. You remember him?"

"That card-nicking son-of-a-bitch? What makes you think I'm going to let him in the door?"

"I'll keep an eye on him. Won't let him steal a thing."

"I hope that's not who you're betting my ten grand on, Crow."

Crow shook his head. "This is a different deal. I just need to talk to him for a few minutes, then we'll be out of your hair."

Zink frowned and said, "I sure hope you know what you're doing, Crow." He ducked under the end of the bar and handed a book of matches to the man with the blue kerchief, who had succeeded in getting a smoke out of the pack and between his thin lips. Crow settled into a booth near the back door and watched the sluggish late-morning action slowly accelerate as the lunch hour drew near.

For the past few days, he had avoided thinking about the cabin on the island in Whiting Lake. Jimbo Bobick had left several messages on his machine, but Crow had put the dream on hold, filing it between the childhood memories and the cocaine fantasies in the basement of his mind. Later he would haul it up and take a look. Now he could not afford the distraction.

At exactly noon, Ben Fink stepped through the door, wearing a pale-beige sport coat and wrinkled blue trousers. He wiped his hand on his lapel and scanned the room. Crow watched from the back booth, remembering his own entrance into the bar's dark interior, knowing he was invisible. The lunch business was starting to happen, a few guys from the printing plant across the street catching a few quick brews, some of them even wolfing down a microwaved hot dog or slice of pizza. The jukebox was spinning a country song, something about ". . . now I drink to remember what I drank to forget." Both Zink and Cory were busy pouring beers and loading food in and out of the two microwave ovens.

Crow had suggested Club 34 because it was convenient—he had planned to talk to Zink anyway—and because he thought Ben Fink would be thrown off his act by the no-nonsense ambience of the establishment. Fink moved into the room with a fastidious frown. Eventually he spotted Crow and wove his way through the tables, chairs, and customers.

"What a lovely spot for a business meeting," he said, looking suspiciously at the vinyl seat.

"My favorite place," said Crow. He noticed Zink glaring at them from behind the bar.

Fink frowned, bent forward, and flicked something off the seat. He slid carefully into the booth. His tie, which had looked like a formal pattern from a distance, was revealed as a pattern of red-and-yellow Superman logos on a royal-blue ground.

"You want something to drink?"

"No, thank you. . . . I don't think the bartender likes me."

Crow nodded and sipped his Coke. He was curious but sensed he would learn more by letting Fink make his approach than by asking questions.

"Have you seen our friend Mr. Wicky lately?" Fink asked.

Crow smiled. He wasn't going to give away anything.

Fink waited for his answer, and his frown deepened. "I see," he said. "How much is this conversation going to cost me?"

"Just tell me what you want," said Crow.

Fink hunched forward and fixed Crow with his pale-brown eyes. "How do you feel about doing work for me, Mr. Crow?"

"It depends on the work and the pay. Especially the pay."

"Have you any remaining obligation to Mr. Wicky?"

"I'm done with Dickie."

Fink smiled and sat up straight. "Yes, I can understand that. I wish I could say the same. Unfortunately, our businesses are somewhat entangled at this point, and there are some things I need to know. Dickie has a client I wish to identify and locate. Dickie describes this person as an old man who lives somewhere in Saint Paul. Dickie also says this person owns a lake cabin somewhere north of the cities. This person had a brother named Vince, who died in 1951. I don't know much more than that. I want to know who he is, where he lives, and the location of his lake cabin. Do you think you could do that?"

"That's all you know?"

"Yes. And that Dickie has recently been in contact with him and will probably be in contact with him again soon."

Crow turned his empty Coke glass with his fingertips, as though he was tightening a knob or trying to screw the glass down into the table. "I'll do it for a flat fee of two thousand dollars, fifty percent up front, results guaranteed."

"That seems like a great deal of money for a job you might easily complete within a few hours."

"I don't want this job bad enough to negotiate with you, Fink. And I get a premium for anything to do with Dickie."

"How can you guarantee that you will find this person?"

"I'm very good at this sort of thing. Oh, and there's one other thing I want."

"Yes?"

"A few of those Stasis Shields."

Fink jerked as if he had been kicked in the shin. "What? Where did you hear about those?"

Crow tipped back his glass, took an ice cube into his mouth, and crushed it between his molars.

Fink winced. "Please don't do that. You could break a tooth. Why do you want the shields?"

"To hang on my wall."

Fink stared at Crow, his pale-brown eyes filled with dead light. "To hang on your wall?"

Crow smiled.

Fink sighed and moistened his lips. "You understand, of course, that you can't take the comics out and read them."

"They're phonies, right?"

"Only if you open the shield. If you use them for selling or trading, of course, it doesn't matter. Did you have some particular titles in mind?"

"Actually, I just want the shields themselves. I'll supply my own comic books. Before we talk about that, though, I want to know one thing. Am I working for you, or for you and Tommy Campo?"

Fink smiled. "You are working for me."

*The THING from the IDOL-HEAD of DIABOLU caused me
to lose my Martian powers and has turned my pal, ZOOK, into
a destructive giant!*

—*J'onn J'onzz, Manhunter from Mars* (House of Mystery #143)

Freddy's new tie looked like a baseball bat. The pattern was wood grain, the tip squared off like the end of a Louisville Slugger, and the Minnesota Twins *M* logo was imprinted on the sweet spot. Freddy couldn't keep his hands off it. A gift from his new friend, Rich.

Wicky watched him fingering the Twins logo with his greasy, sausage-size fingers and said, "Good thing about polyester, Fred, you can throw it right in the washing machine." He cut another slice of pepperoni pizza and offered it to Freddy, who had already finished the other pizza—hamburger and hot peppers—all by himself. They were sitting on the balcony of Wicky's condo, enjoying an early dinner. Wicky liked Freddy Wisnesky. He was like a dog—big, dumb, and vicious.

"Thanks"—Freddy belched—"Rich."

"You're welcome. You want another beer?"

"Sure."

Wicky went to the refrigerator and grabbed two more Mooseheads. He noticed that the cat's water dish was empty. He never saw the cat anymore; it had found a hiding place somewhere, under something or behind something. Wicky was mildly curious, but not curious enough to search. All he knew was that when he put food in the bowl it would eventually disappear. He opened the bottles, poured a few ounces from one of them into the water dish, and brought them back out onto the balcony. Sated with beer and pizza, Freddy was spacing out, staring sightlessly to the south, his mouth slack. Dickie set the beer beside the pizza boxes.

"You want to go see another game next week? The White Sox'll be in town. Your hometown team, huh?"

Freddy returned to planet Earth. "I come from Terre Haute," he said.

"Yeah, well, Terre Haute don't have a franchise, so you might as well go with the Sox. You could do worse. Listen, I was wondering if you could do me a favor, Fred."

"Sure."

"You know those two guys you've been looking for?"

Freddy nodded.

"I think I know how we can find them."

"Where?" said Freddy.

"I'm not sure yet. But when we find them, what I want is, I want you to hold off doing anything for a while."

"I have to take care of Mister C.'s business," Freddy said, his brow knotting at the prospect of conflicting orders.

"I know you do, and I'm going to help you find them so you can do that. But I have some business with them first. I have to take care of my business, then we can take care of Joey C.'s business. You've been trying to find them for weeks. All I'm asking is that once we find them you hold off until they find a buyer for my comic books."

"I dunno," Freddy said. He liked his new friend, Rich, but Mister C. was his boss.

"It's a win-win deal, Fred. I get what I want, and Mister C. gets what he wants. Everybody's happy."

"I gotta ask Mister C."

"Fine. Call him up. But wouldn't you rather wait a few days, then call him up and tell him you've got the job done? You call him up now, he's just going to yell at you like he did last time. Why upset him? Hold off a few days, Fred, then call and give him the good news."

Freddy felt Wicky's words on his mind like a barber's fingers giving him a scalp massage. It felt good to have somebody he liked telling him what to do. He liked it when Wicky called him "Fred." It was better than Freddy, which made him sound like a little kid, and it was a *lot* better than "Dipshit," which was what Mister C. had called him during their most recent conversation.

Wicky was still talking. Freddy tuned in.

". . . so what I want is for you to be my personal secretary for a few days—"

"Personal what?"

"Personal secretary. It means you just sort of hang out with me, like a buddy. And if anybody gives us any trouble, you break their arm."

Freddy brightened. "Sure," he said. "I guess that would be okay."

Catfish Wicky lit a cigarette and blew a geyser of blue smoke at the ceiling. Her eyes were bright, her mouth soft and satisfied. As she watched the plume of smoke break apart on the white acoustic tiles, her mouth curved into a broad smile. She said, "You realize, of course, that we're going to have to give Dickie back his ten thousand."

She turned her head to look at Tom Campo, and both of them burst into laughter, hers throaty and deep, his more like the nervous yipping of a terrier.

"Do you think he's for real?" Tommy asked after he stopped laughing.

"With this comic thing? Probably. You know, he really believed in you all. I still can't hardly believe it. I mean, I thought when I introduced you guys that he understood that the fund was for selling, not for buying."

"A good salesman buys his own line," Tommy said. "Never fails."

"That sounds like something Ben would say."

"It is. He says it all the time. I get pretty sick of it, all the things he likes to say. Hey, how about we call room service and get us some food. My stomach is going, 'Feed me.' "

Catfish reached for the phone on the end table, punched in the number for room service, and handed him the phone. She smoked her cigarette and watched him order sandwiches, beer, coffee, pie, and milk. "You want anything?" he asked. She shook her head.

"I don't think Ben likes me," she said.

"Ben thinks you just like to stir things up. Hell, he don't like anybody, when it comes right down to it. I think he's got some kind of mental problem. All he likes to do is play the ponies. It's like he's got no pulse. If he wins or loses, it's the same. And he doesn't trust anybody."

"Except you."

"Except me, right."

"So what are you all planning to do about Dickie?"

"Ben says find out if this comic deal of his is for real. Then we'll take it from there."

"You going to give him the fund like he wants? And loan him the money?"

Tommy shrugged. "That's what Ben wants to do. He says the fund is history, says we can't milk it no more. He thinks we can do this last deal and come out of it looking good. We put up the cash, sell the collection fast, maybe sell it to Kansas City Walt, and move on."

"You don't agree?"

"I don't know. Ben is usually right. What d'you think?"

"I think Benny is getting too set in his ways, that's what I think."

When the food arrived, Catfish took the blueberry pie.

"I thought you didn't want anything," Tommy complained.

She forked a piece into her mouth. "I didn't know it would look this good. Can I have some of your milk?"

The 7:00 P.M. flight to O'Hare cost Crow $321 out of Zink's ten thousand, but it was far better than spending eight hours on I-90 getting his ass massaged in Sam's truck. Just driving it to the airport had been an ordeal.

As always, O'Hare was efficient, impossible, and utterly disorienting. It took him half an hour to find Debrowski, and even then he probably wouldn't have recognized her if she hadn't been arguing with a young, efficient-looking airport cop. Her rented Lincoln was parked in a Loading and Unloading Only zone, a situation to which the cop was taking justifiable exception. Debrowski's voice was distinctive. Crow walked quickly down the sidewalk, hoping to intercede before she climbed out of the car and punched the poor guy. He threw his briefcase—a battered vinyl Samsonite—into the back seat and got into the car with an apologetic shrug to the cop.

"Let's go, before he decides to tag us."

She fluttered her made-up eyes at him and banged down the accelerator. The cop hopped back up on the curb to get out of the way.

"What was that all about?"

Debrowski laughed. "I guess I have a problem with guys in uniform." She was wearing nylons and heels, and a green dress that might have looked natural on Vanna White. Big white bow on the front, like a birthday present.

"How do you make your hair do that?" Crow asked. Her hair had expanded. Her face seemed to be peeking out of a big blond ball.

"It's a wig, Crow. Aren't I beautiful?"

"Lovely."

"Chrissy has hair like this, only hers is real. It gave us a jumping-off point when I first met her. A woman like that, you always start out talking hair. You think Joey Cadillac is going to remember me?"

"Is it worth the risk? I don't like the idea of him seeing you, no matter how much hair you've got on your head. Your lip looks like it's healing up."

"Makeup, Crow. You can do anything with enough foundation."

"You're enjoying this, aren't you?"

"I never got to play Barbie when I was growing up. Don't worry about it, Crow. There's no way he's going to recognize me. Do I look like Debrowski the chain-swinging biker bitch to you?"

"You look like a mannequin."

"Thank you! You're looking pretty ornamental yourself there, Crow."

Crow wore a lightweight buff-colored silk jacket, big shoulders, over a blue-striped cotton dress shirt. His navy linen trousers were already hopelessly wrinkled, which was why he never wore the things, but they looked expensive. With his faux-crocodile loafers and the fake Rolex watch, he looked, in a casual way, like a guy that might actually have some loose money.

"The traffic is intense, Crow. We're going to be a little late; it's after eight already."

"That's good," said Crow. "Late is good."

During the drive to Chrissy Swenson's condo, she filled him in on what she had learned. Crow listened, watching her drive the Lincoln, admiring the way she attacked the Chicago traffic, one hand on the horn, the other spinning the big steering wheel, moving in and out of lanes as skillfully as any cabbie.

"You think the other players are legit guys?" Crow asked.

"As far as I can tell, except for Jimmy Spencer. According to Chrissy, who doesn't like him much, he runs a chop shop for Joey C. Joey likes to economize on his parts cost. She says Spencer almost always wins, but not big. But it sounds like a fairly straight card game. She says Joey usually wins big, but not always. Thor Kjellgard and Joey's cousin Tony—the guy who owns the restaurant where I met Chrissy—are both surefire losers. Wexler, the alderman, usually drops a few thousand. Chrissy's really looking forward to this."

"So we're all set, then."

"Barring complications, I'd say yes. How are you feeling?"

Crow considered. "Tired and hungry. Just right for poker."

Joey was in an expansive, back-slapping mood, which meant that every time he got within five feet of her he wanted a little kiss and a squeeze. Chrissy didn't mind that so much, but she hated the winking and tongue wiggles he gave to the other players after each brief tableside encounter. She spent as much time as possible clinking things around in the kitchen, staying out of range, waiting for the game to get serious so he'd forget about her. She wished Laura would hurry up and get there.

Joey was telling the guys the burglar-eaten-by-dogs story.

The first time Chrissy had heard the burglar story, it had gone something like this: One night a fourteen-year-old kid decided to climb the fence at J.C. Motors, apparently with the idea of boosting a few CD players. Unfortunately for the would-be thief, Joey C. had a contract with K-9 Patrol Services, and a pair of Rottweilers were on the job. When the K-9 people showed up at six-thirty the next morning to pick up the dogs, they found the terrified kid wrapped around a drainpipe twelve feet up the wall of the office building. The two Rotts were standing at attention below, growling and snarling, as they had been for over four hours. When the cops showed up, and later the ambulance, they had to dislocate two of the kid's fingers to get him down off the drainpipe. He was missing about eight ounces of flesh from his butt and upper thigh, enough for two small breakfast steaks.

Joey had told her that version of the story the night after it happened, almost a year ago. At that time, he had told her that the young burglar had been taken to the hospital and survived with no more to show for his ordeal than a slight limp and a horror of all brown-and-black dogs. Since then, she had watched the tale evolve.

"So I get to work—I like to get in early, y'know—and these two Rotts, supposed to be guarding the place, they're all laid out on the ground, fast asleep, bellies bulging like a couple cooked sausages." Joey grabbed a handful of peanuts from the dish at his elbow, threw a few into his mouth, and bit down on them, looking from face to face. Kjellgard and Spence had heard the story before and were wearing neutral expressions. Cousin Tony and Wexler the alderman were leaning forward, listening with some interest. It was Joey's turn to deal, and there would be no more cards until he finished telling his tale. He washed the peanuts down with his Remy and diet Coke, then continued his story.

"So I'm thinking, I'm gonna have to get myself a new guard dog service. These mutts couldn't protect this place from a damn rat. Then I notice this big stain on my driveway. I go, What the fuck? I think its tranny fluid at first, 'cause it's sort of pink and red, and then I take another look at these two dogs, all bloody on their faces, and I think, These fucking mutts have killed themselves a cat or something, y'know? So I give one of them a kick on account of I'm pissed, getting my driveway all messed up like that. Dog jumps up and starts doing that hunching thing dogs do when they're gonna puke, then he blows breakfast all over the place." Something about the image of dogs vomiting made Joey laugh. Cousin Tony politely joined in.

"I'm going, What the fuck? What the fuck are these fucking dogs doing to my fucking driveway?" He opened his eyes as wide as possible and looked from face to face, demanding reaction from each of them. When he was satisfied that everyone at the table appreciated his dilemma, he went for the big finish. Chrissy sat up and paid attention here, repelled but curious to see how Joey was going to end it this time.

"So I look down at this pile of vomit, and I see something sitting right on top. I just about lost my own breakfast right there, damn near barfed my eggs Benedict all over my fucking shoes!"

Again he laughed, looking around the table.

"It was a fucking *nigger dick*! Turned out some black kid jumped the fence, and these Rotts, they're big dogs, they ate the fucker, bones and all."

"They ate everything?" cousin Tony asked. Tony was in the restaurant business.

"Yeah. Bones and all. So when K-9 came around to pick up the dogs, I told them they owed me a discount, on account of they wouldn't have to feed 'em for a couple days."

Chrissy had to leave the room. She was ready to talk Technicolor herself. Every time Joey told the story, a different body part was up-chucked, but it was always a *nigger* toe, or a *nigger* ear, or a *nigger* finger.

When she came back to the room, Joey was dealing a hand of five-card draw, a freshly lit Davidoff clenched in his teeth. Chrissy took her position at his elbow and watched, waiting for the next player to demand a drink, or more chips, or a quick neck massage. It was going to be a long, smoky night. She thought about her bank account, about the thirty thousand she had socked away, thinking about making it forty or fifty thousand, thinking she could then afford to move on to another guy. The phone rang. She picked it up.

"Yes?" A smile spread across her face. "Sure, Cal. You send them right on up. Thanks."

She turned to Joey, who was looking at her with raised eyebrows. "Your other player is here," she said.

◆ ♥ 29 ♣ ♠
THE RIVER

If you haven't figured out who the fish is in your first half hour at the table, it's probably you.

—Poker saying

Crow entered slowly, letting himself absorb the scene in Chrissy Swenson's condo. The layout was disorienting at first. To his left, down two steps, a sitting area or conversation pit that the rental agent had no doubt described as "cozy" was filled with a white leather sectional sofa. It looked cold and uncomfortable, as if no one ever sat there. The glass coffee table held a copy of *Architec-*

tural Digest. To his right, three green-carpeted steps, eight feet wide, led up to a tiny kitchen, a hallway, and a larger space that might have been intended as a dining area but was now serving as a cardroom.

Chrissy grabbed Debrowski by both hands and whispered, "I'm so glad you're here!" She looked at Crow. "Is this Joe?"

Crow smiled.

"He's *cute*!" Chrissy said.

"You're cute too," Crow said. "Sorry we're late. Laura here had a problem with the traffic."

Debrowski smiled and gave him a light but sharp kick on the ankle.

Chrissy said, "Oh, God, I know. Isn't it awful? You two come on in and let me introduce you to Joey and the guys." She pulled them toward the dining area.

Joey and the guys were finishing up a hand of draw poker. A chubby guy in a white cotton sweater, black hair combed straight back over a bald spot—Crow figured him to be Joey Cadillac—had just raised the pot by two stacks of blue chips. A blond man with a big Nordic face stared at his cards, thinking about it. That would be Kjellgard, the Swede. Joey Cadillac was drumming his fingers, scratching his nose, stretching his neck, puffing on his cigar, waiting for Kjellgard to make up his mind. Crow liked playing against a guy with lots of nervous mannerisms. They were all tells, once they were decoded. The Swede decided to go for it, pushed a pile of chips out into the center of the table. Crow realized then that the Swede was not all that big in his body, but his head was enormous. His small hands flipped over two pair, nines over fours. Joey Cadillac grinned, showed him three deuces, scooped in the chips, emitted a thick cloud of smoke, then looked up at Crow and Debrowski.

"You Chrissy's friends?"

Crow nodded. "Joe Crow. This is my friend Laura."

Chrissy jumped in. "They're from Minneapolis."

Joey's eyes narrowed. He started to say something but closed his mouth.

Chrissy said, "This's Joey. Next to him, that's Jimmy—"

"Call me Spence," said Jimmy Spencer, with a crinkly-eyed smile that made Crow want to back slowly out of the room. The smile was too practiced, too cold.

The slim, elegant-looking man closest to Crow stood up and offered him his hand. "Tony Battagno," he said, with a genuine smile.

"Good to meet you, Joe." Crow shook his hand and liked him immediately. Tony was wearing a suit and tie, his hair was silver on the sides, full and jet black on top. He was a guy who took a lot of time to make sure he looked good, but not in a vain, pretentious way. Crow's sense was that he wanted to look nice for his friends. Tony continued the introductions that Chrissy had started. "This is Bobby Wexler, our prestigious alderperson—"

"How you doing?" Wexler, the chunky alderman, rumpled gray suit with no tie, shifted in his chair and wiggled his hand in the air—a truncated version of standing and shaking hands.

"—and Thor Kjellgard." The Swede with the big head nodded.

Joey said, "You want to sit down, get this game rolling?"

"What's the game?" asked Crow. He took the empty seat between Wexler and Tony Battagno.

"Five draw, seven stud, or Hold 'em—dealer's choice," Joey said to Crow. "No new games, no limit. Twenty-dollar ante. Cash plays, but we like chips. Chrissy's the bank; you buy your chips from her."

Crow turned to Chrissy, who was standing directly behind him. "Let's start with ten thousand," he said.

He handed her a thick packet of hundred-dollar bills. Chrissy counted out an assortment of chips—white, red, blue, and black—and set them on the table in front of him. "What have I got here?" he asked her.

"Whites are ten, reds twenty, blues one hundred, blacks five hundred," Chrissy said. "You want something to drink?"

"Yeah. How about a rum and Coke. Have Laura make it for me, though. She knows how I like them." Crow looked over the other players' stacks. He hadn't yet made his first bet, and already he was looking light. Only Wexler, the alderman, was sitting on a smaller stack.

"The gray chips are worth a thousand?" Chrissy hadn't given him any grays.

"That's right," said Joey, who had at least twenty grays in front of him, in addition to another twenty thousand in assorted smaller-denomination chips. He obviously liked to play behind a big stack.

"Table stakes?" Crow asked.

"Only if you're tapped," said Spencer, whose own stack was nearly the size of Joey's. "Ante up, gentlemen. This is Texas Hold 'em." He gave Joey the cut, then dealt two cards to each player. Crow looked at his cards. Seven, deuce. A beer hand. Tony bet twenty dollars. Crow folded and sat back to watch and learn. Both Bobby Wexler and Thor Kjellgard called the bet without hesitating. Joey raised it up to one hundred dollars; Spencer folded, Tony folded, Wexler and Kjellgard called the raise. Already, Crow was forming his line on the players.

Kjellgard and Wexler were callers on the first bet. They would probably always be callers. They wanted to see the flop every time, no matter what two cards they caught on the deal. Joey Cadillac was clearly a pot jammer and would be the most aggressive player at the table. If he caught good cards, he would make a lot of money. He could also lose big on a run of second-best hands. From what Chrissy had told them, he usually swung twenty or thirty thousand one way or the other. Crow wasn't sure about Jimmy Spencer, but he looked like a tough player. Tough and tight with his money. Joey C.'s chop-shop guy.

Tony looked out of place, too elegant and open to do well in what promised to be a nasty game. Debrowski set Crow's rum and Coke in front of him, then pulled up a chair and sat at his elbow. Chrissy took a similar station behind Joey. Crow sniffed, smelled the quarter ounce of rum floating on top of the Coke, and sipped. The false high hit him in the back of the neck. He felt his scalp lifting, then settling back into place. He watched the hand play out, watched Joey Cadillac turn over a full boat to take Bobby Wexler—who had been playing trip sixes—for an easy five thousand. Wexler lit a cigarette and watched, eyes watering, as Joey scooped the pot for the second time in a row. Crow thought, If he keeps catching cards like that, we might as well just give him our money and hitchhike home. Still, it was good for Joey to be winning the money. The more he won from the other players, the more Crow could win from him. He took a deep breath and another sip of his drink, his hindbrain wishing fervently that the imagined jolt was real.

It took another twenty minutes for him to make Joey Cadillac's shit list.

It was a small Hold 'em pot, Tony dealing, and all the players except for Crow, Wexler, and Joey had folded before the flop. Crow was holding an ace, deuce. The flop came up five, jack, king, giving him nothing but a long shot at a straight, plus an overcard. Wexler bet a hundred, Crow called, Joey raised two hundred. Both Wexler and Crow called the raise. The turn brought another jack. Joey bet five hundred. Wexler scratched his nose with a stubby forefinger and folded.

Crow looked at Joey and considered. Chrissy was blinking both eyes, as though the cigar smoke was getting to her.

Crow said, "Raising it up, Cadillac man." He threw three five-hundred-dollar chips into the pot.

Joey stared across the table at Crow, slowly counted off a stack of chips, and raised back an equal amount. Crow called.

Tony dealt a seven. Chrissy's eyes were bothering her again. Crow bet three thousand. Joey scowled at his cards and threw them away.

"Thanks," said Crow. He turned his cards faceup and collected the pot. Joey stared at Crow's ace, deuce, turning slowly red, color radiating from the cigar in the center of his mouth.

"What the fuck were you doing in there?" he demanded.

"Messing with your head, Cadillac man."

"Listen, Crow, you can call me Joey or you can call me Mister Cadillac. You understand?"

"Sure thing, guy. Hey, you got any more of those cigars?"

Joey took the cigar out of his mouth and looked at it, then flicked his eyes back at Crow. "You take my money, then you want me to give you a cigar? You're lucky I don't stick it in your fucking eye."

"Hey, fellas," said Wexler. "We here to play cards or what? Come on!"

Joey held the glare for a few more seconds, then smiled and laughed. "Just kidding. It's your deal, Bobby. Hey, Chrissy, you want to clip a fresh smoke for my friend Crow, here? I hope you appreciate it, Crow. Cuban Davidoffs; they don't make 'em anymore. Cost me twenty-five bucks each."

"I like a good cigar," Crow said.

"The game is seven stud," Bobby Wexler announced. "Jack, nine, another nine, a lady for Tony, a cowboy for the Crow, dealer gives himself the big ace. That ought to be worth one little blue chip for starters. What do you say, Thor?"

Joey returned his attention to his cards, but Crow could see the flicker of his eyes, every few beats, checking him out.

Something was nagging at Joey's mind, something about Joe Crow and his girlfriend. He looked at his cards, two and six down, with a nine up top. Rags. He checked, then folded when Crow bet fifty on a king of hearts. Something about the guy? Joey watched him light the cigar. The guy looked like a slob, all wrinkled up, but his clothes had some style and he was wearing a nice watch. The face looked familiar, like he was on the TV. Or maybe it was the chick, Laura. Had he met her before? She wasn't bad, nice hair, and that big white bow over her tits made you want to tug it open. Maybe it was just that all the shit in his life lately was flowing down from Minneapolis. The comic book guys, Freddy Wisnesky, and that Rich character. What was going on up there? Were they sending all the assholes south?

Joey watched Crow win a small pot, about five hundred bucks. Joey didn't like his style, whoever he was. Fucking with him, asking him for a twenty-five-dollar cigar like he was bumming a ten-cent cigarette. And the way he was smoking it, holding it like a prop, making big clouds of smoke, not taking the time to savor the Cuban tobacco. He might as well have given him a twenty-five-cent Dutch Master. What did he know about this guy? Chrissy's friend's friend. Could be anybody. Chrissy had said the guy was some kind of businessman who loved to play cards and usually lost. Crow didn't look much like a businessman, and he wasn't losing.

Kjellgard dealt a hand of five-card draw. Joey was looking at trip cowboys, three beautiful kings. He sandbagged, checking, letting Spence open the pot, then raising it up. They folded like dominoes. Joey stacked his winnings, feeling the power that came with a big stack. Fuck Joe Crow from Minneapolis and all the rest of them. This was Joey C.'s game all the way. He shuffled the deck, spread a hand of Hold 'em, peeked at his down cards. Wired bullets. Yeah, this was his game, all right. He looked over his shoulder at Chrissy, giving her a look at his cards.

She was scratching her nose. "You got fleas or something?" he asked. She smiled and dropped her hand quickly to her lap.

Spence and Tony checked. Joe Crow examined his cards, puffing on his cigar, taking his time.

"You gonna bet or not?" Joey asked.

Crow raised his eyebrows and stubbed out the cigar—less than an inch of it smoked—breaking it right in half in the ashtray. "This smokes a little harsh," he said. "These Havanas aren't what they used to be. I think I'll just fold this hand."

Joey's eyes and mouth bulged, then got very small. He stared at the wreck of the cigar, his wired aces momentarily forgotten, and thought about feeding Joe Crow to the Rottweilers.

Crow wished that Chrissy would take it easy with the signals. Anybody looking at her would think she had some kind of nervous disorder. He could feel Debrowski, who was sitting obediently at his elbow, tensing up every time Chrissy went into her routine.

They had agreed on three simple signals, which was all Debrowski had thought Chrissy could handle. The blink signal, several quickly repeated blinks, meant that Joey was bluffing, that he had nothing. Since Joey loved to play in every hand, Chrissy had been doing a lot of blinking. The nose-scratch signal meant that he had a strong hand, a high pair or better, something he could win with. The lip bite, which she had not yet employed, meant that he had a come hand—a four flush or a four-card straight. Considering the energy with which she had conveyed the blink and the nose scratch, the lip bite would be something to see.

He asked Debrowski to mix him another rum and Coke. She took his glass into the kitchen. A moment later, she called to Chrissy for help. He hoped she could calm her down a bit, before one of the other players started to wonder what was going on. The two women returned to their posts. Crow sipped his freshened drink, willing the trace of alcohol to proceed directly to his brain.

The next quarter hour went by without any new contortions from Chrissy. Crow lost a small pot to Spence, then watched the other players battle it out over the next several hands. Finally, while holding a pair of sixes in five-card draw, he thought he saw the blink signal.

Or did he? It was hard to tell. Had Debrowski told her to tone down the signals? Had he seen a meaningless eyelid flutter, or was she telling him that Joey had shit for cards? He couldn't decide. Joey Cadillac opened with a one-thousand-dollar bet. Spence folded; Tony called. Crow considered his position. He wasn't sure he had seen the blink signal. On the other hand, she wasn't scratching her nose or biting her lip. He decided to play the hand. To knock out Wexler and the Swede, neither of whom looked all that interested in the hand, he raised it up to three thousand.

Joey sneered and called. Tony folded.

Both Joey and Crow drew three cards. Crow made sixes and treys, two pair. Not a great hand, but a hand. The odds were, Joey hadn't improved at all. Crow looked at Chrissy. She blinked a few times, raised a hand, touched herself lightly near her nose, let the hand fall back to her lap, shifted in her chair, bit her lip lightly. Each action appeared to be entirely natural, unlike the exaggerated signals he had seen before. She looked bored.

Crow thought, What the hell am I supposed to do with that?

He checked. Joey bet five thousand. Crow considered, and decided to play the hand as if Chrissy had done nothing. He called the bet.

Joey showed him jacks over deuces. Crow watched him gather in the chips, thinking that if he hadn't been paying so much attention to Chrissy's signals, or lack thereof, he would never have been in the hand. Another mistake like that and he would be out of the game.

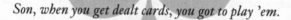

♦ ♥ **30** ♣ ♠

Son, when you get dealt cards, you got to play 'em.

—*Sam O'Gara*

Chrissy was both bored and frustrated. Joey wasn't getting any good cards, or any really bad cards. But he was winning. There were a few times when she could have let Laura and Joe Crow know that all he had was, like, a pair of jacks, but she didn't know how to do that. What was really bugging her was that her nose itched like crazy, and the cigar smoke was bothering her eyes. She was waiting for the big hand, waiting for Joey to make the big play, and hope it was when Joe Crow was in there with something good.

It seemed, a few times, like it was going to happen, but every time Joey tried to buy a pot, it seemed, one of the other players was in there too, or Joe Crow had already dropped, or something else went wrong. There were too many things that had to come together. She knew it would take a while, maybe all night, but that didn't mean she had to like it.

The game had been going on for almost six hours. Joe Crow was winning, but so was Joey.

Thor Kjellgard dealt a hand of seven stud. Joey caught an ace of hearts. She peeked at his hole cards. He bet two hundred. Everybody but Tony stayed in to see his next card. Chrissy yawned.

Crow liked his wired black aces, and he liked the ten of spades he had showing. He liked his fourth card too: the queen of spades. A pair of aces and three cards to a straight flush. Very nice cards. When Joey bet five hundred, Crow raised five hundred. Wexler and Kjellgard both called. Joey had an ace, eight showing, both hearts. He took another look at his hole cards and said, "Raise again." He pushed two thousand dollars into the pot.

Wexler groaned.

Chrissy was blinking, staring right at Crow. Well, Crow thought, there's no mistaking that.

"And four," he said.

Wexler couldn't throw his hand away fast enough. Kjellgard pretended to consider it, faked a reach for his chips, then shrugged and folded. Joey turned his cigar in his mouth, as if he was screwing it into a socket, and smooth-called.

Crow felt his stomach start a slow roll. If it was a bluff, as Chrissy was signaling, Joey Cadillac should have either raised or folded. What could he have? The other pair of aces? Then why would Chrissy be giving the blink signal? Had she misread his cards? Even worse, was it possible that she was working with Joey?

Kjellgard dealt the fifth card, a ten of hearts to Joey and a three of spades to Crow, giving him a four flush to go with his pair of bullets. Chrissy was blinking and biting her lower lip, not a flattering look.

Joey checked.

Crow sorted through the possibilities. The lip bite signaled a come hand—four cards to a straight or flush—and Joey had three hearts showing. If he had a fourth heart in the hole—with two cards yet to come—that made it about a one-in-three chance he would fill his flush. Crow had the same chance at his own flush. But then why would Chrissy be blinking, signaling the bluff? Maybe she had gotten scared and decided to double back, working for Joey now, or maybe she had been working for him all along. But if that was true, he would have lost his money hours ago. And why would she be bothering with the lip-bite signal? The blink would be enough to suck him in.

Another possibility—maybe she was trying to tell him something. Like that Joey had a come hand, which she would signal with a lip bite, but that he was also bluffing. If he was drawing to a flush, or trying to improve a high pair, she wouldn't be blinking, trying to tell him Joey was bluffing. The only hand that made sense would be a gut-shot straight. Bluffing but hoping to get lucky and catch that perfect card. With two cards to come, that gave him about a one-in-six chance. A semi-bluff. Did Chrissy know enough about the game to call it that way?

It was also possible that Chrissy was a complete airhead—so out of it that nothing she did could have any useful meaning. She was giving him the mixed signal again. Crow could feel Debrowski's breath on his shoulder. Joey was waiting, playing with his chips. He looked to Crow like a man who would play a gut shot.

He also looked like a man who could get lucky.

Crow decided to go for it now, buy the pot before the cards could betray him. He pushed out five tall stacks of black chips, almost everything he had. He could hear Debrowski breathe in and hold it.

"Ten thousand."

Again, Joey smooth-called, adding his gray chips to the pot as if they were nickels.

Crow did not like that at all.

Kjellgard gave Joey a nine of diamonds. Joey's cigar perked up. Crow didn't like that, either. He especially did not like the way Chrissy was scratching her nose. It looked like she was going to hurt herself. It looked like Joey had made his inside draw. The thing about gut shots was, if you play them you sometimes make them. Bad beats can happen to the nicest guys.

Crow stared down at his lousy four of hearts, a rag if ever there was one. He looked at his remaining chips—less than a thousand dollars. He waited for Joey to bet, feeling sick, knowing that the odds had failed him once again.

"What have you got there, fella?" Joey asked. "Can you cover a little two-thousand-dollar bet?"

There was thirty-five thousand dollars on the table. He still had one chance in five to make his flush. The pot odds were good. He counted out his chips. Nine hundred twenty dollars. He pushed them forward.

"I'm a thousand eighty light."

Kjellgard looked at Joey—who nodded, accepting the marker—and dealt the final card facedown.

Joey didn't even bother to look.

Crow lifted the corner of his own card. It was black, a jack, a jack of spades. His heart went wild, doing a tarantella inside his rib cage. He had the son-of-a-bitch. It would take a higher flush or a concealed full house to beat him, and he didn't think Joey Cadillac was going to come up with either.

His face remained utterly placid. He looked at Joey.

Joey took the cigar out of his mouth and said, "What the hell. I check."

"Ten," Crow said.

Joey said, "What?" Like he couldn't believe what he was hearing.

"I bet another ten thousand," Crow said.

Joey looked at Crow's cards, then picked up his own last card, checked it, and looked again at Crow's three spades showing.

"That's bullshit. You've got no money on the table. The betting is over, Crow. Table stakes, remember?"

"It wasn't table stakes a minute ago when you overbet my stack," Crow said.

Joey screwed his cigar into his mouth. His eyes, nose, and chin all seemed to crowd around the fuming Havana.

"He's right, Joey," Tony said. "You took his marker."

A new shade of red, starting low on his neck and rising, stained Joey's constricted features.

"That was for a lousy grand," he said. "I don't know this guy good enough that I want to take his marker for ten K."

Spence said to Crow, "He's right about that, fella. That's a lot of money, since none of us knows you."

"I don't got to take any bet like that without you got something to back it up," Joey said, relaxing slightly. "You got to show me some cash."

Crow said, "You want to grab my briefcase there, Laur?"

Debrowski went to retrieve Crow's battered Samsonite from where he'd left it by the front door.

Joey said, "Spence!"

Spence got up and took the case from Debrowski. "Never know what you might come up with here, honey." He opened the case, frowned, shrugged, and handed it to Crow.

Crow removed three flat plastic packages. He dropped them on the table in front of Joey. "These are worth three to four thousand each. There's a signed and notarized appraisal dated last May attached to the backs."

Joey looked down at the Stasis Shields. The one on top showed the same *Batman* cover he had tried to open for Chrissy two months ago. *Batman* #3. He savored the moment for about ten seconds.

"Where did you get these?" he asked.

"I bought them," Crow said.

"From *who*?"

"What difference does that make? They're worth a lot of money. The appraisals are right there. You want to take my bet or not?"

"From who?" Joey was up out of his chair, waving a Stasis Shield under Crow's nose. He was grinning, his face aflame.

Crow pushed back and crossed his arms. "The Franklin Jefferson Investment Group, if you must know. They specialize in rare ephemera."

Joey slammed the Stasis Shield back down on the table. "You dumb shit," he said. "These aren't worth a fucking nickel."

"What are you talking about?" asked Crow.

Joey pulled out his miniature pocket stiletto; the three-inch blade flicked out. He turned the knife in his hand and stabbed it through one of the shields.

"Hey!" Crow said, starting around the table. He was blocked by one of Spence's arms, like running into a steel pipe. Joey ripped the knife across the face of the Mylar shield, tore it open the rest of the way, and pulled out the comic book, which had been sliced along with the shield. Joey shook the comic open; pages fell loose, fluttering to the table and floor.

"See!" he shouted at Crow. "You stupid fuck, you got burned. There's nothing there! It's a fake!" Joey looked at the shredded remains of the comic book and experienced a very bad rush in his belly region. The torn pages were not blank, as they had been with *his* copy of *Batman* #3. In fact, the comic book seemed to be quite genuine.

Crow said, "I guess you're right. There's nothing there anymore, that's for sure." He picked up the white card that had been sealed in with the comic. "This one was appraised at thirty-eight hundred dollars. You want to take it as is, or do you want it gift-wrapped? How do you want to handle it, Cadillac man?"

Joey was staring down at the remains of the comic book. "Those fuckers," he said. He didn't understand what was happening, but he knew he was getting fucked again. If Wexler, Kjellgard, and cousin Tony hadn't been sitting there watching, he'd just have had Spence take Crow down to the parking ramp and do a little Harlem Globetrotters with his head. Crow was looking at him, same stupid expression on his face. The guy looked about half as bright as Freddy Wisnesky. "Where'd you get this fuckin' thing? Goddamn it, quit staring at me like a fuckin' wooden Indian. I'll pay you for your goddamn comic book! Where'd you get it?"

Crow said, "I told you. Franklin Jefferson Investments. Now you want to take my bet?"

Joey gripped the edge of the table, practicing self-control. It felt as though he had a rib cage full of monkeys, clawing at his skin from the inside. He grabbed the remains of the comic in a fist, crumpled it, threw it back over his shoulder.

Spence said, "Be cool, Mister C. It's gonna be okay." He was smiling, one hand on Joey's shoulder.

Joey shot him a look, then forced himself back down into his seat. With Kjellgard and Wexler there, not to mention Tony, there wasn't much he could do. "We got to have a talk, you and me, later," he said to Crow. He threw four gray chips into the pot. "That's for the comic. You wanted to bet ten? Now you're light seven." He picked up his cigar, only three inches left now, and relit it, staring through the gathering smoke at Joe Crow.

After a time, Tony Battagno said, "It's up to you, Joey."

"I know that, goddamn it!" He reached for his dwindling stack and considered the chips with his fingers. He looked again at his cards. A straight to the ten. In light of Crow's raise, the straight didn't look as good as it had a few minutes ago. But he couldn't fold now. Maybe he should raise, really blow the guy's mind.

Fuck it. After the comic book thing, he didn't have the heart for it.

"I call." He pushed ten thousand dollars into the pot. "Let's see 'em."

Crow showed his flush. Joey looked at Spence, then back at Crow.

He shrugged and forced out a laugh. It sounded like an old man's cough.

"Good thing we give it all back at the end of the night, right, guys?" His mouth smiling, his little black eyes dead on Crow's impassive face.

Everybody laughed.

At four in the morning, Thor Kjellgard announced that he was leaving after one more round. He was down only a few thousand dollars, a good time to leave. Tony said that sounded good to him too. He was ready to hit the sack.

"What a bunch of flyweights," Joey said.

Crow said, "I'm out of here too. Sorry, guys. I've got to be back in Minneapolis by tonight. Long drive." He had somewhat over fifty thousand dollars in front of him, nearly all of it from Joey Cadillac, whose stack was down to about fifteen thousand dollars.

Spence had been winning modestly. Wexler and Tony were each within a thousand dollars of even.

Since the hand where Crow had taken him for nearly thirty K, Joey had calmed down considerably, but he had continued to lose. It didn't seem to matter to him anymore. He laughed every time Crow swept in a pot.

Crow didn't want to ride down in the elevator without Thor Kjellgard and Tony. He had the feeling that Joey wouldn't try anything with any of his legitimate buddies in the vicinity. Joey had been acting far too sanguine about his losses; he was playing as if it didn't matter whether he won or lost. Crow was remembering the solid feel of Spence's arm across his abdomen. The real challenge was not to win the money; it was to keep it.

Joey played the last round aggressively, buying most of the pots. No one, at this late hour, wanted to play against him. That was fine with Crow. Let him win a few hands. Crow was happy with his take. Spence dealt the last hand, five-card draw. Crow was ready to fold—he had no desire for a final confrontation—but when he looked at his cards he found four jacks and an eight. He looked across the table. Joey Cadillac was staring at him, his little eyes like black olives.

Tony checked. Crow checked. Wexler bet one hundred, and Kjellgard folded.

Joey raised the bet to five hundred. Spence folded, Tony called the raise.

Crow considered his cards. They were too damn good. He had been watching Spence deal all night, and the guy clearly was no card mechanic. But four jacks? Last hand of the night? There was no way. It had to be a cooler. Spence had probably set up another deck during one of his trips to the bathroom, kept it between his legs, and switched it in somehow. Had Joey cut the cards? Crow couldn't remember.

But he didn't believe the four jacks. You just don't get dealt in four jacks.

Chrissy was scratching her nose again. It was all red on one side. Crow placed his cards facedown on the table and pushed them forward.

"I fold," he said.

He thought Joey was going to explode. He watched Wexler call the raise. Tony and Wexler both drew two. Joey stood pat—no surprise there; he probably had a straight flush. Another round of betting, raising, and re-raising brought the pot up to over twelve thousand dollars, with all three players staying in. Crow was guessing that both Wexler and Tony had been dealt in trips, with one or both of them improving on the draw. Of course, if the deck was a cooler, his dropping out might have screwed up Wexler's draw.

He was right about Wexler and Tony. Tony turned over three aces. Wexler had a pair of fours to his three sevens, making a full house. They both looked at Joey, who threw his cards away.

Wexler dragged in the chips and started arranging them by color in neat stacks of twenty.

"You got to show 'em, Joey. You were called," Tony complained, reaching for the cards and flipping them up. A little flush, ten high. Joey crossed his arms and glared at Wexler.

Crow sighed, thinking about his four jacks. He started to count his chips and made a new rule for himself: *When somebody deals you four jacks, you bet the hell out of them.*

Crow and Debrowski rode down in the elevator with Thor Kjellgard and Bobby Wexler.

"That was some hand you played," Wexler said.

"I got lucky," Crow replied.

"Like hell. Listen, anybody interested in some breakfast? I got to get some chow. No? Kjell?"

At the front entrance, Kjellgard and Wexler turned north toward a twenty-four-hour café that had "incredible hash browns."

Debrowski and Crow headed up the sidewalk in the opposite direction. Debrowski said, "I thought we were goners, that one hand."

Crow looked back toward the building, watching for Joey or Spence, or for somebody else. He was glad that Freddy Wisnesky was back in Minneapolis.

"Where's the car?"

"Up the block, right where we left it. Are you okay, Crow?"

"For now." He had put all the money in his briefcase. Joey and Spence had been sitting on the white sectional, talking quietly, glancing up at him occasionally.

"He's going to come after us," Crow said.

"Let him," Debrowski said. She was loosening up, shedding the meek bimbo persona. "Man, was that ever something! He didn't know what the hell was going on. That was almost as good as kicking him in the head. No, it was better. How much did we score? Tell me again."

"I think about fifty-four." He looked down an alley entrance. No one there. They were only a few yards from the Lincoln. "Hurry it up," he said as Debrowski fumbled with the door key.

Moments later they were moving north on Lake Shore Drive, Debrowski behind the wheel. At 4:30 A.M., the street was empty.

Crow asked, "Does anyone know where we're staying?"

"No."

"Not even Chrissy?"

"Nobody. Crow, don't turn around, okay? There's a Cadillac back there—came out of the ramp—about a block behind us."

"That's it. I knew it. Shit."

"You want me to try and lose them?"

"Just keep going, see what they do."

"They're coming up on us."

"Can you see who it is?"

"Too dark. Tinted windows. Shit, we're gonna catch a red light, Crow. You sure you don't want to go for it?"

"I doubt we could lose them." Crow opened the briefcase and shook the money out onto the seat. He closed the empty briefcase.

Debrowski stopped the Lincoln at the light. A black Cadillac Eldorado rolled up alongside them, to their left. The tinted window lowered to reveal Joey Cadillac's smiling face.

"Roll down your window," Crow said. "Let's see what he's got to say."

Debrowski found the window control and pressed it.

"How you doing?" Joey Cadillac asked, grinning.

Crow leaned over Debrowski. "We're doing fine, Joey." He tried to see who was driving. Spence.

Joey asked, "You want to stop and have a nightcap? Celebrate your big win? There's a place I know, a few blocks over, never closes."

"No, thanks, Joey. I think we'll just be heading back to our place."

"Yeah? Where you staying?"

"The light's green, Crow," Debrowski muttered.

"I don't remember offhand," Crow said. Debrowski took her foot off the brake and eased down on the accelerator. The Cadillac fell in behind them.

"I don't like this, Crow," she said. "Christ, another light. I'm gonna run it."

"Don't. I want to talk to Joey some more."

"What for?"

"Trust me. I've got a plan." He wished it were true. Debrowski's instinct to make a run for it was tempting, but he didn't think the rented Lincoln would be able to outrun the Eldorado, not with Spence behind the wheel. He would have to come up with something, tell them some story.

Debrowski stopped at the light. They were on a section of Lake Shore Drive that was all condos and pricey apartment buildings. The Eldorado eased up beside them.

Crow leaned over and said, "Hey, Joey, what do we have to do to get you off our ass?"

Joey laughed. "In my game we give the money back at the end of the night."

"You want your money back?"

"Sure, why not?"

"Or else what?"

Joey laughed again. The barrel of a shotgun appeared across his chest, pointing in the general direction of Debrowski's head. Spence's craggy face was suddenly visible, looking down the ribbed barrel. So much for telling them a story.

Crow held up the empty briefcase. "How about we split it?"

The shotgun barrel moved back and forth. Debrowski was staring straight ahead, one foot holding down the brake pedal, the other pressing against the accelerator.

This is bad, Crow thought. He had to do something before Debrowski tried to take off and got a face full of buckshot. "Just stay cool," he said in a low voice as he opened the door. "I've got everything under control." He got out of the car, set the briefcase on the roof of the Lincoln. He thought he heard Debrowski mutter, "Like hell."

"You want it all?"

"That's a good idea," Joey said. "Why don't you just bring it on over here."

"Tell Spence he doesn't need to be pointing that thing."

Joey said something to Spence, then turned back to Crow. "He doesn't agree with you, Crow." The barrel lifted and was now focused on Crow's head. "All you got to do is bring the money over here, then you can go back to Minnesota. Nobody wants anybody to get hurt. It's only money. You had a good time playing, didn't you? You want to keep your comic books? I'll let you keep 'em." Joey opened the car door. As the doorpost passed in front of the shotgun barrel, Debrowski took off, tires shrieking. Crow, Joey, and Spence stared after the fishtailing Lincoln with equal measures of astonishment. The briefcase had flown from the roof of the car, bounced, rolled end over end, and landed upright in the middle of the street, twenty yards away. The white Lincoln disappeared down a side street.

Crow took off running in the opposite direction, imagining the buckshot chasing him, tearing through the fabric of his jacket, penetrating his skin, shredding lung, heart, liver. He hoped Joey Cadillac would go for the money, give him time to get lost. His years as a cop had taught him that the hardest guys to catch were the ones on foot. He looked back and saw Joey lifting the briefcase, feeling its light weight, throwing it. Crow was over a block away when the Eldorado made a screaming U-turn, tires shrieking, and came at him. He looked for a break between the buildings, or an open lobby, or anything he could get between him and the approaching Cadillac. The wall of condos was uninterrupted, a barrier as unbroken and unsurmountable as the Great Wall of China. He looked back, risking a full-speed collision with a utility pole.

They were coming. He needed an alley to duck into, but there were no alleys or even cross streets on this stretch of Lake Shore Drive. He threw another look over his shoulder.

A white Lincoln was bearing down on the Eldorado. The Lincoln struck from behind, hard, sending the Eldorado over the curb, across the sidewalk, and into a concrete lion that guarded the entrance to one of the older buildings. The Lincoln stopped on the street. Plastic molding, chrome, and broken glass were everywhere, but the car was largely intact. Crow ran to the driver's-side door and opened it. Debrowski, still gripping the wheel, seemed dazed but uninjured. "Are you okay?" he shouted.

Debrowski nodded. The air bag was hanging like a limp plastic rag from the center of the steering wheel. He looked back at the Cadillac. Steam rose from its hood.

"Move over." He reached over her and unsnapped her seat belt. She slid across the money-littered seat. Crow got behind the wheel and turned the key. After a few long seconds, the engine caught and started. He looked again toward the Cadillac, saw one of its doors swinging open. He dropped the Lincoln into gear and took off up Lake Shore Drive. A howling sound was coming from under the hood, but the car was moving.

"I hope you bought the insurance when you rented this thing," Crow said.

Debrowski was looking around the interior of the car. The front seat was covered with hundred-dollar bills. The two remaining Stasis Shields were on the floor. She picked up one of them. "I feel sort of bad about what he did to that *Batman* comic," she said. "Natch is going to have a fit."

"He'll get paid," Crow said. "That one was only worth about fifty bucks. It had a couple pages missing." He looked at her. "What the hell were you doing back there? I told you I had a plan."

"Your plans are too damn fancy, Crow."

♦ ♥ 31 ♣ ♠

You know, Sam, it's not too soon to think about how you're going to invest your money, and the energy market is now providing some of the most exciting opportunities we've seen in recent years. Just the other day, I put one of my most sophisticated investors into a little thing called Homestead Mining. . . .

—Rich Wicky, investment counselor

Ben Fink lay facedown on his bed with a pillow over his head to block out the squeals, grunts, and thumps. Nine in the morning, and they were at it again. Even the prestigious Whitehall Suites did not have walls thick enough to insulate him from the sounds of Tommy and Catherine fucking their brains out in the next room. It was disgusting. Against the laws of nature. Forcing his mind to other issues, he threw the pillow aside, picked up the phone, and dialed Joe Crow's number. After two rings he heard, "Wait for the beep," and slammed the phone back down. He had been calling all day and had long since stopped waiting for the beep.

Again, he went over Dickie's proposal in his mind.

It sounded as though the comic books the old man had were worth a couple hundred thousand dollars, minimum, even if the collection was not complete, even if the books weren't in such great shape. The notebook had listed items that were rare in any condition at all. *Detective* #27 alone could go for over fifty thousand dollars at auction, if it was in top condition. On the upside, the collection could be worth over a quarter million.

Yes, it was definitely worth looking into.

Dickie wanted them to front the sixty K for the collection, then find him some buyers and unload it fast. They would get their sixty back right away, in addition to a chunk of the sale price. Dickie had mentioned ten percent, but he would almost certainly move on that figure. They could make a nice little chunk. It seemed reasonable. Almost legitimate. Maybe too reasonable and too legitimate.

A better plan would be to approach the old man directly, buy the collection, and cut Dickie out of the loop. If only Crow would get back to him.

A high-pitched ululation pierced the wall—Ben made a sour face—and then there was Tom. He had a few problems with his partner, not the least of which was Catherine. The most pressing issue between them, however, was the bad luck Ben had experienced out at Canterbury Downs. Rabble Rouser, five to one to place, had not. Nor had Golden Fields. On A Lark, the favorite in the sixth race, had failed to show.

Ben frowned at the memory of a very bad afternoon. A heady series of unfortunate and ever-increasing wagers had provided relief to Minnesota taxpayers in the amount of ninety-seven thousand dollars, the last ten thousand of which had gone to support a horse with the highly descriptive and painfully accurate name of Bad Bet.

Tommy, of course, did not yet know of this. Tommy still believed that most of the two hundred thousand dollars they had made off the GGF scam was in their safe-deposit box at First Bank. Would he understand? Ben Fink did not think so. He was most anxious to locate Wicky's old man. He could make the buy directly, turn the collection into cash, and replenish the safe-deposit box before Tommy found out. Maybe even have a few bucks left over.

Or maybe he wouldn't bother to put the money in their box. Tommy had been his partner for a long time, but people change. He would have to think about it.

Once again, he dialed Joe Crow's number.

"Ben is getting anxious," Crow said. "There are six messages from him on my machine."

Debrowski lay on the sofa, Milo purring on her belly. Beside her, on the floor, was fifty-four thousand dollars, divided into four piles.

"What are you going to tell him?"

"I'm not sure. I'll probably put him off until tomorrow, keep him at that anxious pitch." He picked up the phone and dialed Sam's number. "Sam!"

"Son! You're back! Just a goddamn minute."

Crow heard a thud, a crash, and a howl.

"Goddamn dog got my tube steak," Sam said. "You're back!" he repeated.

"We just got in. Have you set up the meeting?"

"Day after tomorrow he's going up north to see the books. I told him to bring cash and be there at noon. Listen, he's been after me to put some money into this Homestead Mining thing. You think I should?"

"The guy never quits, does he?"

"Nope, he don't. I like that. Says I can make a lot of money. Says they got a line on how to squeeze new gold out of mines that have been abandoned. You know, used to be there was a lot of gold taken out of the arrowhead region, specially up on the Gunflint Trail. Richie says these Homestead fellows buy up mineral rights for nothing, then use this new process to force out the yellow. I guess it's a sure thing."

"Don't do it, Sam."

"I figured you'd say that. Say, when d'you think I can get that red fucker back? I want to get that gas pedal fixed before you go run it up the side of a tree."

"Anytime, Sam. My car should be ready. How about if I swing by tomorrow morning, you can give me a lift to the Jaguar place. About nine? Okay. Bye."

Milo had hopped down from Debrowski's belly and was sniffing the piles of money.

"Which one's mine?" Crow asked.

Debrowski pointed. "The short one on the end is for Chrissy, and the one next to it is Zink's twelve thousand."

"I'll drop that off on my way over to Sam's."

"It went good, didn't it?"

"It went great, so long as neither of us ever runs into Joey Cadillac again."

"You going to buy your island now?"

"I'm going to get my Jag out of hock, pay off the IRS, and make the folks at American Express happy. I'm still working on the island. What are you going to do?"

"Probably buy an annuity."

"You're kidding."

"You're right; I am. I don't know what I'll do. That was one nice thing about being a cokehead: you always knew what to spend your money on. Never used to have to think about it."

Rich was showing Freddy how to make a Mondo Martini.

"It's physics, Fred. What happens is, where the outside of the glass is cold, the moisture in the air condenses and freezes, see? Careful when you drink it, now. It's really cold. There you go."

Freddy looked at the martini, a frosty tumbler full of olives and gin. He would have preferred another beer, but Rich had insisted on making him a martini. Freddy tried a sip. It tasted like pine needles.

The Twins had won the night before, beat the Yankees five to four on an eighth-inning two-run homer by Hrbek. Freddy had his Homer Hankie hanging from his shirt pocket, a red-white-and-blue Twins cap perched on his head.

"I like that Hrbek," Freddy said. He punched the air. "Pow, over the fence."

The telephone rang.

Rich picked it up. "Rich Wicky here." He listened, then pointed at the mouthpiece and winked at Freddy.

"Just great, Joey. Me and Fred were just talking about that. Every-thing's all set, you don't have to worry about a thing, we'll get back to you in the next couple days. Yeah, I understand, but I'm afraid you'll have to wait a little while longer. Like I told you before, I have some business of my own to conduct, then I'll put you in touch with them. Keep in mind, I'm not asking for anything for myself here, Joey. This is strictly on the house, but we have to play it my way, or we don't play. Now is there anything else I can do for you?"

He listened, frowned, and scrunched up his brow. "Do I know him? Sure I know him. I play cards with him; he used to work for me. Joe Crow—yeah, that's his real name. How do you know him? Yeah? Maybe we could work something out here, Joey. What's a piece of in-formation like that worth to you? Fine; you think about it and get back to me. Yeah, he's here. Just a minute." He held the phone out to-ward Freddy. "It's for you, Fred."

Freddy took the receiver and buried it in his ear. "Hi, Mister C."

"Who the fuck does that son-of-a-bitch think he is?"

Freddy jerked as though the phone had bit his earlobe. "I dunno, Mister C."

"I ask him a question, I don't need this mealy-mouth bullshit about 'we play it my way. . . .' Who the fuck does he think he's talking to? Listen, Freddy, I want you to ask him a couple questions for me, okay? See if you can't get some straight answers."

Freddy listened carefully, his face contorting as it absorbed each new bit of information. After a few moments, he set the phone down and looked at his friend Rich.

"What's going on?" Rich asked.

In answer, Freddy took him by the arms, marched him through the living room and onto the balcony, pushed him against the steel railing, reached down and grabbed him by the ankles, lifted him up over the railing, and let him hang there screaming. He felt bad about doing this to Rich, but it seemed better than breaking a Mondo Martini against his forehead, which had been his first idea.

"I got to ask you a couple questions, Rich," Freddy said.

♦ ♥ **32** ♣ ♠

I love to sell. Every morning I get out of bed and I look in the mirror and I ask myself, "Is this really what I want to be doing with my life?" And every morning I say to myself, "Yes!"

—James Bobick, realtor

Joe Crow's name came up in the lavender tickler file. Without hesitating, Jimbo Bobick dialed the number on the card, smiled, stroked his chin, and listened to the phone ring.

"Hello."

"Joe! How are you doing? This is Jimbo, up in the lake country! How are you doing?"

"I'm fine, Jimbo."

"Thought I'd give you a buzz, see when you could come on up and take a look-see at this island I got for you."

"This isn't really a good time for me, Jimbo. I've got some business I have to take care of here. . . ."

"Cool! Cool! I hear you, Joe. Hey, I don't mind. I just thought I'd give you a call, see how you were doing, you know? You been playing over at Zink's lately?"

"A little."

"Boy, you sure took me to the cleaners last time! So when do you think you might be ready to look at that island on Whiting? It's still available, you know. The guy wants to sell bad. Might be he'd come down a nice chunk."

"Well . . . actually, I'm going to be up at Ozzie's place on Wednesday. Maybe I can find time. . . . Tell you what, Jimbo—you going to be around on Wednesday afternoon?"

"Sure!"

"Maybe I'll swing by your office, if I have time."

After hanging up the phone, Jimbo made a note on Crow's card, flipped to the next one, picked up the phone, and dialed.

Sam couldn't get over the floor.

"Would you look at that damn floor," he said for the third time. "I could eat hot dish offa that fucker."

They were in the waiting room at Jaguar Motor Cars of Minneapolis, waiting for the computer to total the bill for repairs to Crow's XJS. One wall of the waiting room was glass. They could see directly out into the service area. Crow watched Sam watching the white-coated technicians working on clean, well-cared-for "Jag-you-are" motorcars. It was like visiting the NASA Space Center with a crotchety Orville Wright.

"Lookit there." Sam pointed at a bespectacled, bearded technician who was examining an old yellow E-type convertible, leaning forward and peering into the engine compartment, his hands clasped behind his back.

"He's been standing like that three, four minutes now, just lookin'. How much you say they charge you here?"

"Sixty-nine dollars an hour."

"Damn! Look at him, he's still standing there looking. What do you think he's looking at?"

"I don't know. Listen, you could take off now—my car will be ready in a few minutes. Thanks for the lift and for the loan of the truck." Crow did not want his father to see the bill. The most recent estimate from Charles had been over six thousand dollars, nearly half his take from the poker game. Six thousand dollars to repair a car—Sam would never let him forget it.

"Maybe he's just afraid he's gonna get dirty, you think? You think I should go out there, give him a hand?"

"I wouldn't do that, Sam. Tell you what—why don't you go home now, get ready for the trip. You have to pick up the boxes and tape. You're going up tonight, right?"

"Yep."

"I'll be up about midmorning tomorrow. You told Dickie noon, right?"

Sam was still watching the bearded technician. "Look at that! He reached in and touched something. Now he's wiping his hand on a rag. What a wuss. I bet it could cost you five hundred bucks to get a fucking tune-up here."

More like seven hundred, Crow thought.

"Mr. Crow?" Charles was standing in the doorway, smiling happily. "We're ready for you now."

Melly brought him a fourth martini, saying, "Are you sure you don't want a little something to eat, Mr. Rich? We got a real nice soup today. Wild rice and chicken?"

"No, thanks, Melly."

"How about a little toast, then?"

"Toast? No, thanks."

"Suit yourself, Mr. Rich." She moved on to the next booth, leaving Wicky with his thoughts.

Wicky was perturbed, but the martinis were helping. He'd used up the last of his coke in the process of getting out of bed and was wishing he had another gram or two to get him through the next twenty-four hours. He was still trying to figure out how it would work. He had thought he had it figured, until Freddy Wisnesky had changed the way he felt about living on the twenty-fifth floor. Wicky squeezed his eyes shut and gave his head a violent shake, trying to throw off the memory. He knew, now, how Catfish's cat must have felt.

Freddy Wisnesky was still there in his apartment, eating his food, drinking his beer, waiting for him to come home. Wicky took a shaky breath and followed it with a half ounce of icy gin, then another.

Catfish and Tommy, another painful memory, slipped between the molecules of alcohol and flashed on his brainpan. He finished his drink and looked around for Melly. As always, she was right there. She put a plate of french fries on his table.

"The cook had an extra order, Mr. Rich. On the house."

He knew that the fries had been brought to moderate the effects of the alcohol he had consumed. Melly didn't want him passing out at her table. But he appreciated it. "Thanks, Melly. I'd like another drink." He picked up a french fry and ate it, smiling up at her.

"Sure thing, Mr. Rich."

His mind kept returning to the image of Catfish kissing Tommy. He tried to make it a friendly, sisterly kiss, but even his flexible memory could not erase the lust that had passed between them. He jerked his mind away from one painful memory and landed in another: The call he had made to Freddy's boss, Joey Cadillac. He had a bad feeling about it, like he had made a big mistake getting him involved. He reassured himself. One way or another, whatever happened, the Tom and Ben Show was fucked. He felt a surge of testosterone. The Tom and Ben Show was going down the tube. He didn't even care about the money.

Actually, that wasn't true. If only he could figure a way around Freddy's new attitude. All the nice stuff he'd done for Freddy, and the guy . . .

He shivered, barely avoiding the memory.

He could leave straight from work, just head straight up to Crook Lake, find the old man's cabin . . . No, that wouldn't work. Freddy would be on him before he made Anoka. He needed time to secure the deal with O'Gara before Tom and Ben got there with the money. Timing was everything. He ticked off the agenda in his mind.

Check out the comics, make sure they weren't all chewed up by mice or something.

Meet Tom and Ben someplace nearby. Make it a public place, someplace in Brainerd.

Get the money from them. Wicky took a swallow from the martini that had appeared in his hand, stabbed an olive with the red plastic spear, and chewed thoughtfully. If they thought that Freddy was waiting back at the old man's cabin, they wouldn't want to go near it. They probably wouldn't let loose of the money, either. And the old man had been sticky on that one point—he had to see the cash money, or the comics were going nowhere.

Shit. It made him dizzy to think about it. What had possessed him to get involved with Freddy? He should've got the money and the comics and *then* called in the Incredible Hulk. Now it was looking like he was in the same deep shit as Tom and Ben. Before Freddy, it had all seemed so simple: buy low; sell high. Now the screechy voice of Joey Cadillac had come over the wire and turned it all around, turned his incredible opportunity into a horror show.

He wouldn't get a second chance at Sam O'Gara's comics, especially if the old man found out what they were really worth. Why the hell did the old cocker keep the things up north? Wicky hated the woods. He hated mosquitoes. He took a pull at the martini. Logical, orderly thought was becoming unavailable to him. Fuck it. He'd have to wing it, and whatever happened, well, he wouldn't be any worse off than he was now—his wife cuckolding him, a murderous three-hundred-pound ogre living in his apartment, a phony limited-partnership scam about to blow up in his face.

His thoughts became flash cards. Catfish. Tommy. Joe Crow. The way the swimming pool looked upside down. Freddy bellowing down at him, "How do you get to the cabin on Crook Lake?" Trying to scream back directions while inverted. "Who's Sam O'Gara?" Looking into his downstairs neighbor's window. "Where do I find Joe Crow?" Being shaken up and down. "The comics—how much are they worth?" The swimming pool too far out; he would never make it. He squeezed his eyes tight, tighter, squeezed until it hurt and everything inside was red. His breaths were coming rapidly, his chest felt constricted. He felt for the edge of the table, gripped it with both hands, willed himself to unclench.

Slowly, his eyes opened. Joe Crow, stone-faced, was staring pitilessly across the booth. Wicky closed his eyes again, then opened them, but Crow was still there.

Paying six thousand nine hundred eighty-six dollars and sixteen cents to Charles the Customer Service Specialist at Jaguar Motor Cars of Minneapolis had put Crow in exactly the right mood to talk to Dickie Wicky. His agenda was simple. He would ask one last time for his fifty-seven hundred dollars. When Wicky refused, Crow could proceed without compunction.

"I don't know why you bother," Debrowski had said. "Dickie is one notch down the food chain from a Joey Cadillac. Just do what you've got to do. You need help, you just let me know. I'd love to put it to the little skank."

"I think I've got this one covered, Debrowski," Crow had told her. "You did more than enough already."

"I did it for the money."

"Like hell."

Now Crow sat across the booth from Wicky, watching him make faces, waiting to be noticed. He was sure Debrowski was right, but he had to give Wicky one last chance to slime his way out.

"Joe!" Dickie said after a few shocked facial contortions.

"Afternoon, Dickie."

"Jesus, where'd you come from?"

"How's your cash situation these days?"

"Me? I'm hurting, Joe. This comic book thing. Christ, I'm really sorry about getting you into it. You know, I gave everything I had to those guys. I'm hurting real bad." He looked at the Rolex. "Thanks for not pawning my Rolex, Joe. I thought you were gonna sell it on me for a while there."

"Now's your chance to buy it back." He thought about the twenty thousand dollars cash Wicky had promised to pay Sam the next day.

"I would if I could, Joe."

He was good.

"But you know, it didn't work, what you did." Wicky's face tensed and flushed, his voice rose in pitch and volume. "She's still not coming home, Joe. She's still fucking him. You know who he is?"

"You said you didn't want to know, Dickie."

"I know who he is. It's her brother Tommy. My fucking wife is fucking her fucking brother. My kids could turn out to be monsters, and you don't even tell me?"

Crow was too surprised to point out the error in Dickie's genetic theory. He said, "Tommy is her brother? Are you sure?"

"How the hell do you think I met him? Sure I'm sure. They grew up together. You can't tell by looking at them?"

Crow called up the faces in his memory. The resemblance was there. He could believe it. He said, repeating it for his own benefit, "She's his sister?"

Wicky nodded jerkily, his mouth sucked into a knot, his fists quivering on the table. Crow took a long breath, not knowing quite what to say next. As he watched, Wicky's features seemed to melt. The angry Dickie faded and was replaced by a maudlin, teary Dickie. His fists unclenched and flattened.

"You did what you could, Joe. No one can control Cat. You know what she does with her lips? She rubs Tabasco sauce on 'em to make 'em swell up like that. You kiss her, your lips burn for hours."

Crow swallowed, remembering the lingering heat from her kisses. Tabasco sauce? He was almost feeling sorry for the guy.

"You know what else she does? You know what she did once?" Somehow, he had made his squinty eyes big and doleful.

"No," Crow said. "I don't want to know. I just want you to pay me my fifty-seven hundred dollars."

"I can't do it, Joe." His expression mutated again, to something resembling his business-only face. "I don't have it, and even if I did, you didn't get the job done, Joe. My sister-fucking brother-in-law is still out there with pepper on his lips. You want me to buy you a drink, I'll buy you a drink, but that's all I can do. If you have to sell my Rolex, then that's what you have to do. I'm sorry."

"This watch isn't worth fifty bucks, Dickie. It's a fake, just like your comic book scam, just like you, just like your wife." He stood up, stripped the watch off his wrist, dropped it in Wicky's martini.

Wicky was shaking his head sadly. "Joe, Joe, Joe. I can't believe this. What did I ever do to you?" He picked the watch out of the martini, shook it off, dried it on the lapel of his navy-blue blazer, slipped it on his wrist. "Why don't you like me?"

Crow shuddered internally and walked away, trying to extract a minim of joy from his childish act. What was it about Dickie? Did he recognize his other self, stoned at noon, strapping a martini-drenched counterfeit Rolex on his wrist, lamenting his wife's pepper-laced lips?

33

Friends? Tommy and I have never been friends. It's more like we're married.

—Ben Fink

"Just a moment. I have to write this down. The Pop Top Lounge in Brainerd. I thought you told us the old man had a cabin of some sort." Ben listened, pressing the receiver to his ear. He was sitting on the edge of his bed at the Whitehall, hunched forward, staring down at the gold-and-brown carpeting. "Dickie? I don't think that's going to be acceptable. I have to take a look at these comics. It's not that I don't trust you, but it would be bad business for me to simply give you sixty thousand dollars cash. Yes, I understand that. Take it easy. No, I know, you already told me that. Dickie? Perhaps you could bring the old man to this Pop Top place. We can have a drink and get friendly, then proceed to his place, look over the comics. Well, see what he says. The Pop Top Lounge, three in the afternoon. Okay, Dickie, I'll be there. No, just me. Tommy's not coming. Yes, of course he's in on the deal, but he's asked me to take care of it. Okay. Goodbye, Dickie."

Ben returned the telephone receiver to its cradle, put his ear to the wall, and listened. Things seemed to have calmed down in there. He picked up the phone, called the front desk, and asked to be connected to Tommy's room.

Catfish answered the phone; Ben frowned and moved the receiver away from his ear.

"Let me talk to your brother," he said.

"He's in the shower, Benny-poo."

He hated that Benny-poo stuff. "When he comes out, tell him I need to talk to him."

Catfish said that she would do that. A few minutes later, Tommy was knocking on the door. His hair, wet and combed straight back over his skull, looked like a shiny black bathing cap. He was wearing his Hawaiian shirt, a pair of baggy cotton shorts, and thongs. Several crescent-shaped bruises were visible on his neck. He was grinning.

"What's up?"

"I just spoke with our friend Dickie. The deal's off."

"Off?"

"That's all I know. He sounded drunk."

"Dickie is always drunk. Cat and me, we're going down to the Market Barbecue for some ribs. You want to come?"

"No, thank you. I've already made dinner plans."

"You sure you don't want some company on the drive, Crow? I'm not doing anything tomorrow."

"No, thanks." Crow was in a dark study, drinking coffee, smoking one of Debrowski's Camels, staring at the curling brown-and-blue smoke.

"I've never seen you smoke a cigarette before. Makes you look real fifties. Especially with the undershirt. Kinda sexy."

Crow shrugged. They were sitting in his kitchen, with a sinkful of dishes and a floor that had needed cleaning weeks ago. Milo sat beside his bowl, blinking sleepily, twitching his tail, not particularly hungry but ready to eat should some food happen to fall into his bowl. Crow was wearing a sleeveless white T-shirt and dark-brown trousers. He sipped coffee from a white mug. Debrowski had been trying to cheer him up for the past twenty minutes. It wasn't working. His mind kept returning to Dickie, Catfish, and the rest of them. What he was doing, what he planned to do, seemed, by turns, trivial, impossible, cruel, just, absurd. That he should need these people in his life, even for so short a time, grated at his finish.

"Earth to Crow. You're funking out on me, Crow. Hello?"

Crow stubbed out the cigarette and smiled thinly. "Sorry."

"You worried about your dad?"

Crow realized, with a start, that he wasn't. That he should be. Putting the old man out in the woods with a bunch of desperate con men, he should be worried as hell, but the fact was, he hadn't given it a thought. Sam O'Gara was invulnerable, incapable of taking on hurt, able to shake off the vagaries of life with a shrug of his hard, narrow shoulders. Crow could not imagine Sam in pain. If something went wrong, Sam would fix it with one of the "fuckers" in his ever-present tool chest.

Debrowski said, "He can take care of himself, Crow. Sam's a resourceful guy."

"I know," Crow said. "I wasn't worried about him. Besides, I'll be there with him."

"Is he already up there, you think?"

"He probably got there a few hours ago." It was just after sunset. Sam O'Gara had left town in his red truck early that afternoon. If the truck hadn't broken down, if he had found Ozzie's cabin, if none of the other millions of things that could have gone wrong had not, Sam would be comfortably asleep in Ozzie's bed or, more likely, perusing Ozzie's famous pornography collection. Crow tried to imagine his father staring at a copy of the *Shaved Revue*. No problem. Sam could take care of himself. Crow fixed the concept in his mind, set it forcibly aside.

"You sure you don't want company? I'd kind of like to see how this deal goes down. I feel like I'm involved in it."

"I've got this one covered, but thanks."

"You might need help."

"Sam'll be there. It'll be me, Sam, Dickie, and Ben. What do you think they're going to do?"

"Why don't you want me to come?"

"I don't know." He rolled his shoulders, trying to dislodge the kink in his back. "I feel awkward."

"About what?"

Crow shrugged. "Hiding in the trees, trying to con a bunch of con men, using my poor old dad. It's like you told me—I'm swimming in the sewer with a bunch of losers. I'm too old to be doing this sort of shit."

"You're thirty-five, Crow. That's not old."

"Yes it is. I'm supposed to be grown up by now, acting like an adult."

Ben Fink was waiting at the bar in Harry's Oasis, wearing his gray Mickey Mouse T-shirt and drinking a Perrier. A partially eaten fish sandwich was cooling in the plastic basket in front of him, along with a few limp french fries. He made a sour face when Crow stepped in through the front door.

"I've been here for an hour," Ben said. "Why do you choose these places to meet?" He seemed nervous, agitated. "Next time we meet at a Perkins."

Harry's was not such a bad place, Crow thought. The glasses were clean, even if the carpet was not, and Harry was a nice guy. "Ben, I can't tell you how sorry I am about that. Can I buy you a drink?"

"I have one, thank you. What do you have for me?" His deep voice now carried a strident overtone.

Crow waved at Harry, who brought him a Coke with a straw in it. He wasn't sure what had happened between Tom and Ben, but he liked it. For some reason, Ben was operating on his own, and he was scared. That had to be good.

"Take it easy," he said. "I've got your information about the old man. His name is O'Gara. He lives at 1406 Albury Street in Saint Paul. Dickie's been over to see him twice this week."

"What about the lake cabin? Did you find out where it is?"

"On Crook Lake, up near Brainerd."

"Brainerd? That's where Dickie wants to meet us tomorrow afternoon. The Pop Top Lounge in Brainerd." Ben stroked his beard. "How do I find this Mr. O'Gara's cabin?"

"I don't know. But I have something else you might be interested in. O'Gara has a box full of 1940s comic books in his truck."

Ben paused in his beard-stroking. "How did you happen to learn that?"

"O'Gara had a flat tire. I happened to be in the neighborhood, so I stopped to help him. He had a box of comic books on his front seat. He gave me one. *World's Finest.*"

"What number?" Ben asked automatically.

"I don't know. I left it at home. I don't suppose the comics have anything to do with why you want to get in touch with him, do they?"

Ben frowned. "I hired you to acquire information for me, Mr. Crow, not to ask me questions."

Crow shrugged. "Fine by me."

"Where is he now?"

"He left for his cabin this afternoon. Had the flat on the way out of town. Somebody had been messing with his valve stem. Probably some kids. What's the matter?"

Ben shook his head wearily and sipped his Perrier. "You are very clever, Mr. Crow, but you have failed me."

"I've done exactly as you asked."

"Too late. Let me explain something to you. The old man, Mr. O'Gara, has a large and valuable comic book collection, which Dickie is now going to acquire for practically nothing, if he hasn't already. I had hoped to offer the gentleman a fair price. This is very unfortunate—I hate to see an old man taken advantage of that way."

"If you're really worried about it, you could still make your offer before Dickie gets up there."

"He's probably up there already."

"I don't think so." Crow pulled a Marlboro out of the fresh pack in his pocket and lit it. Smoke crawled gratefully down into his lungs. He could almost hear the cigarette whispering, *We missed you, Joe Crow.*

"What do you mean?"

"I had lunch with Dickie today."

Ben compressed his lips. "You do get around. Was he accompanied by an especially large and unpleasant-looking man named Freddy?"

"He was alone. I had been hoping to collect some money from him. He mentioned that he would be going out of town tomorrow. In fact, he said he had to be up in the Brainerd area by noon. I figure you've got till then to cut your deal."

"How far away is this place?"

"Crook Lake? It's just north of Brainerd. About three hours."

"How will I find it?"

"Do you have the thousand you owe me?"

"Of course. Do you have the location of the cabin?"

"I'll have it for you first thing in the morning." Crow drew hard on his smoke, let a cloud of gray veil his face.

Ben stared distastefully at the burning cigarette. "I didn't know you were a smoker, Crow."

"I'm not," Crow said.

Across the street from Harry's Oasis, half a block down, Tommy was sitting with Catfish in her Porsche.

"I don't get it," Tommy said. "What's the deal with this guy Crow, anyway?"

"He's an odd one," Catfish murmured. "The important question is, what's with Benny-poo? I think he's trying to rip us off."

"Ben wouldn't rip me off. Besides, all he'd have to do is empty out our cash box and fly. We're partners."

"Then why's he talking to Crow? It has something to do with that comic collection Dickie's found. I just know it."

"I don't know," Tommy said.

"I think we should find out, don't you?"

34

You send a gorilla out in the jungle, he's gonna come back with bananas.

—*Joey Cadillac*

Madonna Battagno usually slept well on the nights her husband, Joey, didn't come home. And when he did decide to spend the night in their Hanover Park home, she had learned to tolerate his surly, barking, cigar-smoking, wind-breaking presence. Like all men, Joey was at his best when he was away from home earning money or, if not that, off exercising his vices on more tolerant companions. His amorous and otherwise undignified attentions had been unwelcomed by Madonna since the birth of their third son, which was the exact number she had promised him at their betrothal. Madonna had children to raise, a household to manage, and shopping to perform. Her husband's occasional stints on the home front did nothing to enrich her life.

On this night she was finding him particularly difficult to tolerate. Two o'clock in the morning, and he was lying in his bed, cursing. Every time she started to drift off to sleep, he would mumble some obscenity.

"Fucking Freddy."

And, a few minutes later, "Those fuckers."

Madonna didn't say anything at first. She didn't want to touch him off, and the mood he was in, it wouldn't take much at all to get him throwing the furniture around.

"Goddamn comic books."

"Useless piece a dog shit."

"Goddamn motherfucking Crow."

"Fucking leather bitch."

That was enough. Madonna couldn't take it anymore. It was like he waited in the dark for her to start falling asleep, then jolted her awake with some new bit of nastiness. She turned on the light by her bed and looked across the three-foot-wide no-man's-land between them.

She asked, "What's your problem, sweet pie? Can't sleep? You want to talk about it?"

"No," Joey snapped. "Turn out that goddamn light, would ya?"

"Did somebody do something bad to you? Who are you mad at, honey bunch?"

"I don't want to talk about it."

"Are you sure? You know what Daddy always says, don't you?"

That got his attention. Madonna's daddy was Carlos Bevilacqua, a former priest who now owned, directly or indirectly, most of the Chicago-area GM dealerships. Joey's continued operation of J.C. Motors was made possible through the benign neglect of Carlos Bevilacqua.

Madonna continued, "Daddy always says that when you have a problem at work, you take care of it before you go home. Daddy always says that people who take care of their problems right away are people who can be trusted to get the job done." She smiled sweetly.

Joey felt the dark clouds gathering inside him. He got out of bed and dressed. He had to get out of there before he broke a lamp over Carlos Bevilacqua's daughter's skull and cost himself a Cadillac dealership. It would be close. The woman had no mercy. She left him no slack. He made a promise to himself: When old Carlos died—the sooner the better—first thing he did, he was going to kick the shit out of her.

He needed to go for a drive, maybe have a couple drinks. He grabbed a bottle of Martell on the way out, had a quick hit in the driveway, then took the Brougham d'Elegance for a spin.

The thing was, he decided, her old man was right. Here he was sitting in Hanover Park brooding about his problems, when all the solutions were up in Minnesota. Could he rely on Freddy to take care of things? No way. Freddy was great when you could tell him exactly what to do and when to do it, but managing him from four hundred miles away was impractical, as he had been repeatedly reminded over the past weeks.

Joey looked at the car clock. Two thirty-five.

He thought some more about the Tom and Ben Show.

He thought about Joe Crow, the poker player. He took a hit off the bottle of Martell.

He thought about the little leather bitch; his back was still sore.

Lately, it seemed, everything was going wrong. He turned onto the tollway, brought the big Brougham up to seventy-five, set the cruise control, had another swallow of cognac, and settled into a controlled rage. He could feel the hot spot in his belly growing and added another ounce of Martell. The faces—Tom, Ben, Crow, the bitch—flickered in his mind. He kept returning to the game, seeing Crow's dead-looking expression as he scooped the big one. He saw Bobby Wexler trying not to laugh when he'd ripped up the comic book. Incredible coincidence. Or was it? The image of Crow's girlfriend, what was her name? He couldn't remember. All that blond hair, blue eyes, like every other Minnesota girl. Why did he keep thinking of her face?

A small car, some Japanese thing, flashed by him, going like hell. Joey growled, brought the Brougham up to eighty-five, and reset the cruise control.

Then it hit him. He damn near drove off the freeway when he saw it, clear as anything, right between the eyes.

Crow's girlfriend. Take away the hair, the dress, the false eyelashes. Take away the pink lipstick and make it dark red. Put her in black leather. Give her a fucking bicycle chain.

Joey moaned. The moan became a growl, the growl a scream.

He started shaking and had to bring the Brougham down to sixty. Everything was connected: the comic book guys, the leather bitch, Crow—maybe even Bubby Sharp. A conspiracy to get Joey Cadillac.

A toll plaza appeared a quarter of a mile in front of him. Joey slowed the car, found some change, threw it in the collection basket, and continued up the road. His breathing was returning to normal. He slipped the cork out of the neck of the Martell bottle and tipped another ounce down his throat..

A conspiracy. He savored the concept as he would a peperoncino, letting it burn, knowing he could swallow it at any time. A conspiracy against Joey Cadillac. He let himself fantasize for a few miles. Kicking the leather bitch to death, making Crow watch. Cutting off Crow's dick and stuffing it in her mouth. Feeding the comic book guys to the Rottweilers. He imagined it a few different ways, some of which gave him a hard-on.

He paid two more tolls before his mind returned to the present. The clock on the dash read 3:09. Where the hell was he? On the Northwest Tollway, heading toward Rockford. Joey did some math in his head.

He could be in Minneapolis by 10:00 A.M.

The telephone was ringing. Crow awakened without opening his eyes and listened.

Beep.

"Mr. Crow? Are you there? This is Ben Franklin. It is six-thirty in the morning. I'm awaiting your call."

Crow sat up on the edge of the bed and rested his throbbing forehead in his palms. It was one of those mornings when he woke up with a raging hangover that would disappear once he recalled that he had not had to drink himself down from a coke binge the night before. He focused on his breathing and waited for the phantom pain to subside. It eased by stages, but not completely. He decided it was, in part, the half pack of cigarettes he had consumed the night before. His mouth tasted particularly foul. He decided to quit.

After what seemed like half an hour, he looked at the digital clock beside his bed. Six-forty. The phone rang again. Crow stood and made his way across the room and grabbed the receiver before the answering machine could intercept the call. It was Ben.

"Didn't you just call a minute ago?"

"Do you have the information for me?"

"Hold on a minute." He reviewed the timing in his head. If Ben left immediately, he would be at the cabin by nine-thirty. Too soon. With all that time to spare, he would want to look in every box. "I'll have to get back to you, Ben. I've got a call in to a realtor I know up there. He promised to get back to me before nine."

"That's cutting it rather close."

"Don't worry about it. You can be there in two and a half hours if you push it."

"I'll be awaiting your call."

Crow hung up the phone, then went to the bathroom and let a hot shower bring his metabolism up to speed. He watched the water trailing down his body, turning his chest hair into parallel lines. He made himself a pot of coffee, took it out onto the balcony, and drank it. Reasoning that he might as well finish the pack before quitting, he smoked three cigarettes. He ate an overripe banana and a slice of toast slathered with peanut butter.

At eight forty-five, he picked up the phone and called Ben at the Whitehall Suites and told him how to get to Sam O'Gara's cabin.

Crow took a long, deep breath, held it, and turned the key again. The starter whined, the engine turned over. And over. Thirty seconds later, he released the key. Nothing. He allowed himself a few moments to imagine lifting the car over his head and hurling it against the side of the house. Seven thousand dollars in repairs, and now the damn thing wouldn't start.

Ben would be on his way up north. Dicky would be close behind him. Sam was there, waiting.

Crow climbed out of the car, slammed the door, leaned against the front fender, and considered his options. Only one possibility suggested itself. Crow sighed.

The pool rushing up at him, the sensation of weightlessness, the pressure of giant hands wrapped around his ankles, the soundless screams vibrating his lips, the pool growing larger, looking up to see Freddy Wisnesky's muscled rictus bearing down on him, the realization that they were both falling, plummeting toward the blue and white tiles.

"Mr. Rich! Wake up, Mr. Rich!" The words penetrated the nightmare. Wicky's eyes snapped open. Freddy Wisnesky: The Nightmare Continues. "Wake up, Mr. Rich." Giant hands gripping his shoulders, bouncing him up and down on the mattress.

"Okay, okay!" Wicky gasped.

Freddy stopped. "You was having a bad dream."

"Okay, I'm awake now. Jesus Christ. I think you dislocated a shoulder."

"It's nine o'clock, Mr. Rich. We got to get going pretty quick."

Wicky swung his legs over the edge of the bed, sat up, leaned forward, rested his head in his hands, and waited for his brain to reposition itself.

"You okay, Mr. Rich?"

"Just leave me alone a few minutes, Fred."

"I made you some breakfast. Eggs-in-a-frame."

Wicky felt the matter in his bowel drop a few inches at the thought of Freddy's favorite breakfast. Since the balcony incident, Freddy had been puppyishly eager to please. He seemed genuinely sorry to have put his buddy Rich—or *Mister* Rich, as he had come to call him—through such an ordeal. Freddy seemed anxious for them to put the matter behind them and be buddies again. Wicky was having a little trouble with that.

He was not looking forward to this trip up north. He suspected that with Joey Cadillac involved, as represented by Freddy Wisnesky, there wouldn't be much left for little Rich Wicky. Freddy was evasive on the matter of the instructions he had received from Mister C. When Wicky asked, Freddy told him that he was just supposed to take care of the comic book guys.

"But I can still do my deal first?" Wicky had asked.

"I just got to take care of the comic guys for Mister C.," had been Freddy's only reply.

This had the potential of being the worst day of his life, Wicky decided. Or, another voice in his head piped up, the best. He shook his head gingerly. You just never knew.

Freddy called from the kitchen. "Breakfast is ready, Mr. Rich!"

"Great," Wicky muttered. "Eggs-in-a-frame."

Wind ripped the words to unintelligible shreds, sent them careening past his ear. Crow pushed his head forward.

"*What?*"

Debrowski turned her head. "*How . . . are . . . you . . . doing?*"

"*Fine!*" They were on Highway 10, a few miles north of Saint Cloud, moving at eighty miles per hour on Debrowski's Kawasaki dirt bike. Crow's ass had gone numb back at Elk River. His nylon windbreaker was flapping and cracking in the wind, his fingers were locked around the thin, frayed vinyl seat strap between his legs. He was trying not to think about it. He wouldn't mind riding on the back of a real motorcycle. Something big and solid, like a Harley, or even one of those big Japanese touring bikes. Something with some mass to it and something to hang on to. But two and a half hours on the back of a lime-green 250 cc dirt bike was not his thing. If he didn't have hemorrhoids before, this would almost certainly do it.

They were coming up on a small red sports car. Crow squinted into the wind. A Porsche. As Debrowski pulled out to pass, he recognized the license plate with a start and turned his face away.

What was she doing here?

When they were well in front of the Porsche, he shouted in Debrowski's ear. *"Did you see who that was?"*

Debrowski nodded.

"Was she alone?"

Debrowski shook her head and yelled back, *"Catfish ... and ... Tommy!"* She lifted her left hand and pointed. *"Is ... that ... him?"*

Crow squinted into the wind. She was pointing at another vehicle, half a mile ahead. Was it yellow? His entire body was vibrating. He couldn't focus well enough to identify the color.

They were gaining on the vehicle.

He could now see that it was yellow. A yellow Cadillac.

When he could see the license number clearly, he shouted in Debrowski's ear, *"It's him. Pass him."*

He turned his head toward the left, resting his cheek against Debrowski's back. He felt the little 250 cc engine winding up as Debrowski increased their speed to blow by the Cadillac as quickly as possible.

"Who?" he shouted after they had left the Cadillac behind.

"Ben!"

"Anybody else?"

"No!"

If he had not been traveling at ninety miles per hour on the back of a dirt bike, Crow might have relaxed slightly. They would get there ahead of the pack. He wondered whether Ben knew he was being followed by Catfish and Tommy. Either way, things were getting complicated.

35

THE SCOOP

So what do you think? Can you see yourself sitting out on the dock,
nice comfortable chair, pulling in a twenty-pound northern?

—*Jimbo Bobick, instructing a potential customer in creative visualization*

Sam O'Gara liked Ozzie's cabin. He liked being by the water. He liked the quiet. He liked the squirrels. He thought it would be nice if his son would buy a cabin, someplace he could bring his dogs to, let them run around in the woods. He hadn't seen Chester or Festus since being licked awake shortly after dawn. He heard a distant howl. Dogs will run. Wasn't nothing you could do—they got that call of the wild.

Crook Lake, an eight-mile-long, bean-shaped body of water, had a reputation for good bass fishing and high mercury levels. Ozzie's cabin was on the tip of a long wing-shaped point, almost a peninsula, that jutted half a mile out into the western end of the lake. A weed-choked bay filled the back of the wing; the leading edge was rocky, wind-beaten shoreline. Ozzie LaRose owned the tip of the wing, twenty-nine acres of boggy, rocky, heavily wooded bottomland.

At the entrance to Ozzie's property, a sign, crudely carved into a weathered board, hung from a shaky-looking open gate made from saplings. LAROSE'S ACRES. A few yards past the gate, at the point's elbow, the narrow dirt road made a sudden right turn, almost at the water's edge, and followed the narrowing point another quarter mile to the cabin.

Last night Sam had pulled the sign down and hidden it in the brush. Then he had driven the half mile out to the shore road and used a can of fluorescent orange paint to spray his own name on Ozzie's mailbox.

Sam lit a Pall Mall and put his feet up on the plank table. He was sitting on the screened-in porch, drinking a can of beer and waiting for his son to show up. These kids came up with the damnedest ways to make a buck.

The back of his red truck was loaded with neatly packed and sealed cardboard boxes. They didn't quite fill it up, but damn near. He had used every one of the three dozen cardboard boxes he had brought up and had spent most of last night packing, taping, and loading. He could've done it faster if the magazines hadn't been so distracting, but who could pass up a chance to look at *Clit Cavalcade*? Even more enticing, from Sam's point of view, was *Mopar Mamas*, twelve generously endowed babes posed with their tits hanging over the greatest Mopar engines ever made. His favorite was the redhead on the slant six. Something about the way she was holding the distributor cap. After a while, the acres of unclothed images had lost their power, and he had been able to finish the packing job. Only one of the thirty-six boxes contained actual comic books, the ones they had borrowed from Natch, Crow's hippie friend.

"If you have to open a box for him, make sure you open the right one," Joe had told him. The scheme seemed a bit chancy to Sam, but Joe had assured him they could pull it off with no problem.

"You just be yourself, Sam," Crow had said. "Don't let them push you around. When Ben gets here, he's going to want to cut a deal quick. Just jerk him around for a while, get him good and nervous. He'll want to cut a deal before Dickie shows up—just don't let him start opening boxes, okay? Get him to give you the money, load him up, and get him the hell out of here. Better yet, just give him the keys to the truck. Tell him you'll drive his car back for him. And don't worry—I'll be watching. Anything goes wrong, we kill the deal, okay?"

"What happens when the other fellow shows up?"

"You'll just tell Dickie you sold the collection to Ben. They can work it out between themselves."

Where the hell was Joe? Sam looked at his watch. Damn near ten o'clock. He didn't like this waiting.

That morning, while sitting at the counter at Becky's Sunshine Café, enjoying the Steak and Eggs Breakfast Special, Jimbo Bobick decided not to wait for Joe Crow. There was no percentage in waiting for the customer to come to you. You smell the sale, you go after it. Without further thought, Jimbo left four dollars and thirty-five cents on the counter, got straight into his big Oldsmobile, and headed north out of town on 371. Ozzie's cabin on Crook Lake was only twenty minutes away, which was nothing considering the commission he stood to make if he could get Crow locked into the Whiting Lake property. He would just drop in and say Hi. It was the neighborly thing to do.

"Look, we've got ten miles to go, just up to Brainerd. We'll buy a helmet as soon as we get there."

The highway patrol officer, standing beside his maroon vehicle, gave no sign of having heard her. He was writing carefully in his citation book, occasionally lifting his powerful chin to look through his mirrored sunglasses at Debrowski, at her license, at the bike, or at Crow, who could see that he had decided to write the ticket, and that was that. Eighty-four miles per hour in a fifty-five zone, no helmet on passenger. Crow watched Ben's Fleetwood come into view. He bent over, as if tying his shoe, and turned as the Cadillac flashed by, keeping his face from view. Fifteen seconds later, he repeated the performance for Catfish and Tommy. If the cop noticed, he didn't comment.

Debrowski was shifting her weight from one boot to the other. Crow crossed his arms and leaned a hip on the bike. The more anxious she became, the slower the cop would write. Crow had seen it plenty of times before. He had done it himself. One of the unwritten laws of traffic control was that if you go to the trouble to stop some citizen for speeding, you have to keep him sitting on the shoulder long enough so that he would have arrived at his destination sooner by not speeding.

If they were lucky, if they didn't push it, if Debrowski could keep her feelings about authority figures under wraps, they would be back on the road in five minutes.

Sam would have to fly solo for a while. Crow forced himself to remain calm. He briefly considered telling the cop that he, too, was a cop. Or, rather, an ex-cop. That might help, but more likely it would backfire, especially if this one remembered his name from the papers. It was only two years ago that he'd been busted. Too many cops might have followed that story, and too many might remember.

Debrowski was a few yards away, kicking the ground, sending up sprays of dirt and gravel, puffing furiously on a Camel. The cigarette looked good. Crow reached for one of his own. Hand to pack, cigarette to mouth, lighter to cigarette—the sequence was hard-wired into his brain. Soon he would be back up to two packs a day. He started moving toward Debrowski, thinking to calm her down, when she slammed a fist on her leather-clad thigh and walked stiffly over to the cop.

Crow thought, Uh-oh.

"Listen," he heard her say. "Do you think you could hurry it up a bit? We're supposed to meet some people, and we're late already."

The cop lifted his chin and turned his head slowly to look at her. Crow thought, That's good for another ten minutes, minimum.

Joey Cadillac stared down at the scrambled landscape—rectangular fields of yellow and green and brown splattered with twisting rivers, creeks, and lakes. Lakes everywhere. At least a dozen lakes visible in any direction. Joey commented on this to the pilot, a handsome, happy kid named Karl.

"Land of ten thousand lakes," Karl replied, shouting to be heard over the twin Pratt & Whitney engines. They were in an old Grumman Goose seaplane, practically an antique, but the only thing Joey could find on short notice that would land on water. For eight hundred bucks, Karl had guaranteed to get him to Crook Lake by noon.

Joey nodded. Ten thousand lakes in Minnesota: he'd heard that somewhere before. Chrissy had probably told him. He wondered how they had got the number to come out so even.

Joey had completed the drive up from Chicago by alternating hits from the bottle of Martell with cups of coffee, and with the aid of a Dexedrine spansule from his glove compartment stash. He had kept himself entertained on the drive through Wisconsin by mentally tearing apart and reassembling the conspirators in various creative and unusual ways. Sometimes he had the help of Freddy Wisnesky, and sometimes he made them do it to each other, but most often, and most satisfying, was when he did it himself. Revenge was the tastiest bite of all; Joey savored it in his mind.

He had arrived in the Twin Cities before ten o'clock that morning in a conscious and reasonably coherent state. At least, he was coherent enough to forget about trying to drive the final hundred and fifty miles up to Crook Lake. Instead, he had followed the signs directing him to Crystal Airport, and after flashing some cash around—Joey usually kept a few thousand in his pockets—he had found Karl.

Joey had decided back in Madison, Wisconsin, to begin his aveng-
ing with the Tom and Ben Show, since he might have only this one
crack at them. He wanted to be there to see their faces. According to
Freddy, they were meeting with the comic book guys at a cabin on
the end of Sorenson Point on Crook Lake. Karl had quickly located
Crook Lake on his map, which clearly showed the wing-shaped land-
mass jutting out from the western shore.

"I can put you right there on the tip," Karl had said, touching the
map with the sharp point of his mechanical pencil. Twenty minutes
and eight hundred dollars later, they were airborne.

Joey sat back in his seat and watched the lakes slide by. He imagined what Crook Lake would look like, coming up on the horizon.
He hoped he would get there before Freddy did his thing. The little
.32 caliber Davis in his pocket wasn't much of a gun, not compared to
some of the stuff he had at home, but what the hell—he'd always
wanted to use it.

"Back off, would ya? He's gonna see us."

Catfish snorted and continued to creep up on the yellow Cadillac,
but after a few seconds she slacked off on the accelerator and fell
back until it was almost out of sight.

"If he turns off and we don't see it, we'll lose him."

"We won't lose him."

"The hell we won't."

"I'm hungry."

Catfish dug in her purse, came out with a half-eaten roll of butter-
scotch Life Savers.

"I'm more hungry than that," Tommy said. He took the roll,
stripped the paper away, and put all six of them into his mouth.

"Thanks a hell of a lot," Catfish said.

"I didn't think you wanted any."

"How much farther do you think it is?"

"All Dickie told us was it was a few miles north of Brainerd."
Tommy's knee was pumping up and down.

"Brainerd is coming right up. He's going after those comic books,
I just know it."

"Back off! Back off!"

"I see him. Relax, would you? You're going to wear a hole in my
floor mat."

36

Many gamblers make the mistake of applying their poker strate-gies to real life. Such persons soon discover that, while they may be playing their cards with great skill and subtlety, their oppo-nents are often choosing from a deck containing an infinite number of aces.

At Wicky's insistence, Freddy stopped at a Little Falls liquor store. Wicky had decided that if he was going to listen to any more of Freddy's stories, there was no reason he had to do it sober.

Fifty miles back, trying to make small talk, he had asked Freddy how he had come to work for Joey Cadillac.

"He seen me hit a guy in a bar one time, and so he give me a job," Freddy bellowed, grinning, enjoying the memory, his hair whipping in the wind. He had insisted on taking the blue Eldorado, driving with the top down, the roar of the bad muffler nearly blocking out the sound of the wind. Freddy had gone on to describe the first job he had done for Joey Cadillac: slamming a car door nineteen times on the left hand of a delinquent account, once for each day the pay-ment was late. "That was Mister C.'s idea. Then I told the guy I was gonna come back the next day and do it twenty times."

Freddy had laughed, slapping his huge hand on the steering wheel.

Wicky thought he was going to be sick.

"Mister C., he's so smart. He said to be sure it was the left hand on account of the guy needed his right hand to sign the check."

Freddy had gone on to regale him with other professional success stories.

Wicky bought a fifth of Stoli and a sixer of Mooseheads. He took the Stoli bottle down a full inch before they were out of the liquor store parking lot.

• • •

Ben turned right off Highway 371 and followed County 42, broken asphalt with weeds growing up through the cracks, through the heavily wooded countryside. The map showed Crook Lake as a jellybean or maybe a peanut shape, with a bump of land cutting into the west end. Sam O'Gara's cabin was on the tip of a wing-shaped peninsula known locally as Sorenson Point, or so Crow had told him. Did the bump on the map represent Sorenson Point, as delineated by a lazy cartographer? Ben hoped so. Every few miles the trees would open and he would find himself skirting the shore of a lake, or occasionally traveling an isthmus between two lakes. He turned off County 42 onto a camelback dirt road marked with an arrow sign: CROOK LAKE PUBLIC LANDING.

The camelback ended at the landing, a small beach with a short concrete ramp where boaters could back their boat trailers into the water. A narrow, unmarked road followed the shoreline in either direction. Guessing that he was on the south side of the lake, Ben followed the shore road to the left. Poplars, oak, and white pine chopped up the sunlight into a bewildering spatter; the dancing spots of brightness on the road confused his eyes. Ben didn't like the trees. He preferred the city or, at least, open spaces. The trees felt like a barrier, like a living wall. What was out there? He did not want to know. He felt like an intruder, as if all the beasts of the forest were watching his every move. The Fleetwood, elegant, smooth, and whisper quiet on the highways, moved like a crude tank through these silent woodlands. He slowed and peered down each driveway and logging path, wondering how he would know the road when he saw it. Most of the time, he couldn't even see the lake. He was ready to turn back, thinking he had passed it, when he spotted a mailbox with bright-orange lettering spray-painted on the side: O'GARA.

The road, or driveway, leading out onto Sorenson Point was the worst of all—lumpy, wet, and almost too narrow for one car. Branches raked the sides as the car limped along, its wheels riding in two ruts. Ben could hear grass scraping the Cadillac's belly. Suddenly, the trees opened and he was at the edge of the lake. He hit the brakes, nearly getting his front tires wet, and looked around. No cabin. But the driveway continued—a sharp bend to the right. He backed up a few feet, cranked the wheel, and continued up the driveway another quarter of a mile, until he reached a cleared, rocky area containing a yellow log cabin and two vehicles: an Oldsmobile and an old flatbed truck. Two men were standing beside the truck, watching him drive up. One was a big, happy-looking man with a shiny red face, a kelly-green blazer with gold buttons, a yellow golf shirt, and chartreuse polyester trousers. Even from several yards away, his eyes were intensely blue. The other man, older, wrinkled, and compact, wore a lumberjack shirt and work-faded denim bib overalls. He was holding a crowbar.

Ben stopped the Fleetwood and lowered the window.

"How you doon?" The older man grinned.

Ben nodded, keeping his eyes on the steel bar. "I'm looking for Sam O'Gara?"

"Yep," Sam O'Gara said. "You got 'im." He knelt down on the sparse grass, one hand grabbing the front bumper, and ducked his head down to look under the truck. "Be right with ya." He lowered himself onto his back, then wriggled his body underneath the engine compartment. Ben could hear him muttering, "Goddamn sumbitch mothafucka." He sounded like Tommy. Ben got out of the car.

The man in the green blazer pushed forward a manicured hand. "Jim Bobick. They call me Jimbo."

"Ben Franklin." Ben shook the hand, looking down at the feet sticking out from beneath the truck. A series of ear-wrenching *ka-whang*s blasted out from the underbelly of the old Ford. Ben stepped back a few feet.

"Goddamn fang-fuckin' bastid." Another series of thuds and clangs. After a few tentative scrapes and more muttered curses, O'Gara worm-walked his way out from under the truck and hopped to his feet.

"Did you fix it?" Jimbo asked.

"Prob'ly not, but I sure give the fucker something to think about." The old man cackled and tossed the crowbar onto the hood of the truck. He looked up at Ben. "So what kin I do you for, mister? You selling something?"

Ben extended a hand. "Ben Franklin," he said. "I'm an associate of Mr. Wicky."

O'Gara reached out a large, greasy paw, grabbed the hand, and squeezed. Ben gasped as bone ground against bone. "So you're one a them fellas Richie was talking about," O'Gara said. "He ought to be here anytime now. You want a beer or something?"

Ben took back his throbbing hand and shook his head. "I was hoping we could talk some business." He looked at Jimbo. Jimbo smiled uncomfortably.

O'Gara said, "Jimbo, you mind if Ben and me have us a little one-on-one?"

"I was just leaving," Jimbo said, moving toward the Oldsmobile.

"You don't got to leave," O'Gara said. "Go grab yourself a brew out of the icebox."

Jimbo hesitated, wavered, then shrugged and headed for the cabin.

"So what's this all about?" O'Gara asked.

Ben said, "To get right to it, Mr. O'Gara, I was hoping I could examine your comic book collection and perhaps make you a good, fair offer on it."

"Hell, man, I already got an offer. Everything's all packed up and ready to go." He jerked a thumb toward the back of the truck. "Soon's Richie shows up with the loot, I'm gonna run the whole kit 'n' kaboodle down south."

Ben licked his lips and stepped toward the truck, which was loaded down with twenty or thirty cardboard cartons strapped to the bed.

"That's good," he said. "Would you mind if we take a quick look at the merchandise?"

O'Gara said, "Goddamn it, I just got all them fuckers packed in there. Why don't we just wait for Richie, and I'll drive 'em on down for you. He should be here pretty quick now."

Ben looked at the cardboard boxes. They were crisscrossed with ropes, tied securely to the bed of the truck.

"Has Mr. Wicky made you a firm offer?"

"You think I'd've gone to all the trouble of packing 'em up, he didn't? Richie, he wanted me to haul the whole kit 'n' kaboodle down to the cities last week. I told him I'd have to see some cash before I did a damn thing, but I figured I could pack 'em up, at least; save us all a lot of time later. I sure as hell didn't think you was going to want to unpack the damn things first thing you got here."

Ben looked back down the driveway. He didn't have a lot of time. It was almost eleven-thirty. Wicky would be arriving soon, if Crow's information was correct. Another even more alarming possibility occurred to him—suppose Freddy Wisnesky had come along for the ride? Ben didn't understand what the relationship was, exactly, between Dickie Wicky and Freddy Wisnesky, but if they were going to baseball games together, anything could be true.

The more he thought about it, the more anxious he became. He decided to make his play.

"How much did Mr. Wicky offer for your collection?" he asked.

O'Gara pushed his hands in his pockets and let his head sink between his shoulders, a crafty squint in his eyes. "You don't know? Thought you fellas was partners."

"I want to be sure we're offering you a fair price."

"What's fair?" O'Gara asked, pulling his hands from his pockets and crossing his tanned arms across his narrow chest.

Ben shrugged. Wicky had claimed he'd offered sixty thousand for the collection, but that didn't mean a thing. "I would have to see the comics," he said.

"Goddamn it, didn't Richie show you that list?"

Ben nodded. "A blue notebook. Is it accurate?"

"Hell, yes. Why d'ya think I give it to him?"

"Mr. Wicky has examined the collection?"

"Sure. Richie looked it over good. That's why I figured I'd get 'em all ready to go."

Ben shook his head. "I have to see what I'm buying. You want to sell the books, you're going to have to let me examine them."

Jimbo did not know what was going on, exactly. He had gone to the cabin expecting to find Ozzie LaRose and Joe Crow. Instead, he had met Sam O'Gara. After some confusion—O'Gara mistaking him for Ben Franklin—they had gotten their identities straight. Crow, O'Gara had told him, would be there soon. Whatever was going on now, it was none of his business.

He found a cold Leinenkugel in the refrigerator, cracked it open, and watched through the window as the two men negotiated. O'Gara was jabbing his finger toward the boxes and flapping his arms. Franklin was leaning backward at what looked like an impossible angle, as though blown back by the torrent of words coming from his smaller opponent. He kept looking down the driveway, as if he was expecting someone. From the body language alone, Jimbo concluded that neither of these men was looking for a win-win situation. Neither one of them would make it in the real estate game, he decided. He was thinking about how he was going to spend his commission on the Whiting Lake property, when he saw O'Gara throw up his arms and grab the crowbar.

Jimbo thought, Now *that's* negotiating.

O'Gara squeezed his thin lips together. Both his eyes and his cheeks were bulging. He held himself together for nearly three long seconds before exploding. "You want to see the goddamn comics? I'll show you the goddamn comics!" He grabbed the crowbar off the hood of the truck. Ben sprinted backward ten feet before he saw that the old man was going after the comic books, not him.

"Wait!" he shouted, but O'Gara had already jabbed the chisel end of the greasy crowbar into one of the boxes and ripped through the corrugated cardboard. "Be careful with those!" O'Gara gutted the box, pulling out handfuls of vintage comic books, throwing them at Ben. *Police Comics. World's Finest. Captain Marvel.*

"Okay!" Ben shouted. "Take it easy!" He picked up a copy of *Comic Cavalcade* #50—not a great comic, but not in bad shape. O'Gara was bringing back the bar, preparing to tear into another box. Ben ran forward and grabbed the bar.

"All right, Mr. O'Gara. There's no need to destroy them."

O'Gara scowled and relaxed. Ben started to pick up the scattered comics. They looked to be in excellent condition, except for a few that had been shredded by the crowbar. Quite salable.

"These aren't in perfect condition," he said. "The paper is getting a bit yellow. Fifty thousand dollars seems a bit high, to tell you the truth."

O'Gara's eyes bulged. "Fifty?"

Ben took a step back and said, "Yes, that's the figure Mr. Wicky mentioned."

"Son-of-a-bitch offered me fifteen. A buck a book." O'Gara boxed the air, two rapid jabs and a right hook, about the same height as Wicky's chin would be, had he been there. Ben stepped back. O'Gara said, "You telling me he was trying to rip me off?"

"I believe he was attempting to steal from both of us. You see, I'm the one who was to have provided the money. Mr. Wicky was merely acting as my agent, but since both you and I are now speaking directly, I see no reason why we can't make our own deal. My opinion is, Mr. Wicky's duplicitous acts have served to disqualify him."

"Damn right! He's gonna be here in a few minutes. We can tell him to take a hike. Give him a boot on his rear to get him started."

Ben shook his head. "I don't think we should wait," he said. "Mr. Wicky has an associate, a large man with a violent personality. That man may be with him."

"He has a *stooge*? Is he some kind of mobster or something? What the hell are we talking about here?"

"Let's just say that we'd be best off doing our deal and then clearing out for a while. That is, if we can agree on a price. What do you think?"

"You said something about fifty thousand smackeroonies, my friend." O'Gara made his eyebrows jump up and down.

Ben looked over his shoulder. It was quiet in the woods; the only sounds were those of small waves coming from the shore and the faint scraping sound of leaves in the wind. He did not like being out on a peninsula, at the end of a narrow driveway, only one way in and out. It was one of those moments, he suddenly realized, when he would have to make a decision without having sufficient time or information, like playing a big hand with an unmarked deck.

"If I pay you twenty-five thousand in cash, right now, will you get in that truck and follow me back down to the cities? Right now?"

"Fifty thousand bazookas," said O'Gara, his eyes glazing. "Man, a guy could buy a lot of dog food with that. You show me that kind of cash, my friend, and we'll be rolling south before you can say 'Fuck me, darling.'"

Ben stared down at the smaller man, a leprechaun in a lumberjack shirt, grinning up at him. He looked at his watch. Eleven forty-five. He took a deep breath, walked to the back of the Cadillac, opened the trunk, took thirty bundles of bills out of a black Samsonite suitcase, and stuffed them into a cloth roll bag printed with the Gold's Gym logo. He handed the bag to O'Gara.

"Thirty thousand 'bazookas,'" Ben said. "My final offer." He had brought $72,000 along, the entire remaining assets of the Tom and Ben Show, but he was hoping that the old man would go for the thirty.

O'Gara looked into the bag at the strapped bundles of twenty-dollar bills. He sucked in his breath, reached in, and pushed his hand deep into the bundles. Ben allowed himself a faint smile.

"I'll be damned," O'Gara said, his voice reverent. He raised his head and looked into Ben's tea-colored eyes. "Son, you just bought yourself a whole goddamn truckload of funny pictures."

"I told you we were gonna lose him." Catfish stopped the Porsche in the middle of the road.

Tommy had reached a new level of fidgetiness. His head was jerking back and forth as if he were receiving an electric charge. "Gotta be around here someplace. Go back, try that little road we were looking at." He pulled out his bottle of Tylenol, shook it, poured the last four tablets into his palm, and lapped them up.

"That was an old logging path, Tommy. This is a Porsche, not a four-by-four."

"Okay! Okay! Forget about it! Keep going. It's got to be one of the places on this lake here. How many cabins can there be?"

"Must be hundreds."

"Fuck! Fuck! Now what're we gonna do?"

Catfish had about had it with Tommy. It was like sitting next to a hyperactive Saint Bernard puppy—the only difference was that so far he hadn't pissed on the Recaro seats. She was beginning to understand why Ben was doing his wheeling and dealing solo.

"Let's start looking. You can see most of these places from the road. All we have to do is spot his car. There can't be too many yellow Cadillacs up here."

"Then this one guy, Mister C. tells me to hurt him on account of he did something, I don't know what. So this guy thinks he's a tough guy, a big guy, bigger'n me, and so I kinda ease up next to him, he's standing in line for to see this movie, *Terminator Two*, he's one a them bodybuilders like Arnold, and I drop a quarter on the ground and say, 'Hey, that your money?' The guy says yeah, and he bends over to pick it up, and I hit him back a the head with my elbow. Went down, wham, lost a bunch of teeth on the sidewalk. I didn't even have to do nothing else." Freddy laughed.

Wicky stared numbly out the windshield, holding a bottle of Moosehead between his legs. He had taken the Stoli down to the level where he could listen without envisioning himself in the roles of Freddy's victims. He would never have believed that Freddy could be so voluble, but all you had to do was get him on the right subject, and he opened right up.

Freddy took his foot off the accelerator and slowed the Caddy down to fifty-five. Ahead of them, just coming into sight, a maroon MHP car was parked on the shoulder. As they drew closer, Wicky could see that the cop had pulled over two people on a motorcycle. A man and a woman, the woman arguing with the cop. He watched the scene flash by, wondering what would happen if the highway patrol pulled Freddy over. Terrible things, no doubt.

He took another swallow of beer. The woman had looked familiar. He let his mind run with it for a few seconds, then gave it up, unscrewed the cap on the Stoli, took a hit.

Freddy had thought of another story.

"I ever tell you about the time I hadda do a priest? I hadda cross myself every ten minutes for a week after that one. See, there was this priest . . ."

Wicky scrunched down in his seat, refusing to give meaning to the words. He didn't like priests either, but Jesus Christ! Freddy was remembering and laughing.

An intersection flashed by. Wicky blinked, turned in his seat, and looked back. County 42.

"We got to turn around," he said. "That was the turn."

After a difficult half hour, the cop finished writing Debrowski's ticket and let them go.

"Did you see them go by? That was Dickie and Freddy," Crow said as Debrowski kicked the Kawasaki to life. "What the hell is Freddy doing up here?"

Debrowski signaled, looked back over her shoulder, and pulled out onto the highway. As soon as the cop was out of sight, she brought the bike back up to eighty-five.

"You think Sam can handle Freddy?" Debrowski shouted.

"Yes!" he shouted back. "Maybe," he said to himself. "Maybe not."

Now Chester, he'll take off after anything. And Festus, he don't care what he does, long as he gets to be with Chester.

—Sam O'Gara

"What's that?" Ben said, cocking his head.

Sam O'Gara listened. "You mean that engine sound? Sounds like a car without no muffler on it coming up the drive. Could be Richie, I s'pose." He laughed. "Ain't he gonna be surprised to see you here!"

Ben froze for three seconds, his eyes flicking from side to side. The sound of the approaching car intensified. The front end of a blue Cadillac convertible appeared. He snatched the bag of money from O'Gara, ran to his car, got in and took off, going forward, straight into the woods, aiming the big car at what appeared to be a break in the trees.

O'Gara shouted, "You don't want to go that way!"

Three car lengths into the woods, the left front tire hit a moss-covered rock; the Cadillac slewed to the side, the long tail knocking over a three-inch-diameter spruce tree. Ben wrenched the wheel to the right, trying to avoid a cluster of birch trees, came up over a low hummock, and dove down into a boggy depression, burying the front bumper in wet, mossy peat. He jerked the gear selector into reverse and floored the accelerator. The wheels kicked up a few clods of peat moss, but the car would not move. Ben threw open the door, grabbed the gym bag, and got out.

O'Gara was yelling, "That don't go nowhere, Mr. Franklin!"

The blue Cadillac had skidded to a halt beside O'Gara's truck. Freddy Wisnesky was climbing out of the driver's seat.

Ben looked into the woods—a mass of trees, thornbushes, poison ivy, hungry bears, wolves, moose. . . . Freddy was in motion, walking toward him, less than fifty yards away. Ben's choice was clear. Lifting

257

his long legs high, he bounded into the forest. Freddy hesitated for a beat, giving Ben a sporting ten yards on his lead, then launched himself in pursuit, parting the underbrush as if it was smoke.

O'Gara looked at Wicky, who was sitting in the car unscrewing the top from a bottle of vodka.

"Now what the hell you think got into them two?" O'Gara asked.

Wicky took a hit off the bottle, offered it to O'Gara.

"Russky stuff? No, thanks." He opened the door to the red truck and pulled a bottle out from beneath the seat. Jack Daniel's, with the black label. "I only drink American, son. You want a snort of the real thing?"

Wicky reached an unsteady hand for the bottle, poured an amber ounce into his mouth, swallowed. "That's pretty good," he said. "Say, you given that Homestead Mining any more thought?"

Sam took the bottle back, upended it, swished the whiskey around his mouth, and swallowed.

"Goddamn," he wheezed, snapping his head from side to side. "Ahhh. Homestead? Yep, I been thinking about it. You show me a good price on these here comic books, I'm almost sure to buy some."

"Ben didn't make you a deal?"

"Nope. Tried to, but I said we hadda wait for you. Richie's my main man, I said. I'm sure he'll match your offer, I told him."

During the two and a half hours spent riding behind Debrowski on the open road, Crow had imagined himself flying through the air toward certain death no less than twenty times. Now that they were on a dirt road, the kind of surface the bike was made to handle, he had foreseen his death twenty times in the last five minutes. If doing eighty miles per hour on the highway was frightening, doing sixty on dirt and gravel was pure horror. They came up over a low rise—he was sure they were airborne for at least a second—and saw the lake not fifty yards directly in front of them. Debrowski hit the brakes hard, Crow slid forward, pushing her right up onto the gas tank, the bike skittering over the washboard surface of the road.

Somehow, she kept the machine under control, and they came to a dust-clouded halt twenty feet from the water. Debrowski coughed in the dust, spat.

"You want to get the hell off me?" she said, her voice hoarse.

Crow swung one leg over the back of the bike and stood shakily on solid ground. Debrowski kicked down the stand and got off.

"This must be Crook Lake," she said. "You okay, Crow? You look like you're seeing your tombstone."

Crow said, "Let's get going." His voice cracked, as if he was thirteen again. He pointed. "I think we follow the shore road to the left."

Debrowski climbed back on the bike.

"It's about a mile and a half, a turnoff to the right. There should be a mailbox with 'O'Gara' painted on it. Keep the revs down. When we find the drive, I want to stash the bike and go in on foot. We don't know what we're going to find. I don't want them to hear us coming."

"Do you have anything with you?" Debrowski asked.

"Like what?"

"Like a gun."

"Do I look like I have a gun?"

He could feel her shrug. When they reached the mailbox designated "O'Gara," Debrowski turned up the driveway. Crow tapped her shoulder. She pulled the bike off the path and into a tall stand of nettles. They got off and pushed the bike between two wide-trunked basswoods.

"We've got about a quarter mile to the cabin," Crow said. "Let's see what old Sam's got going on." He started up the driveway at a run, hearing the distinctive, distant howls of Chester and Festus. Howls of celebration, anger, fear, or mourning? He had no idea.

A lifetime ago, Ben Fink had been the number-one hurdler at Knickerbocker High School in White Plains, New York. If there had been a flaw in his technique, it was that he jumped too high and too far. "Time you spend floating around up there, Fink, is time you could be running," his coach had told him.

The tendency to bound high and far was serving him well twenty years later. The uneven, brush-riddled, bog-dotted peninsula flashed beneath his flying feet. Behind him, he could hear the crashing of brush and dead wood. The gym bag gripped in his right hand kept slapping against the passing branches. He hugged it to his chest and concentrated on silent running. Freddy Wisnesky was out of sight, though still audible. Ben turned to his right, thinking to find the driveway, take it back to the lakeshore road, get out of this forest. Every clump of brush, every hillock, every fallen tree, could be concealing a bear, or worse.

As this thought joggled in his mind, he heard a distant howl, a primitive, carnivorous sound that sent violent tremors through his six-foot-three-inch frame. The first howl was followed by another. Ben sailed over an uprooted spruce and accelerated. Whatever they were, he could almost feel their hot tongues rasping shreds of flesh from his long, lonely bones.

38

What you got to do, you want people to do what you want, you want to give them two choices: They do what you want, or else.

—Joey Cadillac

"What was that?" Catfish asked.

"That was Ben!" Tommy said.

The tall man clutching the gym bag had erupted from the woods, crossed the road at high velocity, and been swallowed up by the trees on the other side. The sighting had lasted less than one second.

"Stop the car! Let me out." Tommy opened the door and let his foot drag on the road until Catfish slowed down enough for him to hop out. "Ben!" He looked in at Catfish. "I'll go get him. You wait here."

Catfish watched him disappear into the forest. She could hear dogs barking.

"Like hell," she muttered. She reached over and closed the door. Two spotted yellow hounds crossed the road a few feet in front of the Porsche, entering the trees at the same point where Tom and Ben had disappeared.

Catfish laughed, put the car in gear, and started forward.

Karl tapped Joey on the shoulder and pointed.

"Crook Lake."

The lake grew larger as they approached.

"Where's the point? Show me the point," Joey said. Karl banked the Grumman, tipping the left wing down, and headed toward the west end of the eight-mile-long lake. Joey peered through the windshield. "Is that it?"

"Should be. You want me to set you down right at the end, right? Looks to me like there's a dock."

"Swing us over. Let me see what we got down there."

Karl let the plane drop to two hundred feet and passed by the tip of the point, just off the shoreline.

Joey was staring past him out the Plexiglas window. "I can't see, I can't see."

Karl banked to the right and passed the point on the land side, keeping the right side of the plane down to give Joey his view.

"I see a building. I see Freddy's car, goddamn it! There it is! Put it down, let's go! Shit, I see a yellow Caddy too. They're there! Land this fucker!"

"You want me to bring you into the dock?" Karl asked.

"I pay you eight hundred bucks, you think I want to swim? Let's go. I got business down there!"

Crow crouched and motioned for Debrowski to stop. He could see a flash of baby blue at the end of the drive.

"Dickie and Freddy are here," he said over his shoulder.

"Ben?"

"I can see Freddy's car. Let's fade off to the right here. If Sam's got the deal working, I don't want to ball it up." He stepped off the driveway and into the trees, trying to walk quietly through the sticks and leaves and brush. Debrowski followed. Crow could hear the quiet sound of chains on leather. A loud thrumming sound filtered through the woods—an airplane just off the point. They took advantage of the noise to proceed quickly, but slowed as the sound of the engines faded. They were several yards off the driveway, moving parallel to it. He could hear faint sounds of men talking and, in the distance, Sam's hounds giving voice.

The seaplane made another pass, this time lower and directly overhead, its noisy reciprocating engines rattling the leaves. Crow moved forward quickly, jogging through the woods, then stopped suddenly. He heard Debrowski halt breathlessly, directly behind him. They were looking through a V formed by a pair of mature basswoods. The clearing began a short distance beyond. Sam's truck, loaded down with boxes, was parked at the head of the driveway, ready to roll. Beside it, pointing in the opposite direction, were Freddy's Eldorado convertible and a white Oldsmobile. Sam O'Gara and Dickie Wicky were sitting on the hood of the Cadillac, facing a third man, dressed in a two-tone green suit. The three men were passing a bottle, laughing.

"Where's Freddy?" Debrowski whispered. "Who's the big guy in the leprechaun suit?"

Crow shrugged and held up a hand. He watched Sam take a hit off the bottle, Jack Daniel's, and felt his stomach roll in sympathy. He wanted to hear what they were saying, but they were too far away, their words masked by the wind in the leaves, the waves on the shore, and the buzz of the seaplane. The man in green turned his face to the side, giving them a look at his profile.

"Oh, shit," said Crow.

"What?"

"It's Jimbo Bobick, the realtor from hell."

Debrowski grabbed Crow's arm and squeezed. He looked at her, then looked where she was pointing. Behind them, ten yards off to the side, Ben's yellow Cadillac was mired nose-first in a shallow sinkhole. Crow scanned the woods, suddenly aware that danger could arrive from any direction. The trees were still, revealing nothing. The sound of the seaplane grew louder again.

The only thing he knew for sure was that nothing, so far, was going according to plan.

Wicky took a hit off the bottle and, following Sam's example, wiped his mouth on his sleeve. He continued his story.

"So this guy, I owe the guy a few bucks, you know? Hey, Jimbo, you played with Crow a few times, didn't you?"

Jimbo nodded. He was enjoying the unexpected late-morning cocktail hour but keeping his hits on the bottle light. With no idea what was going on, he didn't want to get too blasted. Smiling vacantly, he listened to Wicky's tale.

"Now this is I guy I known for years," Wicky explained to Sam. "Joe Crow. And he gets all uptight on me about this money, so I said to him, 'Here, take my Rolex. I don't have you paid off in a couple weeks, you got yourself a fifteen-thousand-dollar watch.' I mean, I'm going to pay the guy, so what do I care if he wears my timepiece for a few days? The guy is being an asshole, but hey, I'm flexible, you know?

"So a week later, this Crow comes back at me. 'Gimme my money, Rich,' he says. I tell him I'll have it for him in a few days. So the son-of-a-bitch says, 'Fuck you, I'm gonna hock this sucker.'" Wicky took the bottle from Sam, wiggled his eyebrows, swallowed.

"So what do I do? I get on the horn to the pawnshop, and I say to the pawnshop guy, I say, 'This guy's going to be there in about five minutes to hock a Rolex.' The pawnshop guy says, 'So?' I say, 'So it's a counterfeit.' 'Yeah?' he says. 'How come you're telling me this?' I say, 'And I got a hundred bucks for you if you agree with me.'" Wicky laughed. "Son-of-a-bitch made me give him my *Visa* number! Anyways, a few days later, Crow gives me the Rolex back!" He held out his wrist and turned the gold watch in the sunlight.

"How come he did that?" O'Gara asked.

"I'm not sure. I guess he got pissed. Hey, you know what time it is?" Wicky examined his watch with raised eyebrows. "It's time for another drink!" He reached for the bottle.

Sam, Wicky, and Jimbo were laughing. Wicky was looking at his watch. Past the cabin, through a window in the trees, Crow could see the seaplane coming in low over the lake, heading south, into the wind, the pontoons kissing the water, then it was out of sight.

Debrowski hissed, "What's going on? Where's Ben?"

"I don't know, but I'm guessing he's with Freddy."

"What are we doing?"

"Waiting for Sam to do something."

"Do something? He's getting wasted is what he's doing, Crow. I think I should go talk to them."

"We don't know what's going on. Maybe Sam's closing a deal with Dickie. Maybe Ben and Freddy are in the cabin having milk and cookies. Let's lay low for a while, see what happens."

"We wait much longer, those three are going to be unconscious."

The sound of the airplane taxiing across the water was growing louder. Sam and Wicky seemed to notice it for the first time; Sam was pointing toward the dock. Crow saw the nose of the plane come slowly into view. One pontoon nudged the dock, a door opened, and a man wearing a shiny black sport coat and gray pants jumped clumsily out onto the dock.

Crow said, "It can't be."

"Who is it?" Debrowski asked. "It looks like—"

"It is," Crow said.

Joey was feeling extra good. He had started to think of himself as Joey the Avenger. The two Dex he'd popped just after they took off were doing sprints up and down his arteries, and the last few ounces of Martell, swallowed only minutes ago, had him running smooth as a new Seville. The fact that he hadn't slept all night did not bother him, though he supposed it would later. Right now he had business to take care of, old business, and it was gonna feel good. The comic book guys had been niggling at him for months; now it was payback time. He hoped that Freddy hadn't finished with them yet. He wanted a chance to explain it to them, to watch them regret their sins.

"You stay here," he shouted into the cockpit.

Karl nodded and shut down the engines.

Standing on the dock, brushing his sleeves, straightening his lapels, adjusting his sunglasses, Joey looked toward shore. Three men had come out to the base of the dock to greet him. Joey knew, almost before the particulars registered on his consciousness, that the men were drunk. That they were standing shoulder to shoulder was one clue. That they were rocking from side to side was another. The bottle dangling from the short, fat one's left hand was also a reliable indicator. Much to Joey's regret, none of them resembled either half of the Tom and Ben Show.

The short, fat one was the drunkest. He had greasy blond hair that was pushed carelessly to the side, protruding lips, and tiny pink-and-blue eyes. He was wearing a blue oxford shirt, a red-and-navy rep tie, and red suspenders. Two red patches floated high on his cheeks, making him look like a thirteen-year-old who had awakened in the body of a thirty-five-year-old alcoholic businessman.

The scrawny one, the old man, looked like all the water'd been sucked out of him. Skinny, wrinkly, wiry guy in a lumberjack shirt. He appeared happy. The third man seemed happy too, a big, bald-faced grinner in a sharp-looking green outfit.

"Hey, fella," the old man yelled. "You sure you got the right dock?"

Joey looked past him. He could see the blue Eldorado convertible he had loaned to Freddy.

"This is the O'Gara place, right?" he said. "Which one a you guys is Rich Wicky?"

"Hey, I know that voice!" The one with the bottle in his hand nudged the older one. "You know who this guy is?" He put out a hand. "Mister Cadillac? How d'you do? I'm Rich Wicky. Hey, nice plane!"

"Still no sign of Freddy or Ben," Debrowski said.

"Wait here," Crow said. He ran out and across the clearing, looked in the cabin's south window. Empty room. He circled to the screen door that led in through the porch, then slipped inside. The cabin was unoccupied by the living or the dead. He had half expected to find Ben Fink, or what was left of him. What he did find was an aged and rust-mottled shotgun, twelve-gauge pump, propped in a corner with a broom and two fishing rods. He looked out the window; the three men were walking back up the path from the dock. He pressed the thumb release and pulled on the pump, which moved back with a grinding grit-on-metal sound. There was a shell in the chamber, a paper-bodied number-eight shot that had to be twenty-five years old, at least. He forced the pump forward.

Sam was leading Wicky, Jimbo, and Joey Cadillac toward the truck, pointing, his arms performing whiskey-enhanced gesticulations. Crow went to the screen door and listened. Closer now, only thirty feet away, he could hear them. Sam was pointing toward Ben's mired car.

". . . and they just took off through the woods there, one right after t'other. Prob'ly lost by now, but I wouldn't worry—they just keep on walkin', they'll come out someplace or another." He cackled. "Else my dogs'll find 'em."

Joey Cadillac did not appear to be amused. "What about the other one? Tom."

"Well now, the only fellas I seen here today, 'cept for you fellas, was them two. Don't know no Tom."

"We're supposed to meet him at the Pop Top over in Brainerd, Mister Cadillac," Wicky said. "Later this afternoon."

A series of distant howls floated through the trees.

Joey stared at the woods. "That fucking Freddy, off running with the animals." He shook his head sadly. "So where are these comics everybody's so excited about?"

"I just bought 'em from Sam, here," Wicky said. He pointed toward the truck. "All ready to go."

"They ain't bought till the money's got," Sam said. "You got that money we was talkin', Richie?"

"I'm good for it, Sam, you know I am." Wicky threw an arm over Sam's shoulder.

"I know you are, Richie," Sam said, "but business is business. Maybe Ben, he'll make it on back here. He's got this whole fuckin' bag full a money."

Joey was watching them with a sour, amused expression. "I got a better idea. How about if you two start hauling them boxes down to the dock. I'll take them into, like, protective custody. You two get your deal figured out, then find me this Tom and Ben Show, and I'll give 'em back. How's that sound?"

Sam fitted a Pall Mall into his mouth. "That don't sound so good to me," he said. "Them comics ain't a-goin' nowheres without I get me some fuckin' bazookas."

Crow winced. Even at a moment such as this, he was embarrassed by what happened to Sam's speech when the old guy had had a few drinks. Sam was trying to light up, having trouble matching the flame of his lighter with the tip of the cigarette.

Joey said, "You want some bazookas? How about this bazooka, wise guy?" A small silver handgun appeared in his hand. It was pointing at Sam, pointing at a spot just above his ear, inches away.

Sam froze, staring at the gun, lips impaled by the unlit cigarette. Wicky took two unsteady steps back. Jimbo Bobick, a vacant, uncomprehending smile on his face, watched the other three men as though they were holograms: there but not there.

Joey snapped, "You just hold still now, *Rich*. Now do you boys want to help me get them boxes down to the dock?"

Crow took a deep breath and pushed through the screen door, holding the shotgun at his shoulder, lining up the bead with the center of Joey Cadillac's abdomen.

"Little Joey," he said.

Joey's head swiveled. He started to bring the handgun around.

"Don't do it, Joey. Drop the gun." Crow started walking toward him, looking down the long barrel. Joey froze, but he didn't drop the gun. It was pointed at the ground, just to Crow's left.

"What the fuck're you doing here?" he demanded.

"Put the gun down, Joey."

Joey locked eyes with Crow, then glanced off to his right. "Fucking hell—I knew it!"

Debrowski was coming across the clearing.

"How you doing, Joey?" she said.

"Fuck you."

"Put the gun down, Joey," Crow repeated. Sam and Wicky had eased to the side. Wicky's face was dead white; even the red spots on his cheeks were gone. He was breathing though his mouth, almost panting. Jimbo Bobick, by contrast, remained motionless, his expression one of mild wonder.

Joey stared at the end of the shotgun. "That's some gun you got there, Crow."

Crow tightened his finger on the trigger.

"You know you got a gun full a spiders, Crow? That piece ain't been shot in years. Probably blow up on you, if it shoots at all."

"You can find out," Crow said.

"We were playing cards, I'd call you, Crow."

Crow smiled.

Joey the Avenger felt ready to explode, and he was loving it. Holding it back, keeping the cool on his face, but ready to go apeshit on this guy. Any second now. The barrel of the shotgun was full of spider eggs. The thing looked like it had been rusting away for years. He wouldn't use a gun like that to knock off a 7-Eleven. It was a piece of junk, and this Crow was full of shit.

The more he thought along these lines, the more certain he became. Crow was a bluffer, after all. Joey licked his lips and thought about how he would do it. He would shoot Crow in the face, take his time, see the little black hole appear. Then the ball-busting leather bitch. And the three drunks. Do them all and take the comic books. It was solid, a good payback, righteous vengeance. It was too bad he had missed the Tom and Ben Show, but he could take care of them later.

He laughed and raised the Davis, aligning the shallow silver sights with the center of Crow's forehead. He was feeling the trigger pressing against the flesh of his index finger when he saw the flash from the end of the shotgun barrel and felt something hit him in the chest.

A few weeks earlier, Jimbo Bobick had been driving home from the Grand Casino near Lake Mille Lacs at 4:00 A.M. Suddenly, a deer, a large doe, had appeared in his headlights. He had understood immediately that it would be impossible for him to stop. Time had slowed, and the single second it had taken for the deer to slide up over his hood, shatter the windshield, and travel through the car into the back seat had taken, subjectively, over a minute. He remembered thinking, as the deer was in the process of penetrating the safety glass, that the poor animal looked surprised.

Now the sensation that time had slowed was repeating itself. Jimbo saw Joey's hand coming up with the chrome-plated automatic. He saw the stubby barrel lining up with Joe Crow's forehead. He saw Crow stepping back, bringing the shotgun up, pulling the stock against his shoulder, firing. The sound of the shotgun firing was like that of a paper bag being popped. A cloud of fine lead shot struck Joey Cadillac on the chest, bounced off, and pattered to the grassy earth. Joey staggered back, startled but uninjured. Crow pulled back on the pump to eject the dud, but the paper casing had jammed in the chamber.

Joey Cadillac laughed and again raised the automatic.

This time Jimbo had time to understand that he was about to see a man being shot. Simultaneously, in another sector of his mind, he was watching his eight-thousand-dollar commission on the Whiting Lake property being blown away. In another second there would be no Joe Crow, and therefore no sale. This equation projected itself into the realm of the physical: with a piercing, atavistic shriek, Jimbo propelled his body horizontally through space and hit Joey Cadillac hard on the side of his left knee. He heard the knee pop and the gun fire as one explosion, an intensely loud *crack* only inches from his ear. He rolled away, sat up. Something was wrong with his foot. A red hole in his shoe. Blood. Joey had gone down hard but had held on to the gun. Sitting on the grass, his face contorted with pain, he was holding his knee with one hand, bringing the gun up with the other, now aiming it toward Jimbo, ready to make a new hole in some other part of his body. Though he had acted quickly and decisively a moment before, Jimbo now found himself charmed to paralysis by the small dark hole at the end of the shiny little automatic. He had just enough time to regret that he would never be able to close the sale, when he saw the shotgun flicker through the air like a spinning baton.

The cartwheeling shotgun smashed into the back of Joey's right hand, sending the little automatic through a twenty-foot arc into a patch of dark-green woodbine. Joey stared at his hand, bewildered. His wrist did not appear to be working; the hand hung limp.

Wicky, who was closest to where the gun had landed, picked it up and waved it in front of him like a shield, pointing it at everyone and no one. "Okay," he said, his voice cracking. "Okay!"

"Take it easy, Dickie," Crow said.

"You broke my fucking hand!" Joey said, looking at Crow, astonished.

"Okay!" Wicky shouted. His eyes were wild, pointing in too many directions, his pupils constricted to pinheads.

"Easy now, Richie," Sam said, starting toward him.

"Okay!" Wicky screamed, bringing the gun to bear on Sam.

The sudden crashing of brush jerked everyone's attention from the drunk with the gun. Freddy Wisnesky, his red face bearing dozens of scratches, charged out of the woods, into the clearing. His Minnesota Twins T-shirt was shredded, and his arms were covered with scratches from plowing through acres of thornbushes.

"Frederick!" said Joey Cadillac, his expression a mélange of pain, hope, anger, and triumph.

Freddy was breathing heavily. His eyes rested briefly on the gun in Wicky's hand, then landed on Joey Cadillac.

"Mister C.?"

Holding his hand against his belly, Joey climbed painfully to his feet and jerked his head toward the dock.

"Okay!" rasped Wicky. He was aiming the gun at Freddy. Crow hoped he wouldn't shoot. A guy like Freddy, getting shot would just piss him off.

Joey looked at Wicky, at the gun. "Get me down to the dock, Freddy." As the words left his mouth, the sound of the twin Pratt & Whitneys rumbled up from the shore and the seaplane started moving away from the dock.

Joey screamed at the departing plane. "You son-of-a-bitch, you leave me here, you're a fucking dead man!" He stared at the seaplane, breathing heavily, then turned back to Freddy. "Fuck him. He can't hear me. Get in that truck, Freddy. You're driving." He shot a look at Wicky. "You shoot that thing at me, Rich, and you're fucked." He hopped and limped to the truck, opened the passenger door with his left hand, climbed in. Crow, Debrowski, and Sam were all moving back, away from Freddy, away from the truck, away from Dickie Wicky and the gun. Bobick sat on the ground, gaping white-faced at the blood seeping from the hole in his white shoe.

Wicky staggered to the side, holding the gun unsteadily in both hands. Freddy got into the cab, started the truck.

"No!" Wicky fired the gun. A short gash appeared on the truck hood. "My comics!" he shrieked.

"Get moving!" Joey yelled, ducking his head down. Freddy popped the clutch, and the truck lurched forward.

Wicky screamed, "No!" He pulled the trigger again, shattering the truck's back window.

"Go! Go! Go!" Joey shouted. Freddy found second gear and pressed the gas pedal to the floor. Wicky staggered after them, firing again, missing the truck completely, and again, shattering the driver's side mirror. The truck was bouncing down the uneven surface of the driveway, picking up speed. Freddy slammed the shifter into third gear, keeping his right foot on the floor. Wicky fired again, running splay-legged down the driveway after the truck. "Go! Get me the fuck out of here!" Joey shouted, his head between his knees. The speedometer read thirty miles per hour when Freddy saw the lake in front of him and remembered the sharp turn in the driveway. He took his foot off the gas, but oddly, the big red fucker continued to accelerate.

The sound of the racing truck engine ended with a splash. Crow looked at his father and asked, "You ever get around to fixing that bad gas pedal, Sam?"

Sam shrugged. "I thought I had 'er taken care of, but maybe not."

"What are you guys talking about?" Debrowski asked.

"Let's walk up to the bend and take a look," Crow suggested.

"Jimbo here's got hisself shot up," Sam said.

"My foot," Jimbo moaned, his face bloodless.

"Let me see." Debrowski squatted beside him, carefully removed his shoe, and peeled off his sock. "Looks worse than it is," she said. "You got a groove down the side of your foot now. A little tape, you'll be fine."

"It doesn't feel fine."

"Let's go inside and see what Ozzie's got in his medicine cabinet. Can you walk?"

"I think so." He climbed painfully to his feet and hobbled toward the cabin.

"I'm going to see what's happened with Dickie and company," Crow said. He started down the driveway, followed by Sam. They found Wicky sitting on the shore at the bend in the driveway, staring out onto the lake.

"You okay, Richie?" Sam asked, taking the gun from his hands.

Wicky nodded but showed no interest in standing up. The tail end of the truck was jutting from the water, pointed straight up, forty feet out from the shore. A few boxes were still bobbing on the surface.

"You s'pose those fellas are still in there?" Sam asked.

"I suppose they are," said Crow.

Sam shook his head. "It's too goddamn bad. Ozzie had one hell of a porn collection."

Wicky said, "My comic books. All those comic books."

Sam patted him on the shoulder. "It's okay, Richie. It's just ink on paper."

39

THOUSANDS OF NUDES CLUTTER
CROOK LAKE SHORELINE

RESIDENTS OUTRAGED BY MYSTERIOUS PORNOGRAPHIC TIDE

—*Headline*, Brainerd Northern Sun

Crow and his father left Wicky sitting on the point and walked back toward the cabin.

"Sorry I was late," Crow said. "My car wouldn't start."

"It's that fancy-ass car you got—that's your trouble, son."

Crow nodded. "So how'd we do?"

Sam squinted up at the sun and scratched his four-day beard. "Welp, that Ben Franklin fellow was here and all but gave me a bag of money, but then the big guy in the blue Caddy showed up. Franklin, he took off. Runs like a goddamn deer. Took his bag of money with him too."

Crow nodded philosophically. Somehow it did not surprise him that he was going to come out of the deal with a big zero.

"Do you think he's still out there in the woods?"

"Sure. 'Less the dogs ate him. They'll chase down anything runnin'. " Sam laughed and fitted a cigarette between his lips. They were coming into the small clearing around the cabin. He lit his cigarette and, closing one eye against the smoke, said, "You know, son, you might just want to take a look in that yellow car over there. That money that fellow was offering me, it came out of the trunk. Wouldn't surprise me there was still a buck or two left in there."

Catfish Wicky had been driving in and out of people's driveways for half an hour, searching for the yellow Cadillac. One way or another, she was going to get her share. Two things she could not bear: to be bored and to be left out. She pulled out of one driveway—there had been nothing at its end but a boarded-up shack—spun her wheels in the dirt, and roared up the road, looking for the next mailbox.

"That fucking Tommy," she muttered, angry with him for taking off after Ben and, at the same time, relieved that he had gone. He had been fucking up her life ever since she could remember. At the same time, there was nobody like Tommy. Ever since they were kids. No one else had ever understood her the way he did. Especially not Dickie.

The eighth driveway she tried, a long, narrow, rutted path, Catfish almost ran over her husband. She saw him at the last instant, sitting like a lump in the middle of the driveway, jammed her foot down on the brake, and skidded to a stop.

"Hey." She stuck her head out the window.

Dickie raised his head and stared at her, open-mouthed. "Cat?"

"Who do you think?"

Dickie staggered to his feet and pointed vaguely in the direction of the lake. Catfish followed his gesture and saw the back of the truck jutting from the water.

"My comics," he said.

"What happened?"

Dickie shook his head helplessly.

"Where's your car? Did you come up here with Ben?" Dickie pointed up the driveway. Catfish put the Porsche in gear and drove around him. Dickie stood weaving in place, then started up the driveway after her. His memories of the last hour were neither clear nor arranged in their proper sequence. All he knew for sure was that the comics were gone, and with them his future. He had no idea what Catfish was doing there or where everybody else had disappeared to. He remembered, in a dreamy way, that he had been shooting a gun, but he couldn't remember why, or at who. Perhaps Catfish could explain it to him.

Jimbo was already feeling better. Debrowski had taped up his foot and mixed him a bourbon and water. Jimbo was telling her about the island on Whiting Lake.

"It's Joe's kind of place. Quiet, secluded, no neighbors. Bass, walleye, northerns, you name it. Anything a guy could want."

"That's great," said Debrowski. "I'm sure he's going to love it." She was tired. Crow and his dad were out in the woods, prying open the trunk of Ben's mired Cadillac. "You think you can drive with that foot all bandaged up?"

"I can't get my shoe on. I'd hate to have to stand on the brake. It still hurts like a son-of-a-bitch."

They heard the crunching of a car coming up the drive. Debrowski looked out the window. "It's Mrs. Fish," she said.

Crow lifted a black suitcase out of the trunk. "Feels like there's something left in there."

"That's cash money, son. Take a look."

Crow tried the catches. They were locked.

Sam started back toward the cabin. "Let's go crack that sucker open."

"Wait." Crow heard a vehicle coming up the driveway. Catfish rolled into view and stopped her car a few feet from the front door of the cabin.

"I don't see Tommy," Crow said. Catfish got out of the car and stretched. Debrowski appeared in the doorway.

"You know that one, son?"

"Quiet, Sam."

The two women were talking, but they were too far away—all Crow could hear was the wind in the leaves. Debrowski reached out and put a hand on the other woman's shoulder. Catfish's knees seemed to collapse; she twisted away and took a step backward, rubbing her shoulder. The conversation continued for a few more seconds, then Debrowski went back inside. Catfish crossed her arms, looked down the driveway, kicked the dirt with her toe. Crow hoped she would not look into the woods and see them. He had no idea what was going on, but he was sure he didn't want to get in the middle of it. A minute later, Jimbo Bobick hopped out of the cabin, aided by Debrowski. Catfish watched as, with some difficulty, she inserted Jimbo into the passenger seat of the Porsche. Debrowski said something to Catfish, who shrugged. Catfish was climbing into the driver's seat when Dickie staggered up. More conversation, this time between Catfish and Dickie, then Dickie squeezed himself into the Porsche's tiny back seat. Catfish got behind the wheel. A moment later, the little car disappeared down the driveway. Debrowski looked over at Crow, smiled, and waved.

"You want to tell me what's going on?" Sam said.

Crow lifted the suitcase. "I have no idea."

Debrowski seemed pleased with herself.

"What was that all about?" Crow asked, setting the suitcase on the steps.

She shifted her eyes to the side and smiled faintly.

"I'll go find us a wrecking bar," Sam said, moving off.

"I asked Mrs. Fish to give the realtor a ride into town," Debrowski said. "He couldn't drive with his foot."

"I'm surprised she agreed."

Debrowski shrugged. "Jimbo wants you to meet him this afternoon at five."

"What for?"

"He wants to show you an island. I told him you'd pick him up in his car at his office in town. Since he saved your life, and probably mine too, I told him you'd be there. Okay?"

Crow sighed.

She pointed at the suitcase. "Is that what I think it is?"

Sam came around the corner of the cabin, holding a crowbar.

Without saying a word, he jammed the tip of the bar under the catch and twisted. Forty-two thousand dollars spilled out onto the cabin steps.

"I want to thank you for the lift, Mrs. Fish," said Jimbo.

Catfish's jaw was clamped shut. She pulled out onto the highway and ran quickly through the gears. Within seconds they were doing ninety. Jimbo cleared his throat nervously and decided not to distract her with more conversation. Something was on this little lady's mind. He still had no idea what had transpired back at the LaRose place. He did not know what all the fuss had been about, and he had heard only a few snatches of the conversation between Laura Debrowski, who had done such a damn fine job of patching him up, and this Mrs. Fish. At one point, he thought he had heard Laura say that she was going to shove her head up her cunt and pull it back out through her asshole. Maybe he hadn't heard that one right. Whatever had been said, Mrs. Fish was decidedly perturbed. He turned and looked in the back seat. Dickie Wicky was passed out already, snoring quietly.

"My office is up the road here, about twenty more miles," Jimbo said.

They rode in silence, a forest of mixed conifers to their right, a field of sweet corn to their left. Jimbo let himself fantasize about selling the Whiting Lake property to Crow.

"I'm going to make the sale," he said out loud.

"What?"

"I'm selling a cabin to Joe Crow. I'm a realtor."

Catfish slid her eyes toward him and eased up on the gas. "You do pretty good at that?"

Jimbo was pleased. He loved to talk about his work. "We've moved forty-two properties so far this year, three of 'em for over a quarter mil. People want to move property in this territory, they give a call to Jimbo Bobick."

Catfish nodded and ran a tongue over her lips. "You must make a lot of money."

"I do all right."

A minute later, she said, "My name isn't 'Mrs. Fish.' It's Wicky. Catfish Wicky."

"Jeez, I'm sorry! Laura said your name was Fish. Are you Dickie's wife?"

She nodded curtly, looked back at her unconscious husband, and said, "But we're separated."

They passed a pastie shop, a bait shop, a KOA campground. The highway curved to the west, followed the rim of a small, milfoil-infested lake, returned to its southern heading. Catfish looked back at Dickie, who was still in his coma, then at Jimbo. They were coming up on a small roadhouse: the North Woods Lounge. She guided the car off the highway and parked, turned to Jimbo and gave him her best smile.

"You in a hurry to get to your office?" she asked. "Or do you have time to buy a lady a drink?"

Sam insisted on getting his truck out of the lake as quickly as possible.

"You let it sit there, one hour in the water is like a year on the road, what it does to the metal."

It had seemed a project of incalculable difficulty to the exhausted Crow, but under Sam's shouted, obscenity-ridden directions, the three of them extracted Ben's Cadillac from the woods and then, pulling with both Cadillacs and a rather complicated system of ropes and chains, they were able to retrieve the sunken truck.

Most of the boxes of magazines had been thrown off the truck and sunk; a few of them were still floating on the lake. Sam opened the driver's door, and several gallons of muddy lake water poured onto his feet. Crow and Debrowski got out of their respective Cadillacs and walked back to view the damage. To their surprise, only the remains of Joey Cadillac were present.

"Looks like the big one swum off," Sam said. "Bet he's halfway to nowheres by now." The windshield had shattered and popped out of its frame.

Crow scanned the woods, looking for a large, wet man.

Debrowski's eyes had become fixed on Joey's body, horror knocking aside all other emotion. "What are we going to do with it?" Her voice rose in pitch.

Sam was opening the hood. "I'll have 'er up and running by morning," he said.

Debrowski grabbed Crow's arm. "We have to do something with it, Crow."

"What?"

"*Him!*" Debrowski pointed at Joey Cadillac's dead eyes.

Crow moistened his lips. Joey Cadillac did not appear real to him. The dead man looked like a wax figure in the House of Horrors at the state fair.

Sam said, "You two want to shorten up those chains? I want to get this fucker towed back over by the cabin there, where I can work on her." He hopped into the cab beside Joey Cadillac, pulled the body out of the cab. "I suppose we ought to get rid of him. You want to give me a hand here, son?" Sam was holding Joey by the feet.

"What do you suppose we should do with him?" Crow asked.

"It's your show, son. I'm just the mechanic."

Crow considered his options and made a decision. He grabbed Joey's wrists, still warm. They loaded Joey's body into the trunk of Freddy's blue Eldorado.

"We'll just park the car someplace," Crow said, slamming the trunk. "Let the cops deal with it."

They towed the truck into the clearing near the cabin. Debrowski sat in a lawn chair smoking cigarettes, watching Sam work on the truck. She looked tired. Crow was debating with himself over whether he should keep his appointment with Jimbo Bobick. He didn't like to leave them there, with Freddy Wisnesky unaccounted for, but he felt an obligation to the realtor.

"Don't you worry 'bout us, son," Sam had said. "You go ahead and buy yourself that island. Me and Deb, we'll be here when you get back."

Crow was thinking about that, resting his eyes on the surface of the lake, when a portion of the brushy shoreline seemed to swell, rise up into a dark column, and move slowly toward them. It was Freddy, soaking wet, Twins T-shirt shredded, shoes gone, his face and torso a collection of opened scabs, new cuts, and bruises in assorted colors, shapes, and sizes. Crow stood up. Sam gripped a ratchet handle.

Freddy was not walking well. One foot was dragging. He walked past them, giving Crow and Debrowski a dull, incurious look. He veered away from Sam and the red truck and headed straight for the blue Eldorado. He lowered himself into the car. The keys were in the ignition. He started the engine, put the car in gear, and drove slowly down the driveway.

40

You'd be surprised how many nights I spend sitting on the god-damn sofa, trying to make sense out of the stains on my ceiling.

—Laura Debrowski, talking on the phone to an old friend

The note on the front door of Bobick Realty read: "Joe: Meet us at the landing." A hand-drawn map directed him to take 371 south, then turn on County 9. Crow tore the note off the door and got back in Jimbo's Oldsmobile. After Debrowski's Kawasaki, the Olds felt like the *Queen Mary*. He spent the short drive wondering who else Jimbo had been referring to when he wrote "us."

Whiting Lake was only ten minutes away. Crow found the public landing easily and was only mildly surprised to see Catfish's Porsche parked near the water's edge. Dickie was sitting on the hood, holding his head in his hands. Crow considered simply turning the big car around and rolling out of there, but he hated the thought that Dickie Wicky might stand between him and his island.

There was no sign of Catfish or Jimbo.

Crow pulled up alongside the Porsche and rolled down his window. "Dickie," he said.

Dickie jerked, and his head came straight up as if it was on a wire.

"Joe! Jesus, am I glad to see you." His face loosened, and a torrent of words spilled down his chin. "Where am I? Christ, I just woke up—Catfish's car—what the hell happened? What happened to the comic books? What are you doing here? What is this place, Joe? I wake up and—Christ, am I thirsty! You got a beer, a can of pop or something? Oh, God. Where are my comic books?"

"The comics are all gone, Dickie. You don't know where Catfish is?"

Wicky's face tightened up. He shook his head, moaned, and pressed both palms to his forehead.

"You haven't seen Jimbo Bobick?"

Wicky did not respond. Now that he had the money, Crow was actually feeling sorry for Dickie. If he had liked the guy, he might even have tried to help him, get him into a program. He looked out over the water and shook off the thought. Wicky the drunk he could handle. If the guy ever got straight, he might be dangerous.

From the landing, Whiting Lake appeared to be almost perfectly round. The land rose steeply from the shore and was heavily wooded with a maple, poplar, and conifer mix that would be spectacularly colorful by mid-October. Two boats were in motion along the far shore, trolling for walleyes. A single island was visible. Crow pulled the Olds forward onto the cement boat ramp, his front wheels entering the water, and looked up and down the shore. He could see a rust-colored log cabin a couple of hundred yards to the right. An open aluminum boat with a small outboard motor was tied up to the dock. He backed up, ignoring Wicky's plaintive shouts, and followed the road in that direction.

Ten minutes later and fifty dollars lighter, Crow eased the boat up to the landing.

"You want to go for a boat ride?" he shouted.

Wicky, who was standing in the water already, nodded and held out his arms. He was so happy not to be abandoned, he reminded Crow of a lost dog.

Jimbo Bobick thought he would never have to fuck again as long as he lived. He looked out over his sweat-glistened body and listened to himself breathing. He watched the smoke from Catfish's cigarette exploring the wood-slatted ceiling.

"That was incredible," he said.

"I thought you were gonna split me wide open, big guy."

Jimbo moaned at the intensity of the memory. Even his lips were burning. Another memory intruded.

"Uh, I oughta get over to the landing, babe. Crow's gonna be waiting for me."

Catfish trailed her red nails up his thigh. "He can wait. Don't you want to play some more?" She put her mouth against his ear and breathed. The smell of cigarettes, which normally he despised, now smelled sweet and seductive. She trailed her hand lightly down his belly.

Jimbo cleared his throat, intending to tell her it was all over. He was spent. It would be impossible. But he felt something moving against the inside of his thigh, and it wasn't Catfish. "Oh, lord," he moaned. "Here I go again."

The island was a rocky mound, about six acres, covered with assorted conifers and stunted hardwoods. Crow cut the engine fifty feet from shore. The boat's momentum carried it to a perfect landing at the stubby wooden dock. Crow tied up the boat and helped Dickie onto the dock.

"Nice dock," Dickie said.

Another boat—longer, with a bigger motor—was tied to the other side of the dock.

"So you're really going to buy this place, huh, Joe?"

Crow took in his surroundings—the trees, the rocky, brush-tangled shore, the collapsing boathouse a few yards down the shore. He looked up the dirt path that snaked its way uphill toward the interior of the island.

He could see part of the cabin—a neat, cedar-sided building with a stone chimney. He thought about sitting in the cabin, alone, listening to the wind, watching the water. Would Milo like it? No other cats. No Debrowski knocking on the door, scratching his ears, smoking cigarettes. Crow wanted a cigarette.

"You got a smoke, Dickie?"

"I don't smoke. It's bad for you."

And on this island, there would be no Dickie Wicky. But here he was. Dickie Wicky. Because Crow had felt a moment of pity. Because he hadn't wanted to leave him waiting alone at the landing.

Or because he had wanted company. Because he did not want to run into Catfish Wicky alone.

"Joe?"

Crow twitched and blinked.

"Are you okay?"

"I'm fine. Let's see if we can find Jimbo."

"I hear something coming from the cabin," Dickie said, starting up the path. "It sounds like a train. 'Ka-chunk, ka-chunk, ka-chunk . . .'"

Crow let him go. To him, it sounded like a headboard slamming repeatedly against a wall. He thought he could even hear the squeaking of bedsprings. He stood at the head of the dock until the sound abruptly stopped, then he got back in the boat and shoved off. He looked back at the island several times, feeling flat and gray, without the slightest twinge of regret or desire.

It was nearly dark when the dogs finally wandered off. Tom and Ben waited until they had been gone a full ten minutes before climbing down from the branches of the basswood. The money bag was gone, dragged away by the dogs, or wolves, or hyenas. Neither Ben nor Tom had ever seen anything like them before—vicious, ugly, yellow-spotted beasts.

At ground level, the darkness was blinding. Tom caught a root with his foot and fell headlong into a black patch of unidentified foliage. Probably poison ivy.

"Tom? You okay?"

Tom stood up, his face a pale blur in the dark. "I still can't believe you put it on a fucking horse. You shoulda asked me. I know horses, man. I used to be a jockey when I was a kid. I rode Sweet Citation in the '69 Derby. Youngest jockey on the field. If I'd a known you were gonna bet the fucking farm, I'd a picked out a winner."

Ben grunted. After confessing his betting errors at the track—a few hours in a tree could make a person do the strangest things—he had been subjected to three hours of Tommy telling him how he should have played it. It was demeaning, listening to a guy who used his testicles for analytical thought tell him how to play the ponies. All he wanted was to get out of the woods. He had already written off the money. Freddy could have the goddamn money.

"Which way's the road?" Ben asked, talking more to himself than to Tom.

"How the fuck should I know. I followed *you* into the woods, re-member? What I get, chasing after a guy who would put five figures on a horse named Bad Bet."

Ben stepped over a fallen sapling, and his foot plunged into icy water six inches deep. He pulled his foot out with a wet, sucking sound. The shoe stayed buried in the mud. He bent over and pulled the sodden shoe out with his hand.

"The thing to look for, you're putting your money on a horse, is the youngest filly on the field, and you bet her to place. You do that every race, you can't lose. I can't believe you didn't ask me, man."

Pouring the cold, muddy water out of his shoe, Ben said, "Tomas, would you be so kind as to shut the fuck up?"

It was getting dark. Crow drove back to Ozzie's cabin in a nasty mood, driving the Olds too fast on the unlit dirt roads. He had forty-two thousand dollars in cash and nothing he wanted to buy. Jimbo and the Wickys had soiled his dream.

What should he do with the money? To use it for living expenses was unthinkable, he told himself. He would become a slug, with nothing to motivate him. What could he spend it on? He had tried to give some of it to Debrowski, but she had refused and had even been offended by his offer. And Sam, to his surprise, had refused to take a cent. Crow decided to leave Ozzie a couple of thousand for the pornography collection. Another thousand for Natch, for the box of comics he had loaned them. As for the rest of it, he had the powerful urge to bet it on something.

A raccoon appeared in his headlights, scuttled safely off into the ditch. Crow thought, If that had been me, I'd have just watched the headlights getting larger.

At the cabin, he was greeted with a series of ugly growls. Chester and Festus had returned. Crow talked his way past them, moving slowly, promising the dogs liver for breakfast, but not his own.

Debrowski was sitting in a chair in front of the wood stove, chin on her chest, deep in sleep. He could hear Sam's snores echoing from the bedroom. Crow found a Coke in the refrigerator. He carried his Coke into the main room, sat down across from Debrowski, and watched her sleep. He lit a cigarette. Some of the debris inside him began to settle. He found a place in his mind for Joey Cadillac and put him there, wedged him in firmly. He found another spot for Catfish Wicky and buried her. He smoked his cigarettes and let his thoughts flow to the rhythm of Laura Debrowski's breathing.

At one o'clock in the morning, her eyes opened.

"Crow?" She sounded childlike; Crow wished he had a blanket to throw over her. "Did you see the island?"

Crow nodded.

"How was it?"

"Surrounded by water. I didn't like it."

Debrowski nodded faintly and closed her eyes. Her face was

smooth. The hard lines were gone, or invisible in this light. Asleep, she was at peace with herself.

"You want to go someplace with me?" he asked. "Help me spend all this money?"

Without opening her eyes she said, "Where?"

"Where do you want to go?"

He thought she had fallen back into sleep, but a minute later she said, "France."

"France?"

Debrowski nodded. "I've always wanted to go to France. They all speak French there." Her eyes opened a millimeter, watching him think. "It's very romantic."

"Okay," Crow said. "France. We'll go to France."

Debrowski's lips relaxed and spread across her face in a sleepy smile.

The next morning, they loaded Debrowski's Kawasaki onto the back of Sam's truck. Sam insisted that he would have the truck up and running before noon and that they should go on ahead. Crow argued that they should wait until they were sure he could get the truck going.

"I say this red fucker's gonna be running by noon, that's all there is to it, son. You calling your daddy a liar?"

Crow gave up. If Sam failed to get the truck going, he still had Jimbo's Olds. He and Debrowski drove off in Ben's yellow Cadillac, with the suitcase full of money. Sam watched them go. When the Cadillac was out of sight, he nodded to himself, then, under the watchful eyes of Chester and Festus, began the process of reinstalling the dried plugs, wires, points, and distributor cap. At one point he stopped, wiped his hands on his coveralls, lit a Pall Mall, and smoked it, staring out across the lake, smiling.

"A cabin on a lake," he said.

Chester barked.

"You like this livin', eh, boy? Me too."

Within an hour he had the truck up and running baby-ass smooth. He went back into the cabin, cracked a beer, sat on the porch with the dogs and drank it, his eyes occasionally shifting to the Gold's Gym bag sitting on the wood-plank floor. The bag was filthy and torn—it looked as if it had been dragged through the woods by dogs. When he had finished the beer, he unzipped the bag and looked inside, again, at the bundles of twenty-dollar bills.

"Dogs," he said to Chester and Festus, "what say we run into town and look up that fella Jimbo Bobick. See if a little money down on an island don't make that sore foot of his feel a little better."

Both Crow and Debrowski were drained and enervated; they hardly spoke during the three-hour drive back to the cities. There seemed to be no subject important enough to overcome the inertia of exhaustion, nothing that couldn't wait. The radio didn't work, so they rode in comfortable silence. When they got home, they were both drawn zombielike to their respective beds.

At five o'clock, Crow woke up, late-afternoon sunlight pushing past the drawn shades. It was hot and stuffy in his bedroom. He had a headache again, and his mouth tasted of tobacco. I quit, he decided. He stared at the ceiling, trying to make pictures out of the cracks and stains. . . .

He would have to call a travel agent.

Was he really going to Europe with Debrowski? Had she meant it? People say crazy things when they have been through a traumatic experience together. They fall in and out of love in a day. Had he ever even touched her? The only time he could remember was on her bike, holding on for his life. He would ask her when she wanted to leave for France, and she would light a cigarette and blow smoke in the air and laugh. He could imagine her saying, "*France*? Jesus, Crow, why would I want to go to *France*?"

Crow shuddered. It would be like hitting a full boat, then losing it all to a straight flush. He sat up, rolled off the bed, went into the bathroom, and cleaned his mouth. The flavor of the toothpaste made his tongue squirm. He dressed and started the coffee water, then lit a cigarette to get the toothpaste taste out of his mouth. He would finish the pack, then quit. Ben Fink's suitcase, full of cash, was still on the kitchen table, where he had left it. While the water heated, he thought about flying out to Las Vegas and investing the money in a game of no-limit Hold 'em. If he lost it all, at least he wouldn't have to decide what to do with it.

But before he went anywhere—France, Las Vegas, Australia—he had to get his Jaguar fixed. Probably just a matter of replacing a cracked distributor cap or something. Whatever it was, he could now afford to have it repaired. He felt like a jerk, driving the big yellow Cadillac, and besides, it wasn't his. He'd just leave it parked with the doors open. Within a day or two, it would disappear.

He opened the kitchen window to let in some air. Looking out, he noticed that the hood of his Jaguar was standing open. Someone was leaning over the fender, doing something in the engine compartment. He took a breath, ready to shout, when he recognized Debrowski's leather-clad back. What was she up to? He watched her do something with the wires, close the hood, then go back into the house. Crow grabbed his keys and went outside.

The Jag started immediately. He let it run for a minute before shutting the engine off. Debrowski's face appeared in her window, then disappeared. He locked the car and knocked on her back door. After a few seconds of listening to his own breathing, he heard her voice telling him to come on in, the door was open.

ABOUT THE AUTHOR

Pete Hautman spends most of his time in Minneapolis, Minnesota. *Drawing Dead* is his first novel.